ROLLER COASTER

by

Karin Kallmaker

Bella
BOOKS

2011

Bella Books, Inc.
P.O. Box 10543
Tallahassee, FL 32302

Printed in the United States of America on acid-free paper
First published 2011

Editor: Katherine V. Forrest
Cover Designer: Judy Fellows

ISBN 13: 978-1-59493-169-7

About the Author

Karin Kallmaker's nearly thirty romances and fantasy-science fiction novels include the award-winning *The Kiss That Counted*, *Just Like That*, *Maybe Next Time* and *Sugar* along with the bestselling *Substitute for Love* and the perennial classic *Painted Moon*. Short stories have appeared in numerous anthologies and collections. She began her writing career with the venerable Naiad Press and continues with Bella. She was recently honored with a Golden Crown Trailblazer Award, recognizing her more than twenty years of writing for lesbian readers.

She and her partner are the mothers of two and live in the San Francisco Bay Area. She is descended from Lady Godiva, a fact which she'll share with anyone who will listen, though she admits you'd have to pay her a lot to get on a horse, naked or otherwise.

All of Karin's work can be found at Bella Books.

Details and background about her novels can also be found at www.kallmaker.com.

Acknowledgments

It's called the Theater of Food, so what could make more sense than a story of theater and food? I found a great deal of inspiration in chefs Cat Cora, Elizabeth Falkner, Alice Waters and, of course, Julia Child. I don't think I could have even attempted this book without the lifelong example of my favorite cooks, Mom and Grandma. A pinch of this, a dash of that. It was writer's bliss to claim that every exploration of a new cheese or olive, soup or dessert was essential research.

This book would not have ever been completed without the outstanding support from the Bella crew of women who make every book a delight. Along the long road to its completion a number of readers and other writers gave me ceaseless encouragement for which I am profoundly grateful. For my family, once again, Moogie's done for now.

Twenty-Five, And Many a Woman is Now Alive

Part One:
Staging Area

PROLOGUE

Another carload of shrieking riders soared over Laura Izmani's head. It took conscious effort not to duck. The fading tone of the screaming was then drowned out by the sharp, metallic roar of the rail. The riders were already at the next turn when the air in their wake sent bits of trash scurrying across the wooden planking of the staging area.

The long, snaking line of raucous, eager teens and adults finally moved out of the sweltering access tunnel. She welcomed the fresh air and clean sea breeze, but the lack of shade was immediately apparent. She ran a fingertip over the top of one ear—the tender skin there was already on its way to a sunburn. Her Santa Cruz ball cap was tugged down as firmly as possible over her short-cropped black hair, but it still wouldn't quite cover her ears. She wasn't giving up now, though. She'd already been in the queue for thirty minutes.

There was no way she wasn't going to ride The Great Wave today. Today marked the anniversary of the day she'd left New York to come here. A fresh start was what she'd found, back in the town where she'd graduated from high school only a few years ago. She'd ridden this roller coaster so many times during those years. The memory of it was bright and true and uncomplicated. And before...The Big Mistake. Now that her life was firmly back on track, she was getting on a plane for New York tomorrow morning. The day after that she would see what she could pick up of her culinary training.

Another coaster load of riders disembarked and the line moved forward. She stepped into the way of the group of teens that had been angling at every possibility to slip in front of her. Sorry, dudes, anyone who'd ever ridden the subway in New York knew how to cut off a line jumper. It was all in the elbows.

After a few minutes she was on the final ascending stairs, bearing left because she wanted to be in the first car and she was willing to wait. Along the wall the old-fashioned drawing of a tidal wave looked exactly as she remembered it, as well as the bright red lettering that proclaimed, "The World's Most Fantastic Wooden Coaster! Only in Santa Cruz!"

Finally, the last coaster before hers departed, exiting the staging area to the left. She loved the *clack-clack-clack* of the pull chain ratcheting the departing car up the first incline in its fight against gravity. On her right she was bombarded with the combined screams of the riders on the cars that would slam to a stop in front of her. It had only been a couple of years since she'd ridden The Great Wave, and she'd changed a lot—mostly not for the better, she reminded herself—but she had every intention of doing the entire ride with hands up in exultation.

The approaching train of cars was rounding the final curve with a clatter and screech of brakes when the attendant asked if she was riding alone. After she nodded, the teenager shouted to the crowd behind her, "Any singles? Room for one!"

Laura had already tossed her ball cap on the seat and sat down on top of it when a woman settled next to her. They wordlessly sorted out the seat belts and locked them in place. Moments later they both tugged the bar firmly down across their laps.

After the attendant walked the length of the train, tugging on lap bars along the way, a voice on the loudspeaker intoned brief, unintelligible safety rules. As she remembered, Laura could only make out the part about keeping hands and feet inside the car at all times.

With a jerk the cars lurched forward into the incline tunnel, which was constructed of crisscrossed wooden beams and closely fitted slats. Every joint was studded with huge bolts.

"Not much padding on these seats," the woman commented. She had a white-knuckled grip on the bar.

"It dates back to when people were tougher, I guess." Laura gave her a distracted smile. They emerged from the tunnel and she found herself grinning at the stunning view of the vibrant Santa Cruz Boardwalk and long, pale, curving beach beyond it. She heard the other woman's breath catch too.

"Time for hands up!" She thrust hers in the air, her stomach lurching, anticipating the top of the rise, where the track appeared to drop away to nothing. For a moment there was only sky in front of her, then the car banked hard to the right, wheels squealing on the rails. She yowled with delight as gravity took over.

Twists, short rises, a tight swirl down, then a long steep run across the length of the coaster to a second rise, their momentum augmented briefly by another pull chain, then swooping again— through it all Laura screamed, hands above her head.

One year. *One year sober.* One year of hard work, good food, freedom from temptation, and she knew no drug could ever feel this exciting. The ride was as fabulous, spine-tingling, breathtaking, stomach-churning, *wonderful* as she remembered.

It wasn't over—they surged up the third rise, jerked hard, and were caught by the last chain that would boost their falling speed, climbing more than halfway as high as their initial ascent. She took a deep breath, giving her throat a break from shrieking. Coming up was the ride's steepest descent and the last series of twists before they were back at the staging area. *Clank-clank—*

With a back-breaking jolt the car stopped just a few feet

from the top.

It took Laura a moment to let her breath out. "What the hell happened?"

She realized then that the woman next to her had not released her death grip on the lap bar, and her eyes were tightly closed. Older than Laura, but not by much, she was pretty pale for a white woman, but now her pallor was so pronounced that at first Laura thought she'd pass out.

Then the woman spoke, her voice a thready whisper. "Please, dear God, tell me we're not dead."

"We'll start up in a second," Laura said. She'd never been on a coaster that had stopped before. But surely it wouldn't be long. She gave her companion another look. "Are you okay?"

"No."

"If you're scared of roller coasters, why did you get on this one?" *And why, for heaven's sake, did you get in the front car?*

After a convulsive swallow, the answer was, "I'm not scared of roller coasters. I'm scared of heights."

"Okay. So why the highest coaster in the park?"

"This is my graduation test. I think I'm going to fail."

She was glad to see a little bit of color come back to the woman's lips, but her eyes hadn't opened. "You're not hysterical and you're not throwing up, so what's to fail?"

"Give me a minute and either could happen." Her lips pulled to one side. "She said go to the Boardwalk, take a few rides, it'll be fun."

"Sounds like you want to shoot someone for the advice."

"My therapist. Helping me with desensitization." The last word was sounded out as if it was being repeated for a spelling bee.

Laura looked over the edge of the coaster. It had to have been at least three minutes by now. "It could be worse. This could have happened just a few seconds later and we wouldn't be leaning back against the seats. We'd be hanging against the seat belts and lap bar."

After an unsteady intake of breath, the woman said, "That's not very comforting."

"I'm Laura, by the way."

"Helen. Helen Baynor." With an air of absentminded rote, she added, "Remember the name. Some day I'll be famous. If I survive this."

"I read somewhere that there are three fatalities a year at amusement parks."

Helen's eyes cracked open slightly, then she scrunched them shut again. "That doesn't help!"

"Same article said ninety million people go to amusement parks a year. You have better odds at winning the big Powerball sweepstakes than dying at an amusement park."

"Like that'll happen."

"That's my point."

"We're hanging by a thread hundreds of feet in the air and how come you're not scared?" Helen sounded like she might cry.

"It's not a thread. It's steel on steel." *Why did I end up next to a nut case who's afraid of heights?* "And there's lots of things they can do. There's these locking brakes on the cars that keep them from rolling backward. They could release them and let us go back the way we came. We'd end up..." Laura leaned over the edge of the car, peering at the rail behind them. "We'd end up near a ladder."

"Shoot me now."

"You'd have to open your eyes, probably."

"To get shot?"

"To get down the ladder."

"Not happening. I had them open when we went up the first time. That was it."

Laura cast about for something to talk about that didn't involve heights, death or roller coasters. "I'm training to be a chef."

"Really? Do you like cooking?"

She glared at Helen's profile. "No, but all the glamorous jobs washing dishes are taken."

Helen's lips actually twitched in a near smile. "Stupid question. Sorry."

Laura decided to let it slide. "I was training in New York, but came home for the past year. Well, as much as home is anywhere. I lived here with kind of distant relatives for a couple of years after my mother died so I could graduate from high school." No need to explain that her father had reluctantly found the living arrangement for her, after being confronted with the unpleasant reality of a mixed-race daughter turning up on his doorstep. She'd gotten on her own two feet the moment she could. He'd been embarrassed by her? Well, she had been even more embarrassed by him.

"Where'd you live before that?"

"Jamaica. My mother was a student in Florida when she got pregnant with me. I was born in Florida and we stayed there until I was eight and her money finally ran out. Then we went back to Jamaica." People tended to think that meant she'd lived some place exotic, but the only difference she'd found between the tracts outside Kingston and a slum in Manhattan was better weather.

"I was wondering about your accent—it's faint but comes out more in the cadence."

"Really? I didn't think I still had an accent. Are you like a Henry Higgins?"

"No, though I've studied Eliza's part repeatedly."

"Oh. So you're an actress." Helen was probably very attractive when she didn't look as if vomiting was imminent. No doubt good looks were an asset, and lots of her good looks was due to sable brown hair that brushed her shoulders. It had been pulled back into a ponytail but tendrils had escaped during their ride, curling against her neck and temples. "And you'll be famous some day so I should remember your name—that kind of actress."

Helen nodded.

"What have you been in?"

"I was nearly in *Rain Man*."

"Oh, that was a good movie."

"And almost got to be a hostage in *Die Hard*."

"Yippee-ki-yay, mother—"

"Don't," Helen said. "I have friends who think that's incredibly amusing. Especially since I was nearly almost a hostage."

"So are you rehearsing to be Eliza Doolittle?"

"I'm up for the role in *Pygmalion* for a run off-broadway. But

I'd have to leave L.A. I'd have to give up the idea of being a big movie star."

"Is that a really bad thing?"

"I like the stage more. I always have. But my agent says anybody who is anybody is in the movies."

"So let your agent be a movie star."

A ghost of a smile crossed Helen's lips. "My boyfriend says he doesn't care where we live."

"So why do you stay here? Are you forcing yourself to ride roller coasters to get a part in an action movie?"

"Yes. My agent says I need one big break."

"An unnamed hostage is a big break?"

"It's how the business works." Now that she was talking, Helen couldn't seem to stop. Her color had come back and she seemed oblivious to the passage of time. Laura guessed it had to have been eight or nine minutes now. The sun was mercifully to their backs or her ears would be turning into cinders. She'd have a burn on her neck, though.

"But you could actually be on stage if you went back. Actually working."

Helen nodded. "I'd have to dump my agent—she doesn't know the stage world as well and never did."

"So she got you out here to get into the world she knows. You don't sound happy."

"Two years of not working beyond a walk-on in a commercial. Thank goodness my boyfriend has money. His family lives up north. Cattle ranchers and gold pioneers, very old California money."

If I had someone to bankroll me, Laura thought, I would go after my own Chez Panisse with both hands, and not look back. Helen seemed to only know she wanted to be an actress, which was like herself saying she wanted to be a chef. What kind, how, where, for whom—those were the bigger, harder questions. She'd spent the last year asking herself every one of them.

"Whatever I do, I have to get over my fear of heights," Helen was saying. "A balcony scene—a producer called me directly to see if I was interested in an O.B. *Romeo and Juliet* but I didn't think I should leave L.A. and I turned it down." She chewed her lower lip. "God, was that a mistake? I don't know what to do."

"So you decided the least you could do is ride a roller coaster." Laura let her gaze turn to the palm tree lined streets.

Another smile flitted briefly across the expressive mouth. "That's not crazy, right?"

"I'm not the best judge of crazy."

"I couldn't hide it any longer and there's more wire work all the time these days. So I took desensitization classes and therapy and finished that and was doing pretty well. I can ride in glass elevators now, that sort of thing, when before I would break out in a cold sweat and barf. But she said—phobia therapist—that if I was at an amusement park, what a victory it would be to ride a roller coaster." Her eyes opened a fraction.

"Is your guy really cool about moving wherever you need to for work?" Normally, Laura wouldn't pry, but she didn't want Helen to ask her about her love life. Women in relationships always asked. It was a I've-shown-you-mine-now-you-show-me-yours kind of thing.

"He says he'd go with me. He wants to get married. I think I'm going to say yes." She smiled, finally, a genuine smile and her eyes opened all the way. "I'm kind of crazy about him too. He gets me. And wants me to be famous and as rich as he is and he says that being Mr. Helen Baynor would be the best thing he could want. So I have to be *somebody*. I gotta be a contender."

The dead-on Brando impression made Laura grin. "I am going to run my own restaurant some day. I spent all of this year doing grunt work in a couple of places in San Francisco. Chop, peel, bake. I put away some cash and now I can pay more tuition." And if I keep myself on limited funds, she added to herself, I won't have any to spend on things that are bad for me.

Helen turned her head and they made eye contact for the first time.

She had amazing eyes. That was the first thing Laura thought, and she didn't realize for a moment that she was staring. But they were exceptional—large and expressive, and a color somewhere between blue and gray. Her lashes, lips and brows worked together to emphasize the rapid shifts from fear to humor to affection and back to fear again.

Then she blinked and Laura snapped back to their present predicament and what Helen was saying.

"You don't sound as young as you are. I thought you were my age, from your voice."

"I'm twenty-two next month." Laura wasn't sure if she should be offended. She sounded old?

"I'll be twenty-seven this fall."

"Why, do I sound old?"

"Oh. I don't know. You're so calm when every time the wind kicks up a little bit I think we're going to blow right off the track."

"They've had near gales and nothing's fallen off."

"People do this in gale-force winds?"

"Well, no..."

Helen arched an eyebrow. "You don't say 'like' and 'you know' every other sentence either."

"I could, like, change that, you know, if that would help."

Helen gave her a smile, which faltered when someone in a car behind them started shouting as if someone on the ground could hear. Laura angled over the side to look, but didn't think anything new was happening below. Maybe ten minutes so far? Or it could be fifteen? Her watch was hanging on her backpack, down on the ride platform.

"It can't be much longer."

The shouting continued behind them. Having looked at the track, Laura tried not to think about how they would get down if the ride didn't resume. There were no ladders to this part of the track, no safety walkway. So they had to have a plan to let them roll back to where they could exit the cars, didn't they? To get them from here to somewhere safe to walk down? She opened her mouth to say this, then realized she'd only upset Helen more. She'd have to keep her speculations to herself, for a while at least.

"So where in New York did you live?"

"Queens," Laura said. "Took the bus to work. A bistro near Wall Street. It paid pretty well and they let me do more than prep."

"And?" Helen closed her eyes again, but it seemed more

to fight the relentless sunlight than in panic. "What went wrong?"

"Why do you think something did?"

"It's in your voice. Something went wrong."

When you lie about your addiction you give it power over you, Laura told herself. But a stranger on a roller coaster? Did she really have to? But this is an anniversary, she told herself, and you should start the rest of your life the way you mean to go on. *She seems interested, so she gets the truth.*

"I did something stupid. I didn't know enough to wonder why there was so much cash around. Restaurants are usually cash-strapped, and at New York rents, it's brutal. But there was a lot of cash. Sometimes I got paid in cash. I was working at a better place than my mother ever had, and I was training to be a real chef. Then I found out where the cash was coming from and I thought I was invulnerable and one of the chosen cool people. There are users in my family in Jamaica, but I figured I was smarter than them, somehow immune to the fact that one line of coke leads to another and then to another. I took a freebie and I was hooked." She paused for breath, feeling a little lightheaded.

Helen's eyes had opened. "I know people—talented, together people—who fried themselves on cocaine. Smart people. A couple went from powder to that crack-rock poison. And you've stopped?"

Laura couldn't meet Helen's gaze. "After I burned through everything I had. No more school, and, of course, the restaurant got raided finally—the owners were selling out of the bar. The raid happened when I wasn't there and I never got dragged into it, which was really lucky. I could have a record." She decided not to go into the different treatment someone with her skin color faced on drug charges. She had reminded herself all through her twelve steps that not having a drug-related record hanging around her neck was through the pure grace of God.

"And I had to leave New York because...it's my sense of smell." She had to pause to swallow, because talking about it reminded her of the aroma of oil, garlic, burnt sugar and grilled veal mingling with the smell of the subway and on many nights, the dank, heavy scent of rain on dirty sidewalks. "Restaurant kitchens in New York smell a certain way."

"You mean a way other than with their noses?"

"Wise ass."

"I truly can't help myself. It got me into so much trouble in school. Anyway..."

"Anyway, maybe it's how old they are. Right now that smell reminds me of how great the drug made me feel, not how awful my life became because I used it. I was turning into my kin. But I've been fine out here. The world smells different here. My sponsor said there's research that links sounds and smells to craving triggers and it seemed smart to get away from it all. I'm kind of nervous about going back..."

Helen pried one hand off the lap bar to rest it gently on Laura's arm. "You're stronger than it is. You made it a year and you're not freaking out about this damn roller coaster."

"Actually, one of the steps is admitting you're not stronger than it, God is."

"Hooey."

"Hooey?" Laura looked at her in shock, both because Helen was scoffing at one of the really big steps, not to mention divine power, plus she'd said *hooey* and who said that nowadays?

"Sorry, I don't mean God," Helen said hurriedly. "I mean if you're strong enough to place faith in God, you're already stronger than it is. It's strength, not weakness, that makes a person realize they need help, and ask for it."

"Is that from a play?"

"Maybe. I don't know," Helen said unexpectedly. She smoothed some of her escaped hair behind her ear. "But I think it's true. Granted I've never been in those shoes, so what do I really know?"

"Believe me, plenty of people who've never been addicted to anything have all the advice a person could want about how to kick it. Nobody has a cure. Nobody is forever and always cured. I'm trying to be strong. It's a choice I make every day."

Helen put her hand back on the bar, wrapping her long fingers tightly around it. "Well, sounds like you have pulled it together. Why don't you stay here in California?"

"Because..." Laura had thought about it a lot. "Because I'm

afraid to go back, that's one thing. Kind of like being afraid of heights and proving you're over it by going on a roller coaster."

Helen gave her a wry nod. "Okay, you have me on that one."

"I'm afraid if I don't go back I'll always be afraid, and culinary America is in New York, if you want to learn, and I really do. And if I can't handle it, even feel a spark of temptation, I'm outta there. I have a great sense of smell—that's another reason not to use the stuff. I could have lost my palate and that's my livelihood. So how can I be afraid to learn there, work in kitchens there? If I can't do it, if I start thinking that we had a really great dinner service and wouldn't the best dessert be powdery white stuff, I'll come back here. I could easily become an Alice Waters acolyte."

As she explained who and what Alice Waters and Chez Panisse were she realized she was babbling about things she'd never said outside of an AA meeting. It felt good to tell someone besides her sponsor about her fears, actually, and it was wonderful that Helen didn't seem shocked or put off. Her response was probably atypical—there'd be plenty of people who would think very poorly of her and wouldn't be afraid to say so. No doubt she'd meet them everywhere she went.

She'd made mistakes. She'd made the amends she could. She'd sniffed her mother's life insurance, her only nest egg, up her nose. What should have taken her three years was going to now take six or seven, and self-pity over having to eke out the means to pay for culinary school was not acceptable.

"There's something about live performance," Helen was saying. "The thrill of it. There's a rhythm backstage, this controlled furious outburst of energy all being directed out over the audience. I love being behind the curtain before it rises. There's always a little dip—a warning. Then it goes up and I feel like I'm flying."

"It sounds like a kind of drug." Laura put one hand over her eyes. The sky was an eye-searing blue, even with the sun behind them.

"It is, I guess." Helen gave her a half-smile. "I crave it, no doubt about that. I think about when I'll get it again, I scheme and worry and fuss to have it as often as possible. In between parts I feel like a piece of me is missing."

"Yep, those are the classic signs—but there's one thing you don't do."

"Yeah?"

"You don't do it in private and lie about it." She had done a lot of lying, but not as much hiding. It had been used so openly in the restaurant stock room that there'd almost been no need. She'd been a fool—times were tough and no break in sight. The Reagan and now Bush years were seeing to that. But their customers had happily paid outrageous sums for simple cocktails, and she'd simply refused to see what was under the cocktail napkin and the meaning of the cash flowing from hand-to-hand.

"True. I have a hundred witnesses at least, every time I do it."

Laura wasn't sure why her voice suddenly quavered. "I'm not going back to it. I won't."

"Good for you," Helen said. She opened her eyes and Laura fancifully thought she was being wrapped in comforting blue-gray velvet. "I know you can do it."

Not sure why she cared so much, Laura said intensely, "You should go back to Broadway. Marry the sweet guy and go after what you love doing."

"I don't know if I'm brave enough."

"You're on this damned roller coaster."

Helen was shaking her head.

"You have the money to live wherever you want. So what's the real excuse for not doing it?"

Helen took a deep breath. "I'm afraid I won't be famous anywhere. If I go back and wash out...then I don't have anything at all."

"Except the sweet guy *and* a pile of money. If you don't go it seems to me that you'll have a sweet guy, a pile of money and a lifetime of regret."

"Is that from a play?" Helen frowned.

"Not that I know of—shit!"

Helen swore at the same time as their coaster jolted underneath them. They slipped backward and they both screamed, as did everyone else behind them. The car squealed to a stop again.

Helen was breathing in short little gasps. "I'm going to throw up." She gave Laura a look of pure panic.

"No you're not," Laura said firmly. "Tell me about Juliet. About Eliza Doolittle." Helen gave her a blank look. "Tell me about the first play you were ever in."

Helen was trying, Laura could tell. Her breathing took on a forced, steadied pace and her lips moved as if she was repeating some internal mantra. "Amateur? Or professionally?"

"When you got paid, the first one."

"*Camelot*—anonymous teen. A singing role, before I'd had any voice training."

"Training helped?"

"It did. But back then... 'If an anvil could sing, it would sound like Helen Baynor.'"

"Ouch."

"From a review in the local paper."

"That's mean."

"It was truthful and it hurt." Helen swallowed hard. "My friends didn't tell me the truth so I'm grateful someone did. I took six years of vocal training. My voice got better. I'm no show-stopper, but I can carry an ensemble part. And I've gotten better about reviews. Sometimes they're dead right. Sometimes they're dead wrong. Sometimes a critic ought to be dead."

Laura nodded. "I know what you mean. You can either stick the so-called critic with a cleaver and go to prison or smile and let them choke on your success. I plot to poison people years later when no one would suspect me. It passes the time."

"If I ever need someone poisoned, I'll call you."

Pleased that Helen's color was coming back, Laura decided that getting her to talk was the best way to cope. "So what do you think about *Cats*?"

Helen made a strangled sound that was probably as close to a laugh as she could get in their situation. "It's good theater. I'm not a snob—entertain the masses. But I wouldn't want Broadway to be nothing but *Cats*. There has to be some *Death of a Salesman* or *Angels in America*—that was fantastic, I saw it when it was still a workshop in L.A. It will go to Broadway, to the West End, it's amazing. You have to have theater like that, plus *Cats*. The world would be so dull with only one or the other." Helen took a longer, steadier breath. "I've lost some people I know to drugs, but so many more to AIDS. After I moved out here I'd call up people I'd worked with and they'd read off lists of men who'd died recently. All those funerals. And it's still going on."

"Nobody's doing anything much about it—at least not that I can tell." Laura wondered if Helen would be ready for her other secret. The irony of being able to trust Helen with her drug-use history and yet doubting she could tell her she was a lesbian brought a wry smile to her lips. Would it ever change?

"That's another play—what if I was the Angel? That's on a wire, and being afraid of heights would make it impossible to take the part."

"You're doing great," Laura said. "This will be a fantastic accomplishment. Tell your agent you had a near-death experience and you're going back to New York. Your heart tells you what it wants and you're a chump if you don't listen. I didn't get to go that much, but I saw *Cats* and *Edwin Drood*."

"Drood was good fun—what's that?"

"Loudspeaker." Laura leaned well outside the car, straining to hear. "I think..." She listened as the message repeated. "They're going to finish the run. Oh." She sat back in the car. "They want our heads and hands inside again."

"You mean we're going to go the rest of the way?" Helen's ashen pallor returned. "I was just getting used to this. I could do this for a while longer."

"It'll be okay." Laura peeled Helen's hand free of the bar. "Hold on to me. We're going to be just fine. And it's a roller coaster. You're expected to be scared and scream."

The *clack-clack-clack* sounded ominous as they jerked up the track.

Helen was holding her hand so tightly Laura knew it would ache later. She didn't mind.

"When I am a rich and famous stage actress," Helen said, "I will bring my rich and famous friends to your restaurant because I know you're going to be a rich and famous restaurateur."

"I'll make you a fantastic meal," Laura promised.

Clack-clack-clack.

"I know you'll be fine." Helen squeezed her hand even

harder.

Touched at Helen's blind faith, Laura wasn't sure which of them was acting as the lifeline to the other. She squeezed back. "We'll both be fine."

The chain released their car. Laura screamed too so Helen wouldn't feel so alone. Gravity took over, but neither of them let go.

CHAPTER ONE

Twenty–Three Years Later

Be calm, be cool, be composed. The last thing Laura Izmani wanted was to show her anxiety to the woman on the other side of the vast mahogany desk.

Not looking up, her interviewer scanned the document in her hand again before commenting, "I can't seem to find it on your résumé. That you've worked as a private chef before."

"That's because I technically haven't." She kept her voice steady, striving for her usual modulated tone, but her prospective client chose that moment to make eye contact again.

Laura wasn't the type to stammer and blush over beautiful eyes, but these were not just any pair of eyes. These eyes had stared out at Laura from dozens of Playbills during the ten years she'd worked in Manhattan, and from numerous Internet pages since she'd left the Big Apple more than a decade ago. In the natural light sifting through the study's gauzy draperies, she could tell that the thick, dark lashes were natural and no tinted lenses enhanced what was already an ever-mutating sky blue-to-gray gaze. Wide and expressive, they were the kind of eyes that radiated emotion on connection—then, with a blink, shut it off.

Those eyes had not changed in twenty-three years.

Helen Baynor blinked now, and Laura felt an absurd chill at the loss of focus. She was breathless, waiting for that next glance. *Good lord! Finish your answer, you fool.*

She stumbled, caught herself, then plowed forward, words tumbling out in a goofy rush. "I spent ten years working in several Michelin-rated restaurants in New York, then more than ten moving around in the Cunard line of resorts." Thankfully, she calmed and was able to go on more normally, "It's there that I was called on for private banquets, to prepare custom meals for high-value customers during their stays, and so on. I've also done catering on the side from time to time, but catering and making meals for a family are two very different results, even if they use many of the same skills."

Belatedly, she added a smile, which froze when Helen Baynor once again looked her in the eye.

"Why are you making this kind of change? This is—well, it seems to me that someone who has been an executive chef at some high-profile establishments would find the work of a private chef a bit..." The chiseled, full lips curved into an expectant smile.

"A bit menial?" She was ready for this question too. Maybe captains of industry couldn't fathom why anyone would downgrade their employment, but she thought that Helen Baynor would understand. She let her gaze fall to the lovely bonzai plant at the corner of the mostly empty desk. The other object of note was an oddly painted and unfired clay figure that might have been a human or a gorilla. A child's handiwork, she guessed, by one of the twins, probably, and years ago. "This is the stage in a lot of chefs' lives where they take the money they've been working too hard to spend and they sink it into a restaurant. I could do that. But it's likely I'd lose my shirt—which happens to most restaurants in the first year even when the economy is strong. The way things are now, I can't think of a more foolish risk to take."

Helen Baynor nodded, and her expression remained attentive. That could be an act, Laura thought. She continued her explanation, "Or I'd end up working more hours than I've ever worked before in my life to avoid losing my life savings, and then I'd be fifty and wondering where my life had gone."

She at last scored a reaction: a tiny wince around Helen's eyes. Laura did the math—if she was forty-five then Helen would be fifty next month. Way to go, she chided herself, remind the potential client of her age. But in her mind's eye, Helen looked almost the same as she had for decades. Flawlessly elegant, innately beautiful, year after year. The only significant change was her hairstyle, which had gone from shoulder-length to much shorter, with a little bit of wave that let it curl around her face— easier to accommodate stage wigs, Laura supposed.

"I have substantial savings, and I live a very simple life. No time for living large," she plowed onward. "I've been restless for a while. My repertoire was shrinking to nothing but bland final dishes, even if they did have good quality ingredients. Flair and one-of-a-kind dishes based on what's fresh that day weren't on the list of what management thought was successful, and a change in managers at the latest resort gave me the push I needed. I want to be part of an artisan community where every night isn't a major competition with people you'd otherwise love to call friends. I do have a number of references, and one pointed me toward this area of California. Many years ago, I lived in Santa Cruz, so this region is also a bit like home to me."

Helen glanced at the second sheet of paper. "Your references are impressive. I know the Merchants, and David Connelly is a great friend of the stage."

Laura nodded. "I came into contact with them in Bali. I worked out the base menu for his family so they could all eat the same food while accommodating his daughter's allergies. It mattered to David that family meals not leave her feeling ostracized but not leave the rest of the family feeling as if they were dining on nothing but rice and soy. When they dine out everyone can have all the dairy and wheat they want. At home there's no dairy or gluten available."

"Is that why David lost all that weight several years ago?" This time it was a genuine smile, and abruptly Helen Baynor was not a famous stage actress, she was the kind of woman you'd have a casual conversation with at the coffee shop or grocery or queuing for half-price tickets. The kind of conversation that put a glow on the rest of the day—the kind of conversation that you never forgot. Well, it seemed perhaps Helen had forgotten.

Laura nodded, cautiously hopeful. "A dietician worked out the necessary elements and I turned them into a stack of recipes their cook uses and plays with—so far they're not bored. But that kind of cooking takes time and attention. Your daughter's primary issue is with preservatives and dyes, isn't it?"

If Helen was surprised that Laura knew that intimate detail it didn't show. She recalled it from the late '90s interview with *Parade Magazine* where it had been casually mentioned.

"Additives and preservatives have been a real hardship. They trigger psoriasis and sometimes migraines. She can go months without an event then something slips through. It's been very bad lately. The last chef wasn't as careful as she said she was. We really need a community organic garden."

"That would be amazing—but you'd need land."

"Few people in these parts are willing to part with any." Helen added a smile. "Even if they're all buying organic."

Laura grinned. "Any community that was able to stop Steve Jobs from tearing down his house and putting up a new one on his own land has a deep sense of…community aesthetics."

"That's putting it diplomatically," Helen said dryly. "He is much missed."

"Is it true that there's no decent map of Woodside available online because a Google zillionaire in the neighborhood mucks with the satellite imagery?"

Helen laughed. "If anyone could, it would be him, I guess. We're pretty private people."

"It must be hard," Laura said, choosing her words carefully, "to be in the public eye and try to have a family life that's private."

"It is. That's why I would never turn loose of this house.

Psychologically, it couldn't be farther away from Broadway. When my children were old enough to realize I was famous I decided to move us out of Manhattan. I live the crazy schedule when I'm there, but this is home. I might not be here, but seven days a week it's home for the kids. That's why I need a private chef, four nights a week, one that will closely supervise every aspect of the kitchen and leave it stocked so we can cook for ourselves when I'm home. I need to know I can reach into the pantry, freezer, ice box, whatever, and it's safe. My time is precious, and I want to spend it cooking and being with my kids, not studying ingredient lists for the iso-propyl-methyl-butimate-red-fifteen-invertase-whatever. It just destroys me when Julie has an attack."

"I'd feel terrible to be the cook that put the meal in front of her." She considered what Helen had said. She didn't need to see more than the entryway and this study to know that Helen Baynor's home was a genuine 1920s mansion. When it had been built Woodside was a secluded little town far from sleepy little San Jose. The town was rumored to have once been a love nest hideaway for Joe DiMaggio and Marilyn Monroe. San Jose and the suburbs of Silicon Valley had grown much closer, but Woodside was still secluded.

Laura had seen the glamorous star of a top-rated police show shopping at the local produce market with her famous blonde locks tucked up under a worn porkpie hat. The star had been debating her equally famous movie star husband on the virtues of North American cornmeal versus Italian polenta. If they hadn't been celebrities Laura would have likely offered her two cents on the issue: cornmeal is the same the world over for the most part. *Polenta* referred to cooked cornmeal as specialized in Italian cookery. But they were enjoying their debate and no one else was paying them any attention, so she'd left them to it.

She nearly mentioned the encounter, but then worried she'd sound like she'd been stargazing. The incident had underscored for Laura what the old, heavily secluded enclave of Woodside offered its residents. A star like Helen Baynor couldn't go two steps anywhere in Manhattan without cameras and autograph books thrust at her. Laura was beginning to realize that northern Californians, in 180-degree contrast to the southern part of the state, prided themselves on their refusal to go gaga over even Lady Gaga. It was rumored Paris Hilton had visited San Francisco and left when no one noticed, vowing never to return.

She abruptly realized her mind was wandering. This was *not* a casual conversation, struck up while hanging several hundred feet above ground. She had yet to get the job, and, she reminded herself, she was only interested in the town because of the job. She hadn't gone looking for Helen Baynor's name. David Connelly had given it to her with several others. It hadn't seemed like fate...

"I cook to make people feel good, not sick," Laura finally said. "Given that I'd be cooking for your children and the housekeeper most nights, and I wouldn't be supervising anyone but myself, I would consider it my kitchen, so to speak. And nobody messes with my kitchen."

Helen Baynor nodded, and this time Laura could see a measure of impatience for the conversation to be over. "My household manager is fairly new—she's been with me for about nine months. She'll abide by the rules since she's seen what happens if Julie has an attack. Justin has no allergies like Julie's, but he has no sense of healthy eating. He loves carbs and butter and pancakes and syrup, and can eat popcorn by the gallon. But his father died of a freak stroke and during the autopsy they discovered his heart was failing. A healthy diet is going to help him with a potential genetic time bomb."

Household manager, not housekeeper, Laura repeated to herself. "I naturally default to heart-healthy cooking. I gather regulating their diet comes with the territory somewhat, then."

"My household manager will do that as well, but the person who runs the kitchen has to be on board about a healthy diet for him or he'll just do what teenagers do. There's one other thing, though."

Helen looked up again, this time with a piercing intensity that made Laura's breath catch. "As I said, I am private. This family is private. One hint that you've been a so-called 'source close to the family' for any news outlet anywhere anytime, and you're through, and I can make that 'through' in all of this state and New York. I won't tolerate gossip, photos—nothing about me, this house, my kids, not even what brand of sugar we prefer—showing up in the press. If you want to cite me as a client you'll have to tell me why every time you think you need to. I'm not *National Enquirer* material. Ever."

Without hesitation, Laura said, "I respect that. I respect that completely. Any of my references you call will back that up."

"Good." Helen was suddenly flustered, standing and pushing the few papers on the desk around. "I'll need to make some calls. It's a few—Could you come back at five? I have to go back to New York tomorrow."

"Surely," Laura said. "Do you want me to meet the household manager?"

"Normally, she's the one who would have done this, but her mother had a bad fall yesterday and Grace drove up to Auburn to spend the night. She'll be back by five, though. I don't really know how to do this."

"You did fine, at least I think you did."

"Really? Is there anything I should have asked you that I didn't?"

Laura cocked her head. "You didn't ask what kind of commitment you wanted from me—the duration."

"Until my kids go to college." She failed to hide a moment of stricken realization. "That's just under two years."

"I can commit to that," Laura said. Already knowing Helen Baynor's very public support of The Trevor Project and Equity Fights AIDS, she said, "You didn't ask if I'm a lesbian."

When Laura didn't go on, Helen lifted one eyebrow.

With a smile, Laura said, "I am."

"Good to know. As they say, some of my best friends..." Helen tinted her tone with a touch of upscale Yankee and Laura realized that in that last few minutes she'd seen Helen slip through a dozen different roles, from self-assured woman of means to worried mom to a fleeting nuance of bored socialite. She wondered if any of them was close to the real woman. She'd read everything there was to read about Helen, but hadn't a clue if Helen Baynor, Queen of Broadway, knew which was the real woman.

Laura rose, smoothing her Dolce & Gabbana suit jacket. Like nearly everyone in California she wore jeans. Her pristine white cotton wrap blouse was meant to be reminiscent of a chef's crisp whites, but the jacket did double duty showing off her slender lines and letting her mingle with people who bought their wardrobes at Fashion Week in New York. Numerous stylists had told her she'd lucked out with a shapely head which made her very short cut elegant and fashionable for a dark-skinned woman. No one would ever take her for one of the wealthy elite, but she did look like a successful professional of some kind, with narrow but solid fashion sense.

Not that she got an *us* vs. *them* vibe from Helen Baynor. Her casual pantsuit of smoky gray was definitely designer work, and it fit the trim form perfectly, but at the moment there was none of the employer-servant distancing she had encountered all over the world, especially places where the color of her skin automatically branded her as inferior in the eyes of many. She was certain that if she violated Helen Baynor's boundaries, however, she would be put in her place as an employee. If she got this job, she would not be a member of the family. But she doubted she'd be taken for granted or treated like furniture either.

If she ruled her own kitchen, she would be content. She would sometimes miss having a sous chef to give the onions to, but after the last couple of years of corporate bosses with the palates of two-year-olds, she was very much looking forward to being boss of only herself for a while.

At the door, Helen offered her hand. "It was a pleasure to meet you, Laura. I look forward to seeing you again later today."

"This was both an honor and a pleasure," she answered.

The contact of their fingertips was so fleeting that Laura couldn't think how it made her feel beyond a kind of pleasing numb. The memory of their clasped hands, racing down the roller coaster track, was suddenly very much in her mind. She tried to match the confident but impersonal pressure of Helen's grasp, and with that, she made a dignified exit, walking down the path from the front door—lined with precisely trimmed box hedges—to the large graveled parking area. Her stolid but vastly practical late-model Volvo station wagon, which could hold an enormous amount of cargo, gleamed in the hazy sunshine.

Her seat belt was buckled before she dared a glance at the door. Her prospective employer had not lingered. She let out a sigh of relief.

Clearly, Helen Baynor didn't remember her. She was going to keep it that way, too.

·

CHAPTER TWO

If Laura hadn't needed to linger in Woodside, she might have been tempted to take the westbound two-lane highway that wound slowly toward the Pacific Ocean. The fog was just offshore and there would be hazy sunlight on the beach. Instead she turned east, passing high hedges and non sign-posted country lanes that gave access to large, secluded estates like Helen Baynor's. After the follow-up interview at five, she'd have only a short drive to Atherton, then south to Menlo Park where her residence hotel sat on the edge of Silicon Valley. She might as well find a snack or a quiet place to enjoy a cup of coffee until it was time to return to Helen Baynor's.

There were many vistas, but not many places to pull off the road and enjoy them. In all directions, Woodside was surrounded by soft rolling hills that ended in sharper, forbidding rocky ridges. The hills were encrusted with rows of grapevines, while the ridges exposed their slate-gray teeth through dense stands of old pines ringed with fragrant eucalyptus. The landscape, painted with shadows cast by pillows of coastal fog torn loose from the offshore marine layer, seemed to lounge contentedly in the hesitant sunshine.

As she approached Woodside's small shopping area, she passed understated civic buildings, including the library, and a few adjacent blocks with the most visible housing in the area. She'd already driven the perimeter and knew there was nothing for rent—at least not publicly. If she got the job she'd have to hire an agent to find housing. On her arrival she'd decided that *enclave* was the best way to describe Woodside. It wasn't hostile to outsiders, but there was no place for visitors to put down any roots—not even a discreet bed-and-breakfast. Her temporary lodgings were expensive, and she'd rather have a place to call her own after years of living in small staff residences behind the walls of resorts.

That kind of thinking, she reminded herself, was counting chickens out of thin air. She had to get the job before any other plans were made.

Woodside's three-block main street had no Safeway or Jamba Juice, and even Starbucks hadn't been able to worm its way into its confines. Instead, the coffee spot was called Makes Life Worth Living. It featured a selection of handmade truffles, delicate petit fours or fresh twisted apple bread to go with meltingly good coffee—Laura had already tried them all in the few days since she'd driven into town. Kicking back to catch up on her email and check her Facebook friends with a slice of cinnamon-buttered apple bread and a frothy mocha... She'd found it very civilized.

As she pulled into a lucky parking space in front of the small, open produce market, the scent of autumn was thick in the air. There was a touch of ocean and a little pine sap in the breeze, but a tantalizing plummy richness hinted at the impending grape harvest and crush for the local wineries. She had already visited two of them, and she'd found that many equaled or surpassed her memory of the Napa wines produced sixty miles or so to the north. From here to Santa Barbara were dozens of wineries and a person could spend months getting to know the choices.

Coffee forgotten, she decided to see what the market had to offer today. After all, she'd need to make her own dinner later.

The dank heaviness of root vegetables attracted her attention as she crossed the market threshold. Her stomach growled for pumpkin curry soup and a crusty slice of rye bread. It was early in the season for ripe pumpkin, though. Just as well. Though her residency hotel provided a small kitchen, nearly all of her equipment was in storage. She was able to make excellent meals with a chef's blade, a cutting board, one pan and a heat source. Still, it was a welcome idea, a rich pumpkin soup with pungent bread, followed by a dessert of apples and pecans sizzled together in white wine and brown sugar, all consumed in front of a crackling fire as a harvest moon glowed through the windows.

She had to laugh at herself as she fondled the artichokes. She'd never had that kind of life and it wasn't likely to happen any time soon. Since quitting her post in Florida, she'd driven across country, had some great and some perfectly awful food, and there was no for sure job in her pocket. If she didn't get the job, she'd have to move north to Marin County or south to Paso Robles or Santa Barbara, where she had lists of potential contacts as well. She'd keep exploring the state, making phone calls and meeting people, and trust that something would work out. It could be quite a while before she was processing her own pumpkin for soup.

"Izmanini, right?" A reedy voice jolted her out of her artichoke reverie.

"Izmani," Laura corrected. She smiled at the woman who had appeared at her elbow. "But I also answer to Laura."

"C'mere, Izmani." The woman, no taller than Laura's chest, spun toward a table in the depths of the market. She moved quickly but it was easy to follow the bobbing gray head. Even in a room of tiny old women Laura could have picked her out from the improbable pigtails over each ear.

"You see what I have for you!" The woman gestured at four

stacked crates. "First dibs. Last local corn you'll see this year, okay? Okay."

There was still sap at the base of the stems—it had been cut that morning or late yesterday, Laura was willing to bet. The ears weren't as large as they usually were in large-scale groceries and they were markedly plump around the middle. Some might call it imperfection, but she called it a sign that the seeds were likely not genetically modified. "Can I peel one?"

"Shoo-er." Her tiny guide gestured.

"You know my name but I don't know yours."

"Everybody calls me Teeny. So you call me Teeny, okay? Okay." Her accent was a charming enigma—not quite Italian, not quite Spanish, not quite Caribbean.

Laura selected an ear from the top and peeled back the husk and silks with one firm pull. There was a lot of silk and the ear was symmetrical with pearlescent kernels. She smelled a good bit of sugar. Her nose signaled her stomach again, and she wanted scallops in lime ceviche topped with caramelized corn. Now *that* was a meal she could reproduce in the half-kitchen her hotel room provided. "Fresh, organic and local. It smells good."

"It's good. Even better is their first corn. Everybody wants that. You come back lots and I'll tip you off when it's in, okay? Okay." She wiped her hands on her apron, which, at one point in its life, had been the color of ripe eggplant. Now it was mottled with bleach marks where any number of stains had been eradicated.

"How long have you owned this place?" Her first visit she'd been the one peppered with questions, unable to get a word in edgewise. She'd told the old woman her name, that she'd been born in Florida, that her father was an anonymous American businessman, and her late mother a Jamaican woman who had worked in his hotel in Florida when she was a student. She'd picked out fresh field greens for her own dinner and discussed the various parts of Manhattan where she had lived. Teeny had relatives in all of them, it seemed, and had asked after each one, sure that Laura must have crossed paths with them somehow.

"Never owned it," Teeny declared. Her gaze darted past Laura to scan the market, then fixed on her again. "My husband—lovely

Italian man, may he rest in peace, he owned it. When he died, my son owned it. He wanted to make wine so now my daughter owns it, with her husband. She got all the Italian. My son he got all the rest from my side of the family and he makes a good wine. You go try the whites at his place, okay? Okay."

"What's it called?"

"'Just Outta Town on the Right.'" She shrugged when Laura cocked her head in puzzlement. "He thought it was amusing. I said nobody is going to know what town and he said it didn't matter."

"It's memorable," Laura said. "I'm more likely to remember that than I am Stag's Leap and Leaping Stag and Home of the Stag that Leaps."

Teeny laughed. "You come back, okay? Okay." She darted in the direction of a customer who had decided to restack the heirloom tomatoes.

It was a long way from New York, but Teeny certainly had a welcome eccentricity. Laura smiled at the ear of corn in her hand—and then she had a *brilliant* idea.

Super brilliant. She checked her watch. Plotted the time and fumbled for her headset and phone. If Chef Emery would help her out, she could pull it off in the little over two hours she had to get back to Helen Baynor's house.

He sounded grumpy when he answered, which was consistent with every time they spoke. There was the steady beat of more than one knife on a cutting board in the background.

"I don't suppose I could borrow a corner of your kitchen for about forty minutes?"

"What'll you give me?"

"I'll do prep for fifteen minutes first. You've seen me prep. You know—"

"Deal."

She bought six ears of corn, a sweet onion and two limes. She was sure Emery wouldn't begrudge her a couple of tablespoons of his extra-virgin olive oil and a dash of sea salt. And she'd sweet talk him into ten minutes with the vegetable grill. Her spoils cradled in one arm, she bought a thick, crusty batard from the bakeshop-cum-cheesemonger next door and then pointed the car toward Emery's, the restaurant inside the Woodside Country Club. Long ago, Emery had worked for her at a Cunard resort in the Caymans, and contacting him on her arrival had given her access to a clean commercial kitchen, should she need one.

He greeted her from his six-two height with, "I need onions, fine dice."

"Bastard," she answered, and she didn't bother to make it sound like a joke.

"I can't find anyone who understands what... A... Fine... Dice... Is!" The last word echoed the length of the kitchen and the four kids hunched over the cutting boards tucked their heads down between their shoulders and kept chopping. Emery pointed out the bag and Laura rolled up her sleeves.

Part of her wondered just how this new life plan of hers was working out if she was reduced to dicing onions. She'd run her own kitchens and cooked for Rockefellers and the like. But she liked the smooth feel of an onion's peeled exterior. She marveled, as she always did, at the ring structure of one of the few plants regularly consumed around the entire planet. Any cook, trained or self-taught, professional or amateur, knew onions.

Peel, halve, transecting cuts up to the root, then fine slices for the dice. Root tossed in the compost can. Next.

Ten onions later Emery told her to switch to leeks. They were already rinsed, which was helpful, and far easier on her tear ducts. In fifteen minutes she finished both jobs.

He surveyed her work. "If you persist in this madness of going private, I'll always be happy to hire you to do prep."

"Call me crazy—"

"Nice to meet you Crazy."

"I have a follow-up interview with a very famous stage actress—that's why I need the kitchen. I thought I'd audition a simple snack." She pointed out the ingredients.

"I have no doubt it'll be delicious. But seriously?" He gave her his grouchy teddy bear glare. "You'd rather do that than plan the menu for your own place?"

Laura nodded. "It makes sense to me. It's what I want...right now. A couple of years I could change my mind." She began shucking the corn. "I had to get out of commercial work."

"From what you said of that bastard at the last place—" His head whipped around. "No, no. You're steaming that bacon. Boiling it! It needs to be fried!" With that he left her to her own devices.

She selected the corner farthest from the cowed sous chefs. Emery yelled. It was his only fault as a boss, she suspected. He had a gift for menu design and his irascible nature seemed to endear him to other divas, and divas were plentiful in country clubs. He was happy. She hoped to be happy again too.

She quickly sprayed down and wiped the surfaces and cutting boards, then set a large pot on to boil. Six minutes later the ears of corn were shucked and she'd carefully removed all the silks. She blanched them in the boiling water to bring out as much of the yellow as she could, then plunged them into an ice bath. They emerged looking much brighter and giving off an almost caramel scent.

She checked her watch, then diced her own sweet onion, rolled the whole limes on the counter, then cut and juiced them over the onion. Emery's vegetable grill was impeccably clean and quickly sizzling hot, so she trusted her food wouldn't pick up cross-contaminants. She babied the ears of corn as she slowly rolled them on the grill, letting many kernels turn a mouth-watering toffee brown. Some burst and the sugars coated the rest of the ear to a state of gleaming succulence.

Her real time crunch was letting them cool enough so she could cut whole slabs of kernels off without them falling into pieces. If she didn't succeed she had a Plan B, but there was a wow factor to slabs. She set them on a tea towel and tasted a piece of onion. It was still fairly raw, and she could wish it were sweeter. She needed a little bit of simple syrup.

Emery didn't comment when she scooped out some cane sugar from his supply, then raided the pantry for the clearly labeled organic EVOO. Thirty years ago, olive oil had been a staple only in the mom-and-pop pizzerias. Now there wasn't a haute cuisine establishment that didn't buy extra-virgin by the five-gallon jug, and organic was easy to find in fresh supplies.

She stirred a quarter cup of sugar into an equal part water and set the tiny saucepan on a burner. The corn was still too warm to handle, so she cut the French bread batard into slices about half the size of playing cards. She brushed one side with olive oil and lightly sprinkled it with salt, and set the neatly arranged tray of the fifteen slices that resulted under the broiler.

Time to stir the sugar.

Check the corn.

Taste the onion again.

When the toast came out of the oven she started on the finally cool corn. It was a job that couldn't be hurried, and her patience was rewarded when she was left with slabs of cut corn the right size to go on her browned toasts. She dribbled the simple syrup over the onion mixture, then she spread the result thinly on top of the corn. Each toast would take three or four bites to eat, and two would be nearly a full serving of corn. It wasn't a green leafy vegetable, but corn had fiber and it had what food scientists called high satiation factors—the stomach felt more full after eating corn than iceberg lettuce, for example. There were far worse snacks in the world. It was also the kind of thing she liked to prepare to make eating vegetables fun.

It was already half-past four. If she was lucky, Helen Baynor hadn't had time for a snack and *le maïs sucré sur batard*—sweet corn on toast—would hit the spot. If Helen didn't like it, then the job was probably lost.

CHAPTER THREE

It wasn't easy to find a wide place in the country lane that led to Helen Baynor's secluded driveway, but Laura found one and turned off the engine for just a few minutes. Her heart was thumping loudly in her chest and a nervous flutter tickled her throat. Though she was trying hard not to think about it, the feelings were similar to the first time she'd met Helen Baynor—the only time she'd met Helen Baynor, before today. All the intervening years when she'd lingered at stage doors she just hadn't been able to force her way forward to say, "Remember me?"

Mostly her shyness had been because she'd been afraid Helen wouldn't remember her. The minutes they'd shared had changed her life. She'd gone back to New York feeling like someone had in full consciousness accepted her, had precious faith in her and more than anything, she didn't want to waste that. Those minutes were a secret. They were a treasure, even. It wasn't likely they had had the same meaning to Helen, even if the dreams Helen had spoken of had all come true for her.

But she also feared being remembered, and discovering that Helen's kind words of twenty-plus years ago had been easy to say to someone she'd never see again. People could so easily say *I understand*. That didn't mean they'd welcome you into their home, or near their kids, that they wouldn't see ADDICT tattooed on your forehead every time you walked in the door. Of the few times she'd told colleagues or employers about her drug use as a young twenty-something—let alone the two additional times she'd fallen off the wagon and regretted even more deeply—none had gone well.

A eucalyptus-laden breeze wafted through the open car window and the ice underneath her plated snack cracked and shifted. Funny how life worked out. She'd wondered for years if she'd be remembered, but when it came down to it today she was glad Helen had no idea who she was. She didn't want to talk about mistakes. Nevertheless, not being remembered...it stung, just a little.

Enough of that, she thought, glancing at the clock. Show time. She pulled back out into the country lane and swung carefully around to park once again along the gravel circle. She carried her covered plate cradled safely in the crook of her arm, a trick she'd learned from watching seasoned waiters move through crowded rooms without dropping a thing.

The housekeeper was a tall, ascetic woman in crisp khaki slacks and a starched white blouse, with a severe ponytail of rich, black hair that didn't make up for the years the style added to her face. She could have been thirty-five or fifty—it was hard to say. She spoke in a soft voice that Laura had to strain to hear, introducing herself as Grace Olmstead.

The foyer was slightly warmer than it had been earlier in the day, and the gleaming parquet floor reflected some of its rich warmth onto ivory walls. The plain walls set off two large English landscapes that flanked the large foyer. Her gaze was drawn again to the dramatic staircase and the two-story atrium over her head. It was easy to imagine a glamorous star making a sweeping entrance. To her right was an expansive, high-ceilinged great room done mostly in cream and white tones. It seemed a bit sterile, in spite of plants and vibrant abstracts on the walls, but perhaps when the large fireplace at the end was lit the room would come alive.

The rest of the house was certainly more alive at this time in the day, however. A door slammed somewhere in its upper-floor recesses. A girl's voice cut across the atrium and knifed down the central staircase with, "Stay out of my room, you perv!"

"Stop taking my T-shirts!"

"I didn't take it, it was in my basket!"

Helen Baynor's unmistakable voice, low but likely audible in every part of the house just as it was from the front row to the far balcony in a theater, came from somewhere downstairs. "Knock it off. We're going to have—"

She appeared in a double doorway just beyond the foot of the curving dramatic staircase. With a mild look of chagrin at Laura, she effortlessly continued at her penetrating volume, "I have company now. Understand?"

There was silence and Helen crossed the foyer toward Laura, smiling graciously. "That'll buy us five minutes of peace," she said to both Laura and Grace. "You two have met?"

"Yes, and thank you again for asking me back," Laura said.

Helen's graze lit on the covered plate. Her eyes suddenly sparkled. "Is that food?"

Laura grinned. "It is. Just a taste. Okay, I admit I put maybe a little more into it than I would for a typical afternoon snack, but this is made purely from the ingredients at the local vegetable market—what a great place that is—and a few staples from a trusted kitchen."

"Let's eat and talk. Grace, maybe some iced tea for all of us?"

"I was just going to suggest that," Grace answered, gaze on the floor. She glided from the foyer through the nearest doorway, which meant the kitchen was on the left side of the house—possibly around the rear for a view of whatever gardens there might be.

Helen led Laura to the doorway she'd emerged from, into a formal dining room that was apparently only accessible from the foyer. An enormous oak sideboard could be stocked with food for ten, easily. The room was dim with no natural light, but inset track lighting brought out a golden oak patina in the paneling. The long table would comfortably seat a dozen. It, and the chairs upholstered in mauve velvet that surrounded it, were Victorian. The chair arms were delightfully carved with grape clusters and ended in intricate pineapples. Ornately ghastly, a pain to dust and polish, and yet amusing, Laura thought. A few papers were at one end of the table, suggesting Helen had been working while she waited for the interview.

"I'm honored that you prepared something for me."

"You prepare your lines for a role you want. I cook."

"I take that to mean you do want this job?"

Laura smiled, but kept her tone serious. "I do. I think the two years you need would let me settle in this part of the country for good. I'd enjoy the challenge, and the three days each week you didn't need me would allow me to explore the local culinary scene, get to know growers, travel a little—there are a lot of advantages and no disadvantages that I can see."

Laura believed every word she was saying, but an unbidden pang of guilt sounded for not having reminded Helen of their long-ago meeting. If Helen did remember her, she'd know to ask more questions, and the answers might not sit well. She wasn't being dishonest, Laura told herself, because she knew her mistakes and they wouldn't happen again.

"The two years will fly by," Helen said, her voice losing some of its strength.

The real Helen, Laura was starting to discern, was the one who showed when she talked casually about her kids. None of the Broadway gossip mills had ever linked her romantically to anyone since she'd been widowed while pregnant. That must have been a tough time, Laura thought. The stage was her living, and breastfeeding actresses don't find much work. Yet, she'd had her husband's estate and this fabulous house, and those assets had let her devote herself to her babies and to her career. When she'd returned to the stage, her turn in a revival of *Agnes of God* had been her first Tony. The play had folded, but Helen went from featured player to leading roles.

The tinkling of ice against glass heralded Grace's return. The cut crystal pitcher caught the overhead light, sending a quick flash of prisms across Helen's face. She didn't look on the edge of fifty, Laura thought. Botox might be involved, but so was a good diet, she'd wager. From the lean lines of her arms, shoulders and neck, exercise was responsible as well.

Laura declined sugar and thanked Grace as she filled a tall glass. Indicating the tray in her hands, she said, "I have plenty, if you wanted to call the kids."

"If it's really tasty, no," Helen said, adding a laugh. "They are quite good at foraging for themselves, especially Justin."

"He eats constantly," Grace said quietly. There was definitely a note of disapproval.

"I'd worry," Helen said to Laura, "if he wasn't six-foot-four and one-fifty soaking wet."

"He sounds like a fuel-burning factory." Laura set the covered dish on the woven bamboo mat that Grace produced from the sideboard. "Does he play sports?"

"His feet are glued to a skateboard." Helen's gaze was focused on the dish.

This was it, Laura thought. Her stomach lurched, as if she'd been jolted out of a starting gate. She lifted the lid, hoping the toast hadn't become soggy. "It's very simple."

"It smells delectable—makes me think of summer," Helen said.

Helen wasted no time lifting one of the toasts from the plate, resting it delicately on one of the linen napkins Grace had lined up. "It looks delicious."

"It conforms completely with your daughter's requirements, contains only a minor amount of fat—"

"You're making it sound like medicine," Helen said, just before she took a large bite.

"Can't help it." Note to self, Laura thought, don't tell Helen how good a dish is for her until after she's enjoyed it.

Grace had also wasted no time having a bite of her own. She nodded, her face still impassive. Laura wished she'd make eye contact.

Helen gave an appreciative moan. "So simple, and so yummy. I'd order this as an appetizer any day of the week. Julie is a grazer—she loves finger foods."

In her head, Laura heard the echo of Helen saying, "When I'm a rich and famous stage actress, I'll bring my rich and famous friends to your restaurant." It mattered that she liked the food, and it mattered even more that Helen believed she could trust her kids with Laura's influence. The butterflies in her stomach were swirling madly, and her heart was going *clack-clack-clack* against her ribs.

Helen was rich and famous now. Laura had had her successes, but she'd had failures which were, she vowed, not relevant to cooking meals for a famous actress and her children. *Clack-clack-clack.* She wasn't going to be cooking much for Helen, she reminded herself. Mostly for the kids. It was only a job—clack-clack-clack—and there were other jobs. But this one mattered, even if right now, feeling poised at the top of the track, suspended between up and down, she couldn't say why.

Clack-clack... She was holding her breath, not sure if she would fly or fall.

"Well," Helen said, with a glance at Grace, "I made a few phone calls this afternoon, and your references could not have been stronger. Why don't we give this a try, and let's say in a month we put our heads together and see how it's going?"

She wanted to whoop, but managed to get a grip on her excessive elation by hurriedly sipping from her glass of iced tea. "I think that sounds great," she said, grinning broadly.

Helen smiled back, her gaze almost searching, before turning to Grace. "If Laura's agreeable, why not go ahead and have her start tomorrow?"

"I could do that," Laura said. She looked at Grace as well.

Her face giving nothing away, Grace gazed at a point somewhere between them. "That would certainly get us back to a normal schedule."

"Great. I fly out tonight on a red-eye," Helen explained, "and report to the theater by five. I'm always in the Wednesday through Saturday performances, and I'll fly home Saturday on a red-eye."

"That's grueling," Laura remarked.

"I've learned to sleep on airplanes, easier in first class. The stewards often know me, and that helps. They don't wake me being solicitous and know to bring my first coffee an hour out from landing. And it means I'm home Sunday morning about when the kids are ready to get up. That gives me all day Sunday, Monday and Tuesday with them. With Grace's help, I keep up on their homework, though at their age we're mostly worried about colleges and exams and members of the opposite sex. And when I'm between runs, I'm here all the time, of course. I love New York, but this is home."

Laura tried to commit the many facts to memory. "So I would be here to cook on Wednesdays through Saturdays. Would you like me to leave the outlines of a meal for Sunday brunch?"

"Yes, actually. That way we can snack and catch up. Though we sometimes go out to our favorite organic burger joint." She broke off at Laura's expression. "I know. Sounds like an oxymoron, but Julie can eat there. The sweet potato fries are killer."

Realizing that she would be spending a lot of time with Grace, Laura tried to draw the woman out. "I'd like to inventory the kitchen tomorrow, then, so I can shop. Tomorrow I'll stick with simple food and I can talk to the kids about their likes and dislikes—and yours as well, of course."

"We'll review the budget and their schedule then," Grace said impassively, then excused herself as a phone in the distance began ringing. She was going to be a tough nut to crack, Laura thought.

The doorway was blocked by a tall figure. "Mom, excuse me. I was just wondering what the plans are for dinner."

Helen laughed and gestured at the boy to come into the room. "Your radar is flawless. Justin, this is Laura Izmani, and she's going to be our chef."

Laura rose—Helen had not exaggerated the height. He towered over her by a full foot, but she definitely had broader shoulders. Long brown hair covered most of his forehead and eyes, but he tossed it back to make brief eye contact as he shook her hand. Then, looking very much like his mother, his expressive gray gaze went directly to the food.

"Help yourself," Laura said. She could almost hear his stomach echoing hollowly with imminent starvation. "I promise it won't always be this healthy."

After swallowing a mouthful that obliterated more than half of one slice, Justin said, "This is good. Thanks."

"Would you get your sister—" As Justin's mouth opened, Helen hastily added, "Don't shout. I can shout. Go up and knock, please. Knock, don't pound."

Laura saw the protest in his eyes, but at the emphatic tip of the head his mother gave toward the door he gave in.

"One for the road," Laura suggested, drawing the tray closer to him.

"Thanks." He moved toward the door at a pace that couldn't be called speedy.

"Today, please, Justin."

"I'm going, Mom. You don't want me to spill on the carpet, do you?" With that he shoved the rest of his toast into his mouth and disappeared from sight. The thudding of feet suggested he was taking the stairs two at a time.

"He's really quite charming when he wants to be."

"I have no doubt of that," Laura said. "I've worked with a lot of teenagers in the past. I congratulate you on the meeting of his pants with his waist."

Helen rolled her eyes. "Two years ago I was lucky he *wore* pants. It was as if they burned or something. Mr. Drama." She laughed. "Okay, don't say it."

"Say what?" Laura opened her eyes wide. "Apples falling from trees and little distance between them?"

Whatever Helen might have said in reply was interrupted by the arrival of Julie. She was slender, like her mother, with the same pointed chin and expressive mouth. Laura realized she hadn't ever seen a picture of the late Mr. Browning—both children had his last name and their mother's last name for a middle name. She looked to be Laura's height, right about five-foot-four, and was probably done growing. She'd been blessed with thick, glossy black hair any Goth would envy. Her eyes were brown and more deeply set in her face than either her brother's or mother's, so probably from her father's side of the gene pool.

While most of their expressiveness came from their eyes, Julie's countenance was more closed and Laura couldn't decide if the slightly mulish expression was habitual, or a result of having been ordered to the dining room by her brother, or both.

After introductions, Julie regarded the offer of a snack with suspicion. "Is it okay for me?"

This was the member of the household that wanted details, Laura realized. She didn't blame the girl one bit. "Yes. The corn is very fresh, and the baker certifies the bread as a true French loaf: flour, water, yeast, salt. That's it. Everything else came from a kitchen I trust. No dyes. All fresh."

"Cool." She bit into a slice, but not with the same zest for sustenance that her brother had exhibited. "Thank you."

"You're entirely welcome. I'll be back tomorrow to take some inventory and make dinner. Over dinner I thought you and your brother could tell me about your favorite foods."

Julie nodded but stopped short of a disinterested shrug. She didn't ask for seconds of the toast and after asking her mother about going over to a friend's after dinner, she left the room.

Laura caught the look of concern in Helen's eyes.

"You'll have to cut her some slack," Helen said hastily. "The last chef—I don't know what the deal was. We just got acclimated to a new person in the kitchen and Julie started having attacks. She may not trust you right away."

"I hope to earn her trust," Laura said. And yours, she added to herself. And just as quickly, the enormity of what she'd done finally penetrated. *And what a great start, too, not mentioning that you'd already met.*

She opened her mouth to blurt out, *Do you ever ride roller coasters anymore?*

But Helen was saying, "For this first month, could we meet on Tuesdays at five, just like today? For maybe fifteen minutes? That way if you have concerns or questions, we can discuss them. And I can give you feedback the kids might not have shared with you."

What else was there for her to do but agree and take her leave? She felt like the coaster ride had started without her and she was running to catch up. What had she been thinking? By saying nothing she'd elevated what could have been a minor blip into her personal elephant in the living room. She'd been so thrilled at the idea of being some part of Helen Baynor's life, so star-struck that she'd tripped over one of the basic principles of her sobriety: *When you lie about your addiction, you give it power over you.*

She hadn't lied, well, not exactly. She wasn't ethically beholden to tell an employer. It wasn't her intention to harm or defraud Helen Baynor in any way by not mentioning their first meeting. The important distinction was ensuring that nothing she was doing was setting her on a path to a renewal of self-deception and/or a willingness to court temptation. She didn't think anything she had said, or that taking this job for that matter, would in any way jeopardize her sobriety.

She'd kept silent about that roller coaster ride because she wasn't that young woman any more than Helen was an unknown actress not sure which life to pick.

She drove most of the way to her residence hotel in a daze. In one part of her mind she was furiously making a shopping list. Another part was reflecting on the personalities that made up the Baynor household, and yet another was trying to decide on the very important first meal together. But mostly she could hear the sound of the roller coaster launching down the track and her own hysterical screaming as it veered in a direction she couldn't foresee.

Part Two:
Fighting Gravity

CHAPTER FOUR

"I gave up an hour's sleep for you, so this better be good." Helen Baynor poured another packet of artificial sweetener into her coffee and watched as her long-time agent, Cassidy Winters, dropped into the chair opposite her.

"Suh-wee-tee," Cass drew out, feigning offense that anyone should consider time with her a waste. "Of course it's good. Would I drag you here if it wasn't?" Cass's gaze traveled the length of the Forty-Seventh and Broadway coffeehouse.

"So what's the deal?" Hardly private, definitely grimy, the shoebox-sized bistro was nevertheless a good meet-up place convenient to Helen's condo, Cass's office and the theater where Helen was headed next. It was packed, however, with mid-afternoon shoppers and the table had been hard to come by.

But for that, she'd have chosen elsewhere—being framed in the street window wasn't her first choice.

Cass leaned closer and her sweater slipped off one shoulder, showing off her ultrasleek physique. It was a signature style and Helen counted Cass one of the most stylish women in the city. "There's a rumor that a production company has assembled their backing and probably landed a lease on the Lunt and Fontaine Theater for a revival of *Picnic*. Male star might be Mr. Harry Potter himself."

Helen let her eyebrows drift up toward her hairline. "As the guy from the wrong side of the tracks who can't catch a break in that hard-bitten little town? That casting is a...stretch. Of course it was a stretch for William Holden in the film. He was in his forties playing twenty."

She had an even worse thought and gave Cass the evil eye. "Don't you dare suggest that I angle for the part of the hysterical spinster, simpering over anything male in hopes of getting married."

"It's Tony material," Cass protested. She stirred her coffee, then sipped delicately, leaving bright pink lipstick on the rim of the white cup.

"Not interested. Not even the tiniest bit. I'll play the mother in *Hamlet* first—oh wait, I'm already too old for that. Mother roles go to thirty-year-olds who'll play fifty."

"There's no *Lion in Winter* on the boards, suh-wee-tee. I'm just trying to keep you employed."

"I appreciate that, you know I do." There was never any pretense with Cass. To her, a successful actor was a working one, regardless of the role. She only brought up the potential for nice things like awards when she wanted Helen to take a part she knew Helen wouldn't want. "What about the staged version of that Sandra Bullock movie—*The Proposal*. I'd love that."

"I've heard they have someone in mind for that."

"Some twenty-year-old to play forty-five, no doubt."

Cass's thin brows arched up. "Did you find a gray hair or something this morning?"

"Just feeling it. On the plane I had a hot flash," she admitted.

She had woken up in her seat drenched from the skin out. A sympathetic cabin attendant had brought her a cool, wet cloth.

"I'm so glad I skipped that whole process. Get the plumbing taken out—it saves a lot of bother."

In spite of the blasé tone, Helen could see the brief fear in Cass's eyes. The surgery had eradicated the earliest stages of cervical cancer. Cass's model-on-crack silhouette was only just starting to fill out, but her nose and jaw were still overprominent in what was once a pixieish face, and even she admitted that her naturally buoyant boobs seemed ungracefully proportioned. Her current hairstyle, very blond and spiky, wasn't yet as lush as the wig she'd worn during chemo. Every week, though, she saw an improvement in Cass's vitality and it was good to see her body starting to look like the various parts were meant to go together. Cass joked about it, but Helen didn't think any woman really laughed when it came to the C-word.

"I've always liked Rosalind Russell's work," Helen admitted. "I'd seriously consider anything that suited her, except that caricature of womanhood in *Picnic*."

"Tony material," Cass said again. "It's been a while."

"I'll do a dead body on *Law and Order* first."

"You're not for the screen, remember? That's why you dumped Hollywood, which was *so* their loss."

"That was twenty years ago and then some. Maybe things have changed. But I've never wanted to be about television. A blockbuster movie with residuals, a superhero's mom, I could do. An instructor at some wizard school? Oh—drats, that's over." Helen stirred her coffee and wished their seats weren't in the window. A couple of kids had spotted her and were conferring just a few feet away on the other side of the glass.

Cass shrugged. "You have to put it out in the universe if you ever hope to get it back."

"I know that stuff works for you," Helen began, but Cass cut her off with a stab of her stir stick.

"It's not *stuff*. It works. Ever since I started my dream board and spent time meditating on my wishes, my life has changed. And it got me through chemo."

"I tried—I cut out pictures from a magazine and I taped them to my ceiling," Helen lied. "But according to the universe's clock, I'm still fifty."

Cass gave her a tired look. "Maybe if something were actually happening in your bed you wouldn't be feeling fifty."

"Those parts have atrophied." Helen shrugged. "You know my deal. I have no time for another person in my life. I don't need the complication. I'm really very happy—"

"I know you're happy. You're also the loneliest person I know." Cass gave her a serious look. "When was the last time you were ecstatic? Transported?"

"Last week," Helen answered seriously. "The last time the curtain went up. Why is it so hard to believe that I find it as exciting and enthralling now as I did the very first time I was on a live stage? And I have two kids I love, and a home I enjoy going to. These are the last two years the kids will be home, so I'm making the most I can of them, too."

Cass sighed. "How is Julie doing? I'm glad you got rid of that cook."

"She's gotten really wary of everything. I don't want her to develop an eating disorder, and that does worry me. But the good news is I just hired a new chef—great references and has a skill level that's usually way out of the league of a private chef. She's starting today."

Cass nodded. "You're sure she can keep Julie steady?"

"I hope so. She knows her stuff. Seemed avid about organics and clean food. David Connelly gave her a big thumbs up. Said she was the guru of pleasing the customer."

"Now that's high praise," Cass agreed. "I'll be happy if you don't have to worry about Julie so much."

"I know. If she can't stay stable she will develop some chronic side effects. It seems like every time she breaks out in skin rashes they take even longer to go away. One of these days maybe they won't, and that scares me."

"There wasn't anything in her father's family history, either. You've had so little to go on." Cass sipped her coffee and made a face. "I hope the new girl works out."

"Laura," Helen said. "Hardly a girl, either. She seemed very nice too." She gathered her cup and became aware of a teenager around Julie's age hovering at her elbow.

"Sure," she said in response to the shy request. She wanted to ask why the girl wasn't in school, but took the proffered book and pen and satisfied herself with writing *Life always gets better!* before signing her name with a flourish. "You're welcome, sweetie," she said as the girl stammered thanks.

"Anyway," she said to Cass, "Laura seemed like the kind of person you talked to for a little bit and felt you'd known all your life. Really, really grounded."

Cass waved at the girl, who was still hovering. "Honey, I'm nobody. Honest." She rolled her eyes at the girl's crestfallen expression. "I'm just the BFF."

"And then some," Helen said. In the best friend department anyone she'd known as long as Cass had to rate as best friend forever material. Some intern of Cass's publicist was the BFF to the thousands of followers on Twitter.

The girl still held out her book, and Cass took it, signed and handed it back. Speaking to Helen, she asked, "Shall we get a cab? I'll drop you at the theater."

"I need to walk it," Helen said. "Clear my head, get that New York air in my lungs. Work an airport croissant off my ass." They were on the sidewalk, turning toward downtown, when she asked, "Who were you today in that girl's autograph book?"

"Bebe Neuwirth," Cass said. "I think she bought it too."

Helen laughed. "I'll rat you out next time I see Bebe. Now why can't I get a great character part on a sitcom? Why is that, agent of mine? She's still getting residual checks from the reruns of *Cheers* and *Frasier*."

"Seriously? Do you want me to send you out on them?"

Helen thought about it. Five years ago she wouldn't have considered it. Fifty was looming so large—really, she shouldn't be letting it bother her so much. She wanted her life to stay exactly the way it had been. Her heart knew what it wanted and she listened. "No, of course not."

She signed more autograph books and assorted hunks of paper as she made her way through Shubert Alley and down Forty-Fourth Street on the way to the stage door of the Olympic. Her current production, *Look the Other Way*, was a lighthearted comedy based roughly on *The Front Page*. It wasn't the kind of production to draw promotion by the serious critics, but it had proven to be a real crowd-pleaser, and comedy had always been her first love. The run was projected safely through the fall and holidays, and if Cass didn't come up with a new production for her, she'd sign on for spring dates as well. They hadn't balked at all over her being absent for the two Sunday and one Tuesday performances each week. The rest of the cast was strong and her understudy was garnering consistent praise so ticket sales dipped only slightly for those shows.

Her character, Moxie Taylor, was a mature woman of indeterminate years. The cast was ten in all, plus understudies and a few nonspeaking crowd members in the finale, and she was enjoying the feeling of being in a smaller production, and one where both of her feet were on the ground. She'd conquered her fear of heights well enough to do a balcony scene, but flying around a stage on a wire was never going to work for her.

Their stage door guard, Jimmy—they were all called Jimmy—greeted her with, "Welcome back, Mrs. Baynor."

"Thanks, Jimmy. All's well?"

"It is indeed. There's catering tonight—a bank sponsor I think. Very good crab puffs."

"There's your bailout. Instead of millions, you get crab puffs."

"Don't I know it." He smiled after her, as far as she could tell, content with his world. A long-ago actor, he sported a badly mended hip that limited his mobility. But he guarded the stage door with ferocity and could be relied upon to share gossip—especially the kind an actor wanted to know before crossing paths with producers, directors or backers.

She headed for her small but adequate dressing room. The

below stage area wasn't opulent, but it was brightly lit and clean, and she'd learned not to take either of those things for granted. On the way past makeup she popped her head in long enough to say, "Ready when you are," to the two artists already working on the bit players. The curtain went up in three hours. Even after two months of practice, it was always a last-minute rush to get everything done. But that was the theater. It wouldn't be the theater if backstage wasn't frenzied.

The dresser—Rudy, they were all named Rudy—swirled into her dressing room saying he had replaced a pair of shoes that had started giving her blisters. He whisked them onto her feet, had her walk two steps, and whisked them off again.

"I can scuff the soles," Helen said.

"So can a monkey," he answered. Before the door closed behind him he added, "Sorry, I meant to say understudy."

He had no sooner departed than the director—Nancy, and so far Helen only knew of one director named Nancy—knocked and hurried in. "The bank sponsors bought the entire balcony as some kind of reward. I told you about it last week. Anyway, could you be a perfect dear and come out to say a few words around six fifteen?"

"I'd be happy to," Helen said. "If I get some crab puffs first."

Nancy looked like her head would burst with yet another detail to cover. But she left without disagreeing and a few short minutes later there was a knock. A shy intern—it was no use learning their names, they were never around long enough—delivered a plate of four delectable looking crab puffs. Perfect.

Thereafter, the dressing room door didn't stay closed for more than two minutes until six o'clock, when Helen put up her Do Not Disturb. For ten minutes she pulled herself into a quiet state of mind, following a simple visualization of a deserted beach with only the sound of the surf. Some might have called it meditation, but for her it was simply a calming ritual. At ten after, the dresser knocked, helped her into the wonderfully tailored 1930s *His-Girl-Friday*-style suit, and left again. She took one last look in the mirror.

For a moment she was Helen, hidden beneath lavish eye

makeup and a tight wig of black curls. She blinked and was Moxie Taylor, determined reporter with a story and a man to catch in less than two hours, with one fifteen-minute intermission. She reached for her cell phone, texted, "Love you. Time for the show," to the kids as she always did, then she tucked it—and the last of the Helen who was a mom—into her purse.

The bank people were effusive, and that never hurt the ego. She waved off hugs and smooches with a gesture at her costume and makeup, promising dire retribution on them all if either got mussed. No food, no liquid, and lots of banter with her co-star, the dashing Neil Fortney. Her gaze flicked to the clock as she listened for the time warning. At six forty-five the ushers firmly urged all the bank people toward the balcony. Six fifty the lights dimmed once. She checked her costume, walked the floor to make sure the new shoes were firmly on. Six fifty-five the lights dimmed twice.

At seven precisely, they took places. The audience was quieting. The stage manager crossed directly behind the curtain saying in a low voice, "Curtain in three. There are no announcements. Curtain in three..."

There was quiet on the stage. Neil, like her, preferred it. The quiet let in the murmur of the audience and the hum of the lights.

That hum ran down the back of her neck, and over her shoulders, down her arms. Sounding in her ears was a deep drumming of a kind that she never felt at any other time. She loved her life, loved her children, knew she enjoyed many privileges. In between each thump of her heart she reminded herself she was blessed. But this...

When the curtain twitched downward in warning, she knew that the rest of her life was a holding pattern, waiting for this moment. The curtain rose. Light flooded her skin.

She was alive.

CHAPTER FIVE

Backstage was an ocean of kisses. Air smooching yet another cheek, Helen reflected—not for the first time—that it was small wonder colds and flu went through the theater community more quickly than gossip.

"Did you hear that ovation?" Neil Fortney mopped his collar, then shook another backer's hand. The bank people were milling about again. Crab puffs and champagne circulated freely.

"The crowd was ready to be pleased, that's for sure," Helen said. She thought the pacing had fallen off a little right after the intermission. Neil and she had both stumbled on lines twice, but had steadied. By the time the mobster's hysterical ex-girlfriend had climbed atop a desk to scream out her need to be hidden, all had been well. The prop people had gotten the big safe door working again. It opened smoothly when it was supposed to and stayed shut the rest of the time.

"Helen, I don't think you had a chance to meet this evening's sponsor." Tiffany—they were all named Tiffany in P.R.— touched Helen's arm lightly. "This is Eugene Masterson of First Union Mortgage Bank."

"A pleasure to meet you," Helen said. The name rang a bell as did the sandy-haired good looks. Given the state of the financial world, perhaps she'd heard it in conjunction with an indictment or congressional hearing.

"The pleasure is certainly all mine," he answered. He wasn't making any effort to hide his admiring glance and against her will, Helen found herself welcoming it. So she was going to be fifty next month. Heads still turned.

Her smile was perhaps warmer than it should have been as she asked, "Did you enjoy the show?"

"Absolutely. It's so well constructed, and traditional, too." At her raised eyebrow, he continued, "No big show-stopping numbers for each primary member of the cast, no one flying around the stage on a wire. Just terrific delivery of a great script with imaginative use of the stage and fabulous costuming."

"You're quite the critic," Helen observed with a smile.

"I've seen a lot of theater. I saw you in *Pygmalion*."

"Off-Broadway? My goodness, that was ages and ages ago." Just after her return to New York, she thought, after that disastrous stint in Hollywood. Well, not that disastrous—she'd met Justin, Senior. She had a family and home she loved as a result.

"I went with my then wife," he was saying. "Your performance was unforgettable."

She expressed her thanks while reflecting that he was wearing a wedding ring now, and, in her opinion, standing a little too close. "Theater is more fun when you're with other people. Talking about it afterward is part of the experience." Eugene Masterson... He was the CEO of his bank, she thought, and her spotty memory was suggesting that he had indeed been called to answer for his bank's lending practices. The kind of tall, handsome, successful man, she supposed, who was used to his way in all things.

"I have to admit I've been a fan ever since. Will you be joining us for the after-party? We've taken over Birdland."

"That's such a fun club and the jazz is always good. But I'm sorry, it's not possible. I only flew back from the West Coast this morning and I need a good night's sleep to survive the rest of the week." She could tell he was going to persist so she quickly added, "I like to get back to my place in time to check in with my kids."

Children, she had learned, were the proverbial cold shower.

But not so for Mr. Masterson, it seemed. "Just for a cocktail? I've looked forward to this evening and meeting you for quite some time. I'd put you in a cab the moment the last drop was gone."

"I really am sorry, but it's just not possible." Helen could feel her mental heels digging in. Had he really spent a fortune on a block of theater seats to arrange a casual introduction to her? She didn't find that flattering, actually. It wasn't his money and she'd been around this town too long not to suspect he was a collector of objects. Anything he felt he'd bought and paid for was a thing, not a person, and his forever.

"Perhaps another time," he said, disappointment plain in his eyes.

"Perhaps," she agreed. But not likely, she added to herself, even if a tiny part of her was flattered that he did find her so attractive.

She retired to her dressing room shortly thereafter, and scarcely sixty seconds later her dresser knocked and collected her costume and wig. Clad in only her slip, she rubbed some reviving gel into her hair, which was mashed to her scalp, then she scrubbed off the pancake and greasepaint that started at her forehead and ended at her collarbone. Just as she leaned forward to look closely for any remnants she saw her face flush bright red. Then her forehead beaded and she felt sweat trickle down her back. Her stomach turned into a furnace so hot she looked to see if it was glowing.

She was drenched, head to toe. The gel she'd just applied melted off her hair like the Wicked Witch under a bucket of water.

Thank God that hadn't happened onstage! Or outside in the reception. She doused a washcloth into the pitcher of ice water on the dressing table and mopped at her face. She found herself mopping the rest of her body as well. She already needed a shower—the stage lights made it unavoidable—and that was the one thing her dressing room didn't have. The Olympic was too old and simply not that posh.

She did the best she could, all the minor glow she'd gotten from an admiring man's glance long gone. Hot flashes—she was old, old, old, damn it. The last thing she needed was to have one during a performance. There was always a blogger looking for the insider tidbit, and wouldn't that be a tasty one. *Helen Baynor is hot! Flashing, that is...*

At least she was no longer the color of a raspberry. She scraped her hair back and pulled on her emergency disguise Yankees cap. Tonight she was sliding out unnoticed. That's right, skulking off into the night like a used up old rag, she told herself.

Before she left she fished out her phone and turned it on. She felt instantly better reading texts from both kids. Justin had gotten a 95% on his advanced chemistry test. Julie had loved dinner and said Chef Laura had been all over the world and was interesting to talk to. It was such welcome news.

They were getting older, and so was she. She couldn't stop time, she told herself. She had Helen Hayes and Angela Lansbury for her role models, and thank goodness her career wasn't built solely on her looks. No matter how lined she became, she'd always have her talent, and she would always be a handsome woman. And that mattered.

She pulled the cap down over her eyes, huddled down into her trench coat and went out the main doors, quickly losing herself in the crowds.

CHAPTER SIX

Ten o'clock in the morning seemed like a decent hour to arrive at the Baynor house to look over her kitchen and take inventory. Laura hadn't wanted to disturb Grace before she was ready, but she felt she did need to assert herself as capable of running it for the four days she'd be there as well as the three days she wouldn't. It wasn't that she wanted to avoid scrutiny— she wanted to avoid meddling. A turf war was useless, so she would do her best to win Grace over and earn everyone's trust.

She was also belatedly anxious about the facilities. She supposed she ought to have asked to see the kitchen before agreeing to the job, but it had never crossed her mind that the kitchen would be anything less than acceptable. She was being asked to cook for four to five people and she was certain that

Helen Baynor's estate home had a reliable heat source, quality cookware, consistent refrigeration and counter space. And that was really all she needed.

Grace didn't look annoyed when she answered the door, but she didn't look welcoming either. "You can park your car around the side. There are several bays and one is always empty," she explained. "It will be easier to bring in the groceries from there. The kitchen is this way."

Laura followed her to the left of the foyer, through a charming but chilly little sitting room. The front parlor of a bygone era, she supposed, where a formal and hopefully short visit with an unwelcome guest would be carried out in dreadfully correct—and unheated—circumstances. The chill would encourage anyone to take their leave. It gave way to a small mud room with a door to the garden and garages and then, finally, to the kitchen.

What a kitchen it was.

It had been remodeled recently, she could tell, and the appliances were all retro antique with steel feet and scrupulously clean baked white enamel exteriors. What at first appeared to be an old-fashioned countertop oven, circa 1940, was actually a microwave. Seasoned oak paneling hid both refrigerators.

And the stove, oh the beautiful stove... The stovetop was an Imperial, finished in copper, with eight gas burners ranging from small enough for a saucepan to large enough for a stockpot. It also boasted a grill and an overhead vent in copper, with big brass fittings. Under it on the left was a full-size oven. On the right was a unit with two wide but short ovens, the top ideal for small tasks like a pie or a half-sheet of cookies, and the bottom oven for thawing or warming with a temperature gauge that went as low as 110 degrees.

She resisted the urge to hug it.

Forcing her rapturous gaze away from the stove orgy-waiting-to-happen, she was almost as delighted to see that the long kitchen island had a sink, knife rack and a selection of cutting boards at one end. The other end was surrounded with comfortable bar stools. Over it was a rack of pots, skillets and pans, all beautifully seasoned and admirably battered from everyday use. Looking at the copper bottoms she was quite sure she'd find matching quality mixing bowls and utensils in the many cupboards and drawers.

The floor was light gray flagstone, with cabinetry a retro enamel-white underneath the counters and seasoned oak above. Gray-green granite countertops completed the muted tones, and her gaze was ultimately caught by scattered throw rugs of vivid yellow that reflected the sunny yellow glow from the ceiling paint and lighting. She followed the path of the rugs to the deep bay window at the far end with an unobstructed view of the gardens.

Like something right out of a Florentine or Milanese villa, the landscaping was manicured, complete with winding pathways around a central fountain of a Venus de Milo-esque figure pouring water from a Roman vase. Two umbrella-shaded tables, with chairs, flanked the fountain. A large outdoor patio heater was ready to be lit at any moment. The hedges at the rear separated the garden from what she could see was an expanse of green grass large enough for football scrimmages.

A well-scrubbed oak farmer's table that could seat eight was positioned in the bay window—at last she knew where the family ate most of their meals. And that, as far as she was concerned, was the center of the house.

She loved the room. This was a room where a family gathered and shared food.

Grace may have mistaken her silence for some kind of disapproval, because she firmly said, "I'm afraid if you find something lacking, you'll have to make do. This is exactly as Ms. Baynor wants it."

"I wouldn't change a thing," Laura said. "It's a scrumptious room."

Conquering her awe, she set down her purse and notebook. "I'll just bring my car around and then I'll do some inventory."

Looking anywhere but at Laura, Grace gestured at the pantry. "We have all the staples, you'll find. Shopping and filling the cupboards seems to have been the last cook's greatest skill." With that Grace left the room in the direction of the front parlor.

Laura wasn't going to let the woman's standoffish manner take anything away from her enjoyment of her new playground. Who knows—maybe Grace hadn't worked closely with a black person before and thought she didn't know how to act. She did a quick exploration and found, to her delight, a cupboard that was actually the pass-through that allowed the transit of food from the kitchen into the dining room, cleverly hidden on the dining room side by paneling. She peeked through the crack to see the room where she'd first served Helen food she'd made. How beautiful was that?

The pantry was walk-in and the shelves were crowded with bags of flour, sugar, cereal, rice, potatoes, onions and other staples. Next to the pantry was narrow rollout shelving no wider than two Mason jars. There were four rollouts in all with eight shelves in each, housing the spices, canned goods, boxes of pasta, more flour and sugar—it was very poorly organized, she thought. Short shelf life products were stored behind long-life staples, for starters. No one who had worked in a commercial kitchen had organized this mess. Boxed pasta? With all the time she'd have to devote to making one meal a day, there was no reason not to make fresh and leave a supply of fresh for Helen to cook if she wanted.

She had a big job ahead of her. In order to take an inventory she needed to be able to find things.

First things first. She moved her car into the carport nearest the side door, careful not to block any of the three garages that exited into the same driveway. It looked like the far end of the garage structure was actually a separate residence, probably where Grace lived. It looked spacious and there was even a fenced area creating a private yard for it.

She paused briefly to crumble some of the leaves from the rosemary that grew semiwild on the far side of the driveway and then inhaled the scent off her fingers. Now she wanted some toasted Italian bread with roasted garlic and rosemary-infused butter spread all over it. Some day soon, she promised herself. Using the side door, she carried in a small bag of groceries with the building blocks of her own lunch. If Grace appeared, she was happy to share the makings with her. She'd also stopped to buy fresh bread and real Monterey Jack cheese—dinner could be anything if she had those two ingredients at hand. Spaghetti, omelets...

Mentally girding her loins for battle, she flicked on the

electric kettle to boil water for tea—such an undertaking needed the proper fuel. Then she rolled up her sleeves and started making notes about the contents of the pantry. There was so much in it for a family of four that she doubted its freshness. A couple of the canned goods hidden in the back of one shelf weren't brands that were dye-free. Perhaps a chef who planned inventory this poorly would resort to an emergency can of something thinking it wouldn't matter once in a while. She'd ask for a box and put these in it for the local food bank, along with the near-expiration goods she was sure she'd uncover.

Her stomach was growling by the time she was elbow deep in the pantry. It was no quick fix—she would have to pull it all out to see what was what. She'd already found a six-year-old bag of beans and numerous bags of rice, each older than the last. Helen Baynor had money to burn, but Laura had seen poverty in plenty in Jamaica and outside the walls of holiday resorts all over the world, including the United States. Wasting food was a sin. If there were already five pounds of rice on the shelf she wanted to see it so that no one bought more.

She lined up all the dry goods and decided she had to have lunch. She got acquainted with the grill by cooking two small filets of salmon, and found the utensils necessary to whisk together some blood orange-infused olive oil and rice wine vinegar for dressing on the fish and some greens. She debated whether she should look for Grace and was about to plate it all for herself when Grace returned.

"Can I offer you a small salmon salad?" She hoped she looked confidently settled in as she chose the correct cupboard for plates.

"I'd like that, though you don't have to plan to cook lunch for me every day. You often won't need to be here that early, I would imagine." It almost sounded like a suggestion.

"A special occasion." Since she was being paid a flat sum every week, she didn't see why she wouldn't have reasonable control over when she arrived and left, as long as snacks and meals were ready on time. Laura set the two finished plates on the kitchen island at the end with the bar stools. "It's just simple fare. Maybe we can go over the budget and schedule as well."

"Let me get my notebook then." Grace didn't quite sigh.

When had Grace intended to give her this information, Laura wondered, if not in some way today? Maybe she was misreading the women, but it was easy to do when someone refused to look you in the eye.

Grace had just returned when there was a knock at the side door. She stopped to let in two young Latinas, both wearing polo shirts from a local cleaning service with their black cotton pants. She gave them some instructions in rapid-fire Spanish, then joined Laura. "The girls are here for three hours on Tuesdays, Wednesdays and Thursdays, working on different parts of the house. They do a full-scale scrub of the kitchen on Tuesdays."

Laura waited for Grace to begin eating—a custom her mother had insisted was proper for the cook—but when Grace was slow to pick up her fork, she began eating anyway. "That's why it was so spotless this morning. Who does the dishes on a daily basis? I expect to do a degree of my washing up, of course, and leave some things to soak. I'm a tidy cook. My mother had high standards." Her sunny smile at Grace didn't get her one in return.

"The children do the dishes, including the cook pots and such. Ms. Baynor feels it's important to their life skills."

Laura digested that. "I've worked in a lot of high-end resorts where the kids were spoiled and ungrateful. Justin and Julie are teenagers, but they both said thank you for their snack yesterday. I was impressed."

"They're quite polite."

A silence fell and Laura thought that Grace didn't seem to much like the people she worked for. Or perhaps she was simply a hard emotional read.

Finally, Grace started on her salad. "It's very good."

"Thank you. Do you have any likes and dislikes I can accommodate at dinner time?"

"I'm a very light eater," Grace said. "I prefer low fat."

"Don't we all? I cook that way for myself naturally. How do you feel about spicy foods? Any vegetables you can't stand?"

It was like pulling teeth, but she finally got a few clues from Grace. They finished their salads and Grace offered to show her the household schedule. To Laura's surprise they walked to the mud room—she hadn't noticed the bulletin board opposite the door. Every member of the household had a line on a large magnetic calendar whiteboard, including employees, like the yard maintenance crew, the cleaners and service visitors. Tomorrow a carpet repair person was stopping in at eleven. Grace's days off were Sunday and Monday and across the top was the number for a local security firm, a doctor and a few more numbers with only a name next to them.

"How efficient," Laura said. She casually picked up the whiteboard eraser and marker and changed "cook" to "Laura." She noted that Julie had an afterschool meeting on Friday, and Justin had some kind of doctor's appointment next week. "I'll know exactly who will be home for dinner every day."

"It's crucial to our success." Grace seemed to brighten up, just a little. "This was my idea."

"It's excellent. So informative." She knew she was laying it on a bit thick, but it was the first genuine emotion she'd seen from Grace. "Now, about my budget."

They rinsed their dishes as Grace laid out the monthly family grocery budget and the stores where there was an account for the household. "Please use them as much as possible as it simplifies the receipts."

Laura agreed—the bread and cheese shop was on the list, for starters. There was easily enough money to feed the household, even when buying more expensive goods that she had confidence would only include the ingredients listed. When Grace went back to her part of the house she was relieved. It had been a good chat. They would all get along, she was sure.

By the time Grace slipped out the side door to bring the twins home from their private school in Menlo Park, Laura had brought order to the pantry and rollouts, and acquainted herself with what was in most of the cupboards of the large room. There were a number of unitaskers that she gathered up from the deep confines of several lower cabinets. Egg peelers, tomato dicers, garlic bashers, an electric gravy boat, even a device shaped like a hair dryer that purported to smoke food. She decided on the single most inconvenient cabinet of all and put them in the back to gather dust.

She heard their chatter before the twins entered the door to the mud room. The kitchen was looking fairly orderly, so she turned on a bright smile, offered up English muffin halves topped with toasted jack cheese, accompanied by fat, ripe seedless grapes and wasabi-roasted almonds.

"Hey, this looks good," Justin immediately said. Comfortably rumpled in cargo pants and a well-worn flannel shirt over a black tee, he devoured one muffin half in three bites. With a bready "Thanks" he headed toward his room, snack plate in one hand, backpack dangling from the other, and a growing trail of almonds behind him.

Julie hesitated before taking her plate.

Aware that the girl probably had questions, Laura still said to Justin's departing back, "Yo—you're losing food."

He paused, looked behind him and seemed utterly amazed to see the nuts on the floor. "Five-second rule."

"Gross," Julie said. "I can only imagine where your feet have been."

"I was walking in pastures filled with cow sh—manure. Acres of manure," Justin said as he juggled his plate and backpack and managed to pick up his fallen almonds. "Mmm, I love manure on my nuts."

"You are so sick." Julie tossed her head in a gesture that vividly reminded Laura of Helen. She added primly, "Laura will get the wrong impression of you. No, wait, I guess she's getting the right impression."

"As long as you pick them all up," Laura said. She glanced at Julie, who had retreated from the kitchen to hang her black sweater on a peg next to the door. Compared to her brother she was very reserved in crisp jeans and a cami under a cute little vest. Laura wondered if the polar differences in their personal styles was a subconscious way they tried to be dissimilar, even though, Laura thought, most people wouldn't immediately guess they were twins. They really only mirrored physically in the pointed chins they shared with their mother.

When Julie paused again to consider the snack plate Laura was offering, Laura went on, "The cheese is made in Monterey, and is free of any kind of dye—that's why it's not darker. The English muffins are from the shop on Main Street, where you've always gotten your bread."

"I'm not crazy about grapes, but I get it. They're good for me." Julie took her plate to the table in the bay window and opened her weighty backpack. Several thick books and a slim laptop were quickly spread out. Julie hunched over her binders, frowning and reading as she absentmindedly finished her snack.

Laura continued her tidying up, grateful to be at the stage where things went back in assigned places in the cupboards and pantry. When Julie paused to stretch, Laura broke the silence with, "So what else is on your list of foods you don't care for, in addition to grapes?"

Without hesitation, she answered, "I really hate bulgar. Please don't make tabouleh. And mint in general doesn't work for me. I've tried and I just don't like mint."

"No bulgar—that doesn't break my heart," Laura admitted. "And I'll watch my use of mint. How do you feel about quinoa?"

She wrinkled her brow in a way distinctly reminiscent of her mother. "I don't think I've had it."

"There's a bag in the pantry just dying to be opened. I'll make just a bit of it at dinner and you can tell me. It's a seed that acts a lot like a grain, ends up being similar to couscous in texture. It's really nutty, low in fat and loaded with protein. Kind of a wonder food and it's good for you, but unlike most things described as good for you, it tastes good." She grinned, liking that Julie was still listening. "Especially with butter."

Julie nodded with a glimmer of enthusiasm.

"Chicken? Fish? Shrimp?" All nods in response, but, "Beef?" got a shake of the head. "Why not beef? Politics? Taste?"

"Sometimes it tastes tinny to me. I don't seem to mind burgers, but steaks..." She put one hand to her jaw. "It's weird. And yeah, shrinking planet and all that."

"How about meatballs? In spaghetti sauce?"

"I like turkey and stuff like that in meatballs. I like soy

meatballs too. Justin doesn't like them though. Mom really hates them. She says they taste like poi, but I've never had that."

"I have," Laura admitted. "You have to do a lot to poi to get it above wallpaper paste in flavor. Think mashed sweet potato without the sweet or potato flavors." No soy meatballs for Helen, when she might be having the meal with her kids, then. "But maybe I can make them once in a while, when your brother is out somewhere, since you do like them and I'm sure they're good for you."

"Okay." Julie brightened a little bit.

Justin returned, looking ravenous and hopeful, holding his plate like a lanky Oliver Twist.

"How would you feel about spaghetti and meatballs for dinner? Some broccoli. A Caesar salad. And a little sample of something called quinoa so I know if I can make you a meal using it?"

"I could seriously get down with that." Justin still looked hopeful. "Is that, like, ready now, or how long?"

"About an hour. There are some beautiful apples and I chopped some fresh carrot sticks, and you can have both of them right this minute."

"You've been listening to Mom." His head stuck deep in the refrigerator, he added, "I could make popcorn."

"You'll spoil your dinner." She got up to run water in a large pot. "And yes, your mother said I should be certain to suck all possible joy out of your nutritional intake."

"She's making soy meatballs," Julie said.

"Is not." Justin took a large chomp out of the apple he'd rummaged out of the crisper.

"Is so, really. They're yummy."

Justin gave Laura a panicky look. "Seriously?"

She shook her head just slightly. "There's ground turkey and some ground pork in the freezer, panko bread crumbs and I'm pretty sure I saw buttermilk. They'll be soy-free."

Justin smacked his sister not so lightly on the head. "Liar."

"Made you ask." If Julie had been several years younger, Laura was certain she'd have stuck out her tongue.

He took aim to smack her again when Laura said, "If you have the energy to hit things, I have vegetables that need chopping and washing. I am always on the lookout for sous chefs. Kitchens are for working or eating, plus talking. Not hitting. Break the rules, you get K.P." To the blank stares she added, "Kitchen practice."

"I have stuff I gotta do."

"I see," Laura said. "An appointment with that skate rail I spotted in the carport perhaps?"

"That's for weekends. No, I have homework. Chem and math, some history." With that he got another apple and left again. Laura didn't think he'd make it an hour before he returned.

Julie said abruptly, "Mary—that was the previous chef. She didn't like us hanging out in here when she was cooking."

Laura blinked at that bit of news but only said, "You'll find that I am nothing like the dearly departed Mary."

"Good. I think she was making me sick on purpose. I complain about food a lot. It's not personal." It came out in a rush, and Laura wondered if she'd told her mother her suspicions.

"I get that. All I'm ever going to ask is if you'll give something one bite—it will always be something safe for you." She fetched a glass and filled it with water, then paused next to the table where Julie was working. "I've worked in many settings, and I think I know the difference between when someone is having issues with food they have no control over and when they're being a brat. Lots and lots and lots of people have food issues. I'm the rare chef that won't eat walnuts. I will pick them out every time."

Julie leaned back in her chair and Laura took that as an invitation to sit down for a short chat. "I like walnuts."

"I'll cook with them but I won't eat the result. But the way they make my mouth feel is something I can't really explain and I really don't like it. But try saying to a bunch of foodies that you won't eat a food and it's not because you're allergic, but because of this...funky..." She ran her tongue along the roof of her mouth. "And my gums get kind of squeaky... I can't help but think they make me feel weird because somehow they're not good for me. And you have plenty more reason than I do to worry when something makes you feel odd."

She glanced at Julie and was surprised to see the girl was tearing up. She started to apologize but Julie said, "I'm not a brat. But I think Mary thought I was."

"No more Mary. You got me, girl." She quickly added, "I lived in Jamaica with my mother for years, and *girl* is like *friend*, or *woman younger than me that I'm comfortable with.* I'm sorry. If I say it, it's not because I think you're a child."

"I prefer my name."

That serious streak must really come from her father, Laura thought.

"But I don't mind *girl.* How long have you been back in the U.S.?"

"Hmm, well, I left Jamaica permanently decades ago. But I worked in a resort there for about six months some four or five years ago. Until a few months ago I worked in a very ritzy place in the Florida Keys."

"What happened a few months ago?"

"I quit. Artistic differences, so to speak, and I was tired of that kind of kitchen."

Another glimmer of a smile went with the next question. "You like this kind of kitchen?"

"This is a bloody fantastic kitchen. And I'm going to be exploring working with other artisans in the area, too. It was time for me to reboot."

The clatter of a pan lid over boiling water drew her back to the stove. She went about blanching tomatoes while Julie returned to her homework. Justin flitted in and out for another apple. They were used to meeting new people, it seemed, and having nonfamily members in the house. It was so different from Laura's own experience. Her mother, too, had had an intense schedule with school and two jobs. But there had been no nanny or cook. She'd spent a lot of afternoons and evenings alone with the television and her books. She'd learned to crack and fry eggs at six. Neither of the twins saw her as a servant or social inferior, and that was a relief too.

All was serene in this lovely home. This job was going to work out.

CHAPTER SEVEN

Friday performances always had an extra edge. It was party night in New York and the energy from the audience was markedly higher, for one thing. Helen had never met a performer who didn't respond to that extra surge of applause. No matter how new performers were to the Broadway stage, they all quickly learned that a Friday crowd could turn grouchy if the show's energy didn't match their mood. That meant on Fridays that backstage was overflowing with nerves.

Neil was telling a joke to someone nearby that included bursting into song. Given his impressive voice, it was distracting. The doors were thin and the Do Not Disturb was only so useful. At least there were no VIPs backstage tonight. Getting out her phone to call the kids because she wouldn't be able to later, she was surprised to see a text from Cass. Business on a Friday night? The words, 'One time deal, have to answer now,' were rare from even drama queen Cass, so Helen got out her earpiece and called.

"Can you take a leave of absence from the performance in two weeks?"

"Why would I? Probably not."

"I'm serious." Cass sounded as if she was in a crowded bar and had just moved into the ladies' room. "It's 8K for a couple days' work. And you're on a week-long cruise. And this kind of deal leads to more of their kind. Easy money, sweetie. Only thing better is voice-overs."

"I'd have to go without pay here. Where does that leave me?"

"You're still better off."

"I don't want to piss Nancy off. She's been great about my schedule. That matters in this business. I'd work for Nancy again in a heartbeat and I want her to feel the same way."

"Ask her. That's all you can do. They hired a twenty-something ingénue for this Stars of Broadway cruise and she just *cough-cough* sorry *cough-cough* sprained an ankle, but if you check the society pages she's in Cannes with a new boyfriend *cough-cough* sorry *cough-cough* recovering. I know being a second choice is unattractive—"

"Second or fifth? Be honest."

"Second. Honest." Cass sounded sincere, but she was probably lying and viewing it as part of her job. "To benefit pre-natal screening, care and education for poor women, especially those with AIDS. How can you say no?"

Helen blew out a huge sigh as she wondered just how far down a list some organizer had gotten to find her name. So many screen stars took turns on Broadway that really big names currently in shows were plentiful. "I'll ask after the performance. Now would be suicidal. But I'm not all that enthused either."

"Seven days, leaving from Miami two weeks from today and heading right for Cancun? It's seven days of nothing but sunshine and for a couple of hours out of two or three days you talk to rich community theater activists about the craft, and you have a couple of cocktail and dinner functions where you make nice. Mostly women. You could get three of these a year."

"I know. Mostly women? I really will ask." She hung up, giving it more thought as she punched up Justin's number. Was she in the mood for something like this? Not really.

Justin completely disagreed. She'd told him as a by-the-way but he leaped on the idea.

"Why wouldn't you? Mom, it sounds great. When's the last time you had a vacation by yourself?" She could hear him clicking and typing while they talked.

"I come here half the week. Is that homework you're working on so furiously?"

"Sure, Mom. Yeah, it's homework." His keyboard went silent and she seemed to have his full attention. "We can handle you gone for that little while. Like you always say, your heart tells you what it wants and you're a chump if you don't listen, right? So what do you want?"

"Children that don't throw my own words back at me."

"Dream on."

"What do you think of the new chef? I mean seriously. Really. She's not there, right?"

"Nah, she's downstairs with Julie in the kitchen I think. She is totally fabulous, Mom. I'm not making it up. She's like a Zen master. She's super laid-back except she's kind of a food Nazi, I mean, really, I can't have popcorn before dinner? She keeps saying no."

"Justin, you shouldn't even be asking her. You know better. I know you work it off, but you got some bum genes on your dad's side and you refuse to eat it without butter so there's no choice."

"I know, Mom."

"You don't need to watch your calories so much as you need to watch the bad heart stuff, and for your entire life if you want to live longer than he did." They had had this conversation many times. "Besides, we both know you have it after she leaves and Grace has retired for the night."

His tone grew mulish. "You give me a way harder time about what I eat than Julie."

"Because you're not the same people, my beloved son. And

boo-hoo you have to watch your diet like most of the world. She has to watch every bite. So no pity card here."

"Fu—Freak that noise."

She laughed into the phone. "So you think I should jet off on a tropical vacation?"

"They're paying, right? Nice work if you can get it. And you're the one who says you never ever turn down work."

"All right, all right. Tell your sister her phone is going to ring in a minute."

As she called up Julie's number she could hear him in her head, shouting at his sister. He did enjoy shouting. Two very different people, but they had a wonderful bond—stronger than she had ever hoped for—and she didn't want it severed, ever.

When Julie answered, she immediately said, "You should go."

"Justin told you?"

"Just that you could get paid to go on a totally free trip to the Caribbean and should go. We're cool here. Hey Mom, could we use some of the back field for an herb garden?"

Helen heard a voice in the background, low and smooth, and realized Laura was chiming in. Julie must be hanging out in the kitchen—that was a good thing. What a disaster Mary had been. "What's that?"

"Oh. I wasn't supposed to bring it up. Laura would like to talk to you about it, though. An herb garden, all organic and rotating and stuff. So go on the trip."

She felt a stray pang of jealousy that the perfect Laura had charmed her children so thoroughly in just a few days, but then again, the way to any adolescent's psyche was totally through their stomachs, and that included Julie's very picky one. These are the choices you made, she reminded herself, so you can walk out on that Broadway stage in twenty-five minutes.

"Well, I'll think about it. How are you feeling?"

"I had a really bad headache this afternoon, and the itches," Julie said, "but it was totally my fault. I had some of a vanilla milkshake at school. I was feeling pretty good."

"And you've learned what from this experience?"

"That even white is probably a dye. And if I don't know the source..."

"I'm sorry, baby. But that's the hand you've been dealt." Helen swallowed hard, trying to go on sounding matter-of-fact. She feared for her daughter, feared for the lifetime of dodging illness that Julie faced. "And now I have to go."

"Break a leg, Mom."

She swiveled back to face her makeup mirror. Moxie Taylor stared back, ready to sparkle. But her brain was still thinking about Helen's kids and Helen's worries and, well, Helen's trip to sunny Cancun and Cozumel and other places with equally warm-sounding names. Did she really want to go?

Moxie looked her right in the eye and said, "Don't be a chump."

She laughed at her reflection. Okay. She'd show some moxie and ask Nancy about it after the show.

"Six performances? I can't let you out for six performances on such short notice."

Nancy tucked her straight brown hair behind her ears, all the while glowering, but Helen had expected initial resistance. She'd waited until her perpetually frazzled director had retired to her tiny office after the first wave of backstage air kisses and congratulations had been made. "Look, I already get lots of the but-Helen-and-Neil-get-days-off, and there are people who don't care that you've earned the arrangement, and it was agreed to when you signed your contracts. I let you out on such short notice and you're not hacking up a lung?"

"I can make it look like I am." She delivered a protracted, lung-aching cough worthy of Greta Garbo. Nancy was unimpressed. "But I don't want to do that. I don't want to lie and say I'm sick when you and everyone else will know I'm not. And showing up here with a cruise-ship tan. I enjoy working with you. I know I'm box office, but I'm a realist."

"Would you consider another part to buy my goodwill? Next summer, two weeks, six performances total—off-off-Broadway?"

Helen raised one eyebrow. "Are you trying to get me into a negotiation without my agent?"

Nancy grinned. "Yes."

"What kind of part?"

"The play is *All About Eve*. It's...sort of...dinner theater. Um... in Jersey."

Helen kept her eyebrow where it was.

"A friend is trying an experiment, looking for a market of people who want a night out and a guaranteed good, meaty play with performers they'd never get to see in such an intimate theater and are willing to pay major bucks—tickets auctioned on eBay."

"It doesn't sound economically feasible to me." She gave up her arch, disinterested look. "Interesting, but it won't survive."

"Probably not. But I owe a friend..." Nancy looked hopeful.

"I could always say it's a favor to a friend," Helen conceded. "I suppose—but if something better comes along..."

"I know, I know." Nancy waved her away. "We'll see how it all shakes out. It's entirely possible that what minor financing he has will evaporate before then."

"So I can go on a trip?"

Nancy sighed. "You can go on a trip. I would appreciate it if you told people I made you agree to horrific conditions. Horrible, terrible, career-ending conditions. Now get out," Nancy finished without heat.

Back in her dressing room, Helen called Cass, who was surprisingly mellow. It helped that she sounded like she was on her third margarita.

"Some experimental thing? Okay." The driving beat of house music threatened to drown out Cass's voice entirely.

"Where are you? It sounds fun."

"It is. Some place in the Village—a friend brought me. I can't tell you how glad I am to be able to drink again."

"Don't go face first."

"Maybe not into the drink. But other things, well, who knows?"

"How cute is she?"

"Very cute."

She was glad to see Cass thinking of getting back in the

saddle, so to speak, after her girlfriend of several years had wilted to nothing under the stress of Cass's cancer diagnosis and treatment. Helen decided not to predict a hangover and only said, "Enjoy yourself then."

"If she's willing."

With the connection broken she realized that her dressing room was very quiet. The postperformance backstage noises had quieted—had everyone taken off for various parties without her? She always went out on Friday night, then did penance at the gym on Saturday morning and repairs at the day spa on Saturday afternoon. Her Thursday and Saturday visits to Chanteuse, the miracle worker of Lexington and Third Avenue, easily kept ten years off her face.

A good night's sleep wouldn't hurt, she told herself.

She swung around to look at herself in the mirror. Moxie's wig suddenly felt too hot and her makeup sat on top of her skin. She hoped she wasn't about to have a hot flash. Her eyes looked... old. *Back to that obsession, are we?*

She tried for some of Moxie's aplomb. "Maybe you're not old, dollface. Maybe you are lonely. Cass is the smart one. You need to get out and start dating again. You could be dancing the night away with a very rich banker right now, if you lifted a finger."

She pulled off the wig and ran fingers through her damp hair. "A very rich, *married* banker." That sort of thing had never appealed to her. Plus she didn't believe that a very rich banker would be happy to hear he took a distant place in her life, Sundays through Wednesdays. She really only had two nights a week for dating. She pushed away the thought of intimacy with a married banker—with any man for that matter. It was just...so much bother.

Wiping greasepaint and makeup off her face she reminded herself she was happy. She'd successfully managed career and children on her own for sixteen years and she very much had the life she had wanted. Helen emerged from behind the layers and she decided an evening at home would be the best medicine for this fit of ennui.

A knock on the door was a welcome break from her dour thoughts. Expecting one of the dressers she called out for whomever to enter. Instead, an intern brought in an enormous bouquet of red roses.

She blushed with pleasure. The children's father had teased her about her love of flowers and had surprised her every Sunday with something special. Reading the card didn't diminish her joy in them—married banker or not. The card said, 'Every night is better than the last,' and he had written his phone number on the card as well. She wouldn't call. A polite note to his office would be best.

The card left in her dressing room trash can, the flowers cradled in the crook of one arm, she eventually left the quieting theater after turning down invitations from the few people that remained. In two weeks she was going to be wearing a swimsuit in public, quite probably, and for the first time in a couple of decades. Drinks and dessert were the last things her hips needed.

The stage door was still busy. Neil was just taking his leave of the crowd, and she was immediately besieged, which bolstered her fragile ego. She had signed a dozen autograph books before she realized that Eugene Masterson was waiting at the stage door as well.

Of course he was, she thought. "Thank you for the flowers. They're lovely."

"No lovelier than you, of course."

Oily, she thought. That was it—he was oily. And certain of his appeal. He reminded her of why she didn't miss men and that the children's father had been a different kind of man. Soft-spoken, filled with humor, utterly without ambition beyond making people in his life happy... She missed him, but now she was wondering exactly when she'd started thinking of him as "the children's father" and not "my late husband."

She'd missed what he'd said, darn it. "I'm sorry—what was that?"

"I was hoping you'd let me make up for missing out on Birdland," he said.

"I love Birdland. One night many years ago Bobby McFerrin and Chick Corea were just hanging out, having fun with the piano. They played and sang riffs off of 'Mary Had a Little Lamb' for nearly an hour." She smiled with as much charm as she could muster. "But not tonight, I'm afraid. A headache...and an early appointment in the morning."

"Really, you must let me know when you're free." He was trying and failing to look nonchalant.

"I have your number," she answered. A fan thrust an autograph book at her and she gave the young man a sweet smile. After signing, she said to Masterson, "Thank you again for the flowers."

"At least let me arrange a cab for you."

"I prefer to walk."

He smiled. "Then I'll be your knight and keep the streets safe for you."

"Ms. Baynor!"

She turned to see Jimmy leaning out the stage door. "Yes?"

"Call for you."

Puzzled, she nevertheless seized on the opportunity. "Perhaps another time," she said. She hurried to the door, hoping she exuded the pheromones of a worried mother.

Once she was back inside, Jimmy gave her a cheeky smile. "He was giving you a bit of trouble—the fellow who sent the flowers, I'm guessing."

"I get flowers so rarely that you notice?"

"No, but he paid me twenty to text him when you were getting ready to leave."

"You're kidding!" She wasn't the least bit flattered.

He settled on his high stool to lean on his desk. "I gave it back, of course. But I kept the hundred he finally offered and figured his type could use a lesson."

She laughed. "Thank you, Jimmy. You're a sweetheart." She gave him a hearty smooch on the cheek and decided a brisk walk from the main entrance would lose her quickly enough into the foot traffic that choked Shubert Alley until all hours.

A fine mist required her to turn up her collar so she disappeared, turtle-like, into the crowds.

The walk seemed longer the closer she got to her condo. It was twenty short blocks and several long ones to Fifty-Sixth and just past Lexington, but the almost mile-and-a-half was just what she needed. The cool echo of her footfalls as she crossed the entry hall to the elevators was one of her favorite sounds of New York. A marble floor sounded like no other. The doorman/security guard murmured "Good night, Ms. Baynor," as she passed him. She replied in kind and let her weariness rise along with the floor numbers. At eight she followed the long corridor to her door, one of four, and moments later she was on the other side.

The hot shower was delicious.

Finding herself in her robe and slippers before midnight on a Friday night was certainly novel, though. The rooms seemed cold and empty. Dark, like an unlit stage, it reminded her of her occasional nightmare—that she was onstage and didn't know her lines or even what play it was. She put the roses in a vase and set them on her dresser. They helped.

She made cocoa and added a good dollop of Irish cream and had a rare moment of wishing she had a television. She could surf the web, she supposed, but that would mean getting her laptop out and then she'd be up all night watching some movie she'd seen fifty times when she was supposed to be getting a good night's sleep.

She was so awake that she decided to inflict herself on her children. To her surprise neither of them answered their cell phones. She tried the main number for the house, hoping someone would answer or she'd be up all night worrying.

A warm but businesslike voice answered with, "Baynor-Browning residence."

"This is Helen—is that you Laura?" She was there late.

"It is. How are you?"

"Well. All is well. I was hoping to talk to either of the kids."

"They're right here. I'm being taught the finer points of Texas Hold 'Em." She added quickly, "We're playing for pretzel sticks."

"They cheat," Helen informed her.

Laura's, "Really?" implied that she had suspected. "And I thought it was just twin mojo. But I was told that everyone plays it and I should know how."

"Why aren't they answering their cell phones?"

"Well...I was using my phone to look up the rules and

probabilities, which they said was slowing down the game and I said I'd turn mine off if they turned theirs off. Since I suspected they were texting each other—"

There were shouts of protest in the background.

"And wouldn't you know," Laura went on blithely, "I've been doing much better since we went phone silent."

Helen felt that pang of jealousy again, but it quickly turned into homesickness. What was wrong with her? Hormones—it had to be hormones.

"Here's the tall one," Laura was saying.

"What's up, Mom?"

"Nothing, I just wanted to let you know I'm going on that cruise."

"Way to go! That's totally sick. What do I have to do to get an all-expenses paid vacation on a cruise?"

"Devote thirty or forty years of your life to a single craft until you get good at it?"

"Details." He snorted into the phone and she wondered if he knew that he sounded just like Clark Gable. "Here's Julie."

"Mom!" Her daughter's voice bubbled out of the phone. "I'm so excited. You're really going? That's awesome. You need a swimsuit."

"The horror. We'll go shopping on Sunday afternoon. That means I'll be gone an entire week. You won't see me from a Tuesday night all the way to the following Friday."

"We'll survive, Mom."

That's what she was worried about, she supposed. They wouldn't miss her. "What are you guys having for a snack?"

"Some kind of hard sort of nutty cheese with celery and apple slices."

She made a face at her cocoa. Cheese with celery and apple slices sounded really good. "Don't keep Laura till all hours. She's got a life, I'm sure."

"Got it, Mom. Justin ate all his pretzels so the game is just about tapped out."

"I miss you guys. See you Sunday morning."

She sat for a while, tapping her phone against her knee.

Ennui. Hormones. The clear tick-tock of the kids going to

college. Even though the play was financially sound, she was already anticipating the need to secure her next part and that always made her anxious. Strange, realizing that she thought of Justin Senior as "the children's father" when tonight, for the first time in many years, she was feeling like a widow. She missed him. Those first few years without him had been so hard with two babies.

When she tried to call up his face she didn't get more than his wonderful eyes, but maybe that was because Julie had them too.

Nothing's wrong, she told herself. It's just life.

And if this is what she did with a Friday night to herself, she didn't intend to have any more of them, that's for sure.

CHAPTER EIGHT

Shopping for swimsuits had been as depressing as expected. Every single one she tried on seemed determined to show off all the places she had never intended to show to the light of day again. They all screamed, "About to turn fifty!" She finally settled on a sea green with a pair of white gauzy cabana pants to pull on over it. Nevertheless, the day at the Stanford Mall with Julie, just being girly-girls, had been great fun. Justin had happily spent all of Sunday at the skate bowls in Menlo Park.

Monday wasn't nearly so laid-back. A dentist checkup and dire warnings about her flossing habits was followed by reading up about the SATs both kids had to take next spring. It wasn't until Monday night that she decided to do more than rummage in the fridge for a quick snack. The profound change to the pantry and food cupboards finally sank in.

"Wow, I didn't realize how much Laura reorganized."

"There was a big box for a food bank she took away with her." Julie looked up from her homework. "Laura found stuff I couldn't eat that idiot Mary must have bought."

"Good riddance, then." There was now room on the shelves in the pantry.

"Do you know what stereoisomers are?" She was scowling at a textbook.

"Well, since it sounds like isotope, I'm guessing it's something to do with chemicals." All the spices were alphabetized, she marveled.

"I knew that already. I hate it when they introduce a new term and it's not defined at the first use."

"Hello, it's me, your mother. No science background whatsoever."

Julie wrinkled her nose and went back to her work. She'd always been comfortable with math and science and Helen hadn't been able to help her with either since she was nine.

Laura was nothing if not thorough, Helen thought. It looked like the shelves had even been scrubbed, and all those bags of rice were gone as was the faint but bothersome smell of something in a package gone rancid. She was thinking of making a light pasta with olive oil, the soy-bacon that Julie could eat, capers and grated Parmesan, along with a salad. After such a light dinner maybe she could throw together some cookies for later as a treat.

"We're reading *Romeo and Juliet* in AP English. I have to write an essay. Do you think I'll get an F if I say Romeo is a dope?"

"Not if you back it up. So why do you say that?"

Julie closed up one set of books and stowed them in her backpack. "Juliet's no better. They don't take control of anything. Just make pretty speeches and do nothing."

"They maondke a plan to escape." She checked one of the pull-out cabinet shelves and admired the orderly arrangement of everything from cinnamon sticks to olive oil infusions—oh, there was lemon-infused oil. She'd use it for dinner.

"And trusted people they shouldn't have. And like hello? So

she's dead and he kills himself? Doesn't even go for some revenge. Or stick around for the funeral. If he had they'd be together."

"Could they ever be together? Let's say she wakes up before he kills himself. The priest marries them. How long does he live after that? 'From ancient grudge, break to new mutiny' and all that."

"He's such a loser, probably not long." Julie tapped her eraser on the table. "The thing with Romeo and Juliet both is that they take one look and are in love and then they're, like, all energized about love. They talk about each other, but really, they're thinking about love more than each other. They've grown up in this totally violent world and I think they're both completely Goth and think it's ripping cool that they're doomed."

"Is that your essay preview?"

"I suppose. They wouldn't have been happy if they'd lived. They used falling in love to get out of dying for a stupid reason. What did Mercutio and Tybalt die for? Some old man's honor. A fight they didn't start. They weren't in families, they were soldiers. At least R and J died for something of their own choosing. Oh." She wrinkled up her forehead. "I guess maybe they did take control of their situation. Their goal wasn't love, it was escaping death by family feud. And they succeeded."

"I never thought about it that way," Helen admitted. "I want to read your essay when you're done." She was momentarily disconcerted to pull out the shelving where the pasta had always been stored and find no sign of the usual boxes. She started checking them all methodically, and it was a huge improvement to have everything thoughtfully organized, but really, where was the spaghetti and angel hair? It wasn't until she opened the last one that she found the note taped to the eye-level shelf.

Fresh fettuccine in covered yellow container in the icebox.
Discard any uncooked Tuesday.
Fresh herbs in crisper. Check there first before using dried.
Marinara in Mason jar in left lower freezer.
Homemade mayo in Mason jar, right door. Store-bought
can have oil blend that uses stabilizers not good for J.

Even more impressed, Helen foraged as directed and came up with the pasta. It smelled and looked wonderful. Right on top were instructions for boiling it and the repeated directive to discard or use by Tuesday. She decided not to use the marinara since it was likely a leftover, which meant the kids had had it recently. Further investigation in the vegetable crispers revealed some already diced onion, a clove of garlic, and fresh basil, oregano and thyme.

Ten minutes later the kitchen smelled *wonderful*. It was the herbs, she thought. The fake bacon even smelled good as she crumbled it into the pan with the nearly translucent onions.

"It smells like Laura is here," Justin said as he entered the kitchen.

"Are you saying your mother doesn't know how to cook?" Really, Helen thought, she didn't know if she should like Laura because she was efficient or hate her for being perfect. Surely the woman had some kind of flaw? Maybe she laughed like a drunken donkey or something.

Fresh pasta cooked really quickly, and she had it tossed in the bacon and herbs before she'd even started the salad. "Come dish yourself some noodles, guys. I'll work on the salad."

"If I rinse the greens will that help?" Justin was already reaching into the fridge.

"Sure." Who had stolen her son, the one who thought food magically appeared on plates?

"I think I want to be a chef." He brandished the paring knife.

"That would be cool," Helen said. She was long familiar with his habit of adopting a new passion every few months. Skateboarding had lasted the longest.

"Laura is teaching me."

Julie coughed. "You mean you slugged me and she made you do K.P."

"Did not. And I know what a *chiffonade* is, so there."

"You're not supposed to hit your sister." She watched him pull leaves off a head of romaine and put them in a colander.

"I didn't slug her. I was just playing around."

"It hurt!"

"You're a wimp."

Helen shut it out, knowing it would run its course. Justin was carefully chopping the rinsed lettuce—impressive. She'd been too easy on them in the kitchen. They could work for their supper. Heck, they were probably old enough to make dinner themselves. Lots of kids did. But she wanted their afternoons focused on school, plus finding things like fresh herbs and pasta in the fridge to work with meant there was time for conversation instead of grocery shopping.

One thing was for sure: Laura was a smart cookie. Justin actually looked like he was enjoying himself. She had tried to impress upon him that now was not the time in world history to be a lazy white boy, but he was utterly without ambition—just like his father. And, truth be told, he'd never have to worry about enough having money to live on. But it would be good to see him passionate about something. Surely he had inherited some of that energy from her?

Julie cleaned her plate with an alacrity that left Helen relieved, yet set her heart to aching. She'd trusted a lot of strangers over the years and to have one turn out to be so wrong for them that the kids were actually hurt was like a bad dream. But Laura was looking like a godsend. She'd be curious what Grace would have to say when they met in the morning. She was very glad she'd asked Laura to stop by in the afternoon tomorrow as well.

"Grace is going to pick you both up from school tomorrow," she told Justin. "I'll meet up with you at the doctor's office. I still don't know how you managed not to get your Tdap shot. We were right there to get it in June after your exam."

He shrugged. "Everyone kept saying I was gonna get some shot but I never did and it's not like I was going to volunteer."

"And now instead of skateboarding with friends you're going to the doctor again. Not exactly the outcome you were hoping for, was it?"

He rolled his eyes, probably because he'd heard it all when the postcard from the school asking for proof of vaccination had arrived. She planned to say it again tomorrow at the doctor's office as well. Food might be the way to an adolescent's heart, but repetition was the only way to their brain, most of the time.

"Grace will take you on to get your hair cut," she said to Julie. Her stomach very pleased with dinner, she carried the salad bowl to the sink. "You know what you're going to tell the stylist right?"

Julie handed over her dinner plate for rinsing. "I think so—I want it shorter. Everyone is into long hair and I'm kind of tired of it. You know that picture of you from *Annie Get Your Gun*? That long maybe."

She measured a length of Julie's silky hair along her finger. "About three inches off? It should look good."

"I want it to look like I chose that look. Unlike some people who look like they just rolled out of bed."

Justin didn't answer this obvious insult. As much as they bickered, they did so far less than they had several years ago. Getting too old for it, or just growing up? It made Helen realize that in two years they wouldn't live under the same roof, probably. This was the year of SATs and college applications. It was all going to change and everywhere she looked there were signs.

"So where are you going on that cruise?"

She shook back tears she didn't want the kids to see. It wasn't like her to get teary-eyed. Hormones. "I'm supposed to get the tickets and information when I get back to New York. It leaves from Miami and I'm guessing Cozumel because that's not that far, ditto on Grand Cayman."

"Sounds like fun. Will you go snorkeling?"

"I don't know how—" She broke off to answer a call from Cass on her cell phone. "It's late for you."

"But it's not for you. Crazy day. Anyway, I can definitely send you up for the role of Rosemary in a revival of *Picnic*. Starts rehearsals for the principals in March. Are you interested or not?"

"Not. I just don't want to play a harridan spinster, especially in a supporting role."

"Okay. I was pretty sure that was your answer, but I'm just crossing things off my list. Now how would you feel about the creepy housekeeper role if a stage version of *Rebecca* were to come along?"

"Yes, I'd consider it, sure." It was a delicious thought, actually.

"A lead in *Private Lives*?"

"Noel Coward? Who wouldn't?"

"Well, you're just full of yes for the plays that are probably never going to make it. I'll keep that in mind. Note to self, Helen doesn't want success anymore."

"Helen has made her feelings very clear for the past twenty-something years."

"Coffee. Wednesday." Cass hung up.

She explained to the always curious Julie which harridan spinster part she was refusing to play as they collaborated on mixing oatmeal-butterscotch cookies. Justin returned as the first batch came out of the oven.

"Your timing is amazing."

"No," he said, big shimmering eyes wide, "you are."

"Your sister helped make them."

He treated his sister to the same look. "Amazing. And smart."

"Oh, have some," Julie said. "Before it starts to smell in here."

He had a cookie and then surprised Helen with an enveloping hug. "You are my favorite mother."

She hugged him back. "You are such a bullshit artist. You will go far in life, my son."

"Can I have another cookie?"

"Yes, two more. Let's watch something. I can't believe it's already Monday night."

At least with a TV show on and all of them enjoying milk and cookies she didn't mind the hot flash that came and went, and the kids didn't notice. But she lay awake for a good chunk of the night, thinking about Cass and her dream boards and belief that wishing something into her life would make it so. But wishes didn't stop time.

Their after-school errands were completed in rapid succession, but it was still a little after five by the time she parked the Saab in its garage. The van was already back so Julie was home, post-haircut, and Grace had likely retired to her apartment. There was also a Volvo in one of the parking bays, which meant Laura had already arrived.

Grace had been grudgingly positive about Laura, but that was how Grace was about everything. Nine months and she still didn't understand Grace's negativity. She knew it was too early to tell if the excellent chef was also good with managing her budget, which was all Grace cared about, but Grace hadn't even said she liked the food while the kids raved about it.

Laura was seated at the table in the bay window, reading something on what was probably an iPad. She looked poised and comfortable in jeans and a burnt orange blouse that set off her dark skin. She immediately looked up with a cheerful smile. "I got here early and dropped off a few groceries. I hope you don't mind that I had a cookie—it was just too tempting. The cardamom was genius. I'll remember that."

"Not at all. One less on my hips," Helen said immediately. "I'm glad you liked it. Julie and I made them last night."

"Where would you like to talk?"

"In here is fine. I was going to start dinner. Dang—I meant to stop for some fresh fish."

"There's frozen uncooked shrimp. It looked like it hadn't been there that long. Even frozen will turn out nice with some gentle treatment." Laura closed her tablet. "Let's talk and cook. Two of my favorite things."

"You're not supposed to cook tonight, really, it's not right—"

"I can't sit idle. It would be physically painful to me to do nothing." Laura's pleading brown eyes reminded Helen of Justin. "Torture."

Helen laughed. "What about poaching?"

"Great idea." Laura was already getting out the shrimp and dropping it into a colander. With cold water running over the frozen mass, she said, "I noticed there's no wine in the kitchen."

"I don't drink at home. There's a fully loaded bar in the living room—locked—for entertaining, but I didn't want to get into a debate about wine versus marijuana with the kids when they should have nothing to do with either at their age." She went to the pantry with a large container of vegetable stock. "It looks terrific in here, by the way. I can find things again."

"Thank you. About wine—would you object to my using it in subtle ways in some dishes? It's a dye-free coloring agent, for one thing, and adds umami...savoriness."

"I can see that—good idea. I love *coq au vin*. And mushrooms sautéed in a dark red smothering just about any kind of meat." The vegetable stock went into a cook pot she set to come to a boil.

"I won't go overboard, and, of course, all the alcohol will evaporate. Some white in the poaching stock would be delicious if we had it—I'm all about flavor." She continued to work with the shrimp, which was thawing. "Do you want to poach in the shell or out?"

"In the shell is more flavorful, isn't it?"

"But messier to eat."

"In. Oh, I'm thinking evil things like butter and garlic for a dipping sauce."

Laura grinned. "Sounds good."

The broccoli in the crisper looked fine and Laura suggested simple steamed rice, which she quickly measured and set on the stove to boil. They worked companionably for a few minutes, Helen focused on trimming the broccoli as she listened to the speedy snick of Laura's paring knife mincing herbs.

She found herself trying not to stare. It wasn't that she'd never seen someone use a knife with that kind of skill before. She'd had several dinners at chefs' tables right in the kitchens of some of Manhattan's finest eateries, and she'd been to numerous fundraisers featuring celebrity chefs. It was more the economy of Laura's movements that was so mesmerizing. The pile of finely minced herbs grew, and then without hardly a break in motion, garlic was smashed, peeled and minced as well.

"Practice," Laura said and Helen realized she'd been caught staring after all.

"It shows. How do you think the budget is for food?"

"Quite easy to live within. I did want to ask about stocking frozen goods, like this shrimp. You obviously like to cook, but I can't buy fresh fish for you on Saturday unless you're going to make it on Sunday."

"It would be a shame to have to throw it away, but you have no way of knowing my plans for Sunday." Helen put the broccoli in a microwave steaming basket. "We've been around that conundrum a couple of times, and that's why there's frozen shrimp and chicken. What worked with the chef before the horrible Mary was if you notice I've used something, replace it in two weeks or so."

"Sounds good. You don't like to shop, do you?"

"Not groceries. I guess I'm passing the buck." She set the microwave on medium-high for six minutes. "If I never buy any groceries, then I never have to blame myself if Julie has an attack."

"You're paying handsomely enough to expect me not to make mistakes. Plus I love food shopping. I thought I'd miss the market experience, but you've got a great one right here in Woodside, and there are farmers' markets literally all over the area. I've been down to Monterey and up to Berkeley in the last two days. Beautiful produce, amazing variety even for this time of year."

She watched Laura fetch butter from the refrigerator and pop a stick in a small saucepan. It was tempting to just sit back and admire. She was a talented woman, and obviously single. Well, that was true of Cass, and she was single too. Apparently, lesbians had no lock on the relationship thing either. Maybe she'd gotten her heart broken or something. It would explain the career change at this stage in her life.

Well look at you, the voice of Moxie drawled. What's with looking at a successful woman and thinking she's incomplete if she's not paired up? Ironic, don't ya think? Besides, just because she hasn't mentioned a girlfriend doesn't mean there isn't one, dollface.

The stock was almost boiling and Laura scraped half of the herbs and garlic into it. "The rice has ten more minutes, so we have to wait a bit."

The microwave dinged.

"Oh—the broccoli's done. I should have waited to start it." She felt herself flush a little. "I never get the timing right."

"Obviously, you save timing for the stage."

That was a comforting thought. "I guess you're right. I hadn't thought of that."

"The broccoli will stay warm. Can I show you a few things about the organization scheme?"

They were chatting about produce in Indonesia, of all things, when Julie discovered them in the walk-in pantry. "Is there dinner soon? I'm starving."

"No, the delicious smells are all to drive you mad." Helen lightly touched Julie's hair, now only a scant inch longer than her ear lobes. "I like this. It's very chic."

Julie glanced at Laura. "Are you talking about the herb garden? I was serious—I'll do most of the work."

"Actually we weren't." Laura shooed them out of the now overcrowded pantry. To Helen she said, "Honest, I didn't pay her to nag you."

"I like the idea. Grace can ask the gardeners—"

"I want to dig it myself," Julie said. "I can turn it in as an environmental sciences project for extra credit. And I thought blogging it with photos I could maybe use for a college application extra."

"Julie's been our environmentalist member of the household for years," Helen explained to Laura, who was peeking under the lid atop the rice.

"About five minutes until it's ready. Julie was telling me about her ideas for sustainable gardens. It's fall, so there are things she can plan and measure now, and I think there are some organic soil treatments she can do before spring planting."

Julie and Laura were off to the races, discussing the plants that Julie wanted to include and Laura reining Julie in on her initial idea of how big to make it.

Helen hated to say it, but she had to. "Don't forget, honey, that in two years you won't be here to care for it, so I'd prefer you didn't plant an acre of zucchini."

"Just herbs, Mom." Julie stared into space with one of her usual pensive frowns. "You're right, I guess."

Helen caught Laura giving her a searching look. She turned quickly to the stove. "About time to poach the shrimp?"

"And clarify this butter." Laura turned up the heat under the saucepan of butter.

"Can I make a salad?" Justin asked from the doorway. "I'm good at salads."

"I meant to ask you," Helen said to Laura, "where is the pod that contains my real son?"

Laura laughed, and it was nothing like a drunken donkey. "We don't need a salad tonight," she said to Justin. "Tomorrow night you can branch out into grilled romaine for a manly salad you eat with your hands."

Justin grunted, Julie told him he was gross and Helen decided that Laura was far too nice to hate. She was going to have to look hard to find some imperfections. Maybe she was single because she was hard to live with. She should introduce Laura to Cass, maybe, if that was the case. Two hard-to-live-with people might just make it work if they lived three thousand miles apart.

Part Three:
Corkscrews

CHAPTER NINE

Though Laura tried to fill every morning before she went to the Baynors' with something useful, Friday morning proved to be empty of any pressing To Do items, and she lacked the ambition to make up a new list. The interior of her hotel room was exceedingly dull—she was heartily sick of it. The boxes stacked three deep and six high in all possible places made it crowded and constantly reminded her that it was impermanent. Yes, she could make a meal, but she was tired of barking her shins.

She was stymied in her search for new housing closer to Woodside, however, because the real estate agents weren't exactly jumping to help her out. She didn't know if their "we'll give you a call if we see something come open" attitude was a reflection of a tight housing market, or if her skin color was influencing them. There were plenty of people with mocha, tea and chocolate skin colors in East Palo Alto and it wouldn't be surprising to find that the milky confines of Woodside wanted to keep them all there.

Maybe she should call Helen to ask permission to use her name—she had her number. No, that would be intruding when it could wait. Maybe she should ask if she could drop by before their scheduled meeting on Tuesday. No, that would take a phone call, so ditto about intruding when it could wait.

She really enjoyed cooking for the kids. Grace, not so much, because Grace never seemed enthusiastic about anything except for merchant receipts that were under budget. It was as if all food were sawdust to her. Making dinner with Helen, however, had been surreal. She had so many memories of her on stage wearing many different faces. Helen was a star. But the Helen in her kitchen was the Helen from the roller coaster. Genuine and warm, clearly loved her kids...and why wouldn't she? All of her dreams had come true. It would be strange if she *wasn't* happy and kind and fun to be around, given those circumstances, but in her many postings she'd met a lot of rich and famous people who weren't happy and let everyone around them know it.

Flicking through email proved no diversion. The one from her aunt in Jamaica was routine. Everything was fine, though no one knew where the money would come from for someone's latest trip to the hospital. No one in her mother's family had ever known where the money would come from. It had been years after her mother's death before she'd realized that her family had treated her mother like an outsider, because she had left to get an education and because she'd worked at any job she could find, every day. Yet they'd all been there when they needed money, with a sad story, a hangover from their substance of choice and a weeping child in their arms for emphasis.

She'd always felt an outsider too. She didn't speak Patois and her "rich" mother made her go to school. In the part of Kingston where they'd lived, far from the tourist maps and next to the water treatment plants, "rich" meant less than six under the same roof and both she and her mother had their own bedroom. The electricity bill was paid, every month, and no one ever came to take back the television or car for lack of hire payments. When she'd complained once that she wasn't like any of her cousins, and no one liked her, her mother had said, "They don't get the fish in your kettle and you don't get theirs. We'll go back to America—just a little bit more money, and we'll go back."

The hard part of adjusting to her new life plan was being alone so much. She was used to fourteen-hour work days. She spent far too much time analyzing the how and why of her situation and it never got her anywhere but right where she was. Yes, she'd been an outsider everywhere she went. If it wasn't her nationality—American, but not quite sounding like it—it was her role as a supervisor, and who wants to be friends with the boss. Or it was the outright objections to her mixed race from whites and blacks alike. Here, in one of the bastions of liberal California, she was hoping not to have to deal with that, or at least accept what she could not change in people's attitudes because she had the means to make them treat her with respect.

Helen did treat her with respect, and importantly, so did the kids. If she had to drop Helen's name to get a rental in Woodside, then she would. The lack of a local referral—maybe that was the entire barrier given how tightly closed the community was to outsiders. She'd proceed on that basis until she had some indication otherwise.

She refreshed her email one more time, liking her iPad more every day. She had a laptop that she used in the evenings, but this little gadget meant she could get up and out in the morning without hanging around for boot time. Of course, she was sitting in her pajamas at ten a.m. with nothing to do.

A new email arrived from the head of Food and Beverage at Florida Grand Keys, her last employer. She read Megan's note with mixed feelings. She wasn't surprised her former boss had taken another job elsewhere. He was the type to always get a better job just before hell broke loose on the one he had. That was one of the reasons she'd left. She'd seen so many of his type come and go. If she'd waited him out she'd still be there, but the stress had made her too anxious, and old whispers of easy ways to feel better had started up. She no longer felt the need to test herself with temptation. That was a stupid waste of energy and focus. She'd had the means to leave it behind and her heart knew it was time anyway.

Megan wrote that the new executive chef probably wouldn't last either and that she should apply to come back. Without hesitation she clicked reply and tapped out, "Thanks for the news. I am loving California very much, and have found exactly the post I was hoping for." She asked about Megan's mother's surgery and sent the message, then closed the email app.

"You're not going to sit here for four or five hours until it's time to be at the Baynors'," she said aloud.

A winery—there was a thought. In the mild fall days, most were open Fridays and the weekend. She could easily fit one in and she'd feel better for doing something useful. A couple of clicks let her print a map to the Just Outta Town on the Right winery, the one that Teeny at the produce market said her son ran. Why not?

Braced by her shower, she savored the cool, crisp fall air as she walked out to the car. She'd been told California didn't have much by way of seasonal changes, but this was already more than she was used to. She had the windows down for all of the drive with her iPad playing a favorite collection of steel drum and island music. The island itself might not be in her blood, but Jamaican music never failed to put more blue in the sky.

Her wheels crunched over the soft gravel of the driveway and she was enocouraged by the open doors of the tasting room, which was attached to one corner of a wine barn. An elderly dog was curled up on a cozy looking mat just to the side of the door. It lifted its head as she passed. She clicked softly and added in a gentle tone, "I'm okay. Just a visitor. You sleep."

The tasting room was undergoing renovations and the lingering aroma of wood stain was still in the air. A middle-aged woman in work pants with her arms sunk into a crate gave her a nod and said, "I'll be right with you. We're not doing full tastings today, but if there's something you were interested in, we may have it open."

"Your dry whites. I'm in no big hurry. No worries," Laura said. Okay, she wouldn't get a full range of tastes, but it was still a beautiful day better spent out and about than sulking in her hotel room. "Teeny sent me."

It turned out to be a magic phrase. The woman left her crate and grinned broadly. "My mother-in-law, and she only sends people she has a good feeling about."

"I'm honored, then. I'm Laura." She held out her hand.

"I'm Carol—my hands are covered in crate dust and other things I won't mention that are always in the bottoms of crates." She held them up like they were dipped in toxins. "Let me get my helper to uncork for you. Sue Ellen!"

There was a muffled reply.

"Come open up down here."

Another muffled reply, then a clatter. A moment later a young woman with long blond hair and a bright smile entered from the far end of the room, gliding across the hardwood as if she'd rather be dancing. "Hi. What can I help you with?"

Carol immediately said, "Whites—a full range. She's a VIP."

Laura laughed. "Wow. I've been promoted."

"Seriously," Carol said, "Teeny is really very picky about who she sends to us. She was not happy about the whole idea to buy a vineyard and a bunch of bottles, but now only the very best people get to know we exist. If you talked to her for any length of time, I'm sure you heard the whole story."

"Not a lot—but enough. Family businesses are always full of personality."

"That is an ever-lovin' understatement."

Sue Ellen had meanwhile been lining up a selection of tall green bottles. "How experienced are you with wine? I don't want to prattle on about varietals and sugar content if you know all that."

"I'm no sommelier, but I've worked side by side with them for years."

"Then I'm not going to waste your time telling you how it tastes. This is last year's reisling, which we're really very pleased with. We're the only grower in the area who corks a pure reisling."

The reisling was very light and sparkled on her palate. They chatted about the region's tendency toward chardonnay and merlot grapes as she made her way through gewürztraminer, pinot grigio and, finally, to a deep-bodied, oaky and fruity sauvignon blanc.

"You liked the pinot best, didn't you?" Sue Ellen grinned when Laura nodded. "Knew it. It's all in how people exhale after they swallow."

"I've never noticed that." The tips of her fingers were ever so slightly tingling from the alcohol, reminding her that she hadn't eaten much of a breakfast. She would be glad of the crackers in her handbag. "I'm a chef and I'm going to watch for that now. I imagine it's the same with food."

"You're a chef? Where do you cook?" Sue Ellen leaned on the bar, her snug tee outlining a lithe form. At first Laura had thought she was in her twenties, but now she was guessing early thirties. She had a fresh, blond, does-yoga-religiously look and very lively green eyes.

"I was a chef in resorts, but now I'm trying my hand at being a private chef and learning all there is to know about this part of California. I'd like to settle somewhere nearby. I'm tired of moving around the world."

"But that sounds so interesting. Like where have you been?"

The alcohol was setting off a few alarms. She'd drunk as much as she ever drank at any one time and she was all too aware that alcohol reduced resistance to other things. She ought to have spit out the wine after tasting, as professional tasters did, but she couldn't spit to save her life. But if she chattered for a few minutes the tingle would subside. "As far as the Caribbean, the only large island I haven't lived on for some period of time is Cuba. I've lived in Hong Kong, Thailand, Malaysia, Australia... Monaco. Greece. Wherever there are resorts for the wealthy, I think I've lived there."

"Wow." Sue Ellen crossed her arms on the bar. "That's so culturally exciting."

"Not as much as you'd think. The culture inside a resort often doesn't resemble the culture outside."

"I've never understood why people want to go to a foreign country and stay someplace that's just like home."

Laura shrugged. "California seems perfect to me right now."

Sue Ellen's smile broadened. "Why thank you."

Laura blushed. "I didn't mean—I mean..."

Wrinkling her nose in a particularly charming fashion, Sue Ellen teased, "I'll give you time to mean it."

Nobody had flirted with her in years. Sue Ellen, like California, was a breath of fresh air. "I have to go to work. And so do you."

"Sad but true. Here." Sue Ellen picked up a Sharpie and took Laura's hand. She had three of the seven numbers written in bright red before Laura thought to suggest paper. "That's my four-one-one and I'll leave it to you. I grew up here and I know every leaf and tree."

"Sounds like you'd make a great guide."

"Yes. I would. A great guide. And now my boss wants to know if you want a bottle of the pinot. I couldn't care less—this day is already a total success as far as I'm concerned."

Grinning, Laura said, "A bottle of the pinot grigio—the reserve. And thank you."

Sue Ellen gave her a wink and selected an unopened bottle from under the bar. She told Laura the total as she rolled the bottle in bright blue tissue.

She was very aware of the phone number on her palm as she picked up the wrapped bottle. "Sue Ellen—"

"You can call me Suzy."

"Why is a California girl called Sue Ellen? Isn't two first names more common in the south?"

"My mother was a big fan of *Dallas*. TV show. With any luck it has never aired anywhere you've lived because I am really not a Sue Ellen." Suzy walked with her to the tasting room door.

"What's a Sue Ellen like that you're not?"

"Straight, for one thing. I'm sure there are lesbians named Sue Ellen for real, but women hear my real name and they think I'm straight. Now if I decided to call myself Scully...?"

"*The X Files* I've seen." Suzy had paused in the doorway, gracefully posed against the doorjamb. To get by Laura would have to step very close, and she was shocked by how much she didn't mind the idea.

"If my name was Scully I'd have dates every night of the week."

"I can't believe you don't anyway."

"Leave or you'll say something that will get you kissed."

Things were moving entirely too fast and too pleasingly for Laura to make sense of it. She was in the Volvo—definitely wishing it was a red sports car—and a half a mile down the road before she thought, *What on earth just happened?*

Chicken breasts with almond and orange infusion were sizzling on the grill by the time she'd convinced herself that the exchange with Sue Ellen—Suzy—had only been a bit of fun on an otherwise dull day.

She might have even forgotten about it if Julie, as Laura plated her chicken for her, hadn't pointed at Laura's hand.

"Did you get some girl's phone number?"

"No, it's not that at all." She was a terrible liar and she knew it.

"Sure. And here Mom said you probably had a life and she was right. What's her name?"

"You're assuming it's a woman or did your mom tell you?"

"There's a rainbow bumper sticker on your car. Duh."

"I forgot." Laura had to laugh at herself. "It's just someone I met and she wrote her number before I was sure I really wanted it."

"Pushy then." Julie dished out two heaping spoonfuls of quinoa flecked with diced mushroom. "I love this stuff. Is there butter?"

"No, we never keep it in the house."

Julie rolled her eyes and went to the refrigerator. "So is she pushy?"

"Not in a bad way."

"You like her then."

"Maybe." Really, Julie was a prize question asker. She should introduce her to Teeny. Probably frustrate both of them intensely.

"Well, are you going to call her?"

"If I do, I'll probably not tell you." She wondered if she should summon Justin for dinner. Usually his nose led him.

"Oh. Not my business." Julie didn't look daunted.

"Have you ever thought of joining a debate team?"

Julie frowned. "Why do people keep asking me that?"

Justin appeared behind her, reaching for his plate. "We all want you to get some help."

"Wasn't. Talking. To you." Julie plunked herself into her chair while lasering her brother's back with her eyes.

Laura joined Julie at the table and wondered if Grace would sit down with them or take her dinner to her apartment.

When Justin joined them she checked out his plate. He had likewise loaded up the quinoa, which pleased her, but had skimped on his green beans.

"Shall I get the rest of your green beans for you?"

He sighed, but fetched the steamer basket and added more beans to his plate. "That enough?"

"Yes. Why do we go through this little vegetable ritual almost every meal?"

"Because I like it?"

Laura gave him the look he deserved, then smiled a welcome at Grace, arriving from somewhere else in the house.

She had noticed how little Grace spoke to the kids. She must be very good at her job—certainly the household seemed to run like a clock. If anyone were to ask Laura her opinion, she'd say give Grace some cooking lessons and she would be able to function as a cook for the house. Overseeing groundskeepers and staff did take time, though, and the house was both old and not easily repaired. No doubt finding the right specialist to mend a weak support in the ninety-year-old banister wasn't an easy job, and there was some kind of electrical upgrade going on in the great room. She could only imagine the details.

"This chicken is really good," Julie said. "How come it tastes like orange and...limes?"

"It was marinated overnight in oil infused with orange flavor and some herbs. You're probably tasting the lime kafir leaf, which is a Middle Eastern touch."

Justin complained, "You made dinner before I could help."

"And I owe you something for that exactly why?"

"I'm an impressionable youth. Saddened and frustrated in his quest to be a master chef."

"Don't tempt me," Laura said. "You have no idea what you're getting into."

Her tone heavy with disapproval, Grace said, "Mrs. Baynor has always stressed that the children's schoolwork comes first."

Grace seemed determined to rain on Justin's parade, regardless of what the parade was about. "Talk to your mother, then. I am willing to teach you, but only if you can learn."

Julie snorted and started to say something, but Laura held up a hand.

"Your brother doesn't get to comment on your herb garden, and you don't get to comment on his cooking plans."

Grace left the table, not seemingly in a huff, but Laura still felt the pall of her negativity. Grace would find a way to make skylarks stop singing.

Laura tried to let none of her opinion show in her face. When the kids were done she made sure they cleaned the grill and took her leave.

The number on her hand felt like it was on fire. She should call. They could see a movie—it was late to propose that. But she should call. Tomorrow night was free—all her nights were free.

She waited until after eight, which was clearly too late to make any kind of plans for the night. A cheery voice mail greeting wished her *namaste* at the end. She stumbled through reminding Suzy who she was. "I was thinking maybe we could meet at the coffee place. I mean at Makes Life Worth Living, on Main Street. Tomorrow or Sunday, say around three? Or earlier or later? I get texts at this number so call or text. If you don't then that's okay and I'll see you around."

There. Had she sounded pathetic? Had she sounded over-eager? She felt both. Suzy was very...physical. She'd never really had time to date before, not seriously, no more than a couple of trysts with co-workers who had the same time constraints. People arrived, then they left. The entire industry had been transient.

She jumped when her phone vibrated. Suzy had texted back, "In a class right now. Sunday at three sounds lovely. See you there."

She liked that it didn't say, "In class Sun good @3 CU." It made her feel like she wasn't a decade older than Suzy and therefore they'd have a chance at reasonable conversation and some mutual likes. Beyond the one thing they both, well, liked...

CHAPTER TEN

With a trip looming on her calendar, time seemed the last thing Helen could control. Before she knew it, she was back on a plane to California, wrung out from four busy days in New York. It didn't help her time management that her solution to hot flashes was extra time at the gym, and her cure for the fits of ennui was extra time out at night. After a Friday charity dessert fundraiser turned into a trip to a SoHo bar for some concoction that was the latest rage, she hadn't gotten in before four. Her understudy had sworn it would be worth it.

Of course it hadn't been worth it. She'd been tired all day Saturday and hadn't really been able to drift off on the plane. She now heard the change in the flaps, too, which meant they had passed the Sierras and were starting to descend into the San Francisco air space.

The worst feature of Grace's job, she often thought, was picking her up at the airport at six a.m. every Sunday morning. Grace was far more reliable than a hired car and usually let her crash across the backseat of the minivan for another forty-five minutes of respite.

"I'm so tired I can't sleep, I think," Helen said, buckling into the passenger seat. "I'm so glad you're driving. I'm hoping my own bed will make all the difference. How are things?"

Grace gave her a rundown of the ongoing project in the great room to upgrade the electricity. It seemed to be going on pace, but there was a constant pushback from the contractor about additional costs. "I always tell them that they gave me a bid and have to live with it. The permit fee, though, wasn't part of the bid. So that was paid."

"Any surprises in the homework?"

"No, both children are on track."

Something in Grace's trailing off tone made Helen glance at her. "Is there something else?"

"Justin seems convinced he's getting a car soon."

Helen laughed. "I'm not sure where he's getting that idea. Not from me."

"Laura, I think, has promised him cooking lessons, which will distract from his schoolwork." Grace smoothly navigated the transition from the airport zone to I-280 south.

"He mentioned that—I'm all for it. As long as he's up on his work. No using it as an excuse. No repeats of last year when he found it hard to begin his homework, let alone finish it and turn it in on time. Julie is okay?"

"She's fine. She's put on a pound or two. She's eating a great deal."

"She was getting a little overlean, so I gather she's liking Laura's food. No attacks?"

"None that I'm aware of."

That little bit of news left her feeling more relaxed and she closed her eyes to doze. While it would be nice to have a household manager with the same lightness of spirit that seemed to envelop Laura, Grace's browbeating ways and tight financial management kept all the highly distracting details out of Helen's way. There had been some wonderful nannies in years past who had also managed some of the business of the household, but Grace was the first to take it over completely. The kids, she knew, didn't need a nanny's benign affection the way they had as youngsters, and Grace had started tackling the long-ignored upgrades to the ninety-year-old house.

There was no one up when they arrived at home. Grace went back to her apartment behind the garage and probably wouldn't be seen until Tuesday morning. Helen let herself in the side door and quietly carried her small suitcase up the stairs to her room. Even though this bedroom and the one in New York had most of the same amenities, all the same toiletries and duplicates of lingerie and even shoes, this room was home. The proliferation of photographs across the dresser was one difference, and she always fancied that the little noises of the kids sleeping kept the whole house from having the chill of the New York condo.

Whatever it was, it proved magic, and the next thing she knew her alarm clock was buzzing. It was after ten. She could hear the unmistakable sound of a shower running. Even at this distance from the kitchen, she could smell something warm and breakfasty. Her stomach promptly yelled, "Get up!"

The other grand thing about home was no witnesses but the kids. She pulled on her robe, ran fingers through her hair and went down to see what was cooking. The smell was so stomach-clenching good that she half expected to find Laura, moving her hands in that way she had, busily producing something delectable.

Instead she found her son frowning over the griddle. He had a box of Bisquick in one hand and a spatula in the other and was muttering, "But how do I tell if it's hot enough?"

She gave him a half-hug and peered at the bowl next to the stove. "Is that pancake batter?"

"It's supposed to be. I'm hungry and I thought I could practice on you guys. And I made a coffee cake from one of Laura's recipes. It uses applesauce and yogurt and almost no butter, so low-fat, honest."

"It smells so good my stomach hurts." She ran a little water on her fingers and then flicked them at the griddle. The drops promptly popped and steamed. "That griddle is plenty hot. Might even be a little too hot. But give one a try and you'll see. The first one is always a test."

"But I don't want to waste any batter."

"Unavoidable. If you get lucky and it turns out you can still eat it."

"Be fearless," he said to himself. "If I don't flip it it'll burn and that's worse than cleaning it off a burner, right?" He tried to do it in one quick motion and mostly succeeded, though much of the uncooked batter trailed across the hot surface to cook.

"It's the right color," Helen said. "The batter looks good."

He nodded grimly, gaze never leaving the griddle. A minute later he slid the little cake onto a plate. She quickly applied a smear of apple butter, cut it in two and offered him half.

"Now that is good," she said. "Congratulations. Now make me three more. And your sister would probably like three or four."

"And I get the rest." He made a move to shelter the bowl as if Helen were threatening to make off with it. "The cook gets the rest."

"Is that one of Laura's rules?"

"No, it's my rule."

"I can live with that. After such great pancakes I think we're going to have to save the coffee cake for after dinner. These are good enough to be dessert."

"But I want to have some *now*."

She grinned and wrapped her robe more tightly. What had she been so restless about? Some things—like her son's stomach—would never change. Peering out at the garden she thought it might be a lovely day.

"She's seen you in jeans," Laura said to her reflection. "Not that anyone wears anything else. And she's more likely to like jeans than the designer wear."

She ran a hand over her hair. It was getting scruffy. Why

hadn't she gotten it cut yesterday? It would have been more productive than driving down to Scotts Valley in the vain search for an olive grower and a bistro that had been written up in *Chef's Gourmet*. The bistro had gone out of business. Such was the vagaries of running a restaurant. But the olive grower and tasting room where she had hoped to sample some artisanal oils and infusions simply hadn't been where they were shown on the map, and calls to their number had gone unanswered.

"It's just coffee. To see if she wants to bolt for the nearest door. Or if you do." She peered closely at her mouth in the poor hotel bathroom light. Was that another wrinkle? One of the things she loved about the hue of her skin was that wrinkles didn't show as much as they did on paler skin. Still, those lines were new and they didn't look like they'd been caused by laughter.

She realized she was frowning—that's where those little buggers were coming from. Too much frowning. It was time to get dressed for a coffee date and spend some time with a very lovely woman. Just what she had been looking for, leaving the corporate resorts behind. Life. A life.

Get on with it, she scolded.

Refusing to look any longer at her reflection, she pulled on well-faded jeans and a fitted blouse of brilliant aquamarine. She hoped the blue-beaded wires she hung in her ears would distract from the untidiness of her hair. Her iPad and purse in hand, she marched out to the car, feeling more like she was going into battle than to a date.

Suzy was already at Makes Life Worth Living, seated at a cozy table next to the street windows, and she was stirring something with the lush mixed spice aroma of chai. Her long hair was a buttery wheat hue in the sunlight. Like Laura, she wore jeans and a blouse, but hers was a deep rose and unbuttoned to show off a pretty white camisole, all of which set off her long neck and highly defined collarbone.

"Shall I get us some apple bread as well?" Laura hoped the butterflies in her stomach weren't audible in her voice. "I think I'm hooked on it."

"It's delicious." Suzy pushed her silky blond hair back over her shoulder. "That would be nice."

After she was settled with a Sumatran dark roast and two toasted slices of apple bread, she asked Suzy, "So are you related to the family that runs the winery or just work there?"

"I'm Carol's yoga instructor and when they opened up I helped with some of the decorating and designing the label. I love wine and Carol suggested I might staff the tasting room for a little extra income. The summers get really busy. Right now they're all crazy trying to finish the renovations before they start crush, which is any day."

"Some vineyards are already in it."

"Their own grapes are later, which is good—the temporary pickers are freed up from the big farms."

"It's such a fascinating business. I have a good palate, but the difference between *jammy* and *plummy* eludes me."

"I've met people with really bad palates, but they can describe wine and food like nobody's business. One was even a celebrity chef type. I swear, if they hadn't been completely different colors, he couldn't have told the difference between a chardonnay and a merlot. But he was lovable anyway." Suzy sipped her chai and half-closed her green eyes as she inhaled the aroma. Laura found it oddly charming. "I could live on this stuff."

"Give me coffee, but I make a mean chai cupcake. Cardamom, ginger, fennel, some clove, touch of cinnamon..."

"You'll have to make me one sometime." Suzy's eyes glittered with unmistakable invitation.

Still feeling taken aback by their undeniable chemistry, Laura said, "As soon as I have an oven. I'm still living out of a hotel. It's not easy to find housing in this area."

"Tell me about it. Rentals are rare. I finally found a bolt hole in Atherton. Some friends and I are talking about buying and sharing a house. An investment and a place to live all in one. No matter the economy, real estate is a good investment here." She broke off a piece of one of the slices of apple bread and ate it with relish. "That is so good."

Laura tried not to stare as Suzy licked her fingers. What was up with her? *First woman in years and years to show interest when I can be interested back and I'm a tingling, responsive mess.* "I'll admit it. I really wanted to see you again, but I picked here because even if the conversation didn't go well, the apple bread would be worth it."

Just as she realized she couldn't have said anything less flattering, Suzy laughed. "And how is the conversation going?"

"So far it's better than the bread." Phew, okay, maybe she'd saved herself.

"You haven't had any of the bread." She tore off another piece of the bread as Laura did the same.

"I don't need to." She ate her piece anyway, distractedly thinking it was as delicious as always.

"So why did you pick the South Bay to explore?"

"I went to high school in Santa Cruz and I also had a recommendation for a potential private chef post in the area. So it wasn't as bad as sticking a pin in a map."

"Sure. It's good to have family near."

"Well, there's family and there's family." Not sure how much to reveal, she added, "They're my father's cousins and quite elderly. He paid them to take me in for a few years, after my mother died. I graduated and the next day my beat-up car and I headed for New York to learn more about being a chef."

Suzy looked puzzled. "Your father paid someone to give you a home?"

"And I got an allowance. He never married my mother and when I turned up at his home in Florida, passport, birth certificate and a social worker alongside, he was somewhat embarrassed. Especially being white, like his wife and two other children."

"He sounds like a creep."

Suzy didn't know the half of it and Laura didn't want to think about it. "He was forced to provide for me since Jamaica had dropped me into the hands of U.S. immigration. I was an American with an employed parent close by in Florida." She took another bite of the apple bread and let it soothe her senses. She saw no reason to tell Suzy about the year she'd come back to piece her life back together and the ride on the roller coaster. "So here I am again. I love this area. It has a lot of good memories. The people I lived with were very nice to me."

"You've had an adventurous life. So you went to New York and became a chef and traveled all over the world."

"And I loved most of it."

"Do you like the place where you're working now?"

"It's the perfect assignment—four nights a week. The family is great and I have lots of free time."

"So do you have to be anywhere tonight?"

"I don't have to be anywhere until Tuesday at five."

"How intriguing..." Suzy grinned. "I'm teaching a class in the morning though. That gives us from now until eight a.m."

"For what?"

Suzy gave her a twinkling look over the top of her mug of tea. Just as Laura felt a blush start in her cheeks there was fierce knocking at the window. She looked through to find Julie eagerly waving.

"Is that her?" Julie shouted through the glass.

Helen came into view, obviously chastising Julie though Laura couldn't make out the words. She smiled and waved.

Laura waved back, not sure if she should nod and give Julie the satisfaction. Fortunately, with an obvious rolling of the eyes, Helen dragged her daughter away.

"Who was that?"

"The family I work for."

"The mother looked really familiar."

"She likes this place too." Laura wasn't going to name names.

"So...am I her? The one the girl was asking about?"

Laura nodded. "She saw the phone number and was curious."

"I'm not shy." Suzy wasn't blushing at all, but Laura thought for sure even her eyes had turned red.

"No. I am... A little."

"I'll keep that in mind."

"Would you like to see a movie or something this afternoon?"

"That sounds like fun." Suzy finished her apple bread and Laura drained her coffee while they discussed the possible choices.

On leaving the café, they decided to leave Suzy's car and take Laura's. They were buckled in when Suzy said, "I think we should get something out of the way, even if you are shy."

Laura glanced at her curiously, then butterflies fluttered against her throat. Warm, and so soft... She had forgotten the exquisite pleasure of another woman's lips on her own. She almost startled out of the kiss, but the faint scent of warm spices drew her in. She loved the silk of Suzy's hair against her face and kissed her with tender curiosity until she felt Suzy smiling.

"Sorry if I shocked you."

"Not in a bad way." Grinning helplessly, Laura started the car. This was going to be a very interesting date.

"Cheese, glorious *cheese*," Helen sang over the stove. "Hot griddle and *buh-ter*—"

"Mom! I can't hear my own music," Justin protested from the table.

"While we're in the *mood*, cold carrots and honey *mus*-tard." For an answer she carried over a plate of carrot sticks, then popped the buds out of his ears when he was distracted with the prospect of food. "It's nearly dinner time. Go wash your hands."

She continued singing as she flipped the sandwiches. Grilled cheese sandwiches were her specialty, pure comfort food, with thin slices of tomato and ham. Laura had left her some fresh dill and she'd decided to be gourmet and sprinkle a little on the tomato before assembling the sandwiches.

It was an exceptional fall day. Their impromptu drive into town for the provolone and cheddar cheese that they all liked in the sandwiches had been perfect. She'd felt as if the cool crackle in the air was blowing away cobwebs. She finally felt that while everything was changing so quickly all around her, she had to look for the things that wouldn't. Like grilled cheese and the happy groans the kids made after the first bite.

"That's practically a sin, that's so good," Helen pronounced of her sandwich.

"Almost as good as pizza."

"It's the cheese, the glorious cheese." She cleared her throat.

In unison she got, "Mom!" drawn out to three full syllables.

"Well, if you won't let me sing at the table I guess I should ask about homework."

Julie launched into a diatribe about the unfairness of a chemistry assignment where just because a "bunch of slackers" turned it in late, the teacher had awarded amnesty, and no extra credit for those who turned it in on time. "And there are kids who are not there to learn. They get in the way all the time."

Justin made his great-big-eyes face. "Are you even my sister? You're like an ugly Hermione Granger."

"Hey!" Helen said sharply. "I let you bicker, but none of that. Say sorry."

Justin muttered an apology while Julie scowled.

"One of these days you're going to have a friend ask if your cute sister is dating anyone," Helen predicted.

The very suggestion earned her a unison, "Gross!"

"Laura's girlfriend is really cute," Julie said.

"I didn't get a good look." It was the truth about the glance through the window, though she'd gotten a much better look when she'd run back to the cheese shop for the keys she'd left on their counter. The girlfriend was very pretty, all California blonde head-to-toe, and certainly young. "Laura has a life, and it's her business, sweetie."

"I know that. I'm just saying."

And what would Julie say if she'd seen what Helen had seen on her way from the cheese shop back to the car?

Watching TV, later, her mind wandered back to the look on Laura's face when she'd realized she was about to get kissed. Wonder and excitement and...satisfaction? No, that wasn't it. Even as she continued to puzzle over exactly what she'd witnessed she told herself it was professional curiosity. She'd played in many love scenes, and watched many more. But she couldn't find a reference point for that singular look.

"So we're agreed the movie was not all that good." Suzy pointed at the next stop sign. "If you turn here and double-back on the next block, you'll come right up behind my car."

"Parts were interesting, but it was such a clichéd story."

"White boy finds out he's magical, has a cranky old mentor and saves the world."

"I've seen that story before." Laura followed Suzy's directions. "Done better."

"I still had a great time. And thank you for dinner."

"It was a place I'd been wanting to try, so thank you for joining me in the experiment."

She glided to a stop behind the Saturn sedan that Suzy pointed out. At this point on a fall Sunday evening, the stores were all closed and the streets deserted.

She said, "I'd love to see you again. My appointment on Tuesday evening is brief, so we could have dinner."

"If I suggested breakfast tomorrow would that be moving too fast for you?"

Laura tried to find a way to say yes to the question without saying no to the idea. "I could probably be persuaded."

"But you hesitated." Suzy smiled at her across the car. "I'm very instinctual and tend to leap without looking."

"Does that work for you?"

"It would if I had perfect instincts. Let's say Tuesday night."

"At six?" Laura let out a little sigh of relief. It wasn't that she didn't find Suzy attractive, it was that she was so out of practice and so used to being cautious. If something happened Tuesday night that would still be a record for her. She had nothing to prove to anyone so she didn't need to jump headlong now.

"Six would be perfect. I'll be teaching classes in Menlo Park all afternoon."

"Then we can meet over there."

Her mind was calculating logistics of their meet-up as Suzy unbuckled her seat belt. Remembering their earlier kiss, she turned her head, expecting—and hoping—for another.

Suzy was leaning away, however, her shoulders against her door. She caught Laura's intent, however, and answered it with a low, "If you want a kiss, you're going to have to come and get it."

She whapped her knee on the center console but it was easy to ignore the shooting pain because Suzy's lips were every bit as soft and tender as they had been earlier in the day. Laura braced herself against the door to keep from falling onto Suzy, who was arching into the kiss with a supple lift to her shoulders that brought their breasts into contact.

She groaned when she felt Suzy's hands on her stomach, not moving, but warm and firm through her blouse. Imagining those hands on her bare skin set off an anticipatory shiver in her thighs. Their mouths parted, but Suzy bit hungrily at her lower lip and they merged again.

Suzy's hands moved slightly, edging toward Laura's breasts. She wanted to move down, encourage that tantalizing touch, but she had no room to maneuver. Her arms shivered slightly and another shiver, low in her gut, answered. She was ready for the ride, at least physically. Her aching knee was still protesting, but if she managed to get the other one set more comfortably she could shift and encourage the movement of Suzy's hands.

The thought was formed but instead of a yielding glow of anticipated pleasure she felt instead of a shockwave of cold sweat abruptly beading down her back. Her heart was racing. She broke the kiss and gasped for breath. The world didn't steady.

"Are you all right?"

She shook her head and scrambled back into her seat. She tried to not gulp for air, but there was no controlling it.

Suzy said sharply, "Open your door, get some fresh air."

She managed, gasping. A panic attack. Stupid, childish reaction—a panic attack. "I'll be fine in a minute."

Suzy fumbled in her purse, a miniature backpack, and came up with tissues. Laura gratefully swabbed at her streaming forehead. "Tell me if you need to go the ER. We can be at one in about fifteen minutes."

"I'll be fine. It was a panic attack." She tried to smile. "How stupid is that?"

"Seems like that was pretty severe. Am I that scary?"

Great, she'd screwed her chances with a new woman. "No. It's not you."

"We're over twenty-one. We both would enjoy it, I'm pretty sure."

"There's no question in my mind that we will."

"So why..?"

"I don't know. Believe me, up until then I was getting green lights from all systems."

"Something threw a master switch, though."

Suzy knew nothing about her. How could she think anything but that Laura was way more complicated than any sane woman would want to deal with on a first date? She glanced at Suzy, but Suzy was staring out her window. "I'm really—really, I am out of practice. I think that's all this is. Some part of me is scared and another part of me wants to let things marinate before we cook."

Thankfully Suzy laughed. "Okay, okay. I'll still have dinner with you on Tuesday. I'm willing to give it another try."

"I'm sorry to be, well, slow to boil." She hung her head in mock shame. "I am such a cooking geek."

"Well, I guess you could be worth waiting for. Time will tell. Are you sure you're okay?"

She wasn't going to admit that she was drenched under her clothes and that she could feel perspiration running from her scalp, making her hair itch. Her heart had calmed the moment it was clear that she and Suzy weren't going any further for now. "I really am okay."

Suzy opened her door and fumbled for her car keys in her purse. "I did have a great time tonight."

She watched Suzy's taillights disappear into the night and couldn't come up with a reason to have said no to what would have probably been a night to remember. What was wrong with her? She'd never had a lot of offers but when they'd come along, and she'd been similarly interested, the last thing she'd been was scared. She'd always been able to handle sex, laughs, a little more sex and then the other woman would be transferred, or she would be.

She made her way to her hotel, feeling grimy on the outside and numb on the inside. She'd had panic attacks before, but they had always been related to cocaine. Seeing it being used had set her off twice. She'd had a panic attack at the job she'd just left, and that was when she'd realized how the stress of thoroughly hating the idea of going to work every day was eating at her. She'd been walking across the grounds to the restaurant and listing in her mind the personnel she passed that she knew were dealing to the guests. She'd felt it coming—blind panic. Fear of the monster.

Suzy was not a monster. But it was the same terror.

Scrubbing herself in the shower she realized she wasn't finding any answers. There was only one thing to do: cook. She done it before and she'd do it again—cook until she found answers. She'd always been safe in her own kitchen.

CHAPTER ELEVEN

"So I won't see you next Tuesday. I think I'll be in Costa Maya. Would you be able to fix dinner while I'm gone? That's Sunday, Monday and Tuesday, then the usual days. I fly back from Miami to New York in time for the Friday evening performance, so things will go back to normal. Certainly, if Grace could finish something you left that would be fine." Helen knew she was no match for Laura when it came to speed with a knife, but she finished the jobs of dicing cold boiled potatoes and slicing mushrooms even though Laura's focus on her was making her self-conscious.

"I can easily make sure something's available every night. Really, it's no problem. As you say, I'll either be here in person or there will be something simple to finish." Laura set a mug of tea in front of Helen, the only culinary task she would let Laura do.

She smiled a thank you and paused long enough to take an appreciative sip. "Do you have any advice for me eating food in the region?"

"You can't go wrong with seafood. Spiny lobster is sustainable, definitely try it if offered. Conch is something I think you'd like. I'm fond of conch in cornmeal batter." She scooted up onto one of the bar stools. "Marlin, shark... Tilapia freshly caught in Caribbean waters is nothing like what you're usually served here."

"I knew you'd know. Given that I fly six thousand miles a week, you'd think I would be better traveled, but other than London and Paris and a hiking trip in Ireland the kids still haven't forgiven me for, we've not gone much farther than California and New York." She checked the temperature of her skillet and dumped in the white mushrooms.

"They didn't like Ireland?"

"They didn't like Ireland on foot. Big difference. I thought it was a great way to get in shape."

"Well, I'll have to make them haggis for old time's sake. Are you sure I can't help?"

"No, you can't. And you're welcome to stay. Mushroom hash with fried eggs. Some asparagus and Justin made applesauce-oatmeal cookies last night."

"I have plans, otherwise I'd love to."

Helen gave Laura a quick glance, but she looked as serene as always. A date with the willowy blonde? She was wearing a beautiful sweater that looked new, in leaves of gold and bronze that brought out the milk chocolate tones in her skin and clung in all the right places. If it was a date it was none of her business. "Thank you for Justin's cooking lessons, by the way. It's not in your job description."

"I'm grateful for his help, and I try to make sure his coursework is finished. He's quite patient, which is a gift for a chef."

"I've noticed. I've never seen him so attentive to detail—speak of the devil. Dinner isn't ready yet."

"Can I do something?" He looked at the pile of chopped vegetables and Helen heard his stomach rumble.

"I hope you have better luck asking than I did," Laura said.

"Some of the asparagus are on the large side, which means they'll be woody. So peel those and trim the ends off them all." Helen moved the mushrooms around in the skillet and tried to use her chin to gesture at the drawer where the peeler was kept.

"I'll show him." Laura was up in a flash. "Wash your hands."

She watched in amazement as he not only washed his hands, but rinsed up his forearms as well. His attitude toward germs had always been if they didn't kill him they must be good for him.

Laura's instructions were concise. She demonstrated with a single stalk, then watched him do two, then left him to finish with, "You have done well, my young apprentice." She had obviously taught unskilled helpers many, many times.

"You're making hash," Justin suddenly said. "Cool. Can I have two eggs?"

"Have I ever made you less than two eggs?"

"No, but I want to be sure." He lined up the bottoms of the asparagus stalks and then picked out the small chef's knife to trim them. "I want to have the proper expectations."

He didn't appear to be about to cut off his fingertips, so she turned to Laura. "Did we finish talking about plans? I won't see you next Tuesday, but I think everything is going swimmingly."

"I'm glad to hear it. It's nice to create something and connect with those who get to enjoy it. Plus I get to enjoy it too." She relaxed into one of her easy-goes-it smiles. "I'm liking the area a lot."

If they'd been alone, Helen would have asked her about her date. She felt comfortable enough to ask, woman-to-woman, whereas she hardly felt comfortable asking Grace about her personal life. Laura was just easier to know.

They chatted a few more minutes and Laura took her leave. She watched the Volvo disappear down the driveway and realized she was going to be sorry to miss their chat next week.

Suzy had texted the name of a bistro in Palo Alto, near the Stanford campus, that specialized in Cajun food. The conversation with Helen had run only a little bit longer than expected, but she didn't think she'd be late.

She had given the encounter on Sunday night a lot of thought. She had spent the best part of Monday prepping and sautéing the first day of two-day *coq au vin*. Tomorrow she'd bake it at the Baynors', and if the kids seemed to like that kind of casserole, she'd plan something like that for Grace to finish for them next week. She was annoyed that her distraction had made her forget to ask Helen about using her name to get the attention of a real estate broker. She would have to call before Helen got on that cruise ship on Friday.

Somewhere between frying chicken and peeling pearl onions she had thought she'd hit on a reasonable explanation for her freak-out. She didn't really want to open up her psyche for Suzy's examination—not at this stage—but she owed Suzy an explanation. If she didn't like parts of it then better to know and they'd both move on.

Arriving first, she asked for their table. She'd barely sat down when Suzy showed up.

"What a beautiful sweater," Suzy said. "It suits you."

"Thank you. You look lovely." It was easy to say, being the truth. She thought the dress was called a wrap, and it liked every lean muscle in Suzy's body. The topaz and blue pattern highlighted both Suzy's eyes and hair. One brief liaison in her past had been with the recreation manager from Kenya who had been devoted to yoga. Perhaps that was what had her so entranced with Suzy—she already knew the possibilities of such a fluid, flexible body. And remembering those encounters was not necessarily going to help her composure, she told herself.

They ordered wine as they studied the menu. The waitress was quick, returning with a chardonnay and a merlot.

"We're here for the pickle chips," Suzy told the waitress. She glanced at Laura. "You trust me, right?"

"I do, and I was definitely intrigued. I've had pickles every way except fried."

"They're a revelation." Suzy gave her a twinkling smile.

They decided to share fried green tomatoes and a jambalaya wrap. Laura could tell Suzy was trying not to appear anxious, but her overly casual manner betrayed her.

"I think I know what happened on Sunday," Laura said. She paused to sip her merlot. "This is really very good. Thank you for picking it."

"I'm glad you're not a white-wine-for-fish-red-wine-for-meat kind of girl."

"I worked with too many sommeliers not to know there are no rules when it comes to a good wine." She sipped again. "So about Sunday night..."

"It really was a panic attack?"

"Yes. I have thought about it a lot and I could be wrong, but I think I've never been in *that* situation before."

Suzy's eyebrows arched up. "You've never... Really?"

"I've had affairs, and that's what they were. A couple of dates, intimacy, but they were short-term. I changed resorts sometimes as often as every three months. I worked with people who expected to move on themselves. There was never anybody I ever believed might lead to more. And I'm not saying I expect us to become a long-term couple but there's the chance that we could. And I've never..." She cleared her throat and lowered her voice. "I've never slept with a woman thinking it could be the start of something long-term. Meaningful. And yes, that appears to have terrified me."

"You've never been in love?"

"No. Never." She smiled, glad to let go of what still seemed like an adolescent's secret. "I had a huge crush on an actress for years. But she's straight and will never have me. Alas."

"So's Keira Knightley, but I can dream." Suzy was staring pensively into her wine glass. "So you think that was it?"

"I know it seems a little Ann Landers meets Dr. Phil, but yes, I think that was the trigger."

"Have you had them often? Panic attacks? I'm sure, actually, that yoga could help."

"It could. Lessons might be very useful for other reasons too." She gave Suzy what she hoped was a promising smile. "I avoid the trigger, and so I was really surprised that it happened in that, um, situation."

"You mean while we were making out in your car?" Suzy seemed to be back to her flirtatious self. "Tell me more about the trigger."

The arrival of the pickle chips interrupted their conversation, and they were quickly deep in food memories and impressions of the South Bay. They left the restaurant still comparing notes about French and Australian wines and decided to stroll part of the nearby Stanford campus. Some event was happening at a small theater on the edge closest to them and the area was alive with the bustle of students, all in a great hurry.

It was a beautiful fall evening. The sun had long set but there was still a faint glow along the coastal hills. Laura was glad of her sweater as the air chilled the tip of her nose.

They turned back after about ten minutes. Suzy took her hand as they talked about the learning center where she taught yoga and shared thoughts about the wellness connection between food and activity.

"Though I think nothing bores people more than calling it 'wellness', I can't think of a better way to put it. Bodies need fuel and they need maintenance but they also need to be used." They were approaching Laura's car where it was parked on the street. "Speaking of that... Can I offer you a nightcap. At my apartment? It's not far."

Laura was sure that the jolt she felt in her stomach was just nerves. Nerves and excitement. "I think that would be lovely. My hotel isn't far either but half the room is stacked with boxes."

"I'm parked just down there. Why don't you follow me?"

The drive was short and once they were both parked in the apartment complex's lot, Suzy led her up a flight of stairs and unlocked the door at the top. Her first impression was that Suzy's taste in décor was in all colors of beige and taupe, which might have been dull if not for the many plants that filled the windowsills and tables and a wall hanging in abstract reds and purples. Though not large, the living room was warm and inviting, much like Suzy herself.

In a few minutes they were ensconced on a comfortable futon, sipping wine and not making eye contact.

"I don't blame you if you're a little wary," Laura said. "I would be."

"I guess I am. But I have such a good feeling about you. You're...nice. And I don't mean that like something pleasant and forgettable. I mean like the kind of person who calls when they say they will. Listens and talks equally. Polite, too."

"Thank you." Laura couldn't help but smile. "I would like to think you don't find those rare qualities."

"My ex—well, let's not get started down that road. It's very, very messy."

"How long ago did you break up?"

"A year—well, maybe two by now."

She shifted so she was facing Suzy on the futon, looking for a topic that avoided Suzy's ex's faults but wasn't blatantly leading to the next possible activity in their evening.

Suzy forestalled her by moving close enough to rest her head on Laura's arm along the back of the futon. "I have a thing about skin. I might as well admit it."

"Skin? As in...?"

"Skin. I like touching." She sought and held Laura's gaze. "I like the way a woman's skin feels along my palms."

A nerve in Laura's neck jumped and she might have been embarrassed that it led to a clenching of the glands in her throat except that Suzy was delicious and promising exactly what Laura realized she was starved for. "You'll find that I am covered with skin just about everywhere."

Suzy's low laugh was inviting and she sighed when Laura gently touched her throat. "I gather you won't mind if I touch you everywhere?"

"As long as I can do the same."

"Please, yes."

She brushed her lips along Suzy's jawline. "You won't mind if I use my lips too, will you?"

Another low laugh answered her question.

Used to a more hurried and frantic pace in her past encounters, Laura told herself there was no rush to get anywhere since she and Suzy were definitely heading the right direction. Suzy's palms exploring her back felt wonderful, and when they gave up all pretense of remaining upright she melted into the pleasure of Suzy's embrace. Their clothes were slowly discarded and they shared a deep, mutual groan of appreciation as their naked breasts touched for the first time. No matter the muscle or bones, Laura loved how women were soft on the outside, plush in secret places and warm where they were wet. There was something so sweet about Suzy, something that reminded her of lazy sunsets in Jamaica that had painted her body with warmth.

"Let's move to the bedroom," Suzy suggested in a low voice.

Stretched out on top of Suzy and nuzzling along her collarbone, Laura said, "But I was just getting comfortable here."

"More room there. I can't roll you over here and I would really like to."

Laura lifted an eyebrow. "What makes you think I want to be rolled over?"

"I promise to make it worth your while."

Keeping her actions deliberate enough for Suzy to object, she pinned Suzy's arms to her side and heard her breath catch. She kissed her as slowly as possible, which became difficult as Suzy arched under her and opened her legs slightly. She ended the kiss and whispered in Suzy's ear, "Let's move to the bed then."

Moments later, the tickle of Suzy's hair along her spine and the feel of crisp cotton against her breasts sent flares of desire through her body. Her toes curled and she couldn't help but lift herself to Suzy's hands as they pressed into the muscles along her back.

"This is the best massage I've ever had," she murmured.

Suzy lowered her body until Laura could feel her taut nipples on her back. Her face was enveloped with the silk of Suzy's hair as Suzy said in her ear, "This is *not* a massage."

She felt Suzy's hand between her legs and gasped. In less than a heartbeat she was consumed with need, sudden, hard and direct.

"This is okay?"

"Yes." She managed to get to her elbows. The throb of her arousal was amplified by lightning sparks across the surface of her skin. Words evaporated before she could say them, and trapped in her head was a shimmering fugue of *yes* and *beautiful* and woman and more. She fumbled for the headboard and held on as if she might break.

She was awakened by a light cramp in her calf. By the time she had kneaded it out, without waking Suzy, her need to discover the whereabouts of the bathroom had grown intense. Fortunately, the apartment was small.

As she washed her hands and face the smells and sounds of the night washed over her. Delicious, every moment, and very pleasing to discover that Suzy received with the same degree of pleasure as she gave.

"You might have prepared better," she told herself as she smeared toothpaste around her mouth with her finger and glowered at the reflection of her sleep-mashed hair. If she had bed head then it truly was overdue for a trim. "Find stylist. Today."

Her mouth softened into a smile. Tomorrow would be soon enough—only a fool would rush away when the morning might have more to offer.

Back in bed Suzy stirred and rolled over, cuddling against Laura's warmth. It was moments like these that carried her all the way back to the first time she'd realized that the simple feel of skin-to-skin with another girl left her breathless.

Suzy coughed slightly and after a moment opened one eye. "Morning?"

"Yes it is." She kissed the soft sleepy mouth and felt Suzy's lips smile against hers.

"Do you have to head out?"

"No. I thought I'd make us some breakfast. I find I'm quite hungry, in spite of the lovely dinner we had."

Suzy closed both eyes as she grinned. "It's the exercise we had last night."

"Do you have any skeletons in your kitchen?"

"Nope, not a one."

"Then I'll explore. You can stay where you are if you like." Not seeing a robe she could borrow, she pulled on her jeans and sweater.

She was whisking some egg substitute together with dried chives and a dash of Tabasco when Suzy padded in wearing a light green robe. "I'll make tea. Would you like some?"

"I'd love some," Laura admitted. "Preferably fully leaded. That's with caffeine."

"Morning Thunder, that will do the trick."

They worked mostly in silence until Laura turned out an omelet which she split between the two plates Suzy provided. It wasn't as fluffy as she liked, but there was no milk. Thankfully some shredded Monterey Jack had added a bit more flavor.

"Thank you, this smells great."

It was a pleasure to look at the still sleepy Suzy. Some of her sexual wattage was definitely toned down, leaving behind a sweet and easy smile that proclaimed she was quite content with her world. Suzy's face looked like the way Laura felt inside.

"I am so glad you got over the panic."

"Me too. From the tips of my toes to the top of my head, I am very glad."

"You never did tell me what the trigger is. I don't want to accidentally do that to you."

"I doubt you could. It's about drugs." She tried to keep her tone nonchalant. "I get near cocaine and it makes me very, very anxious. And if I think about it too much, same thing."

Suzy stilled.

The room suddenly felt cold, but there was nothing for it. "I'm a recovering cocaine addict. There's no easy way to say it easily so I'm sorry it's so blunt. It's the truth."

Suzy shook her head slightly. "Are you an addict? Right now?"

"Once an addict always an addict. I don't believe there is a cure." There was masses of literature behind her choice of words, reading she'd done over so many years, but she didn't think Suzy wanted a lecture. She'd hoped that being involved in the wellness industry, Suzy would know more than she apparently did. A knot of fear formed in her stomach. "Or do you mean am I currently using?"

"Is there a difference?" Suzy's tone was flat and her eyes had lost their inner shine.

Not sure Suzy wanted an answer, Laura still gave her one. "There is a world of difference. I am not using. That's why I said *recovering*. I haven't used in years."

"So you're cured."

Laura took a deep breath. "That's not how it works." She repeated, "There is no cure."

"Sure there is." Suzy pushed her plate away, her mouth twisting as she struggled to speak. "I don't want to hear crap about how it's a disease. That's just an excuse. An excuse addicts use to hurt people and then act like 'sorry, I can't help myself' makes up for it."

"You've had an addict in your life, haven't you?" If she'd known she would have probably not said anything until they got to know each other much better.

"It wasn't *my* addiction. I have willpower and self-respect. I was in a relationship for five years and lost her to meth. I had to move twice to get away from her. She stole stuff, she lied. I won't do it again."

Tamping down her own anger, Laura tried again. "If you can calm down we can talk about this."

"You should have told me last night."

"It's not something I announce to everyone. It's a part of me that I deal with every day, but I try not to force other people to." Maybe I should have made a point of it, she thought. She'd told very few people because it just wasn't relevant to temporary relationships. She was all at sea with dating that could lead to for keeps.

She couldn't help but add, with an edge to her voice, "You don't know me well enough yet to realize that I have an astonishing amount of willpower and self-respect. That's why I'm *recovering*."

Suzy was shaking. "I want you out of here. I can't do this again. I can't stand liars. I want you to go, right now."

Laura held up her hands, fighting back tears. This entire scene was the kind she'd really hoped she would never live. *This is not about you,* an inner voice tried to reassure her, but when the door slammed behind her it certainly felt like it was.

Had she misled Suzy? What was she supposed to have said? She hadn't lied, and she'd told the unvarnished truth. The rules of her sobriety didn't insist that she reveal her past, they only warned her that lying about it was a dangerous path. Lots of addicts in recovery didn't tell the new people in their life until significant time went by, and some never told—and that scene she'd just endured was a fine example of why. She couldn't do that again with anyone else she might date. She just couldn't. She'd regretted not telling Helen about it at the interview, but no longer. She loved cooking for the Baynors and she wasn't going to risk losing that.

She cried all the way back to her hotel, mopping at her eyes with a fast-food napkin. She had a splitting headache and her sinuses ached. She took a shower and spent thirty minutes on the bed with a cloth over her eyes.

There had been possibilities with Suzy. For fun, and exploring food and wine and sharing very good sex. *Your cocaine addiction made those possibilities more remote,* she told herself. *Don't blame Suzy or her ex for more than their share. This is about cocaine and this is the price you pay for having a disease.*

She sat up finally, mind circling around the addict's unsolvable equation. It was not her fault she had a disease that made it impossible to control her behavior in some situations. People with other sorts of diseases are usually not told it's their own fault, so suck it up and cure yourself. There was next to no money spent on research into addiction prevention, just money for prevention of using—and those were two utterly different things. Nobody knew why some people could use and walk away while others turned into Pavlov's dog, slobbering and begging for more because the bell was always ringing.

But she was also as willing as most people to think some diseases had an element of self-infliction. Personal choices did cause all sorts of diseases. If she had never used in the first place she might not be sitting here. People should reap what they sow and not expect a bottomless checkbook of compassion and aid to bail them out after their bad choices. But such thinking was why so few even bothered to begin looking for a cure for AIDS. It wasn't until it started killing people who hadn't made so-called "bad choices" that research got decent funding.

The conflict—between accepting she had a disease while never accepting that it was an excuse—could not be solved. That meant living with the ambiguity of it, every day. It meant having compassion for herself and yet always being wary of any voice of inner pity.

She was a good person.

She'd never hurt anyone but herself through her addiction, and she thanked God for that.

She didn't deserve to be a stand-in for the whipping Suzy had never been able to give her ex.

Taking personal responsibility for her behavior was a huge part of her sobriety and sobriety was addiction's kryptonite. It weakened, but didn't kill it. She starved it but the monster could hibernate. She accepted that she did not have the power to slay the monster, only resist it. For her, the monster lived as long as she did.

She finally got up. She needed to occupy her hands if she wanted to get some control over her spinning thoughts. Thinking she'd make herself toast or have some cheese, she saw the red Dutch oven on the top shelf of the refrigerator. A deep breath over the lush aromas of caramelized vegetables and plum-cherries in the wine of the *coq au vin* helped clear her head. It was beautiful and she'd made it herself and she would get past this truly horrid day.

Part Four:
Inline Twist

CHAPTER TWELVE

In spite of the best efforts of her taxi driver to avoid the crowds at the Port of Miami, Helen still found herself in the swelter of bodies queuing up for the gangplank. The *Solstice Eclipse* was massive and the dock was as crowded as Times Square on a Saturday night.

Her instructions, carefully laid out in a letter from Karolina Tavitian, President of Tavitian Productions located in Chicago, referred to a VIP boarding area, but there was no dockside sign pointing to any such oasis. She saw to her suitcases and tipped the driver as beads of perspiration gathered on her forehead. The heat was wonderful but the thick layer of diesel fumes was not.

A luggage hauler trundled by, stacked deep with suitcases

and trunks and yellow luggage tags flapping. Her luggage tags—she'd forgotten to put them on.

She had no sooner put on the bright purple tags than a longshoreman with a clipboard immediately stopped and asked her name. With a whistle and instructions she didn't quite hear her bags were claimed by a young man who added them to a hauler with other bags fluttering with purple tags. Their arrival triggered the attention of a woman in a white ship's uniform who crossed the dock at a brisk pace, hand extended in greeting.

"Mrs. Baynor? You are expected. Welcome to the *Solstice Eclipse*." Helen found herself swept into matching stride as the woman continued in heavily accented speech—something Nordic, Helen thought. "The VIP access is this way."

The ramp where she was led switched back upward, then joined with the regular gangplank with its own line. She could feel the curious gaze of the other passengers on her as she walked by them. It was rather like a red carpet walk.

Her guide explained, "Proceed to the top and show your papers, and a steward will take you to your cabin so you can relax. Your bags should be delivered in an hour or less. Happy sailing!"

She had scarcely expressed her thanks before the woman made a similar foray into the crowd to guide two more people in her direction. They looked familiar, as if she'd seen them on television on an awards show, but she didn't know their names.

Every step up the ramp left the diesel and hot asphalt stink behind. By the time she reached the deck, forty or fifty feet above the dock, she was in a world paved with wood, gleaming with brass fittings and brilliant with men and women in white uniforms.

She was greeted by two assistant pursers who checked her travel documents and wished her a wonderful journey. She was then passed into the care of a harried-looking young woman in a suit who spoke rapidly into a walkie-talkie upon hearing Helen's name. A few seconds later two heavy wooden doors just beyond them opened.

Bemused by the arrival of yet another person who would no doubt wish her a pleasant journey before leaving her in yet another waiting pattern, she was pleased that the new arrival, a brunette about her age, beamed a smile and extended her hand.

"Helen Baynor? Karolina Tavitian. Welcome aboard. I'm glad the directions I sent have delivered you safely." Her designer-cut white slacks and off-the-shoulder top of deep orange set off olive and gold skin and thick, dark hair.

"It's wonderful to be here." She returned the brilliant smile, immediately feeling at ease.

"Do you want to go to your cabin to freshen up? Or join me for a cocktail?"

"Cocktail," Helen said firmly.

"I love a woman who knows her mind." Karolina's cute sandals clicked on the deck as she led the way to the heavy double doors, which she opened with ease and gestured for Helen to precede her. "There's a hospitality bar set up right in here. Our little green room, so to speak. How was your flight?"

"Fine. Flawless, in fact." To the bartender she said, "A mojito, perhaps?"

"Now you're on vacation," Karolina said. She indicated her own glass with a graceful wave of her hand. "Mario here makes a spiffy mojito."

There was a short awkward silence, into which Helen said, "Thank you for all you did to get me here. I know it was all last minute—and I wasn't a first choice, so I can only imagine the logistics on your end."

"It's my job, and it means I get to meet truly interesting people and see a lot of the world. I can put up with a lot of last-minute arrangements in exchange for that. Between you and me..." She lowered her voice conspiratorially. "I think our contributors got a better deal with you here. The first choice has name recognition but..." She shrugged. "She's a name. You're a star."

Helen smiled. "In others words, she's twenty-five and I'm... older than that."

Karolina lifted a sculpted eyebrow. "Not what I meant at all."

"Then shame on me for hearing it. I can't seem to help it— one of the big milestone birthdays happens the day after I get home."

"I wish you many more of them."

Mint tingling at her nose heralded the arrival of her mojito. After thanking the bartender, she quickly surveyed the room. Without thinking better of it, Helen said, "Oh no."

"What?" Karolina turned her head to follow Helen's gaze. She looked back at Helen. "Is that a problem?"

"It could be—my problem, not yours." Just when she'd started to feel as if she could relax she had Eugene Masterson to deal with.

"It is." Karolina touched her arm lightly. "Is he an ex or something? We actually check backgrounds so we don't book people together on these jaunts that have any reason to be uncomfortable."

"Not an ex—I don't have any of those. Let's just say that I've exhausted a lady's ways of putting out the No sign and he's been persistently blind to them."

"Now I'm really sorry. His bank paid quite a fee to sponsor some time ago, but he only joined the guest list last week."

"After you announced—"

"—That you would be joining us." Karolina briefly bit her lower lip, though the rest of her lively face was schooled into a pleasant, welcoming expression. "Well, tonight you and he are both at the Captain's Table. But I'll adjust the name cards. It's a long table."

"I keep telling myself that he's a fan and certainly a man in his position is a viable suitor." She wondered if she ought to be adding stalker to her description of him. "But he's not my type. Just for starters."

Karolina's nod was understanding. "What is your type? What happens on a cruise stays on a cruise, after all."

"It's been so long since I've dated I'm not sure what it is. But I guess I'm pretty sure what it isn't. What about you?"

"He's not my type either," she answered. "Wrong gender, to start with." Her gaze searched Helen's face for a reaction.

"Poor fellow. I'm quite sure he wouldn't want to undergo any of the measures that would fix that."

"Me too." Karolina relaxed slightly. "Even if he was, still not my type."

Helen was glad she'd put Karolina at ease about her sexuality

without having to resort to the trite, "Some of my best friends…"
It pained her that gay people had to carry around that small
measure of armor, always ready for rejection. It reminded her of
the interview with Laura and how forthright Laura had been as
well. She shook the image of Laura kissing her girlfriend from
her mind. "He'd find that frustrating, I'm sure."

She stirred her drink and flashed Helen a twinkling look.
"The kind of guy who is sure he could fix me?"

"I don't know about that," Helen said fairly. Maybe the
mojito was responsible because she found herself adding, "But
if he thought we were an item, he's probably the type to want to
watch."

Karolina said, "Eww," and burst out laughing as Helen
giggled into her glass.

Their merriment unfortunately caught the subject's attention.
Eugene Masterson broke into a smile. Crossing the room with
a wide-armed gesture that was designed to draw attention, he
boomed, "Helen! A pleasure to see you again!"

Air kisses ensued. As before, he continued to stand a little
too close and Helen was excruciatingly aware that there was no
curtain bell to call her to safety. She was grateful that Karolina
didn't leave, even when Eugene shifted his posture several times,
in subtle ways, to turn their threesome into a twosome. Helen
wasn't at all convinced he was doing it unconsciously.

"This will be a wonderful week—are you looking forward to
snorkeling? The shore excursion to the Bitari Resort on Grand
Cayman sounds wonderful, doesn't it?"

"I haven't had a chance to read up on any of that," Helen lied.
Avoiding him was going to be difficult, damn it. "This was all
very rush. In fact, I haven't had a chance to freshen up."

She slid off the bar stool as Karolina quickly made room for
her to exit.

"I'll see you at dinner," Karolina said. Her light touch on
Helen's arm lingered longer than normal and the mirth in her
eyes was unmistakable.

"I'm looking forward to it." Helen gave her a slow smile with
a hint of a wink, feeling wicked, then said brightly to Eugene, "I
hope you have a lovely vacation this week."

She made a quick exit to the deck and walked briskly, just as if she had a clue where her cabin might be. She ducked through the first set of doors she came to, somewhere mid-ship, and ran right into a cluster of white-suited personnel who immediately directed her, in a chorus of melodious accents, to the nearest stairwell along with explicit directions to her suite.

Even as she approached her door she was greeted by the steward—Jeffrey, were they all named Jeffrey, she wondered—assigned to her suite. He took time explaining her dining choices, how to arrange for in-suite food service and laundry, pointed out useful features of the shipboard shower, then asked what she would like stocked in her minibar. He left her with a little plate of chocolates.

The door finally closed. All alone, she stared in amazement at the spacious suite. There was a huge television, but with the beautiful ocean just beyond the large, shaded balcony, who would watch television? She peeked into all the drawers and decided how to unpack and organize. Jeffrey responded immediately to a press of the button he'd encouraged her to use and headed away with her dresses for a quick touch-up with an iron.

She finished unpacking and checked her watch. They should be setting sail very soon. Should she watch from her balcony? She wished the kids weren't in classes or she'd call to describe her stateroom. She satisfied herself by sending them a couple of photos from her phone.

It was the strangest feeling to have no plan. She had to appear tomorrow, Sunday and Thursday. Friday they returned to Miami. Tonight she was requested at the Captain's Table, but other than that she could do as she liked.

Once she figured out what that was, she was sure she'd have a good time.

Helpful Jeffrey told her that it was expected for guests to dress for the Captain's Table but nothing formal. She had brought one full-length gown and several cocktail dresses, now all beautifully pressed. Little black dress number one was perfect. Karolina was a willowy, elegant woman and she wanted to be sure to measure up to her expectations.

She joined the reception and was quickly handed a glass of white wine by a passing waiter effortlessly balancing a tray of stemmed glassware in spite of the rolling motion of the floor. She sipped and looked for Karolina, not immediately seeing her in the crowd. The vaguely familiar couple she'd spotted on the dock earlier were there. She hoped someone told her their names before it became clear she hadn't a clue.

"A beautiful woman like you should never enter a room unescorted," someone said in her ear.

She knew who it was before she turned and kept a polite smile. "Thank you. I was looking for Karolina."

Eugene's smiled with a shrug. "I haven't seen her. I'm sure she's very busy with many guests to talk to. This is quite an undertaking."

"And for a good cause. I was honored to be asked. And thank you for your bank's support."

"It's one of many charities we support."

He opened his mouth to say more when Karolina emerged from a cluster of people, greeting them both with a smile. "Good evening. Mr. Masterson, you look dashing."

"Eugene, please."

"And Helen, I want to know who made that dress."

"I'll tell—but only if you tell me your tailor's name as well." The yellow sheath was stunning—it almost screamed Chanel couture, but the beadwork on the left shoulder was someone else's work entirely. It showed off her petite frame and highlighted her lovely tan. In the low light of the reception her eyes deepened from brown to black and glittered as brightly as the topaz pendant she wore. Her thick hair was twisted in an elegant, looped braid and brushed at her shoulders when she turned her head. All in all, she had the stunning grasp of classic elegance that came with long and steady acquaintance with both money and wealthy people.

"I'd like you both to meet the Havens, two of our other stars for the week," Karolina was saying. She drew them across the room with a gesture at Eugene and the light touch of a hand on Helen's arm.

The Havens, of course—a husband and wife director/ producer duo. She knew their names far better than their faces. Independent movies with a film company based out of Texas, she recalled. Karolina then brought over an actress who had been in the past summer's action blockbuster, which Helen hadn't seen, and an actor she'd met a few times at gatherings, but had never worked with on the stage.

Introductions were made and Helen managed to angle herself around the small group so that Eugene was on the other side of Karolina. The captain stopped briefly to welcome all of them to his ship, then the doors of the small room were opened so that they could move into the large, main dining room. Other diners had already been seated at the many tables, and they made their way en masse to the center table, on a dais, which was already set with endive salads. Part of Helen wanted to gawk and take a picture to show the kids but she instead searched for her name on a card, finding it above the salt, so to speak, but several chairs down from the head of the table. The captain was flanked by Eugene Masterson on one side and the Havens on the other. Next to Eugene was a vivacious young woman Helen hadn't met, then Karolina, then her. With luck, she wouldn't even make eye contact with him.

Introductions were made and service began. She introduced herself to the woman on the other side of her, only to learn she spoke little English, but they politely mimed greetings and clinked glasses when the captain offered a toast in sketchy English and his native Norwegian for a wonderful journey.

"What are you thinking?" Karolina asked her, after congenial small talk with their nearby tablemates over their salads.

"That I work nights and so this is probably the first dinner party I've been to in...two years. I don't entertain at home, which I'm thinking is actually a real shame."

"Why not? I think you'd be a wonderful hostess."

"Attention span." She explained about her schedule, the kids and airplanes. "I want to give them enough of me and I have to say they're turning out okay, I think."

"That's a relief these days."

"Do you have kids?"

"Never thought about it."

Karolina leaned back in her seat to allow the waiter to set a plate in front of her. Helen did the same and realized she was actually very hungry. The sea bass with leeks and fingerling potatoes smelled wonderful and she suddenly wanted to describe it to Laura.

Thinking Karolina had found the question too personal, she mimed with the woman on her right about the wonderful food and discussed the trip itinerary with the Head Purser, who was seated directly across from her. She was surprised, therefore, when Karolina returned to the subject.

"I'm far too selfish for children," Karolina said. "Selfish enough that I knew I didn't want to do it by myself. And since I had a flawless birth control plan, I was able to avoid it."

Helen grinned. "I'm glad that worked out for you. More women should try it maybe."

"I've done my best to convince as many as possible." Karolina gave her a wicked look.

She laughed outright. "With how much success?"

"That would be indiscreet. But enough to keep my credentials in order."

"My best friend, Cass, refers to it as her toaster oven collection."

"I opted for frequent flyer miles."

"I'm drowning in those, for different reasons—I ended up donating them all to Make-a-Wish."

"They do wonderful work." Karolina paused to throw some laughing comment into the conversation on her other side. "I'll be shameless and ask if you know anyone on the board. I'd like to do fundraising for them."

"I used to know two, but they both retired a couple of years ago."

"Drats. I was shameless for nothing."

"Sorry about that."

Karolina's eyes sparkled with humor. "You don't sound sorry."

"It didn't seem that shameless to me."

"Talking business at the Captain's Table? Oh, the horror."

"You'll have to do better than that for genuine shameless behavior."

"Would you like me to?"

Helen blinked. There was a tight and unfamiliar sensation in her chest. "It's not up to me."

Karolina looked as if she was going to say that it was, but abruptly sipped her wine.

It was just fun conversation, Helen thought. Small talk again ensued. There was a brief moment of worry that Eugene would join her after dinner, but the young woman Karolina had seated next to him had a firm grasp of his arm.

She sighed with relief and said to Karolina, "The idea of sitting in a lounge for an hour, after a meal like that, is the last thing on my mind. Would you like to explore the decks a little bit or do you need to spend time with some of your VIPs?"

"I'd love a walk," Karolina said. "I try to avoid desserts but that torte was beguiling."

They took their leave of the captain and she followed Karolina to the wide central atrium. Pausing to look at the stairwell map, Karolina pointed out the promenade and the deck below where it was possible to circle the entire ship. "It's marked in tenths of a mile for those interested in exercise, though I can't imagine coming on a vacation like this and spending time in the fitness room."

"I'll have to," Helen said. "It's the part of the job I never get to stop." What a dreary outlook, she told herself.

"You won't be seeing me there, sorry."

"You look like you visit often."

"Thank you, that's sweet. I should go, but I don't. I walk everywhere that I can, avoid sugar and hope for the best."

Karolina's best had few flaws that Helen could see. She'd been surrounded all her life by beautiful women of all ages, sizes and personalities, and Karolina could probably hold her own with most. She was, perhaps, a bit thinner in the shoulders than someone fixated on classic proportions might like, and she had a cast to her nose that would do a statue in the Parthenon proud, but her features and bearing were, in a word, arresting. Few would forget meeting her.

"One of the things about being an actress that I understood early on is that our talent is useless without a body. All the role empathy, vocal nuance and charisma in the world means nothing if I can't perform. I never took up smoking or any vices for that matter, and I think when I had enough fame and might have been surrounded with temptation, I had two babies."

"I'm afraid I don't know much about your bio off the stage." They stepped over the threshold of the main doors to the deck. "It's warm out here."

"It feels wonderful. It's very much fall in New York."

"Same in Chicago. I'm glad I decided against a sweater, even though the dining rooms are always frigid."

The warmth made Helen's bones feel loose and easy, or was it the wine? It had only been a glass—but she felt half-melted. The deck lights sent streamers of yellow along the polished golden deck and the faraway thrum of the engines was almost completely lost by the sound of rushing water as the ship sliced through the waves.

"Where to begin? My husband died suddenly before the twins were born. I think I was five months along. His mother tried to be helpful, but she wasn't well, and had been widowed for years. I had his money, but I'd have rather had him." She paused because she was finding it hard to call up the once-vivid memories of that time in her life. "We were best friends. Peas and carrots."

"Do you still miss him? After all these years?"

"The place he was supposed to have in my life is still there. It's been filled by the kids to a large degree, I guess, though they have their own places, of course. I do sometimes wonder what life would have been like if he'd lived. He had such a good soul, very gentle and full of fun. I guess that's why I'm just not drawn to the me-Tarzan type of guy. And I've been too busy working and being a mom to look for any other Justins out there."

"My straight friends tell me the good men are all snapped up. They seem to only have choices of married men, or ones who have no real desire to connect more than horizontally. Look—a shooting star."

Helen followed the line of sight from Karolina's pointed finger, but it was gone before she could track it. She wondered what Karolina's perfume was. It was very complex, almost a spice, but there was perhaps a hint of rose as well.

"I know women who don't want anything more than that either." She added wryly, "But then I haven't dated in so long I'm not sure how it's done."

Karolina laughed. "I should talk. I'm not good girlfriend material. I work too much. I'm in a business where taking a break can be fatal, but I love it, every minute of it."

"I understand completely. As a famous restaurateur once told me, your heart tells you what it wants and you're a chump if you don't listen."

"I like that." Her gesture took in the entirety of the world beyond the ship's railing. "I think I'd be a chump to give up any of this. And thank you again for taking a break from what you love to do this," Karolina said. "I mean that. When I thought of focusing on stage stars instead of screen stars that was the first thing I ran into. They work all the time."

"Or certainly try to. By the way, where is Trevor Huntley?" She was enough of a fan of movies that she was looking forward to meeting the multi-Oscar winner herself. She also respected him for his theatrical work; what little he had done had been excellent.

"He doesn't join us until tomorrow when we get to Grand Cayman. Apparently he has a home there. He'll leave us at Costa Maya on Tuesday and return to his hideaway."

They were approaching the stern and the sound of the engines was definitely louder. But the rush of the warm evening air was still welcome enough that they persevered around the deck to the other side. Behind them a Florida island was sparkling with lights, but the map in her packet had indicated they would be striking out directly across the Gulf, skirting Cuba and then heading farther south to George Town on Grand Cayman. Tomorrow would be entirely spent at sea. So far her stomach was tolerating the ship's motion. Cass had warned her that sleeping was the real test.

"Thank you for the beautiful suite, by the way. It's lovely. The balcony is a treat. I'm looking forward to maybe even reading a book."

Expecting Karolina to answer, she glanced over at her when she didn't and was surprised to find her blushing.

"You look guilty about something."

"You hit a very pleasant memory, that's all. Balconies are indeed very useful."

"I see."

They walked in silence for a bit, dodging other couples also circling the deck, and one intrepid soul who was jogging. She didn't need more details of whatever had happened on a balcony that had left Karolina with such a smile. It reminded her of the look on Laura's face when her girlfriend had leaned in for a kiss. She could imagine... Another woman, nothing but the seagulls to see them. Kisses in the shadows, hands...

Oh.

They had reached the first entrance into the ship's inner corridors. Karolina asked, "Do you want to see the late-night comedy act? Or check out the dance floor?"

"No, but another night I'd love to. I'm suddenly very tired." She found a smile. "My body clock is telling me that right about now the performance would be over. Though normally on a Friday night I would stay out for a while."

"This is the right stairwell for you, then." Karolina stopped to look at the posted map.

"I think so too."

"Well, I think I will see if any other talent—I'm so sorry. That's just the word we use. There's talent and guests aboard that I want to be sure are having a good time. My VIPs, as you said."

"I'm talent?" Helen shrugged. "It's okay, that's flattering."

"No, actually, you're Helen. At least that's who I was walking the deck with, I hope. I'll see Helen the Talent tomorrow before her session at eleven."

The distinction Karolina was making between Helen the woman and Helen the actress made her want to escape all the more. "Enjoy the rest of your night then. I hope everyone is settling in well."

"Sweet dreams."

She found her cabin easily and discovered Jeffrey was ready

to bring her a nightcap, which she declined. A shower turned out to be a good idea; the knobs confounded her and she had to ask Jeffrey for a demonstration. She was glad not to do that in the morning when she was sleepy and addled. Scrubbed and brushed, she wrapped herself in the robe the ship provided and stepped out onto the balcony. She didn't peer down at the deck—given her unsettled state of mind she wasn't going to trust that her fear of heights was under control.

Warm air rushed around her wet hair. The ship's lights sparkled off the dark ocean as they rose and fell. In the distance another cruise ship was heading in the opposite direction. Stars touched the horizon, faint and golden. She followed them upward to a breathtaking canopy of white twinkling lights. She hadn't seen this many stars at night in years.

That easy, almost boneless feeling came back. She sank down onto the deck chair, telling herself she was only interested in looking at the stars, but the moment her head was against the chair back she closed her eyes.

Kisses in the shadows. Karolina's kisses. Would they be as sensual as she was? As elegant and warm, with the fire that sparkled in Karolina's eyes? And hands... Hands slipping under clothing. The feel of another woman's hands sliding over her body. The idea of cupping the swell of soft breasts. The sound of her kisses on Karolina's shoulders in the warm shadows.

She was washed over, her bones dissolved and she couldn't catch her breath. The balcony was suddenly too exposed and she stumbled back into the cabin. Shedding the robe she tried to escape the tidal wave under the sheets but it followed her there, rolling her over.

Clinging to a pillow, as the world rocked under her, she thought perhaps it was something she'd eaten or seasickness. It was hormones, she added desperately, a bizarre kind of hot flash. And Cass was right, she'd ignored her libido for too long and now it was acting crazy. Nonsensical attraction, and wholly inappropriate. She'd flirted with Karolina, she'd enjoyed her company, she'd really liked looking at her and it was rude to use her for an out-of-control fantasy of sighs in her ears and her body savored by the knowing touch of another woman.

Just private fantasy, she told herself. Everybody has fantasies of things they don't really want except for the way it happened in the movie screen inside their own head. That's all this was. Just... hormonal lust.

For the first time, with not even two weeks until her fiftieth birthday.

Just hormonal lust. For another woman.

CHAPTER THIRTEEN

Saturday morning after the horrible date with Suzy, Laura stopped at the produce market because she could no longer avoid it. To her vast relief Teeny treated her as always, so she was hopeful that a story about Laura being some kind of low-life had not circulated from Suzy to her boss to Teeny. At least not yet. Instead, they had a jolly conversation about Brussels sprouts and English peas. The former weren't in season but the latter were available because of a local grower's greenhouse. A chilled pea, sweet onion, herb and mustard salad would be delicious alongside a chicken stew with Jamaican seasonings.

She might even be convinced to make her favorite low-fat brownies for the twins to enjoy over the weekend. They'd both loved the coq au vin, and their general friendliness had proved distracting the past couple of days. Though they didn't know why, she was very grateful. Julie and she had marked out the area for her herb garden and made up a list of three things Julie needed to accomplish before the end of October to get her project going.

Landscaping trucks partially blocked the driveway, but she managed to get past them and roll into an empty carport bay. Upon opening the back hatch of the Volvo she discovered that the box containing the shelled peas had overturned and all the precious little orbs of green delight had rolled every which way. *Well, hell.*

She spent twenty minutes dredging peas out from under the seat. She didn't relish the smell of rotting vegetation and certainly the Volvo already had a layered aroma of old fruits and vegetables. It was inevitable in any food preparation environment—sooner or later, all the things that could taste good together built up into a complex and not entirely pleasant smell akin to dried peat. The car interior was due for a deodorizing. In the meantime, she did not need rotting peas in the gestalt.

Finally, lightheaded from hanging almost upside down, she thought she had most of them. It hurt to throw them in the garbage can next to the cars. As she went back for the surviving groceries she realized she had been ignoring the sound of raised voices. Following the sound around the corner of the patio she saw Grace and one of the gardeners arguing, their voices overlapping in Spanish. She stayed out of sight, not wanting to tread into Grace's domain, but she wanted to make sure that nothing more than a verbal sparring was underway. It was easily the most animated she'd seen Grace to date.

A few moments later, Grace leaned close and said something harsh almost in the man's ear, then she stalked back to the house. Laura hadn't a clue what had begun the incident and the man immediately resumed hacking at the hedge. Maybe he hadn't been showing enough skill, but they had both been very angry.

She shrugged off the mystery and went to the car for the rest of her groceries. The potatoes had also escaped and rolled across the back, but they were easily rescued and could be washed. She had set the box on the kitchen counter when she realized she again heard raised voices.

It was none of her business, and she might not like Grace much, but she'd seen her share of what happened when men let their temper get the better of them, and this man sounded livid. They were again speaking in Spanish and the words overlapped at a pace she couldn't follow. She lingered just out of sight at the end of the sitting room and caught a glimpse of the man, his back to the front door as if he'd just entered. It was the supervisor of the gardening crew, his dark face mottled with rage, and one balled fist clutching the bandana he usually wore around his neck.

He called Grace a name that was extremely rude. It wasn't a word Laura would ever utter, in any language, but she knew enough variations that a member of the kitchen staff never ever got away with calling her one.

Grace laughed and cast aspersions on his male anatomy. The tone was getting uglier and uglier, and Laura felt a foreboding chill. She decided she had to intervene—and then her rusty Spanish kicked in and some of what Grace was shouting made sense.

Estúpido Mexicano, that she understood. Then a string of words she puzzled over for a moment and then took to mean, "I have the power. You have none."

He responded with a denial, then said, "There is no more. We die..." No, that wasn't right. He had said they couldn't live. There was no life, no *comida*, not enough for food to live on after they paid.

Grace said he was *suerte*, lucky, fortunate to have only had to pay percentage *diez* until now. Ten, now to be twenty. Then, clear and plain, "Another word and you're all fired."

Grace turned on her heel and headed for the stairs. The man, boiling mad, stood choking on words, then he slammed out the front door.

Left blinking in confusion, Laura puzzled over what she had just heard. Her Spanish had never been great, but it was enough to tell cooks what to do, offer praise and criticism they could follow, understand when she was being disrespected, and deal with vendors who tried to use the language barrier to their advantage. If she had heard rightly, something very rotten was going on.

She went back to the kitchen, not sure what to do. The calm environment and cheerful sunshine belied the sick chill in her stomach. She couldn't forget about it, even though she knew it wasn't her domain.

She began mindlessly unpacking the produce and nearly jumped out of her skin when Grace spoke from behind her.

"I didn't hear you come in."

"I wanted to get through the market before things were picked over," she said.

Grace only shrugged. "Julie is out with friends at the library and Justin is at the school skateboarding. They'll both be back by five."

"Perfect." That gave her plenty of time for brownies before she started on dinner prep. She was glad when Grace left again, not sure she could look at someone who had been leveling racist sneers only a few minutes earlier. What was she going to do?

She had the melted chocolate, egg- and yogurt-beaten sugar and sifted dry ingredients stirred together when she saw the landscaping trucks move to the side yard. The supervisor was talking to his people. The situation wasn't right, and what was more, she was sure Helen knew nothing of it and wouldn't tolerate it if she did. She had met her share of wealthy people who would have cared less as long as their needs were met, but she'd also met just as many who would care that people who worked for them were being extorted by someone else in their name. Helen was definitely in the latter group.

Creeping through the mud room and out the side door, she waited there, out of sight of the house windows, until one of the workers saw her. She gestured. She could see he was tempted to ignore her, but finally he signaled his boss, who turned to give her a glance. She waved urgently, and he said something, then slowly made his way over.

"I'm sorry to interrupt," she began, then she lapsed into what passed for her Spanish, asking him if he and his crew were paying Grace to keep their jobs.

He lifted a brow, maybe surprised that she spoke in a string of street-learned phrases, not the halting perfection of Spanish learned from books. *"Es privado, señora."*

She repeated herself, then added what she hoped was, "I'll speak to Mrs. Baynor myself. She knows nothing of this. This would upset her."

An involuntary smile ghosted across his face, and he relaxed slightly. Laura realized she'd said Helen would be crazy instead of upset. Then he shrugged. There was no hope in his eyes.

"It's not right," Laura said, growing more certain of her language as it dredged up from the back of her brain. "Mrs. Baynor pays Grace to pay you, and Grace takes a lot for herself. That's not how it should be."

He choose his words carefully, probably gauging to her second grade vocabulary. "*Grace no tomar su dinero?*"

"She wouldn't dare," Laura snapped. On the other hand, maybe Grace was just biding her time, waiting to decide if it was safe to blackmail Laura. But she'd learned, all those years running kitchens staffed almost entirely by men, in resorts owned and run by men, that once you bowed to illicit authority and bullies, you always bowed. Because of her mother she had choices and power her mother had never had. She would be damned if she'd bow to someone like Grace. She loved this job, loved...everything about it. But she wasn't going to let Helen be ripped off. She couldn't pretend she didn't know.

"*Un americano, con papeles. Mis hombres...*" His voice trailed away, leaving Laura certain that some of his crew were in the country without documentation and Grace knew that too.

"When do you return to work?" She started to attempt the sentence in Spanish, but he cut her off.

"Past tomorrow. The day after tomorrow."

His English was better than her Spanish, she suspected, so she stuck with it. "I'll talk to you the day after tomorrow then. Say nothing about this to anyone. I'll do my best, my very best, to stop this."

He nodded and went back to his crew and Laura slipped into the kitchen. The oven was ready and she slipped the brownies inside, her head spinning. She had no further plan made when the twins both arrived home and clomped their mutual way up the stairs to various Internet and phone call pursuits, each with a warm brownie in one hand.

Grace had paused in the mud room to write something on the schedule board, then she joined Laura.

"I've got a few errands to run in Menlo Park and I thought I might take in a movie. I'll probably be back after you leave." Her face was its familiar, impassive façade. Laura realized Grace had never once met her gaze squarely.

"We'll be fine," Laura told her. "I won't dash out, but the kids are fine all by themselves for an hour or two."

She got all of the ingredients of the stew into the pot and settled in to read on her iPad while it bubbled, all the while listening for the sound of Grace's departing car. She waited three minutes after the gravel had stopped crunching from the main drive, then picked up an invoice to carry into the study where she'd had her interview.

This was so not her business. It really could wait until Helen came home next Sunday. It was only a week from tomorrow. But she wanted some proof, something to give Helen to examine or ask her accountant to research, and she didn't know when she'd have this chance to look for something again. What if the maintenance supervisor said something to Grace about their conversation? She shouldn't have spoken to him yet. That hadn't been a smart move.

The file cabinet wasn't locked, but she was quickly frustrated by its contents. The gardening company invoices were there and marked paid. Grace was getting her share in cash handed back from the supervisor. Kickbacks happened all over the world—she'd worked in plenty of places where delivery people took cash to bring goods to her kitchen first. But her bosses had been aware that she was paying them and their bosses knew it too. This was different. The workers were vulnerable and Grace was using that to line her own pockets while Helen footed the bill.

Not sure what she'd find, she pulled out the folder marked *Grocery*. Her invoices from the produce market, bakery and kitchen supply house were there, marked with the date and number of the check that had repaid her. But there were also several handwritten notes on white note paper.

'Mid-Coast Meats', one note read. '$50 cash for delivery'.

Another said, '$61 cash to PTA for local honey—fundraiser'
Both were marked with dates of payments.

She didn't know anything about these purchases.

"What are you doing?"

She knew she looked guilty. It was Justin, not looking hostile,
but definitely curious. Laura's gaze dropped to the paper in her
hand.

It read, '$40 cash for bread and cheese'. In just the past
several weeks, Grace had stolen over a hundred and sixty dollars.

Helen was paying out checks for cash outlays that had never
happened, and she thought Laura was the one buying those items.
Grace had probably even given Laura a budget with plenty of
room left for Grace to take the difference. Helen probably never
looked close at the numbers.

"What's going on, Laura?"

She started again, then focused on him. He was just a boy—
nearly a man—already a man in some cultures. But just a boy...
Not the man of the house. Helen wouldn't want him involved.

"I was just checking an invoice. I'm missing something and I
wanted to be sure I didn't pay for it."

"You look like you've seen a ghost."

"Then I really need to work on my tan."

He smiled and watched without any seeming alarm as she
carefully tucked the folder back exactly as she had found it. She
had no idea what she was going to do.

A slight case of nerves compounded by a mild reaction to
the ship's motion had Helen feeling a little bit queasy just before
the start of her class. She'd taught classes before, but mostly for
highly enthused high schoolers as part of the Broadway Gives
Back program. Her audience here appeared to be about eighty
community theater actors and activists, none younger than
forty and most older than she was. Women outnumbered men
about four to one. She hadn't seen this much cruise wear in one
place since the Tonys had featured *Beach Blanket Bingo*. She saw
Eugene Masterson at the back, and couldn't imagine how he had

justified the time away from his work—but that was none of her business.

The ship's smallest theater was a good venue for the workshops and Helen waited in the wings while Karolina introduced her. Today Karolina was wearing cream-colored slacks with a red halter top that showed off her shoulders. One elegant hand held the microphone comfortably while the other rested lightly on her hip as she read from papers on the lectern. "...Her first critical acclaim in *Agnes of God*, a mere prelude of things to come..."

On waking this morning, after a fevered and restless night, Helen had decided that anything she might have felt had just been the romantic aura of a cruise and Karolina's more than considerable charisma. She'd repeated her diagnosis through the quick snack of an English muffin and slice of ham that Jeffrey had brought her, and through her shower and choice of white denim trousers with a silk tank top printed with Mardi Gras-inspired fleur de lis.

The lie had shattered the moment she'd seen Karolina. There were tingles—adolescent, impossible tingles—in the pit of her stomach. She was very concerned that she was about to go out to a performance—not a play, but still a performance—while a part of her brain was thinking about what it would be like to undo Karolina's halter and touch...

"...Tony Awards with more nominations than a person can count. We are so fortunate..."

She had never been distracted by personal feelings. Never felt like a part of her was disconnected. Performing was everything, all-consuming, and she wouldn't lose it for a momentary infatuation that made no sense in her life. She was nearly *fifty*. How could she not...know?

"...A true light of the Broadway stage. Please join me in welcoming Helen Baynor."

She didn't inhale during the air kisses with Karolina for fear of that heady spice-and-rose cologne. It didn't help. She wanted to turn her head and discover if a woman's lips were as soft as she thought they might be. Her audience applauded enthusiastically.

She put on the demeanor of Helen Baynor, a true light of the Broadway stage, and pushed the scared and reeling Helen to the background of her mind. It was the best she could do.

After thanks and commendation to the audience for their support of a charity that ensured babies entered the world as healthy as possible, especially if born with AIDS, she took a show of hands to make sure that her audience members were themselves all performers. Most did raise their hands as having been in a play or other performance in the last five years. Most had done so on stage, a few in front of a camera, and when she asked, a woman in the front volunteered that she had acted in a series that was running on the Internet and before that, she had been on stage with the Beverly Hills Playhouse.

"The number one question I'm always asked," Helen began as part of her prepared comments, "is what I think the most important attribute of a successful actor is. In my opinion, it's not good looks and it's not skill in the craft. I'm not going to name names, but there are plenty of actors who use an unusual appearance to their benefit, and many more who aren't the best craftsmen and yet manage to land role after role. What all types of successful actors have in common is stamina." She took a moment to assess the crowd. Eyes were bright and they appeared engaged.

"Their stamina is emotional. Rejection, fickle fan support and bad reviews don't slow them. Their stamina is physical. They may not be what *Vogue* considers thin, but they are physically robust and able to handle a stage or production schedule without missing their times."

She went on to detail the typical work schedule for an actor on Broadway, then admitted her own was a little less rigorous, but she'd reached a position where she could ask for some leniency. "I was also just plain lucky, and in a financial position where I could turn down a part if my schedule couldn't be accommodated."

Her hour's talk, including exercises for motion and breathing that she'd learned decades ago in an L.A. workshop and a few funny anecdotes of props and lines gone awry and how different performers had coped, stretched to an hour and a half. The audience was enthusiastic and receptive, and she promised them her next session on Monday would cover how to evaluate a character when taking up a new role. If it hadn't been well into lunch service they might have lingered, but instead the audience quickly cleared.

Karolina was effusive, giving her a quick embrace. "That was smashing! You were perfect."

She had to force her gaze from outlining Karolina's lips, and immediately spotted Eugene Masterson bearing down on them.

Karolina must have felt her stiffen. In a low voice she asked, "Is it the bad penny?"

"Yes, but I'm going to deal with it. I'm not going to spend the cruise ducking him." Her body was in danger of melting from contact with Karolina—how could it not show? "Thanks for the smoke screen, but I'll take it from here."

She nodded and let go of her just as Eugene arrived.

His greeting to Karolina was pleasant enough, but laden with a dismissive aura of "I'm here now so you can go."

"I need to see to a few things," Karolina said. "Helen, I'd like to talk to you this afternoon about a scheduling wrinkle. Around two?"

"That would be great. Can we meet out in the sunshine?"

"I'll be the one on the Lido deck with a blue drink that has some kind of umbrella in it." She waved cheerily at both of them and departed.

"I was wondering if we might have lunch together." It wasn't really a question.

"I'm starving," Helen said. "The main dining room?"

"Certainly." He made a courtly gesture for her to precede him up the theater aisle, which was somewhat odd from a man in Bermuda shorts and a Hawaiian print shirt. His sandy good looks drew eyes to him as she led their way to the main dining room. Helen knew most other women would be flattered, but she felt nothing for him and more familiarity was going to breed outright contempt.

In the daylight the view from the windows on both sides of the main restaurant was filled with a sensational blue sky and the green-blue of unbroken ocean. She really wanted to get outside and into the sun for a while.

She supposed some women would be enthused at his show of opening doors and pulling out her chair. It was gentlemanly, but done with an exaggeration that said it wasn't ingrained in him but rather done precisely so that she and others would notice. She couldn't recall the play, but she remembered the line, "Darling, if you're *acting* like a gentleman, then you aren't one."

She ordered the lobster bisque and an artisanal salad from the attentive waiter. Eugene ordered the same and then leaned back like a man well-pleased by his success. "I have to admit I never dreamed that I'd be having lunch with my longtime stage idol."

Yes you did, she thought. You never doubted that you would. "I'm flattered, but that makes me feel old."

"Not my intention in the least. You're a very attractive woman."

And you are so very married, she wanted to say. She chose the more subtle, "Is your wife a fan of the theater?"

"No. She has other pursuits." He settled his napkin into his lap.

"What a pity. I'd like to meet her. Neither of my children have an interest in the stage as a career. What about yours?"

He shrugged his broad shoulders. "My youngest is a thespian of sorts. I think it's more that he likes hanging around with certain elements in the theater world."

"We're an interesting and diverse bunch." Though she didn't want it, she broke open and buttered a roll to busy her hands.

He waited for the delivery of his cocktail and her iced tea before clearing his throat slightly and leaning forward, as if he did not want to be overheard. "This is somewhat awkward, but modern life being what it is... I have to say yesterday I rather got the impression that you were part of the more diverse element of the theater."

Puzzled, she asked, "How so?"

"According to her own website, Karolina bats for the, uh, other team. It's in her bio, several awards from gay groups and so on."

So he *had* noticed their little interchange yesterday. He wasn't as thick with ego as she'd supposed. Really, she tended to like men. She'd married one. She'd worked with perfectly wonderful guys, many, many times. But everything about Eugene rubbed her the wrong way. "We enjoy each other's company."

"But I didn't think you were..."

"Are you asking if I'm a lesbian?"

"I guess I am. I don't want to be obnoxious."

Oh, you've already been that, Moxie Taylor would have said. "Whether I'm with someone isn't really the issue. You're married. That disqualifies you from my thinking of you in that way. My late husband was a very special man and you're..."

He was plainly disappointed and a bit angry, she could tell. "And I'm not."

"You're nothing like him, no. I don't know exactly what I might want in a relationship when my kids are finally grown, but I'm not drawn to you in a way that would make me want to find out. I'm sorry, I know that's not easy to hear, but I'm simply unavailable."

"I don't think 'Ms.' Tavitian thinks so."

She wanted to say that it was none of his concern, but she wasn't going to let him change the subject. He also had a way of saying Ms. that contained a sneer. "That's not really relevant, is it? I'm not looking and you're not available."

"I know..." He cleared his throat. "We both move in circles where people don't follow the usual rules. I am married to the mother of two of my children and we live in completely different worlds at this point. Our paths cross when necessary. I'm discreet and so is she."

Helen held back her answer until after her soup and salad were set down and the waiter had departed. He refused to hear her point and she couldn't imagine spending time with anyone who didn't listen. "I don't care what anyone else in any circle does. I can't overlook that you're married." She tasted her soup and said brightly, "This is delicious."

"I had hoped that as a show person you had a more cosmopolitan outlook on such things." His food was untouched.

She was going to get angry—fine, she was already angry. "I don't think that an emotional relationship of any kind can be started with a cold-blooded negotiation about basic values." She softened her tone but kept an edge of warning. "This merger isn't going to work, and we'll be better acquaintances if that's accepted right now."

He smiled, though it was strained, and won a few points with her for saying, "Perhaps I've been a bit of an ass, thinking you a mortal woman. I've wanted to know you for years."

If some kind of pedestal made him believe that she had zero interest in him, then fine. "I'm not a mortal woman, then. How about you tell me which plays you've seen while we enjoy our lunch? We can look at the gorgeous sea and revel in schadenfreude about those who are sitting at a desk today."

He was, in the end, enough of a gentleman not to sulk openly. By the time they made it through their salads, the conversation had eased. She'd had suitors before but none so arrogantly assured of his ultimate success and so quick to be angered by a hint of failure. He was, as Cass would say, Bad News on a Stick. She hadn't been interested in him before she'd met Karolina and what did Karolina have to do with it anyway? It wasn't like... It wasn't as if...

"I hope you'll let me take you dancing one night this week," he said as they parted. "Just so I can say that I've danced the night away with a glamorous star."

"Perhaps," was her only answer and she was glad to escape to the deck and drink in the sea air.

If they hadn't been moving at however many knots, the temperature would have been unpleasantly hot and the air unrelentingly humid. But the breeze on the windward side of the deck was perfect. Maybe it was time to break out the swimsuit. Glancing at her watch she saw that she'd be able to meet Karolina on the Lido deck right on time.

She wasn't used to wearing as little as a swimsuit. Julie had thought she should get a bikini, but a more sensible one-piece had been the final purchase, in a soft green that heightened the slight red undertone in her otherwise dark brown hair. She wasn't sure she came off as trim and elegant as Karolina, but it wasn't bad for kissing fifty. If she had a hot flash she could blame the sweat on the sun.

She was dressed before she really looked at her face in the mirror. She'd spent hours every day doing just that, watching someone else layer on makeup while she took inventory of new wrinkles, her nose—just a bit too long—and worried if the color of her lips meant she was losing her alluvial pigmentation or whatever the heck the aesthetist at the spa had been talking about. Today she was reluctant to look, as if she was afraid something had changed. That something she felt inside would show.

What was wrong with her? What was the big deal? She knew many gay and bisexual and transgendered people—there were plenty of all of the above in the theater world. This was just a humorous moment in her life, actually feeling like she might be gay, but she wasn't. Was she? And even if she was, why was she freaked out? She wasn't homophobic, but if she wasn't afraid and scared of being gay, then why wasn't she celebrating in the hallways and thinking about maybe having lesbian sex for the first time? What was so terrifying?

Her unchanged face held no answers. Her eyes were the same gray-blue as always. Only her mouth might be different. It looked fuller, softer even.

As she went up the stairs to the pool deck she asked herself how she knew she wasn't gay. It wasn't as if she'd had more than the one experience with sex, which, if she thought about it, was pathetic for a nearly fifty-year-old woman. She'd been married, had very good sex with her husband, created two beautiful babies. For years the sexual part of her had seemed dead, and when it might have come alive she was busy working and being a mother. She couldn't remember the difference between third grade and seventh grade. Even some shows she'd been in blended together. Time flowed like a steady stream that hadn't seemed to change until recently.

She had reached the point of wondering if she was bisexual, and thinking she really was out of her depth when it came to understanding what was what, who was who, and what got called which by whom when she spotted Karolina stretched out on a chaise in the filtered sunlight of the pool deck awning.

One thing crystallized—an L-word did apply to the situation: Lust, with a capital L. Not blind sexual lust for a body colliding with hers, but lust precisely because Karolina had soft, alluring outlines she wanted to touch with her fingers, and curves at her hips that she was thirsty to trace with her tongue. The surge of desire took her breath away and for a moment she thought she was having a hot flash.

She was, apparently, but not that kind.

For a moment she just looked at Karolina's body, drinking in the desire. There was a hum of electricity in her spine. Glancing around the deck there were certainly a great many male bodies and for some she might feel a definite appreciation, but she didn't want to touch them. She didn't think about their bodies with hers, not the way she was thinking about her breasts against Karolina's and her hand touching intimate and warm places.

Fifty, she told herself, you're nearly fifty, and you haven't the first clue about what your heart wants. That makes you a chump.

Your heart? Moxie Taylor mocked her. *Your heart's got nothing to do with this. Tick-tock, dollface.*

No, she answered, there's no rush here. She didn't have to jump into something without careful consideration. She had to think about the kids and her career and her schedule... Her thoughts trailed off the closer she got to Karolina.

She had not known that her body could feel the way Karolina looked, like poured out silk. She had loved being with Justin Senior, she remembered the first time even, and it was a good memory. But that experience had nothing to do with these feelings. This was new. And she was scared. Wonderfully scared.

CHAPTER FOURTEEN

On Sunday Laura approached the Baynor house filled with trepidation. She didn't see how she could go on working with Grace when she knew what Grace was up to. But Helen was reachable only for an emergency, and she didn't think this counted as one. Knuckling under was not her strong suit, and the stress over it had disturbed her sleep more than the hurt from Suzy's diatribe.

It was a relief to see that the minivan wasn't there. Grace must have taken the kids on errands. She checked the schedule board as soon as she let herself in the side door. Justin was at a friend's house and Julie was listed at an ecology day planning group at the school. Before she lost her nerve she hurried to the study, carefully pulled out the folder with the fabricated cash receipts and took pictures with her phone. She also took a picture of the monthly landscaping and housecleaning bills—she didn't put it past Grace to be pulling the same thing on the Latino women who cleaned as she was on the landscapers. Twenty percent of that and twenty percent of the housekeeper's bill was the equivalent of some people's car payments. Plus Grace was getting a salary and living probably for free in the quarters attached to the rear of the garage.

She thought of her mother and was seared with anger. She couldn't change it, she couldn't make it better, she reminded herself. To the empty room she said, "And the last thing you're going to do is head for a bar because you're angry and scared and your mother died for a stupid reason, and after she gave up everything she could have been for you, and endured things you never understood because she loved you in spite of it all."

She repeated that truth to herself as she looked in the folders for any other evidence. Her predecessor, Mary, had turned in perfect receipts, it seemed, but she wondered if Mary had been easier to strike a deal with. What about her made Grace think she couldn't strong-arm her for a cut of her pay? Her friendship with the kids? That Helen insisted on meeting with her? Maybe Grace thought if she crossed a black girl she'd get knifed or something. Kitchens were full of knives, after all.

She laughed out loud at herself. It didn't really matter why Grace hadn't tried to blackmail her for her job. She wouldn't have succeeded. But there was nothing more to find. She only had the conversation she'd overheard, the word of the landscaper and the fake receipts for cash she'd never spent.

Retreating to the kitchen, she put away the groceries and went about breaking down a whole chicken to oven-fry for Sunday supper. If her mother were alive she'd ask for advice, but she knew what it would have been. "Bend your back for what you love. Bend it for what you hate and you'll break."

She wished she knew the name of Helen's accountant—stupid woman, she told herself. It's got to be in the files somewhere. But even as she decided to go back and look the minivan pulled in. Grace and Julie were home.

"Mrs. Baynor—your class was stupendous yesterday morning and we can't wait to get back to the ship to clean up and go to your four o'clock."

"Thank you." Helen peered through the dockside glare as she and the small group of women waited for the next tender back to the ship from the busy cruise port at George Town on Grand Cayman. She recognized the woman from Beverly Hills. "I'm looking forward to it."

"A group of friends and I were wondering if you'd have dinner with us this evening? We've got an early reservation in the Italian restaurant. Then—of course—we're all going to the Evening with Trevor Huntley."

She'd been trying to figure out how to ask Karolina to have dinner with her again, just as they had after sunbathing most of yesterday afternoon away. It appeared that while she had the self-control not to openly drool on the woman, she didn't have the self-control to keep some kind of distance. Maybe the invitation for dinner with others was a sign. "I'd love to. I can't wait for Mr. Huntley's talk either. It seems a shame to make you all leave Grand Cayman early to hear me, though." She glanced at Karolina, who looked crisp and fresh in a white muslin wrap dress and a large sun hat. "Who do I complain to about the schedule?"

"Haven't the slightest," she answered. "Someone in the production company screwed that up." She fluttered her eyelashes innocently before moving away just enough to leave Helen to her conversation.

"We thought we'd meet at the Solar Lounge for a cocktail before dinner. Around five thirty or quarter to six?"

"I'll be there," Helen agreed.

"I'm glad," Karolina said, after the woman had taken her leave to share the news with her friends. "I have to dine with my client rep tonight to go over our financial outlook and I was afraid I'd be abandoning you potentially to you-know-who."

"I think that's over and done with." She hadn't seen Eugene

since lunch yesterday, but she hadn't expected to. "The tender is nearly here."

The small white craft with a bright blue awning over the passenger area was gliding to a halt at the dock. There was easily enough room for all of them for the short ferry to where the *Solstice Eclipse* was anchored. Burly ship's personnel tied the craft and set out steps with smooth efficiency and they helped the passengers from the dock and safely to a seat.

"I like this part," Karolina said. She pulled off her hat and tossed back her hair as they departed the dock as quickly as the tender had arrived.

Helen had to close her eyes. Their excursion ashore had included shopping and a two-hour stay poolside at a very posh resort. Julie would have loved the black string bikini Karolina wore under her white muslin wrap, but as far as Helen was concerned, it was an invitation to delicious sin and she was definitely a wannabe sinner. As they picked up speed the wind was lifting her hair. She looked like some Greek water goddess.

"So do I, though I don't think my stomach is as strong a sailor as yours."

"You're okay, right?"

She peeked out of one eye to smile at Karolina. "Fine. I'm just glad I'm not sitting on the outside rail like you."

Karolina sighed. "Isn't this the life? I'm usually terribly busy but while most of the people on the cruise have demanding standards, they're not demanding—at least not of me." Karolina sounded half drowsy even though the little craft was bouncing across the waves. "I feel positively wicked for stealing this time. Thank you for spending it with me."

She wanted to keep her eyes closed but it was impossible. The thin white fabric was billowing in the wind, outlining the sleek lines of Karolina's shoulders and breasts like a second skin. Just looking Helen was turning to liquid in parts of her body that had been frozen and apparently resentful for decades and were now intent on making up for the lost time. Those parts were trying to do all the thinking and filling her head with images of Karolina's head thrown back just as it was now in the wind, but in response to Helen's touch. The roar of the boat's engines were in sync with the throb in her belly that never seemed to stop. She imagined sounds of whispered encouragement. Twinges of nerves sent unsettling tingles down her thighs, then up to her nipples and back again. It was unnerving and embarrassing. She wasn't sure she could stop it if she tried.

Moxie drawled, "Why on earth would you want to try, dollface?"

The tender was expertly brought alongside the small floating dock that was tied to the lower deck passenger entry. Karolina pushed herself upright. "What a wonderful day."

The gods were having a good laugh at Helen Baynor, she decided. *Oh you queen of no time for sex, no time for love, who acted the part of a woman and didn't spend any time being one unless the parts of actress or mom required it, think again.* You do have a body that's capable of more than commanding a stage.

Even if she... Even if they... She didn't have the first clue what to do. Not a clue, not a one. Distracted and trying hard not to watch Karolina retie her wrap, she didn't notice the raised doorway from the arrival deck to the ship's corridor. For an instant she was sure she was about to plant face-first on the carpet, but her fall was stopped by a stocky, dark-skinned woman passing the doorway, who caught Helen's arm in a firm grasp.

"Whoa there. Are you okay?" She let Helen go.

"Yes, thank you." Without thinking better of it she said, "You're very strong."

The woman, who was almost as broad-shouldered as she was tall and sported hair so short that it was impossible to tell if it was black or gray, said, "And you're Helen Baynor, aren't you? I couldn't believe it when I saw your picture on one of the marquees."

Helen nodded. "Thank you for saving me."

She got a firm, endearing smile in response. "I can call it my fifteen minutes of fame. I saved Helen Baynor's life."

If this woman isn't a lesbian, then no one is, Helen thought. "I'll back you up on that claim." She nodded and got a wink back and only then did she take note of the Human Rights Campaign logo on the woman's ball cap. Well, apparently she had working gaydar.

As she rejoined her, Karolina asked, "Does that happen to you often?"

Did she mean being rescued by a cute lesbian? See, you're not just after lesbians. That woman was adorable and you're still thinking about Karolina, so it's not just women. It's still safe to be around women. You're not going to go back to New York and want to jump Cass. That was *eww* on so many levels.

"Being recognized," Karolina clarified. She led the way down the carpeted corridor to the elevator. "Does that happen often?"

"Away from New York? No, not really." She could still feel the woman's touch on her arm, but it wasn't sexual. It was just human contact. That was a good sign, wasn't it? That she wasn't fetishizing every lesbian she met? She didn't want to get home again and find she was panting after Laura either, that was hardly appropriate, even if Laura was really nice, and interesting, and rather attractive and easy to talk to.

"You're very modest. I find that unusual in a performer." The elevator arrived and Karolina pushed the number for her own deck and then Helen's as the door closed.

Focused entirely on Karolina, she said, "I'm actually not modest at all. I'm very aware that few women on the stage right now have my credentials and abilities. That probably sounds arrogant." She forestalled a protestation with a gesture. "There are two parts to the equation. There's the gift I was born with and I can't take credit for that any more than I can for the color of my skin. It's as if someone handed me a winning lottery ticket that I didn't even buy. But I cashed that ticket in, and used everything it gave me with as much tenacity and courage as I could find, and backed up every advantage it gave me with hard work. Now that I take credit for. That was all a choice and I'm proud of it."

"A woman after my own heart," said someone behind her.

With a start, Helen turned in the small space and found herself face-to-face with Trevor Huntley. He was at least ten years older than she was, and his craggy New Yorker face was familiar worldwide, though not as readily when obscured by a Mets cap and sunglasses. She smiled and held out her hand. "Mr. Huntley, it's a pleasure."

"Likewise. I was asking myself how it is that you and I have never been in a project together." If he noticed that other people in the elevator had suddenly given him more space, it didn't show.

He had a wonderful voice, lighter in person than on recordings, but with round, open tones that spoke of hard training for diction that had become natural to him. Helen thought she would happily listen to him read the phone book. "Let's blame our agents."

"Done."

"You've of course met our host, Karolina Tavitian."

"We met this morning," Karolina confirmed.

He nodded and said to Helen, "This is nice work if we can get it, isn't it?"

"That's what my son said." The elevator stopped at her deck. "Until later."

She also received a nod plus a hint of a wink. Good heavens, the man had charm for miles.

As she showered for her own lecture she wondered just how bad it was that while she had nonchalantly chatted with a megastar part of her had been fantasizing about following Karolina to her cabin and helping her out of her swimsuit. She was starting to be concerned for her focus during a performance.

It would be funny, except it wasn't.

After a restless Sunday night without much sleep, Laura had finally decided on the only reasonable thing she could do. The more she thought about it, the more she believed that what she had found might only be the tip of an iceberg. Grace could have access to emergency accounts or credit cards. Anyone who would steal for so little might actually be stealing more—or with the hope of more.

She waited until it was after nine in New York, turning her phone over in her hands, getting up her nerve. One of the phone numbers on the schedule board was for Helen's agent, and Helen herself had referred to Cassidy as her closest friend. She was a regular visitor over the holidays, apparently, plus when she'd had surgery for cervical cancer, Cassidy had stayed with the Baynors during part of her convalescence. The kids knew her and she knew them, and she was a trusted friend of the family—and, importantly, someone Helen trusted in a business context as well.

She told a baby-voiced receptionist her name and asked for Ms. Winters. They went back and forth over it being a private matter, but as soon as she said she worked for Helen Baynor she was put on hold. A few moments later, a brisk voice picked up the line.

"Helen? What's wrong?"

"I'm sorry," Laura said. "It's not Helen. I'm her private chef, Laura Izmani."

"Oh—sorry. The message was muddled. Are Justin and Julie okay?"

She took a deep breath. "They're fine. I've come across a situation here that I don't know how to resolve. If Mrs. Baynor were due home this week as usual I'd talk to her directly, but I don't think I can let it go until Sunday when she gets back. And it's possible I wouldn't be able to see her until our regular meeting next Tuesday, when she would expect to meet with me."

"Doesn't her house manager handle emergencies?"

"It involves her. I don't have the authority to confront her."

The razor's edge in Cassidy's tone sharpened. "Grace? What are we talking about here? Drunk on the job? Cruel to the kids? What?"

She heard the wariness in Cassidy's voice. If Laura was a troublemaker, waiting until Helen was out of the country was the way to go, and she knew Cassidy had to be leery of everything Laura told her. Who wouldn't be?

"No, far more ordinary. I have proof that she's padding expenses—paying herself for things I never bought and recording them as if I asked to be reimbursed cash. I also overheard her threatening some of the workers with firing if they didn't increase their kickback to her for their jobs. The landscapers. For Mrs. Baynor I think the sum is probably pretty minor, but I don't think she'd like it and anyone who would do that, well, there's no telling what else she might do. I have no idea at all what sums she could take on her way out of town if she realized I knew what she was up to. Or may have already taken but no one has figured it out yet."

"Neither do I. Do you really have proof? I know Helen's accountant. She's here in New York."

"I do—photographs of fake receipts. She says she paid me cash and I'll swear under oath it never happened. And I think the landscaping supervisor would back me up, if he knew Grace wouldn't be able to fire him and his crew. He was very angry when she told him they had to pay more—that's why I was listening. I heard an angry man shouting at a woman—"

"Send me the photos. And don't do anything until you hear from me. I have to say that I'm stunned and I don't quite know what to think."

"I'm not a liar, Miss Winters," Laura said without heat. "I don't have a personal grudge against Grace. Well, I didn't, but now... This was very hard for me to do. I'm used to solving problems like these, but as I said, I don't have the authority. But I understand you have to think about it. I've been stewing over it for two days."

Cassidy gave Laura her email address then added, "I know you had excellent references, but then Grace came from an agency that vets people too." She sighed. "Helen and her goody-two shoes would not like this and she'd kill me for not telling her. But no way am I telling her while she's on that cruise. She'd jump overboard and swim back if she thought anything would disrupt the kids' lives. You may have to wait and keep quiet."

"At least I won't be alone in the waiting. This is rather over my pay grade, so to speak."

"I get that. But please, don't do anything until you hear from me."

Grateful that her pounding heart hadn't been audible in her voice, Laura keyed in Cassidy's email address and forwarded the photos from her phone. There was no going back.

CHAPTER FIFTEEN

When Laura turned on her phone early Tuesday morning, she was surprised to have an email from Cassidy Winters asking her to come to an office in Redwood City at eleven a.m. She looked up the address—it was a CPA's office. Someone affiliated with Helen's accountant in New York maybe? She was willing to go but wished she knew what kind of reception she was going to get.

She fussed over her clothes. The Dolce & Gabbana jacket always gave her courage and she paired it with tailored black slacks. She found the office in one of Redwood City's office parks that also housed hundreds of small to large Internet companies. Walking from her car to the building she took a steadying breath of the cool morning air. The fog was in, blanketing the sky in gray. She hoped it wasn't an omen. She had done nothing wrong and ultimately, though it would hurt a lot, she could walk away from the job and this situation. All that may be true, she told herself, but you're still the black employee complaining that the white one is stealing. There was no predicting how people acted sometimes.

She was relieved to see no sign of Grace or the minivan she usually drove. She realized she had half expected it to be a she said/she said confrontation.

Hoping she exuded confidence, she gave her name to the receptionist and was shown to a small conference room. Scarcely a minute later a large man in a gray suit, sporting an amazing handlebar moustache, opened the door. He stepped back to allow a very thin woman with spiky blond hair to precede him into the room.

"Cassidy Winters?" Laura thought she looked familiar from photographs in the Baynor house, but she looked even more thin and tightly wound in person. "You flew here from New York?"

"Yes. A pleasure to meet you, Ms. Izmani."

"Laura, please."

"I'm Cass. And this is Daryl Kech, a colleague of Helen's accountant in New York. He's going to observe some of the business niceties for this situation."

They shook hands all around, then settled around the small table. She declined a cup of coffee, but watched Cass open three packets of sugar substitute and stir it into hers. Daryl opened a folder, but it was Cass who did all of the talking.

"Here's where we are. Two choices. I tell Helen or I don't tell her. If we tell her she's going to fly home from some impossible place in Mexico and I don't want to do that because this is not an emergency. A fact she won't believe because you can't tell Helen anything when it comes to her kids. So the other choice is I don't tell her until she's docked in Miami on Friday. But if I don't tell her, then I have to make sure that everything she would have done if she were here happens so when she yells at me I can assure her it made no difference that she took care of her career while the rest of us took care of this business."

Laura let out a stunned breath, hoping she had kept up. "You believe me then?"

"Hell yes. The agency that sent the woman to Helen didn't properly vet her. My guy in New York found a conviction—a *conviction*, mind you—for her on just this kind of thing. She did two years for theft in New Jersey, including art. Apparently when she realized the hammer was going to drop she loaded up the car with valuables and took off. So God yes, I believe you. Especially since my guy didn't even turn up a traffic ticket for you."

Daryl touched the papers in front of him. "Our firm has a power of attorney from Mrs. Baynor for certain financial affairs. Using that, we're in the process of closing all access to household accounts that Grace Olmstead has, and changing passwords for online trading accounts in case a list has fallen into her hands. We're also making a quick spot check to ensure that nothing unusual has transpired in the accounts we monitor. I believe that financially all is secure."

"I'm relieved," Laura said. "This was only a couple of hundred dollars—I mean the cash she said she gave to me. But I didn't know where it would lead. It seemed such a small amount for the risk and I worried that it was only a fraction of what she could do."

Cass indicated the folder. "Daryl has a few statements for you to sign. They're for the file and just state what you told me. Whether Helen presses charges or not is going to be up to her. But the first thing she would do is protect the kids. So that's what I'm going to do. They know me and I'll pick them up at school. I'm on the emergency list to do that, and so is a backup person from the agency that sent Grace, but it's not like I'm going to trust that sleazebag operation to do it and not tell Grace. So really, if I'm not going to tell Helen, then I have to be here. Before that, I'm going to meet with the security company and have them supervise and escort Ms. Olmstead from the premises, with the help of the local police if necessary. They're sending a locksmith and the cars will be re...whatever it is they do to make new codes for the door remotes. I've already faxed the school their documentation to bar that woman from being able to pick the kids up from here on out. So. I think I've covered all the bases."

Laura nodded. As Cass had spoken she'd glanced over the papers Daryl wanted her to sign. She was attesting to the veracity of photographs she'd taken, copies attached, and that the summaries of the conversations she'd overheard and engaged in were accurate. She felt fine signing them.

"I have one question for you, Laura," Cass added. "This will be unpleasant with Olmstead. But Helen is such a stickler for consistency and continuity. Every day the kids have to have the same routine. Even more, Julie's diet has to be as controlled as possible. I can't just take them out for pizza for the next four days. Will you be comfortable being around while that woman is removed so you can keep doing what you do? Helen loves what you've contributed to the family so far. She told me so."

Laura blinked. "Of course—I mean I was planning to make snacks and dinner as usual. I sometimes hang out after dinner if they're looking for company or I have something I want to prep for the next day. We play poker for pretzel sticks. And I'm teaching Justin how to cook and helping Julie start an organic herb garden for a school project."

"Wow." Cass cocked her head. "Overachieve much?"

Laura shrugged. "I enjoy the time with them."

"You've already said more about the kids than Grace did the entire time I was there after my surgery. Helen swore she was efficient—"

"She certainly seemed so," Laura said. "The electrical work in the living room is nearly done. Though I wonder now if Grace made private arrangements with the contractor."

"That's something to check—the quality of what's been done," Cass said to Daryl. "The more the merrier."

He nodded and made a note. "I think we're done here."

He and Cass rose to shake hands. Laura felt shellshocked.

"Can you give me a lift to the Baynors'?" Cass had turned to Laura. "Daryl fetched me from SFO and I'd rather not rent a car when I know perfectly good ones are waiting at Helen's. I like her Saab. If I'm stuck here I might as well put the top down and drive to the beach when the kids are at school every day."

"Of course," she agreed, bemused by the rapidity with which

Cass was managing to sort out everything. Once in the car, Cass asked for a more detailed description of the conversation she had overheard. As they neared Woodside, Laura explained that she needed to make a stop.

"There's some produce I want to get. Do you have any food allergies?"

"Heavens no, but I've been trying an immune-system support diet while trying to put back just a few more pounds."

"Lots of dark leafy greens and bright oranges on the plate?"

Cass smiled. "You got it."

"I'll do my best to make that delicious. Justin is turning out a regular supply of desserts, so I think you'll find plenty of calories to tempt you."

"Justin cooking. I have to say I'm amazed."

She coasted into a convenient parking place. "Do you want to come in with me?"

Cass pointed at Makes Life Worth Living. "No, I need a java fix. I don't know what that was in the pot at the accountant's, but it was not anything resembling coffee. Would you like some?"

"Thank you, yes—I'd love whatever the roast of the day is with steamed milk."

When Laura got back to the car, Cass told her, "While you were gone this willowy blond creature walked past the car three times, and if looks could kill..."

"Oh. That was...an ex. Sort of."

"I gather it didn't end well."

Laura kept her voice steady. "No, it didn't. We turned out to be incompatible. Is my being gay a problem for you?"

Cass blinked at her. "Sweetie, *I'm* gay. Helen told me you were—plus there's the bumper sticker on the back of the car."

Laura grinned. "I forget it's there."

The closer they got to the Baynors' the quieter Cass became. On the last turn, where Laura had stopped to gather her wits before delivering her special snack to Helen on the day of her interview, one of the security patrol vehicles was parked. Cass waved at Laura to pull over.

She waited in the car while Cass talked to the guards. After a short conversation they proceeded to the house. The guards swung around to the front door while Laura went around to the side. The minivan wasn't there.

"Grace isn't home," she told Cass.

"Good. The locksmith is about fifteen minutes behind us."

Deciding that it would be a good idea to stay on Cass's good side—the woman was a buzz saw, Laura thought—she headed for the kitchen and stayed there. The locksmith arrived. Another car with more security people arrived. She overheard Cass saying something about "landlord's right of entry" as she and two guards headed for Grace's apartment behind the garage.

The pumpkin she was working on for soup was cut down to chunks and in the oven to roast when she finally heard Grace's voice. She'd been met, apparently. From the window over the sink that looked toward the carport, she saw Grace gesticulating wildly, heard plenty of shouting and a short while later a police car arrived. Then it got very quiet.

When she next returned to the window all the security and police cars were gone. So was the minivan. She glanced at her watch—it was already time to fetch the kids at school.

When Cass returned about thirty minutes later she had the chance to observe the trio as they approached the house. The twins looked drawn and somber. Cass walked as if someone had put fifty pounds on her thin shoulders.

They all brightened at the vision of Laura's English muffin cheese snacks with thin slices of heirloom tomatoes on top. The kids didn't seem much inclined to talk and headed to their rooms, probably to text friends.

Cass slumped at the table and rested her head on her arms. "Wow. That was absolutely the strangest thing I've ever had to do for a client. Or a friend."

Laura set a freshly brewed cup of coffee in front of her.

"You are a beautiful human being," Cass said, sitting up again. The circles under her eyes were dark and pronounced. "The kids were shocked more than anything, but it turns out neither of them liked Grace. They're feeling vulnerable, though."

"I can get that. You had her arrested?"

"Oh yeah. The thieving bitch had Helen's mother-in-law's gold-plated tableware collection under her bed. The storage box alone would go for about five hundred. I figured it was grand theft given the price of gold and called the cops, and then there were pieces of Helen's jewelry she hasn't missed—expensive pieces she didn't put back in the safe. They were insured but some were heirlooms from her husband's family."

"Sounds like Grace was planning to get out of town soon."

"Maybe. I'm glad she didn't." Cass had another sip of coffee. "Divine—what is this?"

"Jamaican Blue Mountain."

"May all the blessings of the saints be upon you. And you've sweetened it just right. I'm going to need four more cups of this to make it to nightfall."

"You look all in."

"The flight left New York at four a.m. and I didn't sleep before then. I'm so glad it's behind us—the worst part. Until Helen gets home and skins me alive."

Uncertain if the skinning might include her, Laura set about the next stage of the pumpkin soup. Keep cooking, she told herself, and hope for the best.

CHAPTER SIXTEEN

"Have you had a good week?"

Helen tucked her notecards from her final lecture into her beach bag and looked up at Karolina. She was framed by a floodlight, making her hair a deep, rich topaz. Though the physical sensation of desire had not diminished over the last couple of days, she no longer felt as if she might lose control over her hands, even though at the moment she wanted in the worst way to touch Karolina's hair.

"It's been so great. The Honduras are beautiful. And all the people have been really good and interested and sincere."

"You were dynamite. So was Trevor." Karolina's voice dropped. "But between you and me, the Havens are headed for divorce court. The chill was palpable."

"I thought so too."

Karolina opened the door for Helen as they left the small theater and turned in sync in the direction of the elevators that would take them up to their suites.

Helen felt a sense of relief mixed with disbelief that it was already Thursday. At sea all day as they sailed back to Miami, it would be the last afternoon spent sunbathing, and the last one spent near Karolina and the source of such profound temptation. While they had snorkeled together yesterday she had found herself searching Karolina's words and gestures for some hint that she was likewise attracted. At least she'd gotten a little more mature about the situation. At first she'd been so poleaxed by her own attraction that she hadn't even cared if Karolina might feel it as well.

She did feel more in control, and the last couple of days she'd had plenty of time to think, imagine, even fantasize—and take stock of the situation. What if she kissed Karolina? What if they danced together in one of the ship's discos? What if someone made a scene about the two women "flaunting" their desire for each other? She might have thought all these years that she empathized, that she understood how it felt when Cass mentioned some idiot harassing her and her ex when they had held hands while walking down the street. But there was a world of difference between empathy and reality. Cass and Laura—and Karolina—carried some measure of that fear around with them most of the time. She understood now why Cass went on cruises and vacations every so often with only other lesbians.

So, she thought, on top of being scared by the enormity of her attraction for Karolina, she got to be afraid of repercussions from strangers and loved ones. She was fearful of what the kids might say, of what fans might think. Who would choose this kind of fear on top of the already treacherous waters of dating and relationships? She was starting to understand why some people fought it. She honestly didn't know what she was going to do. She'd faced fear before, like her fear of heights and the opening night terrors, and had never let it stop her. This was certainly a new role for her.

"Were you going to wear something formal tonight?"

Karolina was leading the way to the main atrium which left Helen to admire her shoulders and back before she caught up at the elevators. "There's our reception before dinner."

"I can't decide," Helen admitted. "I have a cocktail dress and a full-length gown. I think the gown is too heavy, but I'm sure a number of the other women will dress to the nines."

"Want me to take a look at it?"

"Sure. I had the steward press it, but it's velvet—the bodice is anyway. Velvet on a cruise ship?"

"It sounds elegant and very you."

They got on the same elevator with some of the women from the workshop Helen had just finished, and they all chatted until she and Karolina exited on Helen's deck. Only as she turned the corner to her cabin did it sink in that she'd be alone with Karolina. Was a discussion of clothing the lesbian equivalent of etchings? She honestly hadn't even thought of luring Karolina to her cabin under some pretext. As she slid the key card into the slot she stifled a laugh. She'd been brought up to understand that a good girl waited for the man to make the first move. So what happened when there was no man to make the decision? For Pete's sake, it was humbling to feel like a gauche teenager all over again, worrying about the rules and what people would say.

She set down her bag and quickly opened the closet. She wondered if she was blushing. She didn't dare make eye contact with Karolina. "It's right here."

Karolina held the long black gown at arm's length. "It's sleeveless, though I see what you mean about the velvet. One step outside and it'll be wilted."

"It was cold in New York when I packed it. That's all I can offer in my defense."

"What's your other choice?"

"No one has seen this one yet." She reached into the closet for the last unworn cocktail dress. "Little black dress number three."

Running her fingers down the silk, Karolina said, "This is lovely. Tell you what, I'll go with a short dress as well and neither of us will feel so odd girl out."

Not about the dress, at least, Helen thought. "Deal."

As she hung the dresses back in the closet, Karolina crossed the suite to look out the sliding door onto the balcony. "I never get over the color of the sky out here."

She joined Karolina and focused on the horizon. "I feel foolish for waiting until I was nearly fifty to see it."

"It's never too late to do something new."

"I've definitely learned that on this trip."

Karolina turned her head but Helen kept her gaze on the view as Karolina said, "You tried snorkeling yesterday. That was brave of you."

She blinked. "That's right, I did."

"Isn't that what you were talking about?"

"No. Yes, I mean—this has been a trip full of new things." Don't blush, she warned herself. Hoping to head off the physical flush, she thought about curtain tassels.

"For me too."

"But you've sailed through the Caribbean before, haven't you?"

"Many times. But..."

Helen couldn't help it. She met Karolina's gaze and her normal intake of breath turned into a gasp. How on earth did the woman make her eyes smolder like that?

"This is the first time I've been tempted to mix business and pleasure. And I got a good look at how desperate and cheap it comes off when someone's advances are unwanted. I don't want to be that person."

Thoroughly confused, and her heart beating inexplicably loud in her ears, Helen said, "I'm not following you."

"I don't want to be a Eugene. It was bad enough you had to deal with him."

It took Helen a moment to realize what Karolina meant. She swallowed and found it impossible to speak.

"There is the small matter that you're straight, but I really didn't want to make you uncomfortable. I really hope that I didn't. You didn't seem to mind."

"Mind..." Helen echoed.

"Mind that I flirted with you. Oh heavens." Karolina gave an odd half-laugh. "I am out of practice—you didn't realize I was flirting with you?"

"No," Helen said honestly. "I was trying too hard to keep my hands off you."

There was a crackling silence. Then Helen realized what she'd said.

"I'm not—I didn't mean to say that. I'm sorry. It was inappropriate. Please forget—"

Karolina silenced her with a fingertip on her lips. Helen shivered and saw gooseflesh prickle along Karolina's arm. She closed her eyes.

"Helen." Then, just as softly, "Please look at me."

She forced her eyes open, feeling naked in ways that weren't about clothing, stripped bare in a place that had never been opened before. Her lips felt hot and swollen where Karolina's finger still rested on them.

"I have a rule about straight women," Karolina said. "But I want in the worst way to break it with you. I knew I was in trouble the moment I saw you."

Karolina's finger moved across her lips, then she cupped Helen's jaw. Helen couldn't stifle a convulsive swallow.

"You look terrified."

"That may be what passes for sexy for me," Helen managed to say. "At least at this stage in my life."

It was impossible to talk when Karolina smoothed a thumb over her lips. There was a hint of a smile in her eyes. "This is fair warning. I'm going to kiss you on the count of three. If the answer is no, please say so now."

Helen stared at her.

"One."

She took a deep breath.

"Two."

Leaning forward just slightly, she didn't wait for three.

Karolina's lips were as soft as she had imagined and yet nothing like her fantasies. Warm, firm and strong. Her imagination had allowed her to isolate the experience of a kiss from the whisper of Karolina's breath over her cheek or the scent of her heady perfume. Reality was all of that, all at once.

Overwhelming and yet subtle, it was even more arousing, and she had not thought her body could be any more in need than it already was.

She might have tried to say something when the kiss ended, but Karolina kissed her again, this time pulling their bodies together. The sensation of a woman's sensuous body against her own was unlike anything she had ever felt before. It felt as if every cell inside of her was a shooting star. No experience in her life had felt more right.

Kissing Karolina's neck, then her throat, she knew she was losing her grasp on something, but it seemed the only way to catch hold of the passion that was spiraling between them.

"This is okay? This is what you want?"

Karolina's words sounded languid in her ears. She pulled away slightly and was shocked at the half-lidded arousal that was plain on Karolina's face. Did she look the same? Was this happening?

Karolina was unbuttoning her blouse—it was happening. She had never had a clue that skin could handle so much sensation. Her own palms, smoothing down Karolina's now bare arms, over her naked hips, had never felt this alive. Warm hands on her ribs, on her back, more kisses, a struggle for air to find an answer.

"Yes," she finally said. "This is what I want."

"The reception starts in a half hour," Helen murmured. With her arm wrapped over Karolina's body as they lay coiled on the bed, she was pretty sure Karolina was awake. She was also aware that she could find out by moving her hand up to Karolina's breast. Her response to the slightest touch was marked. She'd never felt this powerful before.

"I have to be there," Karolina groaned. "I really don't want to move. That was..."

She rolled over to face Helen, her hair a sexy mess and her mouth looking extremely kissable. "Tell the truth. You've never been with a woman before?"

From powerful to shy in a heartbeat, she shook her head. "It's okay if you don't believe me. I'll take it as flattering."

"I'm not saying there are things that don't get better with practice, but you were...very aware. Sensitive. Responsive."

She felt Karolina's hand slip between her thighs to tease her again. Her nipples hardened and she shivered, unable to mask a moan. "We'll be late."

"I'm no fool." Karolina kissed her softly as her touch became more direct. "Besides, this might only take a minute, if the past predicts the future."

"I've never been like this before." The rocking of the ship was adding to her slight dizziness.

"I'm glad."

"Please." She moaned again. She was such a stupid woman, thinking these parts of her had turned to cement. They were alive and liquid. She pushed against Karolina's hand and felt her slip inside again, pressing against the places where Helen needed her. Against the same places she had found inside Karolina in a moment of breathless wonder. She knew the world was full of beauty and then there was this. Something else entirely.

Minutes later she laughed against Karolina's shoulder. "Truly, this has been a revelation."

"And now we really must get up."

"I don't want to."

Karolina kissed her. "If we get up that means later we can go back to bed."

"Is it a cliché if I ask why this didn't happen earlier? We're in port in Miami at seven a.m. And supposed to be off the ship by eleven."

Karolina kissed her again. "Get up. And we'll talk about that later."

Helen separated herself from Karolina, feeling oddly deflated. Maybe it was just a crash after an incredible high. She slipped into her robe and went to turn on the shower. When she went back to the main room Karolina was already back in her slacks and pulling on her shirt.

"I'll see you in thirty minutes or less," she said.

"I'm looking forward to it."

Karolina gave her an odd look. "We'll talk later. We are two very busy women." She stepped close enough to touch Helen's face. "I want to see you again. But tomorrow you go back to New York. I'm heading home to Chicago."

"Can you divert to New York?" Helen knew it was a mad suggestion the moment it came out of her mouth.

But Karolina didn't immediately say no. "I'll think about. It might be doable. For a night at least. I have to be in Chicago Sunday at the latest."

"That's when I'll be back in California."

It felt good to be wrapped in Karolina's arms, even if it was only for a moment. "We'll see what we can work out."

She got in the shower feeling dazed. She didn't want to wash the scent of Karolina off her face and hands, not yet. She didn't want to go out in public and look like nothing had happened. On the inside she felt scarlet—brazen and bold and vibrant. But the mirror showed her the same face as always. Everything in her life had just changed. Hadn't it?

Part Five:
Brake Run

CHAPTER SEVENTEEN

It wasn't until she was seated in the back of a cab next to Karolina, speeding toward the Miami airport, that she remembered to turn her phone on. The phone chirped and vibrated while it caught up on messages.

Karolina was likewise thumbing through messages. "Let me sort these out, then I'll see about booking a different flight—preferably the one you're on."

"I can't change mine or I won't get into Manhattan in time for makeup." Helen clicked through to her text screen. "A couple from my agent. She tagged them high priority, but then making sure we're going to meet for coffee is a high priority to her..." She gave her head a slight shake and read Cass's message again. Then the next one.

"Is something wrong?"

"Yes." She put her hand on Karolina's arm. "I'm really sorry—I'm not going to New York. I'm going home. There's been a situation with the house manager. Oh my God, Cass had her arrested."

"What?"

"I don't know. I have to call." Helen fumbled in her purse for her headset, then plugged it in and hit talk. One ring, two rings. "Cass, what in the hell is going on?"

Cass sounded wan but buzzed, as if a double-shot espresso had only been partially successful. "Calm down. I just dropped the kids at school. They're fine. We're all fine. Everything has been handled. Laura is a godsend, and your accountants have covered all the financial bases."

"What happened? You had her arrested?"

"She's a thief, Helen." Cass's voice went tinny. "She had your gold silverware, some jewelry, and we've confirmed she was shaking down the landscapers, the cleaners *and* the contractor doing the electrical work, taking a cut from all of them. She's a real piece of work. And as a parole violator hopefully back in New Jersey by now."

Her heart twisted in panic, even though she knew Cass wouldn't lie to her about the kids being okay. "How on earth did you find out? Why are you there?"

"Who else could step in for you? Laura called me to say she'd stumbled on something that didn't smell right—look, I can give you the details when you get here. I already changed your flight because I was certain you would want to come home early. I called your producer two days ago and told her you would have to take the weekend. She wasn't happy but shit happens and this is shit."

"Yes, I do want to come home." For the first time ever, Helen felt a twinge of...resentment. First time ever she wanted to spend the night with someone in New York and now she couldn't.

"Are you sure? You don't sound sure? What's wrong?"

"Nothing, I'm just in a bit of shock is all. Tell me about the flight."

When she hung up, Karolina said quietly, "I take it I should stick with my flight to Chicago?"

"I'm sorry, I'm really sorry." She blinked to hide a sudden start of tears.

"It's okay, it was just a chance as it was." She stared at her phone and Helen didn't know what she was thinking.

"I'd like you to come for a visit, when you can."

"I was just looking—what about two weeks from yesterday?"

The ache in her heart cleared. "Yes. Yes, I'd like that." She thumbed up her calendar on her phone as well and they compared notes.

"So it went about as well as you might expect," Cass said to Laura. "She was fairly hysterical, but not as much as I thought she'd be. I'm glad you can come to the airport with us—and thanks for driving."

Laura accelerated into the fast lane, hoping the traffic would ease a little bit. The drive to SFO wasn't that far, but the 101 was notoriously sluggish almost all hours of the day. "Minivans and I have been frequent companions, plus driving on both sides of the road. You really don't have a car in New York?"

"Nope. Neither does Helen, for that matter. I'm okay driving in the quiet little 'burb where Helen lives, but out here on a California freeway with the big boys—I'd rather not."

Laura glanced in the rearview mirror at Julie. "I love the sign."

Julie grinned. "It was fun to get out the crayons and glue sticks."

"We've been fine," Justin said from the backseat, his voice sounding like he had a mouth full of cookie, which Laura suspected he did. "I don't know why she'd worry. We're sixteen and everything."

"It's the 'and everything' I think," Cass said. She twisted around to look at Justin. "Don't eat all the cookies before we get there."

"I can make more, Cass. There's dough left."

"They're to make Mom feel better. Give me the plate to hold."

"You're holding the sign."

"I can do both." Julie infused her voice with scorn.

"I'm holding the cookies."

"Pax," Laura said. "I'm driving. My rules."

Cass took a long swallow from her coffee. "Could you be less perfect? Or else I'll have to hate you."

"Trust me," Laura said. She thought of Suzy. "I can find witnesses to my less-than-perfectness."

"She swears when she cuts herself." Justin cleared his cookie-choked throat. "Is there any water?"

"Serves you right," Laura said. "And yes, I say bad words when I cut myself. I know better than to have my fingers near a blade." She grimaced at the Scooby Doo Band-Aid wrapped around her thumb. The incident had made her realize there was no simple first aid kit in the kitchen—she'd rectified that.

At the airport she parked in the short-term lot and they traipsed through the underground walkway to the terminal. Helen's flight was landing and Laura expected she would be among the first people off the plane. They took up positions at the security exit, Justin with his plate of cookies and Julie with her big "Welcome Back Mom!" sign that featured outlines of her and Justin's hands and several snowflakes made from construction paper.

Only a few minutes later Helen was visible in the terminal promenade, then she was hurrying toward them with a big grin. Laura was grateful that Helen seemed to only have eyes for her children because she was sure the look on her face was far from professionally distant.

The glow of the Caribbean was all around Helen. Her dark hair had highlights from the sun and her nose was touched with just a hint of red. She'd thrown a coat over the casual slacks and thin shirt that had probably been perfect for Miami, but nothing diminished how beautiful she looked. She wasn't Helen the actress, or even Helen from the roller coaster, Laura thought. Helen the woman, the mother, the person so obviously glad to be home, was taking Laura's breath away.

She expected Helen to hug them all, and she did, but she went back for a second time with the kids and to Laura's surprise, she burst into tears.

"Mom," Justin said, awkwardly patting her arm, "we're okay. Have a cookie."

"I know." She snuffled and patted her pockets, then took the tissue Laura offered with a grateful, watery look. "It's just—I'm feeling a little overwhelmed."

Laura shot a glance at Cass, who seemed surprised at Helen's display of emotion.

"Honest, suh-wee-tee, I wouldn't let anything happen to the kids. You're way too lucrative."

"I know." Helen dabbed at her nose. "I'm blowing things out of proportion. Give me a cookie and let's go get my suitcase."

Justin happily threw himself into the backseat of the van with the remaining cookies and Helen immediately turned almost completely around in the passenger seat to talk to Cass.

"I want to know every detail."

Laura kept her attention on the road. It was drizzling, though hard to tell if it was very low fog or light rain. When Cass told her that Laura had called on Monday with great concern about how much damage Grace could do, Helen reached over to touch Laura's thigh.

"Thank you."

"I wish I hadn't had to, but I'm glad it's worked out. That she didn't steal your mother-in-law's heirlooms, especially."

Cass resumed her story and Laura wished she didn't still feel the exact spot where Helen had touched her. She couldn't clear her head of the image of Helen glowing with happiness as she had walked toward them.

She was over that crush. Wasn't she?

For a moment, Helen felt like a stranger in her own home. She would have liked to think the feeling was about Grace and knowing that she'd hired a thief to work in their midst. She had hoped that the disastrous Mary as a chef was the worst mistake she'd make, but Grace had easily eclipsed that.

She suspected, though, that the feeling of being a visitor had to do with what was going on inside her. She didn't regret sleeping with Karolina, but she was suddenly confronted with the reality of trying to make a relationship work when she'd spent the last decade and more knowing it was impossible. She couldn't fly to Chicago to see Karolina on a whim. If Karolina had the time to travel to California—which was doubtful—she would have to tell the kids. Not that she wasn't going to tell them, but she wasn't ready. Not by a long shot. So that meant seeing Karolina when she could come to New York. Which meant leading a... secret life. Not acting parts in different places, but maintaining separate but real lives as if she lived in two universes without anything but her own wits to aid the transition between the two.

She had no practice at this kind of thing and she couldn't believe that some people lived every day never mentioning half of their life to the other half, like a gay man in the military or a teacher living in an area that would fire her if she spoke of a girlfriend. She didn't like the feeling of disconnection at all— how could anyone endure it for a lifetime?

"What is that absolutely divine smell?" The kitchen was thick with layers of fruity and salty and pungent aromas.

The kids chorused, "*Coq au vin!*"

She spun around to face Laura. For someone she'd known such a short time, the woman had become a rock in her life. "You remembered?"

"I practiced on the kids. They liked it so I thought you would too. It smells like it's close to done—the oven has already shut off."

"That's great, because I am starving. I ate so much on the trip I thought I should try to avoid airport or airplane food. I seriously need to go on a diet."

There was a small silence, then Justin, who had carried in her suitcase, said, "Bad weekend for a diet, Mom. Seriously bad."

"Why?"

Cass tossed her purse onto the kitchen island. "Birth. Day. It's someone's birthday."

Helen let out a chagrined laugh. "I forgot."

Laura had removed a heavy-looking casserole from the oven and now lifted the lid. The delicious aroma intensified. "Everybody wash up."

Her feeling of foreignness faded to a low jangle, way down deep in the pit of her stomach. As she inhaled the comforting blend of herbs and wine she might have almost believed that nothing had changed.

To her embarrassment, tears threatened again once they were all seated and passing around the gently warmed French bread.

"Mom, what is with you?" Julie used her bread to mop up sauce with an alacrity and appetite that made Helen want to cry all the more.

"I'm just...happy. Relieved. Glad that in the larger scheme of things all we had was a thief to deal with. I had a wonderful trip. The people who run cruises and excursions are very careful to separate their passengers from living conditions in the countries they visit, but anyone with two eyes can see outside a shuttle bus. So I'm looking around our home and even as weird as the whole thing with Grace is, she only threatened our *stuff*. Our things. And we have a lot to be grateful for and very little to complain about." She picked up her fork, trying to lighten the mood, or at least get a grip on her own. "I'd have hated to lose your grandmother's gold tableware, but I'm sure I saw families that didn't have a fork between them. We have not one but several complete sets. We even have special forks for cake."

She patted Julie's arm because she was closest and gave Cass a fond look. "We're all healthy. I'm really proud of you and glad to be home. We have this bounty of wonderful food, and thank you, Laura."

She caught Cass giving her the strangest look. "What?"

"You had a very interesting trip."

"I did." She fought down a blush. "It was luxurious. I went snorkeling and I have tons of underwater pictures."

The chatter turned more general, but she was aware of Cass's scrutiny. Did lesbians have the ability to see the "slept with a woman" tattoo she was certain was on her forehead now? That meant Laura could see it too. Paranoia—she was just tired. The last twenty-four hours had been draining and stressful.

The *coq au vin* was divine. The chicken fell into mouthwatering chunks and the deep succulent red wine sauce had turned the vegetables into savory candy. Her stomach was beyond happy.

Half-sleepy, Helen said to Laura, "You should go on one of those cooking competition shows. You'd paste them."

"The kind of show where they give you anchovies, canned haggis, beets and carrot pulp and you're supposed to make a dessert? Not really my style."

"I think those are so cool."

Julie gave her brother a scathing look. "You watch cooking shows?"

"Sometimes. Men. Knives. Fire. Boo-yah!"

Helen laughed and something inside her relaxed. This was home. The kids were great. Cass looked tired, and no doubt would have more to say in private, but perhaps the several days of Laura's cooking was why the haunted postchemo look had seriously faded. And Laura was a blessing—she hoped the blonde she'd seen Laura kissing knew that.

Life would be good, steady, sane, if only there wasn't a secret bubbling inside her.

Justin held the long, serrated bread knife as if it were a snake. "Are you sure? I just learned how to cut watermelons."

"I know you can do it. The key is patience and steadiness." Laura gave him a thumbs up. "In a bakery they have a cutout to drop the layer into and you use a wire held down on the counter to whip right through it. Just... That's right. You're doing great."

Justin's gentle touch still amazed Laura. He had what her mother had called "baby chick hands" and her experience was that male kitchen trainees weren't the people you'd pick first when needing someone to hold a hatching chick. Justin already knew how to firmly hold a cake layer without crushing it, and he was splitting it into two layers as if he'd been doing it for years.

He turned the top layer over and Laura stood next to him to look at the result.

"The crumb is a beautiful texture," she said. Using her fingertip she gently dusted across the cut layers to gather a few to taste.

Justin did likewise. Then he grinned at her just the way she was grinning at him. "That is awesome! Mom loves lemon cake and it's tart and sweet all at once."

"So now you do the same thing to the other layer and we'll let the surfaces dry just a bit. They'll hold the filling better. Besides, we can't spread on the filling until it's slightly chilled."

"I can't believe how much better toasted coconut tastes than untoasted. The filling is sick."

Laura went back to trimming rib eye cuts out of the prime rib the butcher had delivered. The bones were headed to the stockpot for consommé and the rest of the cut she was going to dress for roasting by Helen on Tuesday. The rib eyes she was prepping so Justin and Julie could make them for their mother tomorrow, for her birthday. Julie was taking responsibility for the rice pilaf while Justin made one of his signature salads, and Cass had engineered decorations and a pile of presents.

As a run-up up to the big day, Cass was taking Helen out on the town in San Francisco. She'd said it wouldn't be nearly as wild and crazy had Helen been in New York as scheduled, but she would do her best. Laura was sure the diversion would be welcome. Cass and Helen had been in the study all morning, according to Julie, going over invoices and working with an agency to find someone reliable to step in on Wednesday when Helen had to go back to New York. At a minimum, the kids needed to get to and from school even if they were largely independent. Helen also needed someone to keep an eye on them in the evenings.

It shouldn't be too hard to find someone, Laura thought. The arrangement was pretty sweet. She hadn't realized there was a very nice, fully furnished bedroom with its own bath where Grace had slept when Helen wasn't home. That was on top of the private quarters attached to the garage. The bedroom alone was nicer than some staff quarters Laura had stayed in at the resorts.

Her own gift was, she hoped, suitable. In a long-ago interview Helen had stated a love of the blintzes from a lower Manhattan deli. She'd of course gone to give them a try, found them lovely, and over the years, she'd perfected her version of the blueberry filling and crepe-like wrapper. She had added a farmer's cheese and sour cream blend that melted to perfection when drizzled on top of the hot pastry. The baking dish was in the refrigerator and Justin had all the instructions so Helen could have breakfast in bed for her birthday. She hoped it would be seen as an appropriately professional gift to an employer. Now that it was made, she was worried Helen would ask how Laura had known about the blintzes. It was an intimate detail and... Maybe it stepped over a line. A line only she knew was there.

It was a line she hadn't thought she needed, but every time she looked at Helen last night she had reminded herself it was real, and she had to respect it.

Cass interrupted Laura's worrying by arriving in the kitchen with a dramatic wheezing and then swooning across the kitchen island. One hand weakly waved her mug. "Coffee..."

Helen was shaking her head as she went around the prostrate Cass. "Get up. Nobody believes you don't know where the coffee is."

"I know how to get terrific coffee." Cass pushed herself upright. "Laura, make me some coffee!"

Laura laughed. "Nice try."

Helen was already filling her cup from the coffeemaker's warming carafe. "I'm glad you pay her no attention." She swirled her coffee mug. "I think I just had the last of the coffee, Cass. You're out of luck."

Cass swore.

"You've already had four cups," Helen said. "It's not even two o'clock."

"That late? Crap, I'm behind."

Laura layered the steaks in a container so they could be refrigerated until tomorrow. She glanced at Helen and seized the moment. "While you're here, I've been meaning to ask you for weeks now if it's okay to drop your name with a couple of the real estate brokers. I can't get them interested in finding me a rental in the area and my residence hotel is getting very old."

A look passed between Helen and Cass that Laura couldn't decipher. Helen said, "Well, that's certainly on point. When you're done, come by the study and we'll talk more."

Helen left the kitchen and Cass trailed after, but not before giving Laura a Bambi-eyed look when she set down her empty mug.

The meat taken care of, she washed her hands and coached Justin through smoothing the toasted coconut filling on the first layer. "Let me help move the next layer on top. That's the trickiest part."

Once the four layers were smeared with the coconut blend and stacked, and he was occupied with gently spreading the top and side with a light strawberry frosting, she took off her apron and went to the study. The door was open.

"Thanks, Laura," Helen said immediately. "Have a seat. We've been discussing a mad plan, but I think we can solve several problems all at once. I'm intent on bribing you, in fact."

Cass was leaning back in her chair, looking unconcerned, so Laura relaxed. "What can I do for you?"

"Finding a completely vetted house manager is going to take a week, maybe even a month. I'm not skimping on interviews and reviews, and I'm not taking an agency's word for it that the person I'm hiring has been checked out."

"Given what you just went through, that makes sense to me," Laura said.

"You need a place to live. I have an empty apartment well— it's partially furnished, actually."

Laura blinked. She supposed she ought to have seen the offer coming. "I really don't have the skill set to be your house manager, and I'm not—"

"Not permanently," Helen said. "While I'm hiring. And either way, the living space Grace had is yours if you're interested. I think you'd make a great tenant, but I can understand if you think that makes you too close to your work, so to speak."

"Seriously? That's—very generous. What if the person you hire wants to live there?"

"Grace was the first person who did. It was built originally for my late husband's aunt, but she passed away before I even became part of the family. It was a really fancy storage space for a long time afterward. Regardless, whoever I hire has to live in the house. That's a deal breaker for me now. The kids tell me that Grace would often be gone all evening."

Laura nodded. "I didn't know what to make of that, but I also didn't think it was my place to say I found it odd."

"The kids loved it—no wonder Justin got into the habit of eating popcorn all night. They're really old enough to be mostly independent, but they still need to know they're being... monitored. These are really treacherous years. I keep them pretty short on spending money, but they hang out with kids who can afford just about anything, if you know what I mean. So the next person lives in the house."

Laura took a deep breath and prayed for a steady voice. "Well, first of all, I'd be a fool not to take the apartment. And if it's only for at most a month, I'd be more than happy to stay in the house and do the best I can to cover things for you. I do understand that it's time-consuming. I'm honored that you trust me."

Cass let out a sigh of relief. "Goodie. I can go home tomorrow night. Thank goodness."

Helen was grinning. "I am so relieved. Move your things into the apartment any time that works for you. Everything that belonged to Grace is in a storage locker and the key is with my attorney when she wants to claim it. Probably when she gets out of her New Jersey prison cell. I was hoping on Monday maybe you could talk to the landscapers with me? My Spanish is worse than my Greek."

"You speak Greek?"

"Not a word." Helen batted her eyelashes. "And maybe tomorrow, you could do me a huge favor?"

Laura gave a helpless shrug. How could anyone not be charmed by this woman? "Which would be?"

"Come to my birthday party, pretty please?"

"I'd love to." Laura found herself grinning.

"Take, take, take." Cass rolled her eyes. "It's all about you, isn't it? 'I'm fifty, I want a party, make me a cake, take me out drinking, suh-wee-tee Cass, my best friend.' Huh."

"I do not whine like that," Helen protested. "And I'm not fifty until tomorrow."

Laura was glad their banter was distracting them from her, and it seemed a good time to excuse herself. This was about a job, not about... This was about helping Helen for her family's sake, not about...

Exactly what it wasn't about simply wouldn't form in her mind. She was going to keep it that way, too.

"So do you like this place?" Cass leaned across the small table. The flicker of candlelight was dancing across her face.

"It's lovely." Helen glanced appreciatively around the piano bar again. The jazz was mellow, the large Maxfield Parrish landscape was the length of the entire wall behind the bar, and the Cape Cod she'd already imbibed half of was certainly helping her mood. "How did you discover it?"

"A client picked it for a meet-up the last time I was in San Francisco. It's so easy to find and it's classy. Like us."

Helen laughed. "Not to mention well-preserved."

"That too. So." Cass favored her with a serious look. "We've got the immediate future sorted out. So let's talk about the immediate past."

Helen pretended ignorance of Cass's meaning. "Lunch?"

"The cruise. You've said absolutely nothing about it except it was 'luxurious.'"

"Well, it was. I had a lot of fun. I think I did well for the people who paid to go."

"You're blushing."

She thought about curtain tassels, but it was too late. "Am not."

"When I saw you in the airport, do you know what my first thought was?"

"How would I know?" She had another sip of her drink.

"I thought 'now there's a woman who got laid.'"

"Cass!"

"Did you?"

"I don't know what you mean."

Both of Cass's eyebrows were almost to her spiky hairline. "You'll have to do better than that."

"It's none of—"

"Don't go there," Cass said sharply. "Of course it's my business. I just spent a week covering your family not because I'm your agent but because I love you and the kids. So don't tell me something momentous in your life—like having sex for the first time in *decades*—isn't at least a little bit my business."

Chagrined, Helen muttered an apology. She took another sip of her drink for courage, but alcohol really didn't give a person courage, did it? It tended to make her not care about being scared. But she was scared and not nearly drunk enough not to care. "Okay, something happened. With the person who was running the event."

"Well, I'll be." Cass lifted her glass of merlot in salute. "You're alive after all."

She couldn't help but smile. "Definitely. Very alive."

"So what's with the coy attitude? You don't have to be ashamed of a one-nighter. You're free, you're nearly fifty, for heck's sake."

"It may not have been a one-nighter."

"Oh—too early to tell the kids though?"

"Something like that."

"You're being coy again."

"It was a woman." There, she'd said it.

"You can tell me any—*what?*"

Cass's expression was so comic that Helen laughed. "It was with a woman."

"Since when—I mean, is that the... What are you trying to tell me?"

"That I slept with a woman and it was amazing."

"And you want to do that again?"

"Definitely."

Cass regarded her for a long time, sipping thoughtfully from her wine. Finally, she asked, "Is it the woman? Or because she's a woman?"

"I wish I knew. That's why..." Helen blinked furiously. "I'm not going to cry. Damned hormones. It's all their fault."

"That sounds perilously like something a guy would say."

She gave Cass an evil look. "I'm being irrational. Work with me here."

"So your hormones made you pick out a woman to sleep with?"

"I was very attracted to her. It was mutual, it turned out. That's never happened to me before. I've never—other than Justin Senior, in my whole life, I never felt ... I know it's a cliché but I am in love with the theater. It fills me with passion and joy. My heart has always told me that's what I want. I wasn't looking for a person to give me that."

"And the moment you got away from the theater, you felt it for a woman."

"I suppose so. I know what you're trying to figure out, and believe me, I've been asking myself if I'm gay pretty much every waking minute." She shook her glass to hear the ice cubes clink.

"You slept with a woman, and want to again. There's not a lot more to the definition."

"But there's my marriage. There's the fact that I enjoyed sex with a man."

Cass heaved an exasperated sigh. "I know plenty of lesbians who can say that. They lived straight lives and were happy enough that they didn't realize they were missing something. Besides, we're not lesbians because we had bad sex with men. We're lesbians because sex with women, relationships with women, is our future. It doesn't have anything to do with men— or the past."

"It's really weird not to know who you are." Helen realized how hard she had been working to tamp down the uncertainty and confusion. It felt very good to let it out.

"Maybe you're bisexual. For you, it's the person and their gender isn't as relevant as many other factors."

"I've thought about that. There's just one flaw to that theory." She closed her eyes and focused on the words, searching to make sense of her feelings. "Justin and I had a good sex life. And what I just felt with a woman last week—no comparison. It was transformational. Like passing through fire."

"Well, you *were* a virgin all over again."

She opened her eyes to glare at Cass. "Quit with the jokes."

"I'm sorry. Sweetie, what you're feeling, it's just I've heard it from other women coming out before. I know you feel all alone, but you're not."

"I feel like a chump. I'm fifty tomorrow. How did I not know?"

"That I can't answer. I'm sure with several thousand dollars in therapy you might find out. Does it matter? Did it make you feel good? You sure as hell look like it made you feel fantastic."

She leaned forward, words tumbling out finally. "I felt better than good, Cass. I felt like I'd come home. Come home to a place I didn't know I'd been keeping inside me."

"So that brings us back to the question. Was it the woman?"

"Karolina."

"Or the fact that she was a woman?"

"I don't know that yet. I don't want to get forced into picking someone else's label either."

Cass shrugged. "What I've learned about labels is that you take what fits, and stand up proud. Anyone who disputes your right to define yourself can go screw themselves."

"Even my fans? And producers I badly need to believe I can play a romantic lead?"

"We'll cross those bridges hand-in-hand, sweetie. Let me ask you something, though."

"Sure."

"This Karolina—successful, smart and charming, right?"

"Yes, you're right."

Cass pointed at herself. "Successful. Smart. Charming. Attractive, right?"

"Yes, all true. And I've never had a pang, I mean—that didn't come out the way I meant it."

Cass smiled into her glass. "There was a time when all you'd have had to do was look at me funny and I'd have dragged you to my lair."

"You had feelings for me? Romantic ones?" Helen did not want to have this conversation. She needed Cass as a friend—needed her desperately.

"Are you kidding? Romantic? We'd kill each other in three days. No. Just lustful."

"But you never showed that."

Cass tilted her head. "A: Like you, I was using the evidence of your marriage and production of offspring as proof you were straight. B: You were a client and I knew if I'd made you uncomfortable, ever, I was history. C: I have never, in my life, met anyone as career-focused as you are. D: You spend almost half your life three thousand miles away."

"And you don't really like kids."

"E: I don't really like kids. Yours are an exception, now that they're turning into people. Oh, wait. F: I was with what's-her-name at the time."

"The bitch." They clinked glasses.

"Well, that's something to remember, Helen. If you date women, you should know that they can stomp on your heart just like a man can. There's no guarantee that if you get sick a woman won't ditch you just as fast as Newt Gingrich ditched his first or third or eleventh wife, whatever."

Helen sighed. "I think reason G must be that we were meant to be friends."

"I'll drink to that." Cass drained the last of her wine. "Who knows why we lust after just one person or fall in love with just one person when we meet thousands of people, and many of them have similar qualities? It's a mystery to me."

"I have not drunk nearly enough to even discuss the metaphysics of love and desire."

"Drink up, then." Cass pulled out her phone. "I'm finding us a dance party for girls."

"Oh, I don't know..."

"It's your birthday. You dance. You don't have to do anything else. See? You get to choose how you act."

Cass had adopted a tone of lecturing a small child. Helen finished her Cape Cod while she watched Cass browse for a dance party. She knew she got to choose how to act. She was listening to her heart with every bit of attention she could give it. She wanted to be with Karolina again. She wanted to get to know more about her. Wanted to...

Okay, so she was mostly thinking about having sex again. Was she that shallow? How the hell should she know? She hadn't known she was a lesbian, after all.

Maybe she was all about sex. Sure, sitting here trying to think of ways not to go to a dance party that could be full of uninhibited nubile creatures, yes, she was a babe-trawling cougar. Right.

CHAPTER EIGHTEEN

The days settled into an even rhythm for Laura. She'd moved out of her motel the day after Helen's birthday and spent Monday looking at household expenses and the specifics of the electrical improvements and then going with Helen to the kids' school to add her name to the authorized pick up list. Tuesday, at Helen's urging, she'd taken some personal time to unpack a little, putting the basic necessities in the bedroom in the house, which was next to Julie's and across the central atrium from Justin's. The rest of her things, including all the boxes, she'd settled in the apartment behind the garage. When she drove Helen to the airport late Tuesday night for her red-eye flight to New York, she hoped Helen couldn't hear the singing inside her. She knew it was temporary, but for a little while she thought she might be purely content and at peace.

Running the Baynor household wasn't as complicated as running a commercial kitchen with a staff, that was for sure. The same skills applied here, but she was used to anticipating the demands of the guests and thinking three days ahead. She needed to pay attention to detail, keep orderly track of the household expenses and make sure the schedule was always up to date. A lot of chauffeuring, to be sure, and it wasn't really in her realm of expertise to respond to impending disaster in the form of a missing button on a beloved blouse. But she managed. She knew better than anyone that the job was, overall, cushy. There were a lot of single moms who didn't have a lovely bedroom to themselves and a staff to take care of cleaning.

Saturday was a foggy autumn day, and she had spent the morning helping Julie drive in short stakes to mark out her organic herb garden. The landscaping supervisor, Mr. Ortega, with whom she was now on excellent terms, had agreed to procure the slats that Julie needed and had chattered cheerfully about the maintenance of an organic garden. His English and Julie's high school Spanish met somewhere in the middle. Justin had agreed to make dinner and was doing his best to imitate Remy the mouse chef while making ratatouille. She sliced bananas for roasting in cinnamon and sugar.

Her cell phone launched into the song she'd chosen for Helen's ring tone—"Nights on Broadway" had seemed an innocuous choice.

"How's it going? Curtain is in an hour here."

"It's started to drizzle, I think. Julie is hard at work on her garden and Justin thinks he's a cooking mouse. Hang on..." She dug in her pocket for the notebook she'd started using. "Ready for some questions?"

"Shoot."

"I found two different auto shops with invoices in the folder. The van's check engine light came on."

Helen told her which company to call and answered Laura's other questions on her short list. She also warned Helen that Julie was seeking permission to go on a weekend trip with family friends to a Lake Tahoe cabin early next month.

"The Flynns? Sure, she can go—I'll tell her when we talk."

"Wrapping it up, the building inspector is coming on Monday to look at the electrical. The supervisor is confident it'll pass, so I was going to have the drywall folks and painters come in ASAP to do the repairs and finish. While you're here I really need you to pick out the paint color, so I'm going to put the paint chips out on the desk so you can look. I'm sure you'll have an opinion about the difference between Baltic Sage, Stieglitz Grain and Linen Leather. I might forget to mention it tomorrow morning at the airport."

"I'll do that, I promise. Even if you did remember to tell me in the morning, there's a strong chance I wouldn't remember a word you said."

"I promise to be awake enough to drive. But more than that... no guarantees."

"Tell the kids I'm going to call."

"Will do. Call Justin first—Julie's outside. I'll warn her to expect you."

She'd no sooner called to Julie than Justin's phone was ringing. She listened to him describing his ratatouille to his mother, then answering questions about his schoolwork. Julie came bounding in from the damp outdoors, flushed and glowing. For the first time Laura could see that she resembled her mother—they had the same broad smile and moved with the same bounce when pleased. She was the fully developed color photograph compared to the washed-out, joyless girl she had met. And she knew that she was, in part, responsible for making Julie feel better. It was a very nice feeling.

It was why she'd agreed to stay, to be part of the family. No, not to be part of the family, she told herself. To help the family, and remember your place, she scolded. You're an employee. Valued and respected, but you're not family. *And being a house manager-cum-nanny-cum-personal chef—basically, a mom who gets paid—is not what you quit working in kitchens to do, remember?*

She didn't want to spend a lot of time figuring out why she'd been repeating that to herself for the last several days. And later, finding it difficult to fall asleep, she told herself that it was the awareness of the impending buzz of the alarm clock that made her restless. She had to wake at five, check the flight status and hop in the car to pick up Helen. It was so early. That's why she couldn't sleep.

Even with a Thermos of coffee, courtesy of the wonderful timer on the coffeemaker, she regretted the lost sleep as she drove to SFO. The roads were wet from outright rain, but the showers were supposed to end by midmorning. She'd take a nap later. After all, once she got Helen home safely, she was off duty until Tuesday morning. She should get back to hunting down vineyards and food artisans and exploring and…not hang around wondering if she could help make breakfast. That was something someone who was part of the family would do. And she wasn't…

As much as her thoughts were going round and round in circles, they stopped in their tracks when she saw the weary set to Helen's shoulders as she emerged from the security entrance. She wanted to hug her close, tell her a warm bed was waiting and kiss away the tired lines.

God in heaven, she was in trouble. Big trouble.

It wasn't until she saw Laura just past the security exit that Helen realized how much she hadn't enjoyed being met by Grace. That must be the reason for the rush of gratitude and sheer gladness she felt to see Laura's kind smile. She looked tired and Helen realized she hadn't seen Laura anything but bright-eyed and ready to tackle any culinary task. Well, except when she'd been kissing her girlfriend in her car. She was willing to bet Laura was a fantastic girlfriend. Considerate, thoughtful…

"Thank you for being here. It was a dreadful flight, so much turbulence." She took the travel mug from Laura, hoping it wasn't coffee—she'd had plenty of caffeine on the plane once they'd stopped bouncing up and down over the Great Plains. She didn't want to hurt Laura's feelings by refusing something she'd prepared. "What's this?"

"A cure for airports. Lemon herb tea with cinnamon and lavender. It's supposed to be refreshing to your parched sinuses, ward off germs, settle the tummy and refresh the palate after lots of coffee. No caffeine."

Touched by how dead-on accurate the tea was for what ailed her, she cracked the top and sniffed. "Oh, that smells marvelous." It had cooled during the drive and she took a healthy sip. "I feel better already."

They talked quietly in fits and starts. There was nothing for her to worry about, Helen thought. She was in safe, sure hands. Her children were fine—they sounded so lively and happy on the phone. She couldn't wait to hug them both. In the dark she was glad that the rush of tears didn't need to be explained. She couldn't explain it to herself. With Laura there she felt as if she could finally relax, for the first time in sixteen years. When she went back to New York Karolina would arrive on Thursday and maybe with some face-to-face time, in familiar places, she could put some words to her trepidations. She was trying so hard to listen, but her heart wasn't sending messages she could understand.

She bid Laura a good night when they reached home, even though the sky was showing signs of lightening. Relaxed and drowsy, she was distractedly aware of Laura's footsteps behind hers on the stairs. If anything happened Laura would be there. She could sleep at last.

"You look pretty good for a Wednesday." Cass pointed out a table in the back of their favorite coffee bistro. "I'll get the poison. I don't know where Laura gets your heavenly coffee, but I am deeply, deeply envious."

Helen oozed into the chair, tired from the flight, but otherwise feeling pretty darned good. She knew she ought to make Laura take personal time, and had told her it was okay to sleep in her apartment on the nights Helen was home—to which Laura had invoked the specter of global warming. It was wasteful, she had said firmly, to heat the entire apartment for a few nights a week now that the weather had turned chilly and damp.

She hadn't argued the point because when a new house

manager was found, things would be different. Besides, it felt so good to come down the stairs and find Laura already there. It wasn't just the creature comforts being met—though oatmeal already made or eggs already whipped and ready for scrambling were certainly lovely to find. It was also having the company, someone to talk to. Grace had been anything but warm, for the most part, but in the past there had been several nannies who had also enjoyed that quiet morning time to quietly chat and look at the paper. Laura was more up-to-date on events in other parts of the world than she was, and she knew many cities from the inside. It made conversation intriguing. She couldn't remember when she'd felt this good. Well, except after being with Karolina.

Cass arrived back with two steaming mugs. "All's well at home, I take it?"

"It is. You were right—I fell in the gravy. I feel guilty that I've not made any real progress finding a permanent house manager because Laura is so great."

"She's a nice person to be around, though I wish she didn't feel that she had to try so hard. Like she's always making up for some lack."

"Do you think so?" She sipped her coffee and grimaced. "I am getting spoiled. I thought this tasted good a month ago."

"At first I thought Laura was one of the few genuine what-you-see-is-what-you-get people I've ever met. Most of her is right on the surface. But after a couple of days I started to realize that there's a whole piece of herself she's got locked down and I bet only a really special woman will ever get to see it."

Helen cocked her head speculatively. "She has a girlfriend, you know."

"She does? I didn't think so." Cass wrinkled her brow. "But why tell me? I'm not interested in a three thousand mile thing. I'm pretty sure she wouldn't put up with my spoiled ways one little bit. I'd be on the receiving end of calm, cool, collected explanations as to why I was not going to get my way all the time. I just can't have that." She grinned. "She's way too grown-up for me."

"Sorry, you sounded besotted."

"I'm in love with her coffee. And truly, I could watch her rub butter on a chicken for hours. Those wonderful hands..."

Helen laughed. "I kind of know what you mean. She's got great hands, and now as opposed to two months ago, that has taken on a completely different perspective for me."

Cass gave a knowing laugh. "You are a total lesbian, just so you know."

Helen stuck out her tongue.

"Put that where it counts." Cass gave her a sunny smile over the top of her coffee cup.

"Why do you think she doesn't have a girlfriend? I saw them together in Woodside."

"Long blond hair, probably wears a size zero?"

Helen nodded.

"Laura said that was an ex."

"They didn't look like exes when I saw them."

"I gathered it had ended recently and not well."

"Oh." Laura didn't have a girlfriend? She'd taken the lack of mention as just how private a person Laura was. She didn't have a girlfriend? Were lesbians stupid or something? She was an amazing catch. Creative and gifted, solid and dependable—not to make her sound like a blender, because she was also attractive. Sexy, actually, with the right curves, smooth skin and a smile that said everything would be okay, and such lively intelligence in her dark eyes. And Cass was right about her hands.

"Earth to Helen! You want to come back to this planet? I just asked when what's-her-name arrives. I want to meet her."

"After the show Friday night, I guess." She hadn't really been intending to introduce Karolina to anyone yet. It still felt so new and fragile. "If she's willing. She might want to keep me all to herself, you know."

Cass pursed her lips, looking amused. "I can well imagine."

"You are a pushy woman, Cassidy Winters."

"I never got anything I wanted by being demure and subtle. Have you?"

"Not once."

They clinked their mugs and parted ways shortly thereafter, leaving Helen to make the long walk to the theater on her own.

She usually welcomed it but the wind was sharp, and her ears were feeling half frostbitten by the time she arrived. It was blessedly warm backstage, thank goodness.

Nancy met her almost at the door, her face lined with all the worries of a producer. "Glad you made it back again. All your domestic affairs in order? Because I need to talk to you."

That didn't sound good. "What's up?"

"Neil is leaving us early—and his understudy is serviceable as...an understudy not a headliner, so we have to put out a call."

"You need me for readings or something? Sure—Thursday, Friday and Saturday mornings can be opened up."

They had reached her dressing room, and Nancy gestured for Helen to precede her. "Probably, but I have a different concern."

The door closed, Helen turned to face Nancy, who looked slightly ill. "What's the bad news?" Her brain was spinning with possibilities.

"I don't want to have this conversation, believe me. Neil was supposed to stay through January, but he wants out now and he has an early termination option that I didn't think he'd use because of the penalty."

"Let me guess." She didn't bother to hide her bitterness. "You may be skewing to a lower age demographic in a new male lead. And that means you need an appropriate demographically compatible female lead."

"Only if we cast someone a great deal younger than Neil. But I wanted to be upfront about it."

"That's great. For years I've been telling myself that I was making too much of turning fifty, that everything would be fine. Fifty for not even a month and I'm being kicked to the curb?"

"Be honest, Helen. Could you really play opposite a twenty-eight-year old?"

"That young?" Helen felt as if she'd been punched in the stomach. "Has it occurred to anyone that the script only works with mature leads? That they have life histories that make them closing in on forty, if not older?"

"It has. We're not idiots." Nancy glared back. "Do you think this is easy?"

"What difference does that make, whether you find this easy or not? I'm supposed to pity you? You're still working either way."

"And you might be as well. I was only trying to do the right thing and give you a heads-up. That obviously didn't go so well." Nancy flounced out of the room, leaving Helen staring at the door in dismay.

She shouldn't be upset—this was the theater. This was the way things worked, and always had. She just didn't need the worry right now. There was so much else to worry about. Except home. Home was safe and okay and fine, because Laura was there.

And for a moment, before she tried to turn her reeling mind to the night's performance and the Broadway elixir that was her joy, she let herself feel how much she wished she were at home.

"You were wonderful," Karolina murmured. She was standing just close enough that Helen swore she could feel her body heat, but not so close that anyone would give them a second glance. The press of bodies backstage was pretty bad. It seemed the Broadway bloggers had gotten a hold of the rumor that Neil was moving on to another production.

"Thank you." Her own assessment was that she'd been distracted and dropped three cues. "Your flight was okay? The train was fine?"

"Yes, and I checked my bag at Marriott down the street. I didn't want to be conspicuous rolling around with a suitcase."

Grateful for Karolina's forethought, Helen still wanted to be sure she hadn't misunderstood. "Just your bag, right? You're... staying with me?"

"That was my plan. We can reclaim my suitcase any time." Her gaze dropped briefly to Helen's lips, then she put a little more space between them. "It's very hard to behave."

"I have to get out of this gear."

"I forgot you were you—after about five minutes or so. You weren't Helen at all."

"Thank you, really. That's quite a compliment. Did it bother you?"

Karolina lowered her voice further. "I kept thinking how many women you are, all at once."

Helen spotted a prominent *Times* critic headed her direction. She really didn't feel like answering questions about her own future right now. "Will you be all right if I abandon you for a few minutes. Time to change."

Safely escaped to her dressing room, she stripped off Moxie's clothes and the wig, then quickly scrubbed her face clean. Please, she pleaded, no hot flashes now. The frequency seemed to have abated—who knew? Maybe finally having some very good sex had boosted her estrogen. Regardless, she wanted to get into her street clothes as quickly as possible.

The dresser, who had seen her in just about every stage of undress at one time or another, knocked and claimed the clothes. "Who lit a fire under you?"

"Just trying to get decent." She buttoned her blouse. "I have a friend from out of town I don't want to leave out there with the wolves."

"There are a lot of wolves tonight. Neil has us all in an uproar. I heard they are thinking they can get Justin Timberlake."

"Great," Helen said. "Miley Cyrus can have my part."

She wished for a wig that would simulate her normal hair, not sure what Karolina would make of her sleek Prada bucket hat tied down with a violet silk scarf. She'd gotten a little bit lazy, she told herself, with the long, successful run. She wasn't used to having to play the part of the blithely optimistic stage star who wasn't concerned with the petty day-to-day realities of roles and casting. It was what the critics and bloggers wanted to see and she'd long since learned that if you gave an audience what they expected, they didn't look behind the curtain for the frightened actress desperately praying she didn't look her age.

She scarcely had time to catch Karolina's eye when Neil called out, "Helen, darling, where are you off to?"

"I have to get crosstown to a thing." She blew him a kiss and turned for the stage door, hoping Karolina wouldn't find her presumptuous.

Jimmy was his usual dearish self, and he promptly secured her a cab and ushered her through the stage door crowd to its door, deftly including Karolina in his protective sweep. She paused only once to sign an autograph, then fell laughing and breathless into the cab where Karolina was already seated. Jimmy shut the door and they pulled away into the night.

"I'm so sorry, but I simply had to get out of there. I hope you don't think I was being high-handed."

"I was flattered," Karolina said. "I thought it was because you couldn't wait to be alone."

"I can't," Helen answered in a low voice.

Karolina traced a line along the back of Helen's hand. She turned her hand over and marveled at how her body prickled and tightened in response to Karolina's fingertip across her palm.

The cab driver said something, startling Helen out of her daze.

"I'm sorry, could you repeat that?"

"Where to?"

Flushing, she gave him the address of her condo and he quickly turned toward Midtown.

Karolina leaned very close and whispered in her ear, "I have seen a great many late-night specials about what goes on in cabs."

The thought made Helen want to ease open her thighs, but she whispered back, "There isn't a cab driver in this town that doesn't have a camera phone."

"What a pity. You'll just have to wait."

Her breath caught at the liquid fire in Karolina's eyes. She felt heavy with desire. Unlike on the cruise ship, she knew exactly what she wanted. She knew what it felt like to be pinned underneath another woman's body and open herself to kisses, to touches. She wanted to feel Karolina's soft hair against her thighs. And she wanted to do all those things to Karolina, to explore her and feel again a kind of power that she had never experienced before.

Under her coat she was sweating. Karolina's tracings across her palm and along her arm were making her nipples ache. She feared loss of control but wanted to revel in abandonment. It was a complex mixture, and it was so hard to think when her body was screaming *now, now, now.*

The doorman met the cab and welcomed her home after another triumphant appearance. Moments later they were alone in the elevator.

"You stay over there." Helen pointed at the far corner. "I can't breathe."

"I do prefer my women breathing," Karolina answered.

"You look so good." She did, too, wrapped in an elegant trench coat in a deep green that made her eyes glitter.

"So do you."

"I'm a mess," Helen protested. "I need a shower."

"We can do that."

The elevator doors opened and Helen managed to find her key. The condo was cold, but she quickly turned up the heat. "It'll get warm in a—"

Karolina seized her by the shoulders and kissed her. Their hands found ties and zippers and belts. She heard a blouse rip, wasn't sure which of them it was, and then they were on the soft carpet, half on top of their coats and shirts.

She pleaded, said words that had never come easily to her but were so right.

Karolina pushed her legs apart and said, "That's exactly what I'm going to do."

Her breath was ragged in her throat. She wanted to scream but couldn't manage more than a hoarse shout. Karolina held her close, mouth on her breasts, while she touched again places Helen still couldn't believe could feel so much—could need so much. She climaxed with another shout, then Karolina was laughing and kissing her face.

"Let's move to the bed and do that again."

Helen found no reason to argue.

It wasn't until sleep had nearly claimed her that Helen realized they'd forgotten something important. "Your suitcase," she murmured.

Karolina made a sound that said she was barely awake. "I

guess I'll just have to go about the house naked."

"Delicious thought." She resisted sleep long enough to add, "We can ask the doorman to arrange for it to be delivered."

"Oh, but I want to be naked."

Helen laughed quietly and let her hand explore Karolina's delicious backside. Karolina stretched in response and then shifted suggestively. Helen laughed again and said, "Not so sleepy after all?"

They'd just reached a satisfactory state of not-really-asleep when the phone rang. Only a few people knew the number and it jarred Helen out of her singular focus.

"I think I have to get that," she murmured apologetically.

Karolina groaned. "I'll expect you to make up for this."

"Oh, I will." She kissed her soft lips quickly, then leaned across the bed for the handset.

The line crackled, then Cass's voice slapped at her ear with, "I had to hear about it from a gossip columnist! A *gossip* columnist. I could kill you!"

Oh, hell. "Cass, I'm so sorry. I should have called you—I just got distracted."

"What on earth could possibly distract you from what the hell you're going to do if you get replaced in the next thirty days?"

"Maybe I have a life, Cass."

"You? You're kidding, right? Wait—you're not alone. Crap, the new girlfriend arrived tonight?"

"Yes, and I didn't find out about it until right before the show. Oh jeez." With the fever for Karolina's touch sated, her brain began to operate properly. "I forgot to text the kids even."

"Can I have the honor of meeting with you tomorrow morning? Let's say ten?"

"There's no reason to be sarcastic. Of course. I'd like you to meet Karolina."

"Another time. This is a business meeting. Maybe you could come by my office?"

Annoyed, Helen agreed because it was the only way to get Cass to hang up. Besides, when Cass was angry the only cure was to let her stew. She'd be a little more pleasant-minded in the morning.

"What was that all about?"

"Changes in the play." Helen tried to lose herself in the warmth of Karolina's embrace, but even as they snuggled close and Karolina drifted off to sleep she knew it would be a while before she joined her.

CHAPTER NINETEEN

"The Halloween dances were apparently acceptable, but neither of the kids had much to say when they got in last night." Laura stifled a yawn. This was her fourth Sunday of picking Helen up and she was still not used to it. Keeping one hand on the minivan's steering wheel, she snagged the coffee mug and drained the last of it.

"It can't be particularly comfortable having your sibling at the same event. I'm surprised they both went. They usually switch off." Last week Helen had opted to crash on the backseat of the van—she'd looked exhausted—but this week she was buckled into the passenger seat.

"Well," Laura said slowly, "it's possible both of them were really there sort of on a prearranged meet-up with someone else, not really a date, you understand."

"Well, if they've got boy or girlfriends they're really going to hate me for a while."

She gave Helen a curious look. Her month of filling in as house manager was just about up, but Helen hadn't said anything about replacing her. She didn't want to push. She didn't want this time to end. She didn't want to give up these quiet drives with Helen, the easygoing conversations they had in the mornings or the quick phone calls. But she knew it was temporary, and this job was not what she had planned to do with her life.

"Sounds like something big is in the wind," was all Laura said.

"Yeah." Helen stared out the window, giving Laura time to reflect on all the phone calls she'd noticed between Helen's cell phone and a number with a Chicago area code. She hadn't been prying—it was her job to check the bill for irregularities, and she'd done that by comparing it to the previous month's. Was Helen dating someone finally? Was that why she had seemed distracted and a little bit subdued? Hadn't there been some high-powered executive on that cruise that Helen had mentioned, offhand? She'd been almost too casual about it.

"Is there someplace we can get some breakfast? I know it's six o'clock on a Sunday morning, but I need to talk to you and I don't think I can sleep until I do."

"I can make—"

"I know you can." Helen gave an odd little half laugh. "I think Justin would wake up if he smelled food. And I'd like to talk just by ourselves."

"Well, there's always a diner, or the Golden Arches."

"You darken that establishment's door?"

"I'll confess to an Egg McMuffin now and again."

Helen laughed. "In New York there's this Greek diner just down from my condo that makes this egg and spaghetti breakfast with creamed spinach and feta cheese that I have to tell you looks revolting on the plate and I scarf it down in about three bites."

"Comfort food is comfort food." Laura took the next off-ramp, which dumped them into Burlingame. She skirted the old-town main street where nothing would be open and found an industrial park smack up against the freeway where early morning deliveries were already being loaded. Right in the middle was a brightly lit deli with an open sign.

"The Smelly Deli. Best coffee in the Bay Area, it says. We've hit the mother lode. Look, they even have a banquet room," Helen noted.

"Life is a banquet and most poor suckers are starving to death."

"How apropos," Helen said, leaving a puzzled Laura to follow her inside.

They had mugs of coffee and plates of eggs and toast in front of them before Helen seemed to want to take up whatever it was she needed to say. Laura had a sudden dread—had she somehow found out that Laura was the recovering cocaine addict she'd met on the roller coaster all those years ago? Had she lost Helen's trust somehow?

Helen had a bite of her sourdough toast, but looked as if it were sawdust in her mouth. "The first thing that's happened is that this Friday night is my final performance with *Look the Other Way.* I've known about that for three weeks or so, but I was hoping when I told the kids I could tell them I was being cast in something new. It was silly—I know I could have told them about the uncertainty. But a long time ago I knew someone who'd lost everything and yet she'd gotten right back up, listened to her heart and made a plan. I've always tried to do that. It's what a strong person does. But I've never been thanked for my services and shown the door because of my age before. I still can't believe my producer caved so easily given my box office draw."

Shocked, Laura said, "I'd read that Neil Fortney was moving on to something new, but there wasn't anything about you being replaced." Laura hoped she didn't sound as if she'd been poring over the Internet for news about Helen, even if it was sort of true, mostly.

"They kept that hush-hush because there was a chance they'd replace him with someone who fit with me, age-wise. According to them, that is."

"But they got Greg Littleton—he's thirty-three? Thirty-four?"

"Thirty-four. And I'm fifty. And I guess some people thought that in spite of my talent and history that I'd come off desperate instead of funny in my plans to trap him. They recast Moxie this week with some thirty-something former soap actress and paid off my contract. Whatever. And I exercised my right to end the run on Friday. I could have made it two more weeks, but I decided I could use a vacation now rather than later."

Wondering if Helen would be in California all the time, then, Laura decided not to ask questions yet. Helen was tired and obviously depressed—maybe she just needed to talk. She peppered her eggs and offered the shaker to Helen, who tended to put pepper on everything. A place like this couldn't survive if they didn't know how to produce good scrambled eggs, and they were as simple, hot and filling as she had expected.

"Cass and I put our heads together and she turned up a couple of successful off-Broadway producers who want to move up to Times Square ventures, but need more backing and some star power. As close to a sure thing as they could get. Under other circumstances, I wouldn't be a guinea pig for unproven producers, but the details got better the more they talked. It looks like it's going to happen, and very quickly."

Laura cocked her head. Helen didn't look pleased. "And that's a bad thing?"

"No, actually. It's a good thing. But it changes everything. It's a revival of *Auntie Mame*."

Laura smiled. "That's why my banquet quote was apropos. I see."

"I'm perfect for it. Perfect enough that I'm willing to invest some of the capital, which a lot of actors are doing these days to get production credit and some production control. It means living in New York for the next two to three months at least, probably longer. Rehearsals, venue checks—I'm one of the producers now, I guess. I've made that bed and I have to jump up and down on it singing hallelujah. I've kind of always dreamed of being Mame... When I got older." She let out a large sigh. "And now I am."

Laura wiped her fingers on her napkin, then patted Helen's hand. "Ambivalence is a bitch, isn't it?"

"To say the least. I'm really very excited about it, underneath it all. But it means the kids living in New York because I won't be able to fly home for even two days a week. As wonderful as you are for all of us, I won't be a stranger to them, not after all these years of somehow making it all work."

Laura hoped the utter dismay she felt didn't show in her face. She felt paralyzed.

"I talked to their school administrator, and they can work out a transition to a private school in Manhattan. I really, really don't want to disrupt their junior year but I don't see another choice where I stay working. Julie has her herb garden planned, all for nothing. It might seem silly, but Justin's skateboarding tribe is really important to him. I don't want this to hurt their lives. But I can't afford to get canned because people think I'm too old to dazzle. I have to bounce right back in their face. I *am* box office, damn it."

"They're strong kids, Helen," Laura managed to say. "Lots of families have to move at a moment's notice. Everyone adapts." So I'm out of a job, Laura thought to herself, and there's no reason really to have the apartment if I'm not working in the area. All good things must come to an end, she tried telling herself, but her toast actually did taste like sawdust.

After a hard swallow, she said, "Talk to them. They understand what sacrifice is. They need to make some—and this is not a walk in the park for you. It's risky. And you will miss your home as much as they will."

"If all goes well, I may be able to modify my schedule, but I'm doubtful. This could be how they end their high school years. Two months of their junior year is already gone."

"Time surely does fly." Laura quickly had a bite of eggs to stop herself from talking. It was hard to see Helen wince.

"I want to ask you something I've no right to ask. It's completely off the wall, but it can't hurt to ask, can it?"

Laura gave what she hoped was an encouraging smile. Did Helen want her to caretake the house or something? "So ask."

"Will you come to New York with us?"

Laura's stomach lurched like she'd just been launched into the sky. She froze with her fork halfway to her mouth, and it took all of her self-control not to throw her hands up and scream *yes*, not caring where the ride went as long as it was with Helen. From the depths of dreading that they'd come to a parting of the ways and realizing she was going to spend a long time trying to unlove Helen, she was suddenly on top of the world.

But it wouldn't be *with* Helen, she told herself. Helen wouldn't be on the ride with her, holding her hand. She would only be nearby. Helen would be counting on her, trusting her, needing her, but not in the way that Laura had begun to crave.

There was desperate hope in Helen's eyes. "Just until we know for sure if this is a go. Probably through January? But if you can't I understand. It's not like this is why you went to culinary school or worked for all those years to have a great reputation and incredible skill. I have no idea what your heart tells you it wants. But I have to ask. It would just make it so much easier to get life settled because you know us, you know the kids, you know Julie's diet and you could—"

"I could get the sources of food that's safe for her figured out. I know better than anyone that in New York what someone says they're selling you may not be what arrives in the box." There, she thought. She would be doing something still related to being a chef. And she'd walk away with a stellar reference. Those were good reasons to say yes.

Of course, a great reason to say no was that she was pretty sure she was in love with Helen Baynor, the woman who looked worried and tired and hopeful and about to cry. Every professional instinct said she knew what happened when women put their professional lives on hold for emotional reasons. They lost ground and opportunities. It was a fool's choice.

"I don't know what to say, Helen, honestly," she hedged.

"It's crazy. Forget I asked. It's a huge imposition. You have a life you're trying to get onto a new track, and you've no lions to slay in New York, and maybe you're seeing someone and I have no right to presume you'll say yes. I know it's not about money. I can throw a lot of money at you, but that's not what drives you. I could tell that the day we met. I don't know what to say except it would be wonderful to know I had you to count on." Helen gave an almost disbelieving laugh. "I respect everything about you and I think I could look for years and not find another you. I haven't a clue what I did right that brought you into our lives."

They were wonderful words to hear—if only they'd been meant differently. Laura realized she should tell Helen that they'd met before, just come clean about it because it was so stupid that she hadn't. What would that sound like, though? And her other secret: "Hey Helen, guess what, you've let a recovering cocaine addict into your family's circle, surprise!" And she could spend the next two hours trying to explain why it didn't matter. So if it didn't matter, why did she have to tell? It was such a stupid, useless merry-go-round.

She didn't think she could bear it if Helen reacted the way Suzy had, that was for certain. That was the bottom line. Besides, Helen looked as if she would break right now. Her ego was shattered and yet she could answer the insult to her age with a triumphant signature performance—success was the best revenge. It meant turning her family upside-down at the same time she was perfecting a new role and trying some aspects of producing, stretching herself in new ways where there was no script to guide her.

"You've come to mean so much to the kids, and to me," Helen was saying as if she was too tired to stop the words. "But I don't want you to feel like I'm emotionally blackmailing you and making the fact that I need you desperately more important than your career because how self-centered would that be? I try not to be a diva except in the theater itself where things actually go more smoothly if someone's the diva and everybody else just better get on their marks and stop whining."

Helen paused, then gave herself a mock slap. "I'm babbling. I'm so tired. You think about it. You don't have to decide now. I'm going to shut up."

"I'll go," Laura said, and then she laughed—she couldn't help it.

So she was seven shades of a fool. It was just a couple of months out of her life and the simplest truth was that if she said no she'd regret it for always and forever. She reached across the table to clasp Helen's hand. She swore she could hear *clack-clack-clack*. "We'll both be fine."

For a moment she thought Helen might remember because

she squeezed her hand so hard Laura knew it would ache. She didn't care. But then Helen let go so she could rub her face.

"I'm a mess. And I'm so grateful, so incredibly grateful." Her eyelids drooped.

"Let's get you home and into bed," Laura said.

Helen was asleep before Laura even made it back to the freeway. As she drove the sky was brightening and she could steal glances at Helen's face.

Seven shades of a fool, she reminded herself. That's what you are. She'll never love you the way you want. You've only put off the inevitable for three months. If you stay longer than that, she'll start to wonder why.

Life was strange with twists and corkscrews, ups and downs. As much as she hated the very thought, she thought she would rather Helen shun her for her drug history than pity her for a love that would never be returned. She tried telling her heart that every lesbian on the planet knew falling for straight women was trouble, but her heart wasn't listening.

Doing something you love and knowing it was for the last time added layers to every minute Helen spent in the Olympic Theater on Friday night. She had wanted to have the kids fly out and see the final performance, but the PSAT exams were tomorrow and they were more important. In another way she was glad they weren't there, because she wasn't sure how steady she was going to be, not given all that was at stake in the one-upmanship of backstage Broadway. Plus she loved Moxie—loved being Moxie. She'd miss her. She'd miss Jimmy and even Nancy, with whom she'd mended fences somewhat. She liked the theater itself, old with history, right off Shubert Alley. She walked streets that Helen Hayes had walked and she wanted to go on doing that.

Karolina had made it, though, and while Helen was glad she hadn't been alone last night and Karolina would be with her for the late-night cab ride to the airport before they went their separate ways in the terminals, she knew something was wrong.

The sex was right, it had felt wonderful and even more natural to her. She didn't know what she had expected, but it seemed to her that nothing had changed...and shouldn't it have? Shouldn't something have deepened between them? Shouldn't she be a little more upset that it would be several weeks before Karolina and she could possibly get together again, and even then it was not for sure? Karolina had likewise not seemed concerned.

Backstage was crowded with press, many of whom were there to watch her skulk off after the performance into the darkness. She gave herself a mental shake. Sure, there were those who couldn't wait to see the back of her, because she took parts other people wanted and if she'd just get off the stage people would stop comparing lesser performers to her. But there were many genuine well-wishers, and she was going to give them the scoop on *Auntie Mame*. Cass was there to deflect and answer questions, and she was arriving with Helen's secret invited guest, because two lights on Broadway was always better than one.

She was very excited about the future, and couldn't wait to start rehearsals, but she had nine days to get the kids packed and moved and the house settled. Laura was constantly in her thoughts, and every time she called home it warmed her, unaccountably, to hear Laura's calm voice.

Looking at Moxie in the dressing room mirror for the last time she took a deep breath and banished the bitterness and grief. Tonight there was no time for her brief meditation. This was the first night of a new performance. Time to turn the page and focus on mitigating the damage to her family for the choices she had just made. "You've been good to me, doll," she said. "Let's go show them exactly what they'll miss."

She breezed out of her dressing room and into the heart of the gossip mill siege. Moxie gave her good armor and all critics knew that touching a performer in full costume and makeup before the show was bad-mannered. She didn't have to endure air kisses and false hugs—those would come later. Instead, she laughed, bantered and kept her distance as she raked the crowd for Cass.

The buzz of voices suddenly rippled away from her and she turned her head to see Cass and Trevor Huntley, who looked just as relaxed and tanned as he had on the cruise. What a dilemma for the press. They had a genuine event with Helen's final performance but here was a really big-name stage *and* movie star right in their midst. Why was he there? Who should they be focusing on—the dithering buzz made Helen smile. Trevor made it easy for them by making a beeline for her and planting a huge kiss on her cheek.

Her dresser shrieked in dismay and pulled out puffs and swabs. Voices called out to both of them, asking what exactly was going on. She left it to Trevor as she submitted to the minor repairs to her makeup. She'd evidently made a very strong impression on him during the cruise, and he had responded immediately to her email asking if he'd like to make some waves up and down the Great White Way. Their agents had conferred, then they brought in the lawyers for her, Trevor and the co-producers. With everyone acting professionally and driven by a decent respect and a modicum of trust, everything had been arranged in just a few days.

"Mrs. Baynor—lovely, talented Helen." Trevor was very good at laying it on thick. She'd told him it made him a natural-born producer. "Wonderful Helen and I would like to announce that we are now partners."

The room erupted with a barrage of questions. Cameras flashed. Her makeup repaired, she leaned lightly on Trevor's shoulder in a jaunty pose typical of Moxie. Trevor managed to look pained that it was too loud to speak and an almost immediate silence fell.

"We are now partners in Wisdom Productions, and our first event will be the sumptuous restaging of one of Broadway's most successful plays, *Auntie Mame*. Helen herself will take on the part I believe she was born to play."

The hush continued and Helen felt a flutter of panic.

"Wait for it," Cass muttered.

There was finally a collective sound, not like a confused Scooby Doo, thank God, but rather a collective "ah" as if fireworks had popped overhead. The pandemonium returned, then the stage lights flashed.

Oh poor press, Helen thought. Now they had to stay until

after the play. Moxie winked at Trevor. "Thanks again for giving up that sunny island of yours to be here."

He returned her wink with one of his own. "My dear, all the sunshine in the world couldn't compare to you."

Moxie took her place on stage. The electricity in the audience was like flashes against her skin. Helen basked in the stage lights and gave herself completely over to the moment. The moment the curtain went up the audience erupted into applause.

The fire inside her met with the energy from the crowd and she burned, bright and pure, through every minute.

When the curtain went down she slowly became aware of the clamoring applause and shouts of "Hel-en, Hel-en." They took a cast bow, then the other cast members drew back and she stood alone, not afraid to let tears glisten in her eyes.

And because Moxie was no fool, she waved them to silence. "New York audiences are the best any performer could hope for. Thank you for your fabulous support. I can't wait to be back among all of you as your Auntie Mame next spring!"

The rest of the night was a blur. Cass was there to answer more questions, and Trevor was obviously enjoying every moment of being a producer. He was besieged with cards from agents and reporters. Helen was able to refer everyone to Cass— at least for now.

The one moment that stood out for her, when time seemed to go back to operating at a normal pace, was when she introduced Cass to Karolina. They said all the right things to each other but Helen was painfully aware of the lack of warmth on both sides. Cass was being her usual hostile and suspicious self, and Karolina—harder to read—seemed to not really care whether she and Cass hit it off. When she'd met Justin's closest friend, the one who would later be Justin's best man, she'd been supremely aware that she wanted him to like her because it would make Justin happy, and his happiness had truly mattered to her.

Some things were so right between her and Karolina, she thought. The sex was amazing and they made each other laugh. Her own discomfort told her that she wasn't comfortable with a sex-and-good-times understanding, though. She knew what those hateful bigots said about gay people, and she had never believed them and wouldn't start now. If she was a lesbian, she still deserved happiness, and relationships that were as complete and fulfilling as she could make them.

Alone with Karolina finally, drained and wired all at once as their cab sped across Midtown toward JFK, she smoothed the skin on the back of Karolina's hand. She had amazing hands, and her fingers had done things Helen hadn't known were possible. Karolina hadn't said much, so Helen broke the silence with a quiet, "It's okay."

"What is?"

"That you're halfway hoping this is the last time."

The yellow lighting on the ceiling of the Queens-Midtown Tunnel flickered across Karolina's face. She looked surprised and chagrined. "Am I that obvious?"

"I know you have a very busy life."

"I wasn't looking for you, that's true. You kindled quite the fire." Her lips curved in a fond smile.

"That was mutual. And I'm okay with it having run out of gas."

"Your life is already chock-full, Helen. I just didn't want to seem love 'em and leave 'em—I didn't want to turn you off women because I'm not the marrying kind."

"I won't be turning off women." Helen leaned closer, not wanting the cab driver to overhear. "I will always thank you for that enlightenment."

"*Je ne regrette rein?*"

"I don't regret one single moment. Can I ask you one thing? Not because I'm ashamed, but because, well, you saw what the press can be like. I haven't had much private life to keep quiet, but I still value my privacy. I'd appreciate it if you were discreet."

Karolina nodded. "I wouldn't want anyone thinking I use the fundraiser events I arrange as a hunting ground of some kind. But I have one proviso."

They cleared the East River and emerged onto the expressway. At that late hour traffic flowed quickly and Helen relaxed, letting go of the perpetual worry that she would miss her flight. Laura was waiting for her and she hated to drag her out of bed needlessly. "Which is?"

"If you run for public office on an antigay platform I will out you in a heartbeat."

Helen laughed. "I'll consider politics if and only when I'm turned away from the last dinner theater in West Palm Beach."

Karolina held her hand tightly for a moment. "I am a little bit sad."

"Me too."

They parted with a gentle kiss. Women had such soft lips, Helen thought. They smelled so good. Inwardly, she was shaking her head at herself. Really, how could she not have realized this before?

So, she asked herself as she buckled herself into her seat for the long flight, if you don't have a girlfriend, who do you have to tell that you've figured out this surprising new thing about yourself? With all the upheaval of the next few weeks, she decided she would wait to resolve that question. The wild ride of the last few days had reached a lull, courtesy of an airplane. When she got home it would be a race to get ready for the moving van.

The moment the edict to remain full, upright and locked ended, she pushed her seat into the semireclined sleep position, tucked a pillow between her face and the bulkhead and decided for the next few hours she could relax. She smiled into the pillow and fell asleep thinking how nice it was knowing that Laura would be at the airport.

Part Six:
Heartline Roll

CHAPTER TWENTY

Every return to New York still held some anxiety for Laura. She hadn't been back in years, and yet the city held a dread magic for her. It was The Big Apple, a place where art in all forms, from performance to happenstance to painting to architecture, lived, breathed, walked. It was in the signs hanging on food trucks, the plants lining the sidewalks outside the Flower District shops, and the voices of the street vendors hawking tickets for the Improv. Midtown Manhattan was filthy, half under construction, crowded, hard as diamond and brimming with life energy. In all the places she had ever been, none matched Manhattan in passion for creative expression.

The past week and a half had been frantic. Julie was despondently resigned to the move, especially sad about leaving her friends and her herb garden project. Justin was still resentful, and trying not to be, because his after-school two-hour skate-a-thons with friends were cut off and the scuttlebutt was that skateboarding in New York wasn't even close to sick. She'd heard him protest to his mother that if they lived in Manhattan for long he'd never get a car.

Laura had mollified him somewhat; she'd promised him an inside look at some of the most famous kitchens in the city— she could mine her Facebook friends gathered from her decade working in Manhattan and the years as a resort gypsy. She'd met very few chefs who didn't love to show off their kitchens. It had been a very long time since she'd smelled a New York kitchen. She was pretty sure it wouldn't do more than remind her why she was sober. The difference between *pretty sure* and *absolutely certain* always caused anxiety, though.

They were in two cabs, traveling in tandem from JFK to Helen's condo. The small moving van with the carefully chosen items everyone had deemed essential to surviving in New York was at this point somewhere in Pennsylvania. Helen had constantly reminded them all that New York wasn't the hinterlands, and anything that could be bought was available in Manhattan. Having room for it, however, was an entirely different matter.

The condominium building was technically in Midtown on East Fifty-Sixth Street, halfway between Third and Lexington Avenues and just a few blocks from Bloomingdale's. But Laura could immediately tell that it had more in common with its cousins in the Upper East Side than it did with most Midtown properties. The foyer décor wasn't overly opulent but it was in flawless condition, from the pale marble tile to the settees and an antique writing desk which had been modified to include a charging station—anything a resident or resident's guest might need to make waiting a few minutes in the lobby bearable.

The doorman had a full array of security monitors behind his desk. He knew the twins, and Helen introduced him to Laura and he said he'd follow with the rest of their suitcases. They squeezed into the elevator with one rolling bag each.

She hadn't known what to expect from the condo. Helen didn't seem to have anything memorable to say about it beyond that the kids had, once upon a time, liked how close it had been to FAO Schwarz. It was certainly large by New York standards. The living room was spacious and a formal dining room was set off to one side. The kitchen, behind an old-fashioned swinging door, was to her right, and a hallway with a window at the end for light led to the four bedrooms and she'd been told each had its own bath. A powder room was adjacent to the small foyer. Looking around, Laura understood Helen's nonchalance. It was cold, for one thing, and sterile. It wasn't a home.

Wasn't a home *yet*, Laura thought. She was exhausted from the flight but she had one sure fix for the tired and long faces. While the kids dispiritedly trundled to their rooms with their suitcases and Helen did likewise, after pointing out Laura's room adjacent to hers, she made a beeline for the kitchen. A quick look confirmed that Helen never cooked. There weren't even cans of soup.

She made her way to the door Helen had pointed out and liked her room well enough. It wasn't as large as the one in Woodside, and there was no sign of electronics—the kids had made it plain they expected a television and cable to be added to the living room in short order—but it was comfortable and had its own small bathroom.

She heard suitcase latches popping but she left hers closed and went to find Helen. Peeking into Helen's room she found it much like her own, though larger with a small sitting area, and decorated in the same costly and classic taupes and beiges. Here, at least, there were photographs of the kids, an abandoned water glass and beauty products on the dressing table. Someone lived in this room.

"I'm going to run out for about ten minutes," Laura said. "You'll be glad I did, I promise."

"Okay." Helen gave her a puzzled but trusting look.

She hurried out the door because she did want to be quick about her errand and to put some distance between her and Helen. Those looks were always from Helen the woman, and they made Laura's breath catch. For her, the attraction was palpable. It hadn't seemed so huge inside the house at Woodside, but the condo was small by comparison. Suddenly her longing to be wanted as more than a reliable employee, or possibly even a friend, had seemed to paint the walls in shivering reds.

It would be easier when Helen went to work. They wouldn't be in close quarters. She kept repeating that as she went into the market on the corner and found applesauce that was just cooked apples and water, quick oats, eggs, unbleached flour, white sugar, plain Greek yogurt, dye-free molasses, vegetable oil and raisins with the welcome ingredient list of "dried grapes, no preservatives." A half gallon of organic milk made the bag heavy, but it was a short walk and she was glad to know the nearest grocery had good quality staples. Given the neighborhood, she'd hoped that was the case. She would have liked to get butter, but she didn't know the brands, and coloring agents were so common that she wanted something that stated it was certified dye-free.

She found the family gathered in the large living room—it had a high ceiling with crown molding and she supposed a real estate agent would call it a "great room" but it was no comparison to the scale of the great room at the home in Woodside. Helen was making a list and the words "flat screen" were issuing from Justin's mouth. He eyed her grocery bags as she went past them into the kitchen. It was much, much smaller than she was used to, but there was still plenty of space to cook meals for a family of four. The table was spacious and occupied the eastern corner of the condo with a large picture window that would let in all the morning sun.

She was finally stumped by the lack of cookie sheets, so she thought she could make do with the griddle pan, which was oven safe. It only took two minutes before she had an audience of three.

"Are you making cookies?" Justin looked hopeful. His stomach growled in spite of the generous first-class airplane meal they'd been served.

"Yes I am, oatmeal-applesauce."

"Cookies?" Julie echoed. "Is there milk?"

"Yes."

"Cookies." Helen gave a tired laugh. "I could kiss you."

"They're vegetarian," she said inanely as she stirred the applesauce and oats. How many cookies would it take before

Helen really meant it? She'd make cookies every day if she thought it would work.

As eager as she was to roll up her metaphorical sleeves and tackle perfecting the role of the iconic Mame Dennis, Helen found herself spending almost all of her time the next several weeks working with the two co-producers, Patrick May and Casey Milk. They interviewed costume, set and marketing designers and asked for drawing mock-ups from their favorites. They also negotiated and finalized the venue. The St. John Theatre was about a block from the Olympic, but slightly more modern. With just over eight hundred seats, it was equal in size to the Olympic as well, and they all felt that they had every chance of matching the run numbers for *Look the Other Way*. Trevor flew back to New York for Thanksgiving week and met with them several times. Otherwise he participated via video conference.

Her hours were routine, though, and that meant every day in November she came home to the kids, and did her best to take away as much of the sting from the sudden move as possible. She tracked down an indoor skateboard park for Justin and bought him a pass. And though there was a waiting list, Julie was in the queue to volunteer for a community garden. Truly, they had made very little fuss considering how unhappy they were, so she cut them extra slack when it came to time on their computers and the phone with California friends.

What she marveled at still was how different the condo felt. It wasn't just that the kids were there, and they squabbled and watched videos and left abandoned plates and dirty clothes anywhere they fell from their hands. There was something else at work. Home had always been in California, and for so many years she had found it at the end of a plane ride. Now it was a short cab ride and she was where she could relax and talk, laugh, think about something other than the theater because she had an intelligent and interesting woman to talk to. Laura made cuisine and culture in Sopot, Poland, sound fascinating—for the first time, Helen could feel the itch of wanderlust. How fun it would be to see the world with someone as inquisitive yet practical as Laura.

Midtown was draped in holiday lights and it seemed like an almost magical time. She'd triumphed over the depths of despair over her age because she had, well, moxie. Moxie and money, she reminded herself. As far as her career was concerned, she had again listened to her heart, her gut even, and it would all work out. That is, if none of the ten thousand little details went wrong.

The best part of most evenings was watching Laura make dinner. It was still like watching a dance performance. She'd contribute some small part of the labor—tonight it was dicing cold roasted carrots so they could be repurposed into a tomato sauce that was bubbling on the stove—but mostly she'd watch Laura. She'd seen Laura make pasta a dozen times already and it was still a miracle. It looked like such a mess, then knead-roll-pat-cut *et voila!* There were fistfuls of noodles.

"So we decided to go with the original play's décor time frames, after an intense debate about whether we should try to modernize parts of the production."

"I'd miss it if it weren't the Roaring Twenties at the opening, I think," Laura observed.

"That was part of our discussion. We're going to sell tickets to lots of people who've never seen the original or the movie, but for the critics and older audience it will be very familiar. It's a fine line between freshening something up to keep it sharp and losing the tie to its history. Besides, I love those goofy chairs where Mame hoists the guests up and down."

Laura grinned as she molded her dough into a ball. "One of my favorite scenes. But then I don't think there's a scene I don't like. I'm certainly hoping I know someone high enough up in the production company to get opening night tickets."

It was Helen's turn to grin. "Just so you know, the first of January I go on a diet. Seriously. Mame wears those gorgeous long lines and I won't get the vocal control I need if I'm wearing a girdle. Ugh," she added. "Gym tomorrow. I don't suppose you want to go to the gym, do you?"

"I can't go to the gym for you," Laura's expression was

deadpan.

"No, silly, I mean join me. It would be less boring. And I've just realized I haven't asked you lately if you're okay here."

"Helen, you asked me while we were making pies on Thanksgiving. The answer is still yes, I'm doing just fine. But I wouldn't mind some gym visits."

She abruptly wanted to tell Laura about Karolina. She'd told Cass the news that they'd broken up. Cass's reaction had been sympathetic, but she'd admitted that at first glance, Karolina hadn't seemed interested in more than an uncomplicated good time. Laura didn't even know that Karolina existed and somehow that seemed wrong.

"Here's trouble," she said as her phone rang. As she answered the call she said to Laura, "I was just thinking about Cass and guess who's calling?"

"Tell her yes," Laura said.

Without preamble, Helen said, "Laura says yes."

"Doesn't she get sick of feeding me?"

"We worry about you putting on some pounds. You've lost it all again."

"Nervous disposition."

"But it's not good for you. You need some fat armor because the cold and flu season is upon us."

Cass's tone grew more acid. "I didn't call to get a lecture. But yes, I'd love to come for dinner. Tell me she's made pasta."

"She has. So why did you call?"

"P.R."

"As in I need some?"

"You do. You haven't been seen in a hot spot or in the company of the Bee-yoo-tiful People for weeks now."

"I'm so happy being at home," Helen said.

"Who cares if you're happy? I have a series of theater tickets for you, a couple of pairs, and a couple of sets of four. Say yes to every fundraiser cocktail party invite you get since you do have time to go now. And I think you should have a party. Invite some very A-list gossips and wow them and send them off to tell all their blogging friends that you are the woman who puts the shine on Broadway."

"You mean like a holiday party?"

"Whatever you want to call it. Two weeks from now."

"Can we haggle about a date when you get here?" The doorbell rang. "Hang on, I have to get the door."

"Sure."

Helen peeped through the security glass, then yanked the door open. Cass hung up her phone and was shedding her coat even as she crossed the threshold.

Ignoring Helen, Cass made a beeline for the kitchen. From the doorway Helen watched Laura greet her and they chatted, then Laura said something that Helen didn't follow, but Cass laughed. They looked...very comfortable.

Taken aback by how unwelcome the thought was of a budding romance right under her nose, she said to Cass's back, "I'll go get my calendar."

One thing she didn't like about the condo was her office, actually the small formal dining room, just off the living room. When the movers had delivered the printer and files it had quickly become a hodgepodge of school papers at one end of the table and the middle completely covered with folders and portfolios related to *Auntie Mame*. There was no other place for it and the situation had no solution beyond moving or asking Patrick and Casey if they would move their production offices—the official home of Wisdom Productions as well—from New Jersey to Manhattan, and let her move in. But it was made all better by stopping to inhale the mild scent of the carnations that Laura had brought home from the market and arranged in the foyer.

When she returned to the kitchen Laura was smacking Cass's hand away from her cutting board, which appeared to have slices of a rich blue cheese. They couldn't be dating. Cass's days were far too busy, and Helen knew where Laura had been every night—here. With a clang she realized that after they'd settled in, Laura had not gone back to a schedule where she got days off. She's your employee, Helen told herself. You're treating her like family which is good and she seems happy and all, but it's totally unacceptable. She's not your sister filling in while you're in a pinch. Besides, you're not in a pinch anymore.

And she's not your sister. She's a friend and nice people don't take advantage of friends or employees. Annoyed, she decided it really didn't matter what label she used to describe Laura. Laura deserved a private life. Even more annoyed, she decided Laura and Cass would make a lovely couple.

Workouts at the gym with Helen turned out to be good for Laura physically, but emotionally they took a toll. All around them were hard bodies of every shape and size, and a lot of women seemed to find the gym a social mecca where flirtation was more or less commonplace. She didn't get a lot of second glances because, like Helen, she dressed to work out in ordinary sweats, old T-shirts and a ball cap on her head. No slinky, sweat-slimed Spandex for either of them. What made it so hard was that Helen was devastatingly sexy in a sweaty T-shirt and a faded hoodie. Her skin glowed with energy and her eyes were bright with determination. Just the real woman, completely alive.

This was bad, she told herself. She'd devoted herself to making sure everyone was happy and she spent all her time in a state of ecstatic dread. Helen seemed not to notice anything strange in her demeanor at least. She was sure she'd given herself away when they'd been making pies for Thanksgiving. Helen had fed her a bite of filling for the apple pie and her stupid nipples had hardened and she'd blushed. Granted a blush didn't show on her the way it would on a white woman, but it had been a hot flush she had felt burning in her cheeks and along her neck.

She'd been saved by the oven timer, and if she didn't stop staring at Helen doing yoga she was going to blush again.

It was a long, long way to the land of Calm, Cool and Collected. Cab rides several times a week, coffee and breakfast every morning, dinner almost every day, a trip to Helen's day spa for facials, late-night chats over some sliced fruit and a bit of cheese—she loved every minute. Tonight they were all going to see *Wicked*. At least when the kids were around her reaction didn't seem as intense. She had some propriety left in her.

Towels still wrapped around their necks and bodies steaming

in the cold street air, Helen once again proved her mastery at calling cabs. A drizzle had started and the dank smell was one of her least favorite realities of New York in the winter. She didn't mind snowdrifts, steady rain or even treacherous iced streets, but the mix of human and animal waste, exhaust and half-wet grime made her feel slightly ill.

"When are you going to take a day off?"

Laura blinked at the abrupt question. "It hadn't occurred to me. I spend a lot of time reading during the day, which I love. Plus it's a ten-minute walk to some of the best restaurants in the world. I've met up with some people I used to work with, had lunch—I do get out, Helen. Don't worry about it."

"Oh. Well, if you wanted a night out, certainly, we can cope."

Laura smiled. "I'll keep it in mind." Was Helen tired of her being around? Had she figured out Laura was enjoying the company just a little too much?

"Are there any restaurants you think Julie would be safe eating at?"

"Yes—that's partly why I've been making the rounds, and also to set up some tours for Justin. He's really interested in cuisine. I don't think it's a passing fancy."

"I don't either. He's been watching Alton Brown at night and the other day he said he wants to take more organic chemistry. A year ago I would have said he was my drifter. Julie has always wanted to remake the world. She wants to create solar cells and stack gardening—I don't know what that is. Something about growing plants in the equivalent of little apartment buildings that went upward instead of sideways. She's so imaginative."

The cab turned the last corner toward home. "Well, I think she could eat safely at two or three places for a special occasion, especially if we book ahead and explain the need. They're the kind of places that would plan a daily special that happened to accommodate her but would appeal to a wide customer base."

"That sounds wonderful." Helen suddenly looked stricken. "Not that we're bored with your cooking."

Laura laughed. "I didn't think that was the case."

The cab pulled up in front of their building and Laura

scrambled out. Helen was checking her phone and glancing at her watch. Laura left her full access to the hot water for a shower and checked her cupboards to make sure she had her dinner ingredients. They were eating early so they could get to the theater early.

It seemed like only a few minutes later that Helen was calling that she was on her way to the rehearsal studios they'd rented. Laura went to the door to lock it after her and tried, unsuccessfully, to ignore the weak feeling in her knees from the mingled aroma of Helen's shampoo and light perfume—almonds and cherries and notes of apricot.

She shook herself out of her daze. The smell of her post-workout body was going to kill what lingered of Helen. Besides, she wanted to be done with her shower before the building's twice-weekly housekeeper arrived.

With five minutes to spare she finished drying her hair, then checked her email until the housekeeper, Fan, knocked. Laura didn't know any Vietnamese, but she was pretty sure that Fan was the name the woman gave to keep from hearing her real name mangled. They communicated mostly by miming, including many nods and smiles.

Grateful that she'd acquired cookie sheets, she slid one with scattered slivered almonds under the broiler and set the timer.

"Lady please?"

She turned to find Fan holding a dress still in a dry cleaner's wrapping.

"For cleaner?"

Laura shook her head. "No. I don't think so."

"Okay be thanking you." Fan hustled away again.

Laura decided Helen must have been thinking about what she'd wear to the theater tonight and left the dress out. She checked the almonds and realized she hadn't given her own wardrobe much thought. It wasn't as if it was a date, but she was going to be seen in public with a very beautiful woman. She didn't want to embarrass Helen, and her beloved Dolce & Gabbana jacket had been seen many times. Maybe she ought to spend her afternoon at Bloomingdale's.

CHAPTER TWENTY-ONE

"It's not that often I forget I'm watching a play," Helen said to Laura at intermission. "This is a dazzling production."

"It is, isn't it? I heard so many good things about it I was afraid it was overhyped, but no, it's wonderful. So many beautiful layers to the story, friendship and persecution of difference—but it doesn't get lost in those elements either. Like *coq au vin* isn't about chicken or wine."

Helen laughed. "How apt. You should be a theater critic who describes everything in terms of food. I think more people would understand."

Laura gestured at the crowd surrounding the merchandise sales counters. "I think I want a T-shirt. I'll be right back."

Helen watched Laura work her way toward the counter and

wondered if the black, form-fitting jacket was new. The clean lines with touches of iridescent sequins at the collar and ends of the sleeves looked great over the tailored amethyst slacks that showed off her curvy hips.

Her reverie was broken when Julie followed after Laura saying, "I want one too." Julie had had a lot of fun dressing up for the theater, focusing her makeup with a little black dress of her own and stack heels that didn't make her ankles look *too* wobbly.

Left alone with her suit-and-tie wearing son, she smiled at him, aware that she'd been seen and there were a few phones out and pointed their way. "Is it okay being out with your famous mom?"

"Kind of annoying, but I don't really mind."

"You look very Cary Grant." She patted his suit jacket.

"Who?"

"Don't play dumb."

"I'd rather dance like Fred Astaire."

"Keep cooking and you will." He gave her a puzzled look and she added, "When Laura cooks it's almost like she's dancing."

He still looked confused but she was saved from further inane remarks to her son by the arrival of a producer she had once worked with when the twins had been perhaps a year old. She introduced Justin, agreed he was very tall and yes, time did fly. Justin was polite and casual. A theater critic horned in, asking for some inside details about *Auntie Mame*, and she let slip the name of their newly chosen set designer, Henri—they were all named Henri—which sent him away quite happy. Cass would be proud.

They were all settled in their seats again when she remembered to check her phone, which she had, of course, set to silent. Cass had texted about a fundraiser at the Tom Kat for Feed-Kids, a charity that underwrote meal delivery to extremely ill children and their families. She loved the cause, but the idea of a soirée later that evening was a bit tiring.

"How would everyone feel about making a brief appearance at a party after the play?"

"If it's not too late," Julie said. "I know it's not a school night, but I don't like staying up late like you guys."

Justin asked, "Is there food?"

"I can take the kids home while you go," Laura said.

"Don't you dare. We all go or no one goes. Who's in? Yes, there will be food and no we won't stay for more than an hour."

"Then I think it's a social imperative," Justin said.

The vote ended up unanimous. She texted Cass the happy news, then tucked her phone away.

"Cass will be there," she said to Laura. Though she watched for a reaction, Laura merely nodded.

The lights went down and she breathed in the welcome dark. Laura was wearing a new cologne, she thought. If gold had a smell, that was it. She tipped her head slightly and the scent came to her again. She felt dizzy, but then the curtain went up and she lost herself once again in the play.

The Tom Kat turned out to be an exclusive bar just off Broadway at Forty-Second Street, complete with an A-list and a bouncer enforcing entry. Helen said her name and in they went, leaving Laura deeply glad she'd invested in some new clothes. Her outfit was still off the rack, but the pieces were Michael Kors and Vera Wang and had come from the hushed private shopping designer boutique in the recesses of the fourth floor. At least she wouldn't embarrass Helen.

To her relief they bypassed the main bar and went as directed up the stairs, where they were greeted by a hostess whom Helen apparently knew. She introduced Justin and Julie, then drew Laura forward to say, "And my friend, Laura Izmani, the chef."

She only realized then that she was glad not to be introduced as the Baynor Household Manager. She didn't want it to define her life. So, her inner skeptic asked, what exactly are you going to do about it, then? Every month you go on doing the job, the more that's what you'll become.

She ignored the little voice and was glad to escape some of the press by moving deeper into the room with Helen. Happily for Justin, it was closer to the catered food. She caught Julie's worried sigh and so joined her at the table.

"I feel like some fresh fruit—pineapple and mango, yum." She quickly tasted a couple of the cheese offerings and pointed out the Parmigiano-Reggiano and wheel of Camembert. Both were never made with any kind of dye. The bread looked like it was real French but the server didn't know the source and the caterer wasn't there to ask. Julie made do with her limited choices, and was really pleased when Laura returned from the bar with an icy tall glass of 7-Up, the only kind of soft drink that had never bothered her. Justin meanwhile loaded up with canapés, stuffed jalapenos and several items he confessed he hadn't a clue about.

He eyed Julie's plate and said, "I think it would be so easy to make food you could eat and that everyone would still like. I'm sorry there's not much for you to choose from. It'll be a real drag if we go to more parties."

"Well, this is better for me, I guess. Sometimes all I can think about is frosted doughnuts. At least Laura is making the food for mom's party."

"And I promise you'll eat, girl. Oh, there's Cass at that table—the one in the middle."

With the kids being at a loose end because they knew almost no one and were so young, and Helen working the room like the pro she was, Laura shepherded them over to Cass and the tall, pale man she was talking to.

Introductions and air kisses were made. Georg turned out to be a costume designer who was chatting Cass up fast and furious about showing his portfolio to Helen. Upon hearing that Helen was in the building, he made an abrupt departure.

"I suppose I should have saved her," Cass said. "But she's a big-time producer now. She can have the fun of dealing with the Georgs."

"He'll have to move fast. Helen wants to get out of here in another forty-five minutes, max."

"I want to get something from the bar, but it's been a really long day and I didn't want to give up this cozy seat. Will you linger here until I get back? Can I get you anything?"

"No, I'm good."

Cass nodded, then froze as she rose from her chair. "Oh hell, I had no idea *he* would be here."

Laura followed Cass's gaze.

"Who's that?" Julie asked.

"Mr. Big Banker who was being a little too persistent in wanting to date your mother."

Helen looked a little bit like a deer in the headlights. Laura's hackles rose. The guy was standing about six inches too close.

"I could pretend I'm eight and tell my mommy I need to talk to her." Julie lifted one eyebrow and, for just a moment, was the spitting image of her mother.

"Your mother has been handling his type for years. Give her a chance to work it out. I'll be right back."

Cass crossed the room, pausing briefly to touch Helen's arm, then pushed her way between Helen and the guy to continue to the small bar. Helen didn't look desperate to be rescued, but Laura wasn't about to stop watching.

"Who knew that Manhattan was such a small place? We seem to run into each other constantly, in New York terms." Helen hoped her smile looked remotely pleased. No more, no less.

"I really had no idea you'd be here, Helen, but what a pleasant surprise." Eugene smiled benevolently at her, but was really crowding her space with the intimidating body language that set her teeth on edge. She doubted he crowded men of his acquaintance. "After the recent news about your new production and partnership with Trevor Huntley I realized that of course you needed to spend more time with him on the cruise. What a good business decision on your part."

So, he'd decided she'd not given him the time of day in favor of Trevor? Whatever, Helen thought. "We did get acquainted on the cruise, and then when this opportunity came along it was good to already have some sense of each other's production capabilities."

"Time well spent." His tone was oily and she realized he'd had at least one drink too many. About that time a cute redhead, not more than twenty-five, twined her hands around his arm. He gave her a glance and said in a grown-ups-are-talking voice, "Go play for a few more minutes."

She pouted and left.

Helen cleared her throat and prepared to do the same, especially when Cass paused, then pushed her way between them, ostensibly going to the bar.

"I'm so glad that I was truly mistaken—it was laughable, thinking you and that woman were perhaps an item. A very attractive item, but you're a real woman, all the way through."

She didn't like the way the conversation was going. "Exactly what is a real woman?"

He laughed. "Maybe it's like art—I know one when I see one."

She was pretty sure he meant that his penis knew one when it saw one. She told herself to walk away, but part of her just couldn't. "So essentially you're saying I must not be a lesbian because you're attracted to me?"

All those HRC galas and GLAAD events she'd attended as a straight ally had taught her all the signs, but she heard the words with different ears now and they made her a very different kind of angry. With the anger came fear, irrational, but still real. He could not destroy her world or take her children away. She had nothing to be afraid of, but thinking so and knowing so were two different things.

He gave her a maddening and indulgent smile. "Besides. You're not part of a freak show." His gaze flicked to Helen's right.

She glanced and only saw Cass chatting with the bartender. "I don't know what you mean."

"The man trying to be a woman—trying so hard to look normal it's freakish. The super high heels, the overdone nails, the ridiculous eyelashes. That's not what's attractive about a woman."

That he was trying to compliment her for her womanly attributes was completely lost in a haze of anger because he was talking about Cass. Her voice rose as she asked, "Are you assuming she isn't a woman because you don't want to do her? And that makes *her* the freak show?"

He raised his voice as if Helen couldn't possibly have understood him because she still disagreed with him. "I'm saying that's not a real woman."

She intensified her volume without raising her pitch and could hear the room slowly quieting as people eavesdropped. "Not only is what you just said distastefully homophobic and transphobic, it's very clear that you don't like women."

"Is that why you've been so standoffish? You think I'm gay and I want you for cover?"

"Oh my lord—is there no end to it?" Helen no longer cared if he saw her naked contempt. Maybe the alcohol had stripped away his civilized veneer, but whatever the reason, she fully saw the ugly, grasping truth of him. "Men are not gay because they don't like women. Women aren't lesbians because they don't like men. You, on the other hand, don't like women except to bed them, which means they're toys you use until you're tired of them."

His eyes narrowed and he raised his voice. "You're saying I don't like women because I'm not attracted to that emaciated drag queen with fake equipment?"

She glanced at Cass, who was white as a sheet with anger. The room was silent though the floor below her feet was pounding with the music from downstairs. She knew her kids had only ever seen her this upset on stage, acting, but the rage she felt had to escape.

She drew herself up and stepped back slightly as if he smelled. "For your information, that woman is a cancer survivor. When her surgeons removed her uterus they were certain she was a woman, and she's still more woman than you will *ever* enjoy. If you're the alternative, all women would be lesbians."

She shifted her weight and lowered her pitch so the words would carry. "And I know a number of gay men who are better men than you will ever be because they *like* women. They like people. They know how to love. The only love you'll ever have is what your money can buy."

She took a breath, not sure what to say next, but Cass stalked over to them, her glass of wine trembling in one hand. With her other hand she yanked down the wide collar of her cocktail dress. "*These* are my one hundred percent original equipment breasts. And *this* is my drink in your face."

Cass's aim was good and Eugene spluttered and swore into his face full of wine. There was a horrified silence but then several men began laughing and yelling, "Brava!"

Cass covered herself up and took a bow. The poor representative for the charity was frozen in shock, but the young woman who'd been clinging to Eugene earlier rushed up, horrified.

"I'm so sorry about the mess." Helen felt as if she were channeling a combination of Moxie and Mame. "But how fortunate your daughter is here to help clean up."

To Cass she said, "I think we should be going."

"Indeed, our work here is done."

Helen paused only long enough to tell the speechless charity representative that a big check would be on the way before she swept down the stairs and out of the club.

Once on the street, Justin said, "I thought these parties were really dull. I didn't know there were naked boobies."

"There usually aren't naked boobies, though I'm usually hoping for it," Cass said. She didn't seem the least embarrassed. "Tonight was the right time for naked boobies."

Laura slung her arm around Cass's shoulder. "That was magnificent. You too Helen," she said with a backward glance. "What an ass. You were like a one-two punch."

"Would you believe that man is the CEO of First Union?"

"You're kidding! That's awful—bad enough that he'd think such stupid and hateful things, but how bright can he be if he actually says them out loud?" Laura let go of Cass but not before Cass gave her a one-armed squeeze.

"Alcohol was involved," Helen said. "Let that be a lesson to you, my young ones. Mood-altering substances often lead to stupidity."

"And naked boobies."

Cass swatted Justin.

"I thought it was cool," Julie said. "Are you okay Mom?"

"Yes," Helen muttered. "I'm having a hot flash. Maybe because I got so hot under the collar." She shucked her jacket and fanned the cold night air down her blouse.

Laura stopped walking. "Hey, I know this place. They do desserts including vegan options which are almost always dye-free. They have a tofu silk brûlée I thought was scrumptious."

"Does that mean Julie can eat?" Justin immediately turned to the door. "Anything to support my sister."

"You mean support your stomach." Julie looked pleased, though.

Helen mopped her forehead with napkins while they placed their orders at the counter. Justin proved resourceful at scrounging chairs to make up a table for five in the crowded café. Helen was aware that people were whispering her name, but so far everyone kept their distance, perhaps because she was clearly with her family. Laura had found a gem of an eatery. Most of the desserts were as expected, but they did indeed have several choices that were dye and preservative free, including a lush chocolate mousse that put a twinkle in Julie's eyes.

She was glad that her outburst didn't seem to have scarred the children, but she was still feeling the adrenaline surge and that disconcerting twist of fear. After Cass's wine had splattered Eugene's suit, she had been momentarily afraid he would accuse them both of being lesbians.

It would have been true and she wasn't going to lie about it. Ever. But it wasn't how she wanted the kids or Laura to find out. For anyone to find out.

They shared yummy noises when their desserts were delivered.

"Guys," she said, after a bite of sumptuous red velvet cake, "I have to tell you something about what just happened. That all started because he was interested in dating me. He turned up on the cruise and I kind of let him get the impression I was interested in someone else—the woman who organized the trip. It did get him to leave me alone. Mostly."

Julie glanced at Cass, and Helen hadn't a clue what she was

thinking. "Did she mind? The other woman? Being used as asshole repellent?"

Cass snickered and Justin laughed outright.

"No, not at all. The funny thing is that I discovered I wasn't lying. It wasn't a cover. The more time I spent with her the more right it seemed. You know I haven't dated in a long, long time, and mostly that was because I just didn't have time." She couldn't bring herself to look at Laura.

Justin put his fork down. "What are you trying to say, Mom?"

"I think I partly didn't date because I wasn't looking at the right kind of person."

Laura spilled her water. "Oh, heck." She hurried to the counter for more napkins.

Julie looked at Justin with one of those twin glances that had always disconcerted Helen. Then Julie said, "You get to be happy, Mom. It's only a little bit weird because, I mean... What about our father?"

Laura returned to mop madly at the table. Cass helped her push sopping napkins into a pile.

"I want to be really clear about it—I loved your father. I know that I did. I was very happy with him, and if he'd lived who knows, I might have never realized I was interested in women. He was a special man, maybe one of a kind, even. I've never been attracted to another man in my entire life."

"So, Mom, without further damaging my youthful sensibilities with revelations about your sex life—"

Helen stuck her tongue out at Justin.

"Is this woman you met going to be coming to dinner or something?"

"No, it didn't work out. It wasn't long-term."

Julie snorted into her dessert and nudged her brother with her shoulder. "Our mom had a one-nighter."

"I know. Gross."

Helen looked at Cass. "I have been dreading this conversation for weeks and instead of trauma over their mother being a homo-sex-u-al, they're giving me a bad time about having a brief affair?"

Her comment sent the twins into a fit of the giggles.

"It's official," Laura said. "You've had too much sugar." She glanced at Helen, her eyes gleaming.

Cass muttered under her breath, "And some woman on a cruise ship got a toaster oven."

Laura choked and spluttered into her napkin.

Julie recovered enough to ask, "What was she like, this woman?"

"She was very smart and quite attractive. Cass met her."

Cass nodded. "I'm glad you told them, Helen. I nearly said it tonight to that jerk—that his pestering you had made you gay. He'd have believed it because there's no way he could possibly be irrelevant to you."

"So how attractive was she?" Julie persisted. "There's a lesbian teacher at my school and she's very pretty, but I don't know if she's mom's type."

"Oh for crying out loud." Helen focused on her red velvet cake, which was delicious and satisfying and a real treat. Deep down there was a steady thrum of joy building, though, and she found herself smiling at her fork.

"A very attractive woman," Cass said. "She was the kind of woman who could wear white, use chopsticks to eat sushi dipped in soy sauce and not get a drop on her."

"She sounds elegant and poised." Laura's expression was uncharacteristically bland.

"She was," Helen said. "And a very busy, successful woman. It was a mutual decision to stop seeing each other."

"So I don't get a new mommy?"

"Finish your dessert, young man. Who raises these kids to be so smart-mouthed?" Helen gave Laura a mock accusatory look.

"Hey, don't look at me. They were that way when I got here."

Cass said something that Helen missed, but it made Laura chortle again. Inside she felt ridiculously as if bluebirds were singing or magic sprites were dancing, and whatever it was it felt terrific. Maybe she was just a big chicken, and hadn't let herself feel anything for women until she knew it was safe. Heck, she could marry a woman in New York now, if she wanted. If she fell for the right woman.

She glanced at Laura. She couldn't help it. Her stomach tightened and abruptly she had answers to questions she didn't think she'd asked. She was such a chump.

Cass nudged her. "That's a funny look."

"What?"

"I don't know. Kind of a 'I could have had a V-8' look."

"Just thinking about costumes," she lied.

CHAPTER TWENTY-TWO

With Helen's party on the schedule for Sunday evening, which wasn't a "school night" for most of the guests since Broadway theaters were dark on Mondays, Laura geared up in her prep work by renting commercial kitchen space starting the Friday before and over the weekend. There was no way the condo's refrigerator would hold it all. She'd arranged for a server to work with her starting Sunday at two, and Justin and Julie had also said they'd help with transporting the food and the set-up. Helen and Cass were on point for flowers, service rentals and working with the string quartet when they arrived. The guest list held only thirty people, but they were a Who's Who of Broadway opinion makers and Helen was sparing no expense and not missing any details.

The kids had agreed—with some relief—to make themselves mostly scarce for the evening, though Justin had said if there would be more naked boobies he wanted to stay. Laura smiled to herself remembering that perfect moment when the red arc of Cass's wine had caught the light just before it doused that idiotic ass's face and shirtfront. She kept herself focused on that because otherwise she'd get the shivers again remembering Helen's announcement.

It was one thing to be hopelessly in love with a straight woman. And quite another to be hopelessly in love with another lesbian. When there was no chance of being loved back, a person could stay out of the game. Helen could return her love, it seemed, but wouldn't unless Laura had the guts to ante up and eventually show her cards.

She didn't know what to do. Nothing while she was Helen's employee, that was for sure, she told herself.

So she cooked.

For food service on Sunday night she planned to spend all of Friday on pastry for savory tarts and desserts, plus breaking down her basic produce and doing its first prep: sauté onions, leeks and shallots, roast garlic, char and peel roasted peppers and so on. It would be a long day, but with all the space she needed and a large commercial refrigerator to throw it all in, she could work very, very quickly. She'd promised Justin food if he would help her out tonight, but time would tell if he'd show up or text that he was heading out with new skateboard buddies to explore before it got dark. She expected a text from Julie that she was safely at an after-school club meeting and then another that she had arrived safely home.

She paused only long enough to devour some lunch, then pulled the last of the tins of mini-tartlet shells out of the oven and added them to the tall cooling rack. She'd let them rest, then plastic wrap the entire rack and roll it into the refrigerator. The workspace was warming up as other people arrived to use their allotted space and fired up their own grills and ovens. She belatedly remembered to hydrate and was grateful to find a sweatband in the pocket of her apron. It had been a while since she'd been in the real fire—and she had missed it.

Just after two her phone rang with the kids' school on the caller ID. A brisk but calm voice asked for Helen.

"This is Mrs. Baynor's household manager. You can speak to me. It's in the paperwork."

"There's a medical situation with Julie and we really think Mrs. Baynor should be notified."

The rest of the room dimmed. The phone threatened to slip out of her suddenly slick hand. "What do you mean? I'll notify her immediately. Tell me what's happened."

"She's broken out in a severe rash and we're concerned about measles—"

"She has food allergies. Has she taken an antihistamine?" She cradled the phone on her shoulder while she hurriedly washed her hands. "Let me talk to her."

"She's in some distress—I'm sorry. The school nurse says we need to call nine-one-one. She's starting to have some trouble breathing."

Laura said a bad word. Her heart was twisting and pounding. "Where will they take her?"

"We need to talk to Mrs. Baynor."

"Tell me where they're taking her—until I can locate Julie's mother I'm the medical decision maker. I'm all you've got. So *please* tell me."

"Lenox Hill."

She hung up. No time for niceties. Every cab driver in New York knew where Lenox Hill Hospital was. She threw kitchen towels over the top of any open bowls, made sure all the burners and ovens were off and shrugged out of her apron. She reeked of sweat and onion. The old hoodie she pulled on didn't help much.

"One of my kids had to go to the ER," she told the woman at the next station.

"I'm here at least until midnight, hon. Wedding tomorrow. I'll keep an eye out on your stuff." Laura barely had time to make eye contact with the woman and couldn't have said later if she was tall, Hobbit, black or purple.

She found a cab by throwing herself in front of one. Once inside she tried to call Helen, but got her voice mail. Today she was in New Jersey with the other producers on a long call scheduled with Trevor. She went to her next source.

"Cass, there's some kind of emergency with Julie. I'm going to Lenox Hill. I can't reach Helen. Do you have numbers for Patrick or Casey or their office? That's where she is."

"I can find them. What should I tell her?"

"The school thought it was measles. I think it's allergies. She was having trouble breathing and they wouldn't tell me anything."

"You focus on Julie. I'll find Helen."

The cab driver was a sympathetic Pakistani man who explained at length his choice of route. "I know this is faster this time of day. Friday you can't go on the FDR."

"Thank you," Laura said several times and thought irrelevantly that people were the same the world over—for the most part they were kind. She hoped her food and knives were still there when she got back, but they were only things. They could be replaced.

She was terrified but that felt far away. Her mind churned with difficulties—what if the hospital took one look at the disheveled black woman claiming medical rights to an unconscious white girl and refused to act? Surely they would do anything necessary to save Julie's life. Had someone from the school gone with her? Her copy of the papers that let her act in Helen's place to make decisions for Julie were back at the condo. She had her wallet with ID and smelled like a pub kitchen. Julie must be so frightened.

What could it have been? Had the jam on her PB&J not been honest about the contents? Should she make all their jelly in the future? The all-natural cheese puffs hadn't bothered Julie before, but maybe they'd changed a formula without updating the label? That sort of thing happened constantly, which was why she was leery of packaged goods, but Julie liked them and they were one of the few things that made her feel "normal" when she unpacked her lunch.

No call from Cass. "How much farther?"

"Two blocks. I take you 'round to ER otherwise very long walk. My boy was here last year."

"Thank you so much. I really appreciate it."

"I hope your daughter is okay. She'll be fine." He pointed at the photo of his kids taped to the dash. "God is good."

She took it as kindly as it was meant and didn't correct him. She was perfectly aware that Julie was not her daughter and never would be, but she cared for her and loved her for her tenacity and seriousness.

Her phone chirped—Justin. "Laura, what's up? Someone said Julie went away in an ambulance?"

He sounded scared. "I'm so sorry. I've been frantic trying to get hold of your mom and pretty scared myself." She tried to calm down for his sake, and she told him what she knew. "Can you get a cab from school? I gather it's not that far for you?"

"Yes, I can get there—wait, my friend Tim says his ride can bring me there."

"Good. I truly don't think this is serious, but—"

"If she needs blood or a lung or something, that's me." He hung up.

She could kick herself for not having been the one to call him. Some parental stand-in she was. Still no call from Cass.

The driver wove his way almost by magic to deliver her to the doors of the ER intake. At the ER desk she asked for Julie Browning and boldly lied that she was her aunt. She wasn't going to give them an opening to make her sit and wait in some distant area. The lie got her handed off to someone else who took her through the double doors.

She didn't like hospitals. She'd been stitched up after bad cuts once or twice, but her real dislike dated from a badly sprained wrist from childhood. They had still lived in Miami and her mother had taken her to an emergency room. She remembered the smells that had burned at her nostrils and someone in pain had been screaming, and that had frightened her. The doctor or nurse or whoever had been the one to tape her wrist had made her feel like a waste of his time. He'd said something to her mother that had made her mother reply, in a subservient tone she'd never heard from her mother before, that of course she had insurance. Of course her daughter was an American.

She shook off the past—it was hard, her head was spinning—and tried to listen to the nurse. The woman was round and no taller than Laura, and had a nice smile. "I'll tell doctor that you're here."

She led Laura to a curtained bed in a long, bleak room of about eight similar drawn curtains, checked the chart, then peeked inside. She drew back and looked doubtfully at Laura. "Are you next of kin?"

"I have the medical power of attorney until her mother arrives."

"Laura?" Julie's voice sounded thin. "Is that Laura?"

The nurse decided to take the situation at face value, and she let Laura into the small area.

Julie's skin was like translucent paper—what wasn't covered with livid, angry hives. She was on a drip of some kind, which surprised Laura.

"Oh girl." Without hesitation she put her hands lightly on Julie's matted hair, smoothing it from her face. "Baby girl, how are you feeling?"

"Awful. I itch everywhere and my head is pounding."

Her phone began to play "Nights on Broadway." Thank goodness. "Your mom, finally."

"Is she okay?" Helen's voice was like a laser and Laura had to hold the phone away from her ear.

"I'm with her now, yes, she'll be okay. Uncomfortable—very itchy."

"What the hell did you feed her?" Helen's voice faded. "No, take me to the train station. We'll sit in the Lincoln Tunnel for hours."

"Helen, are you there?"

"How did this happen?"

"I don't know."

"I'll be there as soon as—bloody hell! Damn it, I said the train station! Go back!"

The line went dead. Laura took a deep breath. "Your mom's frantic," she said to Julie, then she realized that Julie had dozed off.

A doctor tweaked open the curtain and Laura stepped out to speak to him.

"Why is she sleeping?"

The Latino doctor wore a resident's tag and looked like he had yet to see thirty. "And you are?"

She kept her voice brisk and professional. "I'm Laura Izmani, a member of Mrs. Baynor's staff. She's on her way as fast as she can, but I have a power of attorney if you need any instructions."

He nodded. "There's nothing life threatening going on, though I take it this is the most severe attack she's ever had?"

"That I'm aware of, yes."

"Then get her to her specialist ASAP. The next bout could be very, very dangerous."

"That will happen, I assure you."

"Good." He quickly reviewed her treatment. "The steroid for her respiration made her wired, and it does tend to make the itching worse, so we gave her a fairly strong sedative, which will also help with her headache. That's why she's dozing. Probably your arrival made her realize she could relax."

"When her mother arrives, I'll ask for you," Laura told him. He nodded and left the ward, passing Justin in the doorway. Justin was nearly as pale as Julie was.

"She's okay. Sleeping—peek if you want," Laura told him.

He settled somewhat after seeing her, but Laura didn't like how pale he was. "Let's find a place to sit and wait for your mom. She's frantic."

"I bet."

There was a soda machine in the closest waiting room, and he perked up a little after some root beer. Fortunately, he was recognized by a school administrator who introduced herself to Laura and asked, before taking her leave, that Laura update them if Julie's condition should worsen.

They sat mostly in silence and Laura told herself it was only natural for Helen to first think this was Laura's fault. She had been mentally scouring over every ingredient she'd handled in the last two days, looking for the culprit, but nothing came to mind. None of the party food was even where it would get to Julie, so it couldn't be that she'd missed anything there.

Helen had every right to be upset.

She'd dealt with upset clients before. This was no different.

She told herself it was convenience only that had Helen texting Justin with her progress and Justin texting back updates, meager as they were. Her own phone remained silent.

Justin and she took turns checking on Julie, who continued to sleep. Allergic reactions were exhausting and it was probably best for her to sleep through as much of the itching as she could.

When Helen finally arrived Laura thought she was braced for the impact, but instead of finding a calm and professional distance she wanted a hug in the worst way, and her arms ached to hold Helen as well.

"She's this way," was all she managed to say. "She's been asleep all this while."

Helen opened the curtain and though Laura didn't think most people would see it, she could tell that some of the color had drained out of her lips and cheeks. Her surface expression was only a mask of confident motherhood. Her baby would be fine. Nothing was wrong. Inside, Helen was terrified.

Julie was still asleep, so in a whisper, Helen asked, "What caused this? What did you miss?"

"I don't know. I've been over it and over it in my head and I can't think of a thing."

"You'll have to find out." Helen's whisper was sharp as a whip. "This can't happen again."

"I'll do my best—"

"Do better than that. That's what I pay you for."

Crying will not help this situation, Laura told herself sternly. "I feel terrible about this."

"Not nearly as bad as she does."

"Mom."

Julie's voice spun Helen in place. "Honey, how are you feeling?"

"It's not Laura's fault. Don't yell at her."

"I wasn't yelling."

"Yes you were."

"It's not important," Laura said.

"I had a doughnut. With pink frosting. After lunch. I've been so good for so long I thought maybe it wouldn't hurt." Julie wiped away a tear, then sat up in bed and held out her arms.

Helen scooped her up, hugging her tight.

Between gulps, Julie managed, "I thought it wouldn't be bad. Maybe I'd itch a little. I upchucked my lunch on the way to English class. It's so embarrassing. Then I don't remember much. It was just one little doughnut. Mom, I'm so sorry. I'm sorry."

Helen rocked her. "Oh sweetie, you can't do that, you know that. Please don't do that again. You might have died. What if you'd been alone?"

"What am I going to do when there's no Laura?" Between sobs, Julie added, "I can't go to college."

"Sure you can," Justin said. "Hate to tell you but whole bunches of people learn to cook for themselves."

"Shut up," Julie said, wiping her nose. "How about I live with you and you cook for me then?"

"Only if you pay me." He made a face at her and Laura thought he was finally looking more like himself. If Julie was well enough to abuse him, then his world was getting back to normal.

"We can work this out," Helen said. "Your brother's right. It's not fair, but you'll learn to cope. You're smart and independent and you'll manage. Learn to find doughnuts you can eat even if the frosting isn't pink."

"I itch everywhere. Even the roof of my mouth itches."

"That sucks." Justin looked at Laura. "Can we make pink frosting with pomegranate juice?"

"That would end up a bluish frosting. We can get some intense reds with beet juice." With that Laura did the only thing she could think of that would keep anyone else from seeing that she was going to cry.

She made her way to the nurses' station, asked for the doctor assigned to Julie to please come back and talk to Julie's mother, and then she went to the restroom and sniveled in one of the stalls until she felt more composed.

By the time she got back to Julie's bedside, Julie was asleep again. Helen was talking to Cass, who broke off the conversation to give Laura a quick hug. "You must have been worried sick too."

Why couldn't she be in love with Cass? For all her high-strung narcissism, she was fun and very often kind. "I was. I was obsessing about the stupid jelly on her sandwich."

Helen put her hand on her shoulder. "Laura, I am so sorry. I was worried sick, but that was no reason for me to blame you. Even if it had been something that got by you, I know it would never be lack of diligence on your part."

"It's okay. I was blaming myself."

Cass rolled her eyes at Helen. "Were you a total bitch again?"

"I don't think I was a *total* bitch."

A nurse gave them a warning look and they migrated back to the waiting room.

"You were being a little bit bitchy, Mom."

"You hush or I'll think of something you need to be punished for."

"See?" Justin appealed to Cass.

"I need to get back to the kitchen," Laura said. "I left everything in disarray and am counting on the kindness of strangers that my food and knives are still there."

"Let's go with you, at least for a while," Helen suggested unexpectedly. "I have to do something with my hands or I'll freak out completely. Julie will sleep through the night now, they said. Apparently they had to—" She cleared her throat. "At one point in the ambulance they had her on assisted respiration, making her lungs inflate. So they want to keep her for the night. The hives on her face are already better, though."

Laura nodded, feeling the same flutter of fear that she could see in Helen's eyes. "I can put you all to work, believe me."

"Is there something to eat there? If I get some dinner, I'm in." Justin looked hopeful.

"There is a ton of food there. Totally sick stuff."

"Cooking? You're all going to go cook?" Cass fastened up her trench coat. "I'm out of here. See you Sunday at four or so— but call if something changes here, okay?"

"Thanks again, Cass."

"You are my favorite client," Cass said over her shoulder.

Laura only looked at Helen once in the cab. In its relative

darkness she felt as if she didn't have to hold quite so tight to her own control, and it was evidently having the same effect on Helen. The worry in her face was enough to set Laura's heart to aching. She was hurt by Helen's hasty judgment, but had already forgiven it. The chance to shed a few tears in the restroom had helped drain off some of her anxiety.

Helen, though, was showing signs of cracking. She'd seen her with bedhead and hot flashes, licking food off her fingers, with toothpaste still smeared along one side of her mouth, her slip showing—all the very human aspects of Helen that had separated the star Helen Baynor from the woman who occupied Laura's waking and sleeping mind. But she had never seen Helen with a smile frozen like ice on her lips, and heard her voice twisted tight by short, shallow breaths. She suspected that only Justin's presence was keeping Helen from losing it.

She paid the driver while Helen pulled herself together enough to get out of the cab. Justin bounded into the work area while Laura profusely thanked the woman in the next station for her vigilance. She found some Cotswold cheese, making Justin immediately happy. As he chewed she set him to wrapping the food tray cart in plastic wrap before the tart shells got any drier. Helen nibbled on a piece of cheese, but given the slightly numb expression on her face there was no way Laura would let her handle a knife. She didn't think she wanted to handle one herself, not for a while.

"I have some almonds." She rustled in one of the many boxes. "Oh, they're raw. Hang on." She dropped several handfuls into a small bowl, tossed them quickly with liquid smoke, rosemary and salt, then poured them across a cookie sheet and popped it under the broiler. She set the timer. "Four minutes to hot nuts."

Justin cackled. "That's what she said."

"That doesn't even make sense," Laura protested. She felt lightheaded and giddy. She should probably have something to eat too. She wasn't sure how it happened but she had a palm full of flour and somehow it ended up all over Justin.

"I can't believe you did that!" He dusted the powder off his cheek and shoulder. Then, with a maniacal laugh he returned the favor.

Laura coughed out flour. He'd been more generous than she had. She heard Helen exclaim, "Justin! Don't you dare!"

Laura got one eye open in time to see that Helen had the plain outline of her hands on her face and her hair was dusted white. Justin stopped to laugh, pointing at both of them.

Helen marched to the flour bin and pelted him twice, then aimed a handful at Laura. Laura sidestepped and most of it went in her ear. She returned fire and Helen spluttered out, "I have flour in my bra!"

They all plunked down on the mats. Laura couldn't breathe for laughing—Helen had a distinct Cruella de Vil hair streak and Justin was covered. She ran her hand over her head. Flour on sweat—it felt like she had gravy on her scalp.

"Which way is the restroom?" Helen scrambled to her feet.

"I'll show you. My God, I'm a mess."

"You started it," Justin protested. "Can we order pizza?"

"Maybe," Helen hedged.

"Maybe means yes, right?"

"Smart-ass kid," Helen muttered when they reached the narrow corridor along the back of the building. "What am I going to do with the both of them?"

Laura tried to sound nonchalant. "I don't know where they got the smart-ass quality from."

Helen abruptly gulped for air and burst into tears. Though she had half expected Helen to break down at some point, it was so sudden that Laura was caught off guard. There was nothing to do but offer a shoulder. Helen clung to Laura like a lifeline and Laura held her close, smoothing her back and murmuring, "Hush, hush."

Helen was trying to say something, but the words were lost on her first attempts. Finally, she managed, "Why are you telling me to be quiet?"

"I'm not—oh. Hush means it'll be all right, everything is okay. My mother would always say it after bumps and scrapes." Her aunt had said it when she'd come to tell Laura that her mother had drowned.

"I feel such a fool," Helen said. She finally let go of Laura and leaned against the dingy wall outside the restroom. "I am so sorry, so sorry about what I said."

"You were frightened. I'll get over it." Great, the closest she'd ever been to Helen and she smelled like rotten onions and was covered with sodden flour.

Helen wiped her face with her hands. "I'm a mess."

"We both are."

"And Cass said you were the grown-up."

"She lied."

Helen wiped at the flour on her neck with her wet hands, making a paste. "And I'm the selfish one. I made my kids move across the country because I'm afraid to get old and then my daughter acts out and makes herself sick. I didn't care how the move affected them—"

"Stop it," Laura said quietly. "Of course you cared."

"It didn't stop me from ruining their lives."

"You're being melodramatic." The words were out before she could stop them.

Helen was clearly offended. "What?"

"You're not taking into account the impact on them if you'd walked away from this opportunity. If you'd gone home to Woodside to lick your wounds for who knows how long."

"They'd be living their very happy lives."

"With an unhappy mother who has never not known what her next role would be."

"I could have faked happiness."

"I'm sure you could, except your kids know you too well. I'm just saying that regardless of what you decided, their lives were going to change, and maybe not for the better either way. You can't know which was the better choice. You'll never know. I guess that comes with the parenting territory."

Laura ran her hands over her hair again. They still came away covered in white. "My mother made many, many sacrifices for me, Helen. When she found out she was pregnant, she told the father. He tried to have her deported by telling the INS she was a prostitute. She hid out until I was born so I would be unquestionably an American citizen since my father was fighting acknowledging me. When I was eight my mother moved us back to Jamaica. For the longest time I thought she ran away from Miami, but she had actually swallowed her pride and taken me to Jamaica so I could be around family because she felt she wasn't being a good enough mother. I was alone too much and someone had reported her to child services. She couldn't know that when she went home her family would treat her like a leper. They despised her for leaving them, but they leeched off of her while they belittled her high-a-mighty ways."

She'd heard the phrase applied to their little house, the scrupulously clean rooms, the healthy food, and her mother herself. *High-a-mighty.* "At the time I didn't get that she'd humbled herself in the hopes of giving me something important. What I live with is that she was utterly miserable in Jamaica. Beaten down. And I'd give anything for her to be able to do that over and make the choice that kept her strong."

She stopped abruptly, overwhelmed by the memory of what she'd found in the papers sent to her after her father's death. She had thought her mother weak for running home to Jamaica. Had resented moving, hated the way the other kids treated her. Reading through those papers she could only remember that she'd been a brat, adding to her mother's burdens. She'd whined and complained and stopped saying "I love you."

Helen put a hand on her arm. "Are you all right?"

Somehow she managed not to fold herself into Helen's arms. She wanted to be held, just for a minute, wanted someone else to tell her "Hush, hush," and pat her back.

She found a smile. "Just tired. And I wish my mom had lived a lot longer. I think a lot of things would have been different for me. And I could have given her so much."

"You'd have been a great daughter." Helen gestured at the restroom. "You want to go first?"

"I suppose. I don't want to leave Justin alone with the food for too long."

She laughed out loud at her reflection and managed to get some of her head under the faucet. Marginally better for it, she looked at herself closely. It had been a long, stressful day. She was emotionally drained. She could still feel the warmth of Helen's body against hers, a memory as exquisite as it was excruciating.

CHAPTER TWENTY-THREE

Every time she was alone with Laura, Helen wanted to tell her again she was sorry for how she'd acted at the hospital. There just didn't seem a way to bring it up with Laura so busy getting ready for the party. How could she for a moment have thought Laura had been sloppy, like the incompetent Mary? Even if she had mixed up Julie's food, how could she have thought Laura wasn't already excoriating herself for it? She hadn't needed Helen dumping on her too. And then, as if she hadn't been mean, Laura had held and comforted her when she'd finally broken down into tears. The moment Laura's arms had gone around her she'd felt completely safe.

It was clear to her all of Saturday morning that Laura was bothered by something. She looked wan at times and she wasn't her usual cheerful, somewhat sardonic self. When Helen had arrived home with the very itchy and unhappy Julie, Laura had immediately supplied a warm bowl of soup and toast to help rinse the taste of hospital food out of her mouth. Julie had confessed to eating nothing at all and inhaled the soup. Laura hadn't looked eased in mind, though. Helen could just kick herself—from the very first day Laura had been more than an employee, in thoughtfulness alone.

It probably wasn't a good idea that she was spending all day obsessing about Julie, and then for a change of pace obsessing about Laura. She managed to pull herself together when Laura left to work at the commercial kitchen, leaving Helen to take delivery of rented china, a few tables and chairs, and barware. The florist down the block delivered a huge supply of cedar and ivy boughs with holly sprigs and Christmas roses, all to decorate the tables and entry. She also talked to the string quartet's leader when he dropped by to check the space they would occupy. Laura was completely handling the food, so Helen was also supervising the bartender.

All in all, Helen concluded, parties were a huge pain. She'd rather give an impromptu performance with lines she'd never seen before. On the good side, she'd started getting calls from people on her guest list who wanted to bring a friend or two as well. Cass's feeding of the gossip mill had indeed turned her "little party" into one of the highlights of the Broadway holiday social season for the lucky chosen few. Laura had assured her the food would stretch to sixty, if necessary.

The day wore on in fits and starts. Justin called from the rental kitchen to ask permission to hang at a friend's for the night after he finished there. He promised to be home in time to be of use tomorrow as well. She tossed together a salad for herself and Julie and promptly dozed off in the middle of Julie's holiday favorite *Elf*.

Keys in the front door woke her. The DVD player had turned off after the movie ended—to her surprise, it was after ten. Laura was struggling in with a large and unwieldy box. With a quick glance at Julie, who looked as if she would sleep all night on the couch, Helen went to help.

"I figured I might as well bring back some of my equipment tonight. No wasted trips." She shifted the box awkwardly. "It smells fantastic in here. I love cedar and roses."

Helen skittered ahead of her, holding the swinging door to the kitchen open, then clearing enough space on the small center island for Laura to deposit the box.

"I brought samples. Is Julie up?"

"She's sound asleep on the couch. I guess the movie had the same effect on both of us."

"How is she doing?"

"The hives on her face have almost completely faded. She has a really bad patch on her throat and another on her belly, though."

"I hope they go away too. Here."

Used to sampling from Laura, Helen didn't hesitate to let her pop a wedge of a small tartlet into her mouth. A rich, intense savory goodness exploded along her tongue. Mushrooms infused with black pepper and ginger? "That's delicious. Wow. What else is there?"

Laura smiled. "You look just like your son."

Glad to see Laura looking more cheerful than she had this morning, Helen pretended offense. "Are you saying he and I are gluttons?"

"I didn't say that, you did."

Helen gave her a mocking glower, then happily tried a bite-sized puff filled with soft goat cheese and topped with a fig and balsamic compote. She was surprised by an added tang of cranberry. She licked her lips. "You know, you could make a living at this cooking thing."

"Could I? I'll have to give it some thought." Laura was busily stashing her knives and small equipment back where they belonged.

"I really am sorry about yesterday," Helen said. There was no point in dithering, she decided. "I was out of line."

"It's okay, Helen."

"I hurt your feelings."

"Yes. But I got over it. And you were scared, which gets some slack from me."

"You were scared too. You'd have made a good parent yourself, you know."

"I never had the least interest, to tell you the truth." Laura slid the last mixing bowl into a cupboard. She leaned against the counter, shoulders drooping. "There was the natural limitation— no easy access to the male contribution."

"Indeed, that makes conception very difficult. Even with it, after we decided to start trying it took Justin and I a couple of years."

"To tell you the truth, if I'd known kids could turn out as special as yours I might have considered it. They are great kids." Laura was staring across the room, her eyes half-closed. "Okay, yesterday wasn't Julie's finest hour. She was frustrated and she paid a high price for a silly thing like pink frosting. I get why she tried it. Nothing bad has happened in a while and so you think you'll...test it. See if something that was bad for you is still bad for you."

Helen busied herself getting a glass of water. She leaned against the counter just a foot away from Laura, studying her profile. She knew a lot of very important things about this woman, but she still had the feeling there was much more to learn. It could take years, and she didn't have years. She had to let Laura leave at the end of January. Laura had every reason to leave and not look back.

She's honest, dedicated and passionate, Helen thought. Remembering the flour fight of last night, she had to add 'playful' to the list. Intelligent, goodness yes—Laura's brain was full of information about food and the history of cultural cuisines, and she could discuss cooking as both a science and an art. She always seemed to know a play when Helen mentioned one and was far better read and more curious about the world. All Helen knew about was theater, theater and more theater—pretty dull.

I know she's kind, Helen told herself. Kind and thoughtful. Unbidden, she added, *but I don't know how she likes to be kissed.*

The thought had crept up on her unawares, though she knew it had been lurking for days, even weeks. Had she hesitated telling the kids about her self-discovery in part because it meant telling Laura? She didn't want Laura to think she was telling her because that meant they could now consider romantic possibilities—coming out as a pickup line? What kind of cliché would it be to sleep with a household employee? She wasn't going to act like a bored socialite, corporate king or politician using his own staff for sexual exploits.

She should say nothing more and go to bed instead of gazing at the woman like she was ice cream.

If she'd been scared she might have found a reason to leave the room. Had another snack—done anything to break the long silence. Wanting Karolina had been shattering. It had felt risky and dangerous, no matter how welcome. Looking at Laura's strong profile, weighing the totality of this woman in her heart, she wasn't frightened that she wanted her in ways that she'd never wanted anyone before. Laura might reject her, might not be interested, might be eager to get on with her life and then she would leave. It would hurt, but Helen wasn't even afraid of that pain. She was only afraid of being gnawed away by regret for failing to listen to her heart. After all these years, when she was finally looking at a prize beyond measure, she didn't want to be a chump.

She traced the outline of Laura's lips with her gaze, then the curve of her hairline behind her ear. Karolina had been fireworks and sparkle. There was fire inside her now, but it was deep. There was a voice singing in the depth of her heart, opening places she had left dark and empty. She ached in her bones to touch Laura, explore her, find out what would pleasure her. The look on Laura's face when she had been about to kiss that blonde in her car—Helen wanted to see it again, directed at her. She wanted to be craved that way, by Laura. She wanted to know she had somehow managed to twine her way inside this complicated woman until she was as necessary as air.

She didn't even know where to begin or how to earn such a gift. What did she have to offer in exchange?

Laura turned her head suddenly, her gaze sweeping over Helen's face. Helen realized that if her thoughts showed it was too late to hide them. She leaned toward Laura, unable to stop herself.

The sudden blare of the television separated them. Laura

stumbled to the opposite counter. Helen gasped for air as if that would make her brain work.

The TV was muted as quickly as it had started up. Julie was awake, Helen realized.

"It's okay," Laura said. "See you in the morning. It's okay."

Helen had no idea what was "okay." She watched Laura pull off her coat as she left the kitchen. She heard her say, "Hey— you're awake. I'm wiped out. There are some snacks, all safe for you. I have to get a shower and some sleep."

By the time Helen made herself go to the living room the door to Laura's room was shut.

Julie was looking at her curiously. After a moment, she asked, "Snacks?"

"Sure. Help yourself. I think I'm going to turn in too. Tomorrow will be a long day. Don't forget to take your meds, okay?"

"I'll remember." Julie clicked off the TV as she rose from the couch.

Helen leaned against the closed door of her room. She could hear the shower running in Laura's bathroom. She wanted to go to her. Wanted to spend the night rolling in her arms. But this was not a cruise ship far away from the people in her life where she could luxuriate in passion. This was her life, and her kids' lives. And Laura's life. What did she have to give that Laura could possibly desire? The glamorous life in New York—the one thing that Laura didn't seem to want?

It would have been so easy to kiss Laura, as easy as smiling.

Moxie Taylor mocked her for a fool.

Sleep was impossible.

The only reason Laura slept, she was certain, was because she was exhausted. Her body was as tightly stretched as a bowstring. When she woke after a few hours she was washed over by the smell /of Helen's hair and the soft wonder of her smile in the kitchen last night. She didn't think she was wrong—that look had been an invitation. All so romantic, she thought, if it weren't for the highly erotic thoughts that followed, including stripping Helen naked, pushing her up on the counter and feasting on her, touching her, asking her what she liked... She might have done just that if they hadn't both realized they weren't alone.

There was the party to get through. There was too much work to be fantasizing about what she thought she had seen in Helen's eyes. She was so besotted and lustful that there was no way she could judge any look that Helen gave her. For all she was capable of gauging, Helen might have wanted another bite of tart. Helen was not interested in wild acts of abandon on the kitchen counter.

Bracing, cold tap water splashed on her face helped her to focus. There was no time for this today. She had to get all of the food over from the commercial setup and the final prep going for all the hot hors d'oeuvres. She had wassail to taste and spike. There were a half-dozen Wagyu steaks to sear and slice down to top an *amuse-bouche.* There was yellowfin to prep for ceviche in lime and garam masala. Dozens of tart shells yet to pipe with one of three different cheese blends, and the last big task: breaking down and cleaning pineapples, plums, oranges and grapes, and whatever else she had acquired for a sumptuous fruit cornucopia display around the ice sculpture that was being delivered late in the afternoon.

She decided it was wise to save her shower until as late as possible. She was going to be a mess in short order. A plain T-shirt and jeans would suffice as the kitchen was going to get very, very hot. From the cooking, she scolded herself. Hot from the cooking, not the smoldering glances and the smoky need that was churning inside of her.

Helen's voice floated to her from the living room as she left her room. "Help me move this table over there, then we can cluster these rentals on this end. We want people to have places to put down their plates and drinks while they talk, but not sit. Once people sit, they won't budge. We need mingling!"

Julie was leaning over the large teardrop-shaped coffee table that anchored the center of the room. "Oh good, more hands," she said as Laura came in. "This thing weighs a ton."

Between the three of them they got it shifted. Laura said,

focusing just left of Helen's ear, "Looks like you've got this under control. I'll get started in the kitchen."

The doorbell rang and she escaped.

A half hour later a cheerful Justin joined her. He quickly understood the finesse of piping filling into tarts. He didn't have the precision she would need later for the meringues and toppings, but he was gangbusters with basic filling and completed the task as quickly as she would have. Next she set him up to slice artisanal cheeses for two platters. Flatbread crackers were already baked and ready for rustic presentation with the fruit display. After that she'd have him season and roast the mix of cashews, pecans, almonds and chestnuts.

The hours flew by at an alarming pace. The doorbell rang constantly with deliveries. Helen's stylist would be one of them, and the florist and the liquor delivery. Helen finally did come into the kitchen, but she spoke to Justin and left again. At two, Laura reluctantly put down her knife and asked the doorman to get her a cab. Time to start moving the food. Fortunately, by the time she arrived at the rental kitchen her helper for the afternoon and evening was already there. Rex took the assignment seriously, and proved both strong and thorough. The van service arrived promptly as well—another miracle. They loaded the rolling trays and boxes and turned back to the condo to be met by the doorman and Justin who helped transfer everything safely into the lobby.

At five the ice sculpture was delivered. At five thirty Laura managed a belated shower and dressed carefully in her chef's whites. At six the server helper arrived, decked out in traditional black, and quickly memorized the flow of beverages and descriptions of the food. At six thirty the string quartet members and the bartender arrived. Everything was nearly ready, except for the million last-minute things.

She was arranging the fruit and ice sculpture table when Julie began hovering.

"I feel useless," she said. "Isn't there anything I can do?"

"In a bit I could use help attaching the greenery to the tables. Right now I really need markers written. You have lovely handwriting—could you do it?"

"Sure!" She brightened considerably. "You mean like what

kind of cheese is what?"

"Yes, and the names of the dishes. Let me show you."

In the kitchen, she handed all the small ceramic tiles and their little stands to Julie, along with the dry erase markers. "Justin knows what everything is, so ask him if I'm busy, okay?"

"You bet. Is there anything I can't eat?"

"Everything is safe for you—down to the last bite and drop. Stay away from the wassail." She raised her voice. "That goes for you, too, Justin."

"Aw man, I was looking forward to getting holiday hammered."

"Don't even," Helen said from the doorway.

Laura salivated when she looked at her, and couldn't make herself stop. Her hair was swept into an elegant, formal updo with tiny white snowflakes. Her ears and throat glittered with diamonds. She was wearing a holiday hostess gown of red velvet, trimmed with white, like something out of *White Christmas.*

"Is everything going okay?" Helen asked. "I'm so nervous. The bartender is here—Mario. All bartenders are named Mario. Cass is running late—she's the one who loves this kind of thing."

"I'm here," Cass called from the living room. "It's going to be fine. Have a drink!"

"Double standard," Justin and Julie chorused.

"Don't start with me," Helen said. She disappeared from the doorway.

The doorbell began ringing steadily at seven thirty, thirty minutes after the official start. At nine the great room was crowded with at least sixty-five people, and they spilled into the hallway and dining room as planned. Laura kept the kitchen door closed, but some people still wandered in looking for even more food or simply to escape the noise. The server was good at her work, circulating in a business-like manner to collect abandoned plates and glasses, then more engaging with the guests when taking out something hot. The display around the ice sculpture was replenished by the helpful Rex while Laura kept an eye on the formal dessert table. The bartender seemed to have his station all under control. The string quartet sounded lovely, she thought, though she had never been much of a Mozart fan.

Cass was busy charming a number of people. Laura recognized a few for herself—big promoters who were the type of people who got awards for their good work from charities throughout the theater world. There were a few actors she recognized, but most of the faces were a blur. At one point she heard Helen singing "Let It Snow," but she had no time to stop and listen.

Justin hadn't retired to his room as planned. Instead he'd showered and reappeared dressed all in black, like the server, and took over all the heating duties for the hors d'oeuvres, leaving Laura free to focus on presentation. Julie was chatting with people about the food and helping herself liberally. There was plenty and it was good to see her eating without hesitation.

It was just after eleven when Helen joined her in the kitchen. "What do you say if we push back coffee for an hour? Is there enough food?" Helen gestured at the counters still laden with trays of hors d'oeuvres ready to be circulated.

The great room was still packed—no one would guess it was a Sunday night. Theater people, Laura thought, ran on a different clock. "There's enough. If you delay much later, though, people will start to hunker down into an after-hours party mode instead of going elsewhere to find amusements for the remainder of the night."

Rex returned for another platter of sliced fruit. "The display under the ice sculpture needs to be replenished."

"Go for it. Let me know when there's one left."

He had no sooner cleared the door when the server came in, left an empty tray and picked up another. She gave a twirl on her way back to circulate.

"It's great to have the help. They've been super," Laura told Helen.

Since they were alone again, she risked looking at her. The red velvet, the white fake fur against her throat, her hair sparkling with those darling little snowflakes—she still looked fresh as a daisy. Laura was fairly certain she herself was looking just a bit wilted.

"I think you're right," Helen said. "I want to be a good

hostess, so let's hold coffee until just after midnight. Then we'll stop the music, sober them up and move them out."

Laura nodded and would have walked away, but Helen put her hand lightly on Laura's forearm. "Thank you. I couldn't have done this without you. We make a good team."

She finally met Helen's gaze for the first time that day. There was a deep, steady glow that made her feel just a bit faint.

She would have said "You're welcome" but Helen abruptly pulled her close and kissed her, hard.

She was so surprised she let out a muffled gasp.

Helen let her go just as suddenly. "I'm sorry. I don't know what—"

"It's okay—"

"I just—I mean, it's not—"

Laura kissed Helen back, just as hard.

Helen stumbled back and put a hand to her throat. "Are we—was that—"

"Now we're even," was all Laura could think to say.

Rex came in, followed by Justin. Helen ran for the door.

She tasted like red lipstick and mint, Laura thought, and her hair smelled of rose and apricot. She hadn't a clue why Helen had kissed her, but she wasn't the least bit sorry for kissing her back. In fact, a little imp of delight was doing a jig.

At five after twelve the server began circulating with coffee, sugar and cream as the string quartet finished a medley of holiday tunes and packed up their instruments. It was the universal signal to all well-bred people that the party was winding down. Time to sober up and think about leaving.

Spending a great deal of time reliving the scant second of Helen's lips pressed to hers, Laura removed all the remaining hot food, replated the cheese and crackers to a smaller display, then did the same to the desserts. She also added small gold boxes that would hold two or three of the little bites if a guest wanted to take a treat home with them. Once she offered the tiny tongs and a box to one guest, others quickly followed suit. Julie was happy to tie them shut with a ribbon, from which hung a gift tag in Helen's handwriting that read, "Thank you for sharing a holiday evening with me—Helen." Cass was a genius.

By twelve thirty the crowd had thinned to a quarter of its full size, and more were headed out the door. She estimated that in perhaps five minutes everyone would be gone. She sent the server, bartender and Rex home with thanks and large tips. From Cass's effervescent smile, she gathered the evening was a success.

Still reliving the taste of Helen's lips and wondering exactly what the kiss meant, Laura went back to the kitchen to organize rinsing the rented china and barware so it could be restacked in their containers for pickup. She had thought she was alone but a long sniff drew her attention to someone seated on the far side of the small kitchen island.

She didn't recognize the man—trim, white, ponytail, pushing fifty but trying hard in faux beatnik black to look thirty-five. His cool factor was diminished by the remnants of white powder around his nostrils. On the beautiful black marble of her favorite pastry board there was the trace of a line of cocaine and a line yet untouched.

Deep down, part of her wanted to ask if she could have some. It was small, like a needle, deep like a needle, sharp like a needle. She had to deafen the monster, get away from it. Her mind screamed *run* but her feet wouldn't move.

He looked at her, eyes bleary from the momentary glaze. Her stomach twisted with another sharp yearning. That euphoria had no equal, though she could imagine melting into afterglow in Helen's arms might feel that good. It wasn't nearly so unhealthy a thing to crave. But that was probably never going to happen, the monster whispered. Cocaine was a gift, a guarantee of fantastic highs that never had to end.

She made her choice, not for Helen, but for what she had to do or she would never be with Helen. Never make it to the rest of the life she wanted.

She picked up her eight-inch utility knife and turned on him.

His eyes were steadying. The euphoria was already fading. But after the euphoria was a flash of vulnerability followed by a long surge of confidence and energy. She had to get rid of him while he was still woozy. He sniffed and gave a small cough, spurring her to action.

She stabbed the knife into the small round of cheese in his line of sight, making sure she had his attention. He watched her sort through the large ruby seedless grapes, then gently pinch one free from its stem.

"That fine marble surface you're using is my pastry board." She plucked her knife out of the cheese and put the grape in the middle of his second, untouched, line.

He was still too out to protest and she rolled it along the white powder until it was dusted with the stuff. It was on her fingers. She could taste it if she wanted, so easy, the monster hissed.

"A knife is a very subtle tool. You can hack up a cow with one. Sharper the knife, the easier it is. Or you can slice a grape to serve twenty."

The first slice was slow, then she increased her speed until the *tat-tat* of steel on marble pinged against her ears. "It can be done in seconds."

She tipped her knife against the grape and it relaxed into the slices she'd made. Deftly, she swept the flat of the blade over them, fanning them out the long way so that they stretched out on top of his entire line of coke, purple blood rinsing into the poisonous white.

"Hey—there was no call for that!"

She leaned over him, in his face, her head perilously close to the little bag still intact on the counter. She could smell it now, though the grape was mercifully more powerful. "Listen to me."

"What's your problem?"

"If you *ever* defile my kitchen again with your shit I will slice you into so many pieces they'll never be able to prove that it's even you. Do you understand me?"

"I understand you're a crazy bitch!" He pushed back, looking at the ruined line in dismay.

She snatched up a plum. "I'll start with your testicles."

The plum slices oozed juice onto the board. She quickly restacked them on top of the baggie with the rest of his stash.

At least an ounce, maybe more. With little effort her knife went through the plum and the baggie, making complete contact with the board. Up, down, up, down until her knife had cut the baggie and coke thoroughly into the plum.

"When I'm done, they're going to look like this."

"Fuck you! That was my last bit."

"Guess you're going to have to leave, then."

She was so angry and frightened of what she had all over her hands that Justin's voice made her jump.

"What the hell is that crap?"

"Cocaine," she said numbly. She couldn't look at him. She was sure that her craving showed. "I'm getting rid of it."

Justin moved between the man and the kitchen island. "Get the hell out of our house."

He stepped forward almost chest-to-chest with Justin. "Who the fuck are you to tell me what to do, boy?"

"He is my *son*." Helen's voice rang from the kitchen doorway. "Leave or I will call the police."

"Over a little bit of blow?"

"Be glad," Cass said, slipping into the room by ducking under Helen's arm, "that your producer has already left."

"You're kidding, right?" Laura could tell he was getting the full surge of confidence that came with the rest of the hit. "He'd join me."

"Not in Helen Baynor's kitchen, he wouldn't. Not around her children."

With a little push Laura lifted the heavy cutting board from the counter and took it to the sink.

Hot water. Bleach. Bleach for her hands, and the blast of the acrid chlorine drove the memory of other smells out of her nose. She deliberately inhaled enough to make her nostrils sting.

"What about my three hundred in coke that just went down the drain? That bitch ruined my whole supply."

"Call her a bitch one more time and—"

"Justin," Laura said sharply. "He's a user. You can't argue with him. You can't win. He's gone. The drug owns him."

"Hey mate." Another man Laura didn't know pushed into

the room. He took his apparent friend by the shoulders. "It's time to go. Let's head for SoHo. That little club with the great drinks. Let's go."

"She ruined my stash."

Had she whined like that when she was high? Had she looked so pathetic? Laura scrubbed at her hands with the bleach. She hoped the tingle on her fingertips and palms was the chlorine, not the drug.

The newcomer gave Helen an apologetic look as he pulled at his friend. "Let's go. It's time to go."

None of it had gone up her nose. She'd stared down the monster, but she was going to go to pieces if she couldn't get it off her hands. She doused them with bleach again and scrubbed with the scouring pad.

Someone said her name, close to her ear. It was Helen.

Helen put her hands on Laura's under the running hot water, stilling them. "Laura, stop it."

"Don't touch my hands—it's on my hands," she said. "I didn't use any, I swear."

"No one thinks you did. Laura, honey, stop."

"I can't. I have to get it off."

"You're bleeding. Stop." Helen didn't let go though Laura tried to jerk her hands away.

"I can't stop." Her throat was tight with fear. Her vision was down to pinpoints. From far away she knew she was having a panic attack. "I can still hear it."

Cass was the one who shook her, just once. She said, fiercely, "We love you. You're not alone."

Helen shut off the water and Cass wrapped her hands in a clean towel. She gulped for air, felt arms around her and heard Helen, finally, murmuring, "Hush, hush."

Long ago words circled in her head and she gave into angry, frightened sobs. *Sobriety is something you do for yourself. Sobriety is no one else's job. Sobriety is a choice.*

When she finally lifted her head from Helen's shoulder the party was very over. Only Justin and Julie remained with Cass and Helen. They looked scared.

Her attempt at a smile must have failed because no one

smiled back.

Helen gave her a compassionate look. "What was that about?"

"No," Cass said. "She needs to sleep. We are all exhausted. Time for talking tomorrow."

With an odd look, Helen let Cass pull Laura away.

She remembered the murmur of voices, the dull clank of dishware rattling and doors closing. She was tucked in her bed in her T-shirt and panties. Her hands were hot. The sheets were cool. Someone turned out the light.

CHAPTER TWENTY-FOUR

Helen woke with a start. With a groan she saw that the clock said it was still before seven. The kids needed to get up for school.

Her head felt like lead. She thought that at most she'd only been asleep for an hour or so. She hoped they'd fared better. Laura was probably still asleep—at least Helen hoped she was. Whatever had upset her so much last night, it had taken a heavy toll.

Both children had overslept. She roused Julie into the shower and lured Justin to the kitchen with microwaved hors d'oeuvres. There was a howling wind outside the windows but brilliant sunshine was pouring across the breakfast table. She found hats and coats, anticipating the argument about wearing them because in California it was a point of pride not to need such things, and set them next to the door. After that she swapped her robe for basic sweats and a hoodie—it was too early to care about anything but being warm.

The kids were both in the kitchen now. She had nearly pushed open the door when she realized they were talking about her.

"I always thought Cass was in love with Mom." That was Justin. "And I wondered if they were really a couple, I guess, when I first realized that they could be. But I really don't think anything ever happened."

"I'm not all that surprised that Mom is gay," Julie said. "Do you ever wonder about Mom and Laura?"

"No—thinking about Mom's love life makes me a little queasy. I don't want the details unless it means more eats like this."

"I want our mother to be happy and all you want is for your stomach to be happy."

Only mildly guilty about eavesdropping, Helen pushed her way into the kitchen. "Did you guys get enough breakfast?"

The duet of "Yes, Mom" implied she had asked a stupid question. Julie had heated up more leftovers from the party—the delicious goat cheese puffs with fig jam. Well, Helen thought, it's a better breakfast than a PopTart.

They both acquiesced to hats and coats and she walked them down to the lobby to wait for the car that would take them to school. When it didn't show on time, they managed a cab. She'd have to call and complain. Reliable service was essential.

She scurried into the elevator, which was slightly warmer. She'd ask for something super-warming for dinner. Glad to be alone for the short ride up, she chastised herself, "You're just like Justin, thinking with your stomach. Do you even love this woman? Or do you love her cooking?"

The answer was in the shiver between her legs and the sensation of thick heat running down her spine. It was the same feeling that had overwhelmed her last night in the kitchen, looking at Laura's strong and beautiful face. Never in her life had she thought she would die if she didn't kiss somebody, but she had felt like that last night. Like an adolescent with no self-control, she had kissed the woman with no warning. What must Laura think?

Laura, she reminded herself, had kissed her back. It had been almost playful, almost as if Laura knew it was the only way to shut Helen up so she could get back to work.

Was Cass in the picture? Cass had been so gentle with Laura last night. If Laura loved Cass that would be hard, very hard. She'd be happy for them both and completely miserable at the same time.

Why had Laura flipped out like that? It had been so out of character—something had definitely snapped. She was exhausted, and that was your fault, Helen chided herself. She hoped she didn't have to get Laura exhausted again to garner another kiss. Today, while the kids were at school, they had a chance to talk. Yes, talking was important. All she wanted to do was...talk.

When she stepped inside the condo she smelled coffee. She found Laura wrapped in her dark green terry cloth robe, sipping from a mug and seated at the breakfast table. The sun was dancing all around her and cast her skin in a deep, rich gold.

"That smells good," Helen said quietly.

"I hoped you'd be back. I can't believe I slept this late."

"It's not even half-past seven. I can't believe I'm up. Besides, you're entitled. You were really worn out."

The silence Helen had been dreading fell. She didn't know where to start.

Laura had another swallow of coffee and said, "I freaked out last night."

Helen would have rather talked about kisses, but she would let Laura set the topic. "Cass was right. Whatever it is, you don't have to be alone."

"It's a solo job. No one can do it for me."

"That's not the same thing." She joined Laura at the table, sitting across from her. The sun felt gloriously inappropriate to the chill in the room. "Are you and Cass in love?" She instantly regretted the question. Could she be more self-centered?

Laura looked at her then, eyebrows raised. "Why on earth would you think that?"

"You and she—last night she put you to bed."

"That was Cass? Oh. I like Cass, I like her a lot. I think she likes me. But that's all there is." She frowned into her coffee. "Just because we're both lesbians and we like each other doesn't mean we automatically fall in love."

"I know that."

"I don't love Cass. Not romantically."

"Good." She hadn't meant to say that, not at all. Maybe she ought to have scripted some of this conversation—it would have helped.

"Why is that good?"

"Because... Because you're not right for each other. That's why. That's why...it's good. And everything." You're babbling, she told herself. She felt thirteen. "Tell me about last night, then. About..." Her gaze went to Laura's hands. They were more scraped and raw than she had thought.

"I was afraid that the coke would get into me because I'd touched it. I'm not sorry I ruined his stash. I hope he doesn't make trouble for you."

What had possessed Laura to hurt herself that much? "Neiman is an ass. I don't know who brought him along, but he wasn't on the guest list."

Laura's eyes darkened and there was a glimmer of tears. "I can't be near it, Helen. I know in my heart that I will never use again. Alcoholics can handle watching other people drink— many of them. But I can't be near cocaine. The self-doubt saps my confidence. A daily confrontation with the reality that the temptation never completely goes away—it's corrosive. I don't want that in my life."

Pieces of the puzzle of last night met up with Laura's earlier words and the truth finally assembled in her brain. Idiot, she thought, obsessing over your own feelings when Laura's trying to tell you something, something really huge. She felt a shiver in her heart, then was washed over by an immense stillness. The sunlight dimmed. Words formed across her mind's eye as if her brain had a typewriter: *She is an addict.*

Her first response was visceral. That idiot Neiman and Laura had nothing in common—except they did. A bad something. She didn't know where to look or what to do with her hands. No script, nothing to guide her. That Laura didn't use drugs didn't change the fact that she was an addict. Laura said she'd never use again, but last night she had been so upset—and not at all the Laura Helen was realizing she loved.

How many young talents had she seen fall into the pit of drugs, alcohol and parties? They were drawn to the atmosphere as if it were the only one in which they could breathe. Most lost their roles and disappeared into the streets. She'd been party to the sobbed apologies, the contrition, the acceptance of responsibility during temporary sobriety, then the misery after falling back into using again.

"What..." She cleared her throat. "What all did you use?"

Laura's expression was wooden. She kept her gaze on her hands. "It has always been cocaine. It will always be cocaine. There are addicts all through my mother's family in Jamaica. Somehow, it's in my blood. To crave it."

"Do you?"

"Almost never."

"Almost?"

Laura snorted. "That's the problem. *Almost*. That's what my addiction has become. The difference between almost never and never."

"I didn't expect this." She blinked back tears.

Laura's lips had gone almost gray. She put a shaking hand to her head. "I have wanted to tell you but I could never find the right time. The last woman I told threw me out on the spot."

The California blonde? Cass had said it hadn't ended well. Was that what had gone wrong? What a fool, Helen thought. There—though her head was spinning, she knew that anyone who didn't hear Laura out, didn't try to understand, was a fool. "Why did you use? I guess I mean when and why."

Laura leaned heavily on her elbows. It twisted at Helen's heart to see shame flicker over the face she had only ever seen confident and proud.

"The first time because I was young and stupid. I thought I was smarter than my addicted, wastrel relatives. I had my mother's brains, and I worked and was on the way to making something of myself. I thought I wouldn't get hooked. The second time was even stupider, and I'd even been warned. We're all warned that there will come a day in sobriety when you're convinced you're cured. It's like Julie and the pink frosting. She ate it hoping she was cured. So you use to prove you're not an addict anymore. I'm not..." She shrugged. "I'm not a functional addict. Some people are. I have two uncles I could never tell were high. They use and go about their lives, only partially impaired. Not me. I get really manic, then crash. I managed to find a sponsor. I started over. I was still in the AA system—back then that's pretty much what there was for all substance abusers. It didn't seem so hard to crawl back and I did it."

Laura was silent for so long that Helen prompted her with, "Is there more?"

She nodded and a tear spilled over, shining like an impossible diamond in the incongruous sunlight.

"Did something bad happen to you? Push you over some kind of edge?" If I learn what that is I can protect her, Helen thought.

"No, that's not it." She took a deep breath. "I mean, yes, I went over an edge, but I did it to myself. And even now it still hurts. Mostly the impotence I guess. That...I was too young to see what she had done for me."

"Your mother?"

"She died when I was a teenager."

"I know," Helen said softly. "You said the other night."

"About eight or nine years ago my father died." She gave a ghost of a smile. "I fell off the wagon shortly after that. I've been sober for three thousand forty-two days since."

"But you hardly knew him. Why would his death drive you to..."

Laura turned her palms up. Her face was a mix of pain and shame. "I knew he was a bastard just from how he treated me when I got shipped back to America after my mother died. But I really had no grip on what a bastard he was. My Jamaican kin hoped I'd get sent back to them with money to keep me there, but instead he decided to hide me from his own family and mine. I was glad not to go back to Jamaica. I had no more contact with him and I didn't want any. I asked for nothing from him once I could support myself—which was when I graduated from high school. There is nothing of him in me except DNA."

She closed her eyes for a moment, then looked down at her hands. "A few weeks later I got a letter from a lawyer with a nominal inheritance check to make it so I couldn't claim I'd been forgotten. I gave the money to a girls' school. But after that I got another packet from a different lawyer. Since both parties were now deceased and the suit hadn't been—oh, there's a legal word for it that I don't remember. Anyway, my mother had tried to sue for support for me all along. Because she wasn't a citizen she had a lot of trouble, plus she had very little money to pay a lawyer. Ultimately, she failed because she took me out of the jurisdiction, to Jamaica. But in the documents were her sworn statements about how..."

Her voice broke and Helen went to the sink for a glass of water. Laura accepted it with a murmured thank you. Their fingertips touched. The longing to hold her was so intense that Helen shuddered. Though she could focus on what Laura was saying, there was a fugue in her head. *Protect myself, protect the kids, protect myself...* It might be too late for her, but she had to protect Justin and Julie. She knew that Laura would never deliberately hurt either of them. That was the problem with addicts—once they used they could hurt everyone around them without meaning to. It tore at her heart, the idea that she might have to protect them from the one person they had all grown to trust without question.

Laura spoke again, her voice thick with old and bitter grief. "He had coerced her. He took her for another illiterate near-slave from the Caribbean who existed for his pleasure. She was in the U.S. on a paper-thin student grant that required she have a job. He threatened to fire her and report her to INS as a prostitute, which he'd done before to other young women he employed. She...capitulated. She was a math whiz and all she wanted was to be a teacher. It wasn't a big dream, was it? Not so much to ask."

"No, not so much for anyone to ask," Helen said gently.

"When she told him she was pregnant, he still told the INS she was a prostitute. He tried to get her deported while she was pregnant. It took all the fight she had to stay, stay long enough to have me *here*. My life was immeasurably changed, in every aspect, because I was an American citizen. She gave me that when my father tried—with all his resources—to keep it from me. And we stayed for eight more years because she worked all the time and couldn't be deported because I was a citizen. Every day, nights, weekends, as a hotel maid. I knew when I was in the first grade how to walk home from the bus, let myself in, make dinner for myself. A neighbor checked on me and locked me in. I learned how to be alone. But someone reported her to child services—it said in the papers—and she decided to go home rather than risk me being forced on my father. She didn't trust him. But I didn't know anything about any of that. All I knew was that she had dumped me among people who hated me. I missed America. I was mean to her, and a brat. Cruel and selfish. And then she died."

More tears escaped but Laura didn't seem to notice. "I was so angry with her for taking me to Jamaica. She drowned at the beach. I thought she was *weak*, but all she wanted was something better for herself and me—and she didn't ask to have me. She didn't get pregnant because she was sleeping around. That bastard—he—"

She took a long, shuddering breath. "I didn't look up a meeting, I didn't try to call a sponsor and I should have. I hadn't spent any time creating a support net for myself if things got too much because I was arrogant and sure I was stronger than it was. No, instead, I went to a bar. Someone was dealing, *of course* someone was dealing. I got drunk and then I bought, which is the classic, stupid cocaine addict pattern. Young and stupid is one thing. But thirty-something and twice back from using and falling into it again—that's something else. I didn't think I could be such a fool. But I was. And I can't deny that I could be again, in spite of all my intentions otherwise. I was stupid once. How can I trust myself, really?"

Her mouth was twisted with a self-loathing bitterness that shocked Helen. How could Laura hate herself when she was such a strong and competent woman?

"I knew better and I still walked in the front door of that bar of my own free will."

Helen let out the breath she'd been holding. "And that won't happen again?"

"I don't want it to. With every ounce of fight I have in me, I don't want it to. But I live with my own stupidity. I can't escape myself." After a long moment Laura went on, "One thing that might get an addict to stop using is the certain knowledge that the next one will kill her. I couldn't smell anything for four days and it was two months before I could fully smell and taste sours. I thought my life as a chef was over. It was the only life I ever wanted for myself. I spent days sobbing in AA meetings—I was in Italy of all places. I damn near lost my job but I faked it and prayed." Her word tumbled together. "My father tried to crush my mother, and look what I'd done with her sacrifices. Throwing my life away when she'd given me everything. I didn't think I deserved to get my sense of smell back, but I did. Literally, by the grace of God, which I've enjoyed far more than my fair share of. I never want to use again, Helen. I don't know how to make you believe me when I can't trust myself enough to believe it. But never again. The monster never dies, but I will not let it be the death of me."

Seeming to have run out of words, Laura slumped forward to rest her forehead on her arms.

Helen automatically sipped her coffee but couldn't taste it. She wanted to say that none of it mattered, that she believed in Laura and trusted her, but if she did, wasn't that dismissing one of the strongest shaping forces of Laura's life? "I want to be sure I'm hearing you." Hell, was she resorting to psychobabble? "If you'll never use again, I don't understand what was so upsetting last night."

Laura raised her head. Her eyes were bleak, like a night without stars. "Just because I will never stop fighting the monster doesn't mean I'm not afraid of it. I *am* afraid of it. I know how strong it is. Pretending it doesn't have the power to kill me gives it more power. I don't ever want to put myself in harm's way again. Sometimes..." Her voice broke. "Sometimes running away is the best way not to lose."

Helen's heart was hammering so high in her throat she couldn't speak. For the first time in her life she considered that something might mean more to her than even the next time the curtain went up. Without Laura, without the pulse of Laura in her life, all the stages went dark. How had that happened? Yet another thing she'd thought impossible.

She reached across the table to cover Laura's hands gently with her own. "I don't really know how to put it all into words. Guess I need a script sometimes, huh?" Laura gave her a wan smile. "I understand what a struggle this is, I know it isn't easy, and I know I really have no idea just what the struggle does to you. But I know you can do this, and that you have done it. But you don't have to do it all by yourself. It's like having an operation—it only happens to you, but you're allowed to have someone else bring you soup and love."

She steadied her voice, because the most important thing she needed to say was still to come. "I don't think I can handle it if you leave me. I—"

The front door slammed. It was so unexpected that Helen jumped. Laura scrubbed at her eyes and pulled her robe more tightly closed.

"I wondered where the kids were," Laura said. "Did they go for breakfast or something?"

Justin and Julie appeared in the doorway. They both looked mutinous, caps askew, coats still buttoned and backpacks dangling from their fingers.

Helen's mind was instantly filled with terrorist attacks and pandemics. "What's wrong? What happened?"

"Mom." Julie gritted her teeth.

"It's winter break." Justin snorted.

Julie added, "There's no school."

Laura burst out into near-hysterical laughter.

"Oh my Lord!" Helen clapped her hands to her face. "I completely forgot."

"It's not funny," Justin said. "I could have slept in."

Laura, between chortles, managed to say, "Just as well. Everybody's up so we can get to cleaning."

"No way," Julie said. "I don't want to spend the first day of winter break up to my elbows in dirty dishes."

Laura went off into peals again.

"I'm so sorry," Helen said. She was glad to see Laura laughing. She loved the sound of it.

Calming somewhat, Laura pointed out, "But that's why we're not on a plane home right now, remember? We don't leave until tomorrow."

It was all coming back to Helen. Clearly, she should have started the day with coffee—at least she had the excuse that the schedule board was hidden behind the stacks of empty crates for the rented china. It was also abundantly clear that she and Laura were not going to finish their conversation even though she felt as if her heart were outside of her body, ready to be sliced open if Laura decided leaving was the only safe thing for her to do. She had been so frightened last night—would she run? Couldn't Helen convince her that it was safe to stay?

She desperately wanted to convince Laura to stay.

"Okay. Duly noted that some people don't want to do chores. I don't either. Laura has earned a day off, too."

Laura was shaking her head. "If we all pitch in for twenty minutes, we'll be done getting the rented stuff ready for return. They're coming at ten. I don't know who put the food away last night, but that was the worst of it."

"Cass and I did it," Helen said. "Perhaps not too carefully."

"We'll have most of it for dinner," Laura said. "There's a whole plate of that scrumptious yellowfin just waiting and I am not letting it go to waste. We could have bought a small island in the Pacific for what it cost."

Helen eyed the pouting children. They had every right to be upset with her. However, there were limits to her guilt. "Neither of you remembered either."

Julie became the spokesperson. "That's because we turned off our alarms and then someone woke up our bodies while our brains were still sleeping."

Helen couldn't help but laugh. "That'll get you…sightseeing. I think we should pick something we've not seen and just go. Statue of Liberty? 30 Rock? MOMA, maybe? And then we'll find treats somewhere."

"Don't you have meetings?" Justin looked dubious but hopeful at the word treats.

Helen glanced at Laura. "Helen the Mom is going to have Helen the Diva get her out of her obligations for the day. I will make them up before I come home on Friday as scheduled. Deal?"

The kids slouched off to their rooms. Laura was standing at the sink, hands on hips as if she were about to turn in her robe for battle armor.

Helen rolled up her sleeves and said softly, "We'll talk later?"

"I need to think," Laura said.

"But you'll come with us on an adventure today?"

She only nodded as she reached for the first stack of plates.

CHAPTER TWENTY-FIVE

The old-fashioned elevator, with a seated attendant calling out the stops, had an impressive enough lift that Laura's stomach dropped. It wasn't a roller coaster, but her heart was lurching around in her chest enough that it might well have been. Maybe it wasn't the ride at all, but the fact that Helen was pressed next to her in the crowded car and the knowledge that so far, Helen wasn't pushing her out of her life. She'd been somber and careful during their conversation, and her confusion and uncertainty had showed. But she hadn't been accusatory or even angry so far.

She remembered the kiss, vividly. But the kiss was before Helen knew the whole truth. It was possible that Helen wasn't going to freak out, but that didn't meant she would still be interested in more kisses. She could make no plans based on a chance of...more.

Her own terror from the previous night was fading, but she couldn't just shrug it off as an anomaly. Every time she bumped her sore hands she was reminded of her blind panic. She had to decide—feelings for Helen aside—if it was safe to stay. Well, certainly until after the holidays. Tomorrow she would be leaving with the kids for California. Suzy's diatribe had been quite a test and she'd found plenty of ways to quiet the monster. But could she come back to New York after having had a very bad episode? Could she come back to New York if Helen made it clear the kiss had been a mistake?

There was hope, Laura reminded herself, because last night she had won. The monster had surprised her and she'd won. It had been very, very hard. But she'd won. And there was hope because Helen was standing so close and didn't seem to mind at all.

She touched the elevator wall, tracing the outline of the building that was inset into the marble. "I love art deco."

"Linear symmetry," the attendant said promptly, "is the hallmark of the art deco style. The Empire State Building was designed in the nineteen-twenties when art deco's sharp lines replaced art nouveau's curves. The building was opened in 1931."

They had passed the fiftieth floor already. Laura liked the flutter of the indicator lights. Talking about the building staved off talking about other things too. "I lived in Manhattan for nearly a decade and I never did this. And it's right in the middle of everything."

"I don't know why the kids opted out," Helen said. She looked charming in a bucket hat tied with a scarf. "Well, Justin is obvious, he wanted to have the ice cream downstairs and was just waiting to ditch us. I thought Julie would want to come up to take pictures."

"I'm sure when we get back to ground level she'll have several T-shirts she wants to buy from the shop where we left her. Plus she took lots of pictures from the deck at 30 Rock."

As the elevator slowed the attendant announced, "We're

now arriving at the main observation deck. Please exit to your right. There is always a brisk wind and today's is quite strong. Remember to secure your hats and scarves."

She was glad of the warning and yanked her beanie down. The moment the elevator doors opened on the eighty-sixth floor the wind made itself felt. Pennants of New York's state colors, bright blue and warm gold, snapped overhead. She was glad of her thick jacket and gloves, but her blood was so thin from all the years working in warm climates that she knew she wouldn't last long.

Laura pointed and pulled Helen toward the left. "There's 30 Rock, where we just were. I wonder if we can see the Statue of Liberty. I'm all turned around."

A lattice-work safety fence patterned in diamonds surrounded the promenade that encircled the floor. In all directions the city and rivers were spread out below them. The railings were wrapped in faux ivy and tiny white lights for the holidays, and every dozen feet or so there were large mounted telescopes fixed on other landmarks.

The sky was free of clouds and the sun so bright that she wished for sunglasses. She could see rooftops in all directions with gardens and holiday decorations. Both rivers were a dark, glittering blue, and in the distance the Statue of Liberty was visible, no more than an outline against the gray harbor waters.

Laura's arm was linked with Helen's as they reached the edge. It was simply the most beautiful day. Ever.

Helen leaned close to prevent her words from being stolen by the wind. "I thought we might be able to talk—continue our talk. But it's too cold and windy, isn't it?"

Laura replied, her lips only inches from the tantalizing curve of Helen's ear, "I do want to talk more." She turned so they had their backs to most of the other occupants of the deck.

Helen suddenly slumped against her. "Oh dear heaven."

"What's wrong?" Laura touched her shoulder in alarm.

"It's twelve degrees up here and I'm having a hot flash. I feel like inside-out baked Alaska."

"I'm so sorry."

Helen pulled off her gloves and hat and unbuttoned her

coat. "At least there's air conditioning." She fanned herself as the bright red color in her cheeks began to fade. "This is a beautiful city, but I don't want to live here forever. I already miss home. It's not like... Last night wasn't my life. Only a flash of it."

"I know. But your life is changing."

"Yes, but the fact that I wouldn't let someone knowingly into my home with drugs won't. That was a freakish thing to happen. And now that I know the whole story, I would never participate in exposing you to temptation. You don't have to do it alone." She left off fanning herself to touch Laura's face. "I want to be there for you."

"I don't want to be a pity case."

"Pity is *not* what I'm feeling."

Laura swallowed hard and spoke before she thought better of it. "Please. Please kiss me."

Helen brushed her lips against Laura's, who ignored the weak voice that said maybe neither of them was thinking clearly. She kissed Laura again, light but direct, then again. Laura slid her arms around Helen and pulled her closer. Their lips parted and the wave of desire and aching heat rushed through Laura. She pulled off her gloves so she could put her hands in Helen's beautiful hair and hold her.

When they finally parted time seemed to work again. Helen's eyelids were heavy with an unmistakable longing that tightened Laura's belly and thighs.

"I've been wanting to do that for a while," Helen admitted.

"I've been wanting to do that for years," Laura murmured back.

"What does that mean? Years?"

Time to come clean. "I saw a number of your plays, from *Romeo and Juliet* to *Agnes of God* and *Tequila Sunset*. And I wondered what it would be like to kiss Helen Baynor, the Queen of Broadway."

Looking hurt, Helen pulled back slightly. "And what was it like?"

"I don't know," Laura said. She brushed her lips along Helen's jawline and whispered in her ear, "Turns out she wasn't there. Turns out she wasn't real. I want to kiss Helen. Just Helen."

Helen's beautiful eyes were more blue than gray, maybe because they were filled with the sky, Laura thought. Helen arched her back to find Laura's mouth again with her own. Time began to race, soaring through her blood. Nerves jumped and sparkled and now she could hear her own heart pounding as it danced in her chest. The world was spinning and wheeling around her.

"You're making me dizzy," Helen whispered when she could.

Cold noses and chilled faces didn't negate the heat of Helen's mouth as Laura kissed her. If anything, the wind was blowing away her fears and on a glorious day kissing the woman she loved seemed like the only rational thing to do. She felt Helen laugh against her mouth and let her go. She hoped she looked as sexy and pleased as Helen did. "I think that's a good thing."

"As long as you hold on to me."

"Try and stop me." Laura pressed her cheek to Helen's, then leaned back to look at her. "Now tell me the real reason why it's good that Cass and I aren't in love."

Helen's lashes fluttered. "Must I?"

"I'll tell you my reason if you tell me yours."

Helen stuck out her chin, looking just a bit like Julie. "Okay. Fine. I think I'm in love with you. There. I said it."

"Thank goodness. That's my reason too—I think I'm love with you." She pulled Helen close again, laughing. She felt as if the sunlight and wind had swept through her bones and left her pure and whole. So much of her was already Helen's to claim. The monster was nowhere to be found, for now. The love of a good woman, the conviction of her own will and a busy, useful life would see her through. It was a wealth of riches, more than she had ever dreamed she could hold in her arms.

"Say it again," Helen said in her ear. "Say it again."

"I love you."

"Are you sure? I'm not such a great person. I'm so self-centered and vain. I spend half of every day worrying about my wrinkles and ass. Honest."

Laura laughed again. "Helen, I'll be happy to share the worry about your wrinkles and ass. I will check out your ass every day—every hour, if you'd like."

Helen pushed her away with a shy smile. "I like."

They grinned at each other like idiots.

"Okay," Laura said. "Now what?"

"I would like to give the kids twenty bucks and send them to the movies," Helen said.

"I like that idea," Laura said, trying to be serious. "But a two-hour movie isn't long enough." She moved closer to claim Helen's mouth for another, earthier kiss. "I want to take two hours just undressing you. And spend all night finding out what makes you feel good."

"Dear heaven." Helen clung to her, flushed. "Maybe it's the altitude. I can't think."

"And I thought it was me. Though we are far up." She peered over the side but the arc of the building made it impossible to see the street directly alongside them.

She shifted and Helen stumbled into her. "What's wrong—"

Helen had one hand wound in the lattice. She was drained of color and even as Laura watched, sweat beaded on her forehead in spite of the cold wind. Her eyes were screwed shut.

How could she have forgotten? "Helen, honey, it's okay. I'm here. You won't fall. Everything is safe. I'm here. Hold on to me."

She thought she heard Helen say "I'm okay," which was a big, fat lie. Her lips were pinched and blue.

Trying to get Helen to transfer her death grip from the lattice to her, Laura said, "Tell me about Mame Dennis. Are you going to do that play within a play? What's it called?"

"*Midsummer Madness*," Helen said through gritted teeth.

"Are you going to wear the bells for bracelets?"

"Yes." Helen seemed to take a deep breath, but her eyes remained closed. "I'm not afraid of heights."

"Yes you are. You've just gotten better at hiding it over the years. It's okay. We're on a steel frame floor in a steel building that has survived everything that's been thrown at this city for over eighty years."

With a choked-back whimper, Helen said, "I can feel it moving."

"That's the wind. What was it like to play Juliet?"

"That's ancient history." Helen's grip hadn't loosened on the lattice.

"I'm starting to worry that you're going to freeze to this thing. C'mon, honey. Let's walk to the inside wall, far away from the edge. It's going to be fine."

"I feel like such a fool. I just—forgot. How does a person forget not to look down?"

"I forgot you were afraid of heights too. It's been a long time since you tested it like this."

"At least I'm not on a roller coaster. Did I ever tell you about that?"

Laura laughed—Helen did remember it. It seemed so absurd that it was her last secret, the only thing she hadn't confessed. She gave it up at last. "You didn't have to."

Helen's eyes snapped open. "You're the famous restaurateur!"

Helen didn't even seem to notice that Laura had gently broken her grip and moved her away from the edge of the deck. "I'm not famous. And I never did own a restaurant. I did become an expert chef though. And you became a rich and famous actress."

"And you made food for my rich and famous friends. It all came true."

"It came better than true." They reached the inner wall and Laura plunked Helen down on an icy cold but very solid metal bench.

"In my head, for years—you're my famous restaurateur. Don't be a chump, you told me, and I did it, I went after what my heart was telling me. Why ever didn't you remind me of it?"

Laura loved the way Helen said *my* famous restaurateur. "Not a day of my life has gone by without remembering that you believed I'd be okay."

The color had come back to Helen's face. "You haven't answered my question."

"I wanted the job based on who I was today." The wind was making her ears feel like seared ice cubes.

Helen blinked, then fixed Laura with a steady look. "You didn't want me to remember that you'd told me then about being an addict."

She nodded. "I wanted the job. I asked my contacts for referrals and there was your name. I took it for fate and I didn't want to screw it up."

Helen simply looked at her. "I feel so dense. All I have ever remembered was that this woman kept me from freaking out when we got stuck and told me not to be a chump. I didn't remember her name. I didn't remember what she looked like except for her hands. All I could remember was her hand holding mine."

They both moved to entwine their fingers. A shock went through Laura, like a connection was finally completed.

"I don't want to be your household manager anymore," Laura said. "I need to quit."

"I know," Helen said. She tightened her grip and pulled Laura closer. "I'll find someone else."

"Not necessary. I won't do it for money. But I'll do it for love. We'll figure out a way that I keep my hand in the culinary world, and college isn't that far off. We can't see that far into the future. So we'll take it day by day, production by production, year by year."

"I can see into the future," Helen said. "You're in it."

Laura put her forehead against Helen's. "Mine too."

"Shh. You're making me laugh."

Helen felt like she was committing a slumber party prank as she let Laura in the door of her bedroom. "Do you think the kids heard you?"

"Maybe. I don't think they care."

"I have to confess one thing," Helen said. Laura's hands were already on her hips, hot and strong through the silk of her negligee. "I'm apparently not, um, I can be very, um—I'm not quiet. I didn't know that until…you know."

"Good," Laura said. "I look forward to finding every possible way to make you not quiet."

"But not tonight. I don't want the kids to hear. It's got me a little uncertain."

Laura turned the lock on Helen's door. The low light of the

bedside lamp brought out the dark, glistening depths of her eyes. She has such beautiful skin, Helen thought. She was dying to lick her way across Laura's collarbone.

Her smile slightly wicked, Laura said, "I think that means you'll just have to figure out how to be quiet for the night."

Her heart was beating so hard that Helen felt slightly faint. Even her scalp was tingling. "You're going to have to do the same," she warned.

"I hope so." The slightly sardonic smile was more familiar and Helen relaxed, just a little. She undid the loose knot of Laura's robe, finding a skintight gold cami and matching panties. The swell of her breasts and hard nipples took away what was left of Helen's breath.

"I want to feel you with my hands," Laura murmured. She shrugged out of her robe, then pulled Helen into her arms. Her hands swept around to Helen's backside. "Time for the first ass check?"

Helen burst out laughing. "Please don't ever say that in front of anybody else!"

Laura snickered in her ear. "I'll just look like I'm thinking it and watch you blush."

Helen broke free and pulled Laura to the bed. Their laughter faded.

When the bed was against the backs of Helen's thighs, Laura went to her knees. Her hot breath through the silk set Helen on fire. She'd worn nothing under the negligee. There hadn't seemed any point. She clutched the back of Laura's head, near swooning. Laura's hands were caressing her calves. She frantically pulled up her negligee—how could she have ever not known that she craved a woman's mouth on her? That she could feel so complete, so loved, so treasured? So taken, consumed?

With a little push she found herself sitting on the edge of the bed. Laura stopped only to shush her, then her tongue went back to teasing and swirling, sometimes subtle, sometimes hard. Laura's fingers explored her too, slipping and sliding in a game of delicious torment. Helen pressed her hands over her mouth to dampen the volume of her moan as Laura slipped inside her. She thought she might cry. Laura was pushing her further onto the bed. Her fingers felt so good and she pulled Laura down on top of her with a hungry mewl.

"Yes," Laura whispered. "Yes, I will. Hold on to me."

She loved the shape of Laura's head, her beautiful black hair—she hadn't realized it would feel so sexy and sensual against her body. She could feel Laura's nipples against her breasts and the sensation made her thirsty. They shared an electrifying kiss and tasting herself on Laura's lips sent a surge of pleasure rocketing down her spine.

"Yes, there," Laura said. She lowered her head to run her tongue across Helen's nipple, which tightened against the damp silk.

She gritted her teeth to hold back a shout. Please, please, please, she wanted to beg.

Though she said nothing, Laura still seemed to hear her. She pushed a little harder, bit down on Helen's nipple and held on as Helen exploded off the bed.

Her breath was ragged in her ears, and that was all she could hear for several moments. She was aware of Laura shifting to spoon behind her, arms holding her tight. There were light kisses on her neck that weren't the least bit soothing, not when one hand was moving lightly over her breast.

It was so easy to relax into Laura's arms. She stilled the wandering fingertips.

"Really?" Laura's voice was languid. "You want me to stop?" One fingertip brushed under her nipple in a gesture so knowing that Helen felt utterly naked.

"God, no. I just thought that…" Laura's hand swept down her ribs, over her hip and between her legs. "I don't know what I was thinking. Don't stop."

Her sizzling nerves weren't as fire-hot, but this time she felt more, and deeper. The sensual pressure of Laura's fingers made her shiver, and when she gasped quietly, Laura came back to that place again until Helen was writhing in her arms, sobbing again for breath. She nearly broke Laura's grip as another climax jolted through her.

It took all her strength to finally turn over to kiss Laura. Her arms were like lead weights. Her eyelids wanted so badly to close. She tried to sound displeased, and failed completely. "Look what you've done."

"I'm looking. I love what I see."

"Really, you should try not to be so perfect. You'll spoil me. And that's the last thing this diva needs more of."

"If you think you've been spoiled before this, you are in for some pleasant surprises. I'm going to love spoiling you, in every way I can think of." Laura kissed her on the nose. "You're pretty adorable when you're sleepy."

"I'm not sleepy."

"If you had pants on, they'd be on fire." She brushed an air kiss over Helen's lips.

"You are beyond sexy. Lesbians are idiots, and I'm pretty glad because you were single and I got you."

"I'm not perfect," Laura said. "Really. Well-established fact."

"Perfect for me." She knew she said more, and she heard Laura laugh, but the room was getting dark and she was so warm.

Laura wasn't prepared for the sensation of waking up in Helen's arms. Once Helen had fallen asleep she'd managed to pull some of the comforter over them, laughing quietly to herself that they hadn't even made it under the sheets. She searched her heart and found nothing but happiness. Then another sensation intruded and her happiness blossomed into joyful desire. Helen was gently tugging up her camisole.

"Oh, so you are awake." The bedside lamp was still on and Helen was tousled and bewitching in the soft glow. "It's okay if you're not. Your body is."

"Lecherous woman."

"As often as I can be. I have a lot of years to make up for."

Laura's chuckle of agreement turned into a hiss as Helen's lips, then tongue teased at her nipple. Sharp, rich pleasure drove away any lingering drowsiness.

Remembering Helen's relative inexperience, she murmured, "I love that."

Helen smiled as she arched up to kiss Laura softly. "So do I."

The sensation of Helen's breasts against hers was so delicious that Laura reached for them, but Helen pushed her hand away.

"None of that," she said. "I'll just roll over again."

"And that's supposed to keep my hands off of you?"

Helen pushed her knee firmly between Laura's. "Your hands are full of magic so you keep them to yourself."

"Sure." With a wicked look she slid her hand down her own stomach with a clear destination. "But I'd rather it was your hands doing this."

Helen lifted one eyebrow, but when she didn't intervene, Laura carried through on her bluff. She knew how wet she was and certainly knew how to touch herself, but she wished she hadn't started down this path—she wanted Helen to feel her.

"You keep doing that," Helen murmured. She sat up long enough to pull off her negligee, then her hair tickled across Laura's stomach as she settled between Laura's knees. Then Helen's tongue was sliding along the same places her own fingers were stroking. She groaned loudly, bit it back and clenched her teeth. She opened herself, lifted her hips and Helen was inside of her too. Finally, Helen knocked her hand away and covered her swollen center with her mouth as her fingers went deeper.

She tried not to hold her breath. She couldn't help it. She knotted her hands into the bedclothes and held on tight. Her climax left her shaking but she was proud of herself for not having let go of the scream that had bubbled up inside of her.

Instead it was Helen who shouted, "Yes!"

Still shaking, Laura beckoned to her, laughter mingling with her gasps of pleasure. It was safe to feel ecstasy—this had no price. No penalty. The small knot inside of her where she always suspected anything that felt too good finally unraveled. "Hush. C'mere. Hold me."

Helen gathered her up. "That felt amazing."

"You're telling me? Can we get under the covers?"

"Oh my Lord, that feels so wonderful," Helen murmured into her shoulder, once they were settled. "Sheets. You. In the morning I'll get a ticket on your flight. If Trevor Huntley can do nearly all his producing from sunny Mexico, I can surely do some of mine from California. I'm not letting you get too far away."

"Tell the kids?" Laura yawned. "In the morning?"

"Mm-hmm. Make them pancakes. They can be bought with pancakes."

Laura sighed. "I want to go to sleep so I can wake up and know this hasn't been a dream."

Helen kissed her shoulder. Laura slipped her hand into Helen's. She was never going to let go.

EPILOGUE

"The camera loves that boy," the assistant whispered to the director. "When we get to number three, he should get some face time."

Helen had to agree. On the monitor Justin looked absolutely adorable and she wasn't just saying that because she was a very proud mother. Relatives weren't usually allowed into tapings of a cooking competition show, but she knew the producer and two chairs had become available once she and Cass had signed an agreement not to reveal the outcome before the program aired.

It didn't matter. Helen already knew the outcome of the *Sliced: Family Feuds* sweeps week special. Twenty minutes to make an appetizer out of a fruit, some fish, wheat cereal and coffee beans—child's play for her two stars. She watched Laura's hands on the flour and knew that coffee-scented pasta would be perfect. In the past four years, only the one batch of pumpkin pies had been less than perfect, and Helen accepted much of the blame. Laura had been distracted and not heard the timer's two-minute warning, or when it went off for real, and sounded one more time five minutes later.

It had taken several hours to clear out the smell of burned pie from the condo and reset the smoke alarms. As Laura had said, "Worth it."

All of the contestants had been introduced to each other before the taping began, as well as to the judges. While they had all been settling in, the host had stepped over to ask her for an autograph, saying that he couldn't go home to his boyfriend without it since they had already seen *Auntie Mame* five times. Helen never grew tired of it. She might never grow tired of it. Audiences certainly showed no sign of tiring either. With tickets selling out in hours, her decision to close two weeks out of every three months had been easy to implement. Nobody related to the project was suffering financially. If Mary Martin could play *Peter Pan* for decades, there was no reason why she and Mame Dennis couldn't be inseparable.

She'd finally seen Paris, Warsaw and Tahiti, and spent luxurious weeks at home in California too, all with the woman she loved. That woman right there, Helen thought, as she watched the host finally approach the cooking area where Laura and Justin were frantically working.

"Chef Izmani, you've been an executive chef all over the world and 'The Food's the Thing' is one of the most sought-after private caterers in New York," the host was saying genially. "Tell us about your goal here today."

"I have always loved the flavors of Jamaica and believe there is a spice combination that can make almost anything taste good." Laura smiled and gave him her full attention, completely ignoring the camera only feet away. Her hands, however, never stopped kneading the pasta dough.

"Tell us about your choice of helper."

"Justin Browning is my wife's son, and after he finishes

college, he wants to go to culinary school. I have every confidence that he will be instrumental in helping us win today."

The host, in his trademark black-framed glasses and narrow tie, darted around Laura's work station to push the microphone in front of Justin. "Do you have any particular interests or point of view in regard to your culinary future?"

With a sideways smile and a half-sleepy look that made the assistant next to Helen sigh again, Justin said, "My sister has severe allergies to preservatives and dyes. I want to create food that's safe for her and is so good that it becomes commonplace. Chef Izmani has taught me for years that it's easy to cook without them, and everything tastes better from fresh."

"Admirable, young man. I hope your sister appreciates you."

Cass stifled a snort.

The cameras moved down to the final contestants, and then Laura and Justin were conferring over something. Justin dashed to the pantry and returned with one arm full of more ingredients and a blender in the other. In the short time he was gone, Laura had peeled whatever that fruit was. Helen had never heard of Buddha's hand.

She caught Laura looking in their direction, but didn't dare distract her. In her opinion, the camera loved Laura too.

When the twenty minutes expired the cameras were turned off and dishes quickly carried away to the judging table and for close-up still shots. A makeup artist moved between the contestants buffing away shine with a powder puff.

"Be right back," Helen whispered to Cass.

"I knew you couldn't make it the entire taping." Cass turned a winsome smile on the director, who was quite attractive.

Stepping over cables and skirting the hand-held camera operators, she was able to sidle up to Laura and Justin. "You guys are doing great."

Laura grinned at her. "I'm a wreck. This is *way* harder than it looks on TV." She elbowed Justin. "You better appreciate this."

"I do. I will." He rubbed his side in mock pain.

"Did you walk all the way over here to tell us that?" Laura gave Helen a hard look.

She sees right through me, Helen thought. "Of course."

"No, you just want me to check out your ass when you walk away."

Justin let out an exasperated gasp. "You two are so freakin' gross. It's just nothing but sex, sex, sex."

Heads swiveled in their direction as conversations paused. Helen assumed an innocent demeanor as she walked back to where Cass was still flirting with the assistant. As long as Laura checked it out she wasn't quite as obsessed about her ass, wrinkles or gray hair. She didn't fear the future these days.

She heard Laura say, "I am not staring. I'll focus. Don't worry."

Cass gave her a sidelong look when she sat down. "He's right. It's gross. You should pass out insulin."

"Can't help it. Like you and what's-her-name." She nodded at the director.

"I got her number. Her name is Kim. Isn't she cute?"

"They're all named Kim."

Cass smacked her on the leg. "Julie will be sorry she missed this."

"It's finals week at Smith. Justin goes back to M.I.T. this weekend."

She glanced at the monitor for Laura's station. She and Justin were waiting to be called to the adjacent set to be scored for their first round by the judges.

As Helen watched Laura turned her head to stare directly into the camera.

She winked and blew a kiss.

Cass heaved a sigh.

Helen blew a kiss back. Cass and her kids and even judges and critics—they could say whatever they wanted. This was the ride of a lifetime and she was going to enjoy every minute with her eyes wide open and Laura's hand in hers.

Publications from
Bella Books, Inc.
Women. Books. Even Better Together.
P.O. Box 10543
Tallahassee, FL 32302
Phone: 800-729-4992
www.bellabooks.com

CALM BEFORE THE STORM by Peggy J. Herring. Colonel Marcel Robicheaux doesn't tell and so far no one official has asked, but the amorous pursuit by Jordan McGowen has her worried for both her career and her honor.
978-0-9677753-1-9

THE WILD ONE by Lyn Denison. Rachel Weston is busy keeping home and head together after the death of her husband. Her kids need her and what she doesn't need is the confusion that Quinn Farrelly creates in her body and heart.
978-0-9677753-4-0

LESSONS IN MURDER by Claire McNab. There's a corpse in the school with a neat hole in the head and a Black & Decker drill alongside. Which teacher should Inspector Carol Ashton suspect? Unfortunately, the alluring Sybil Quade is at the top of the list. First in this highly lauded series.
978-1-931513-65-4

WHEN AN ECHO RETURNS by Linda Kay Silva. The bayou where Echo Branson found her sanity has been swept clean by a hurricane—or at least they thought. Then an evil washed up by the storm comes looking for them all, one-by-one. Second in series.
978-1-59493-225-0

DEADLY INTERSECTIONS by Ann Roberts. Everyone is lying, including her own father and her girlfriend. Leaving matters to the professionals is supposed to be easier! Third in series with *Paid In Full* and *White Offerings*.
978-1-59493-224-3

SUBSTITUTE FOR LOVE by Karin Kallmaker. No substitutes, ever again! But then Holly's heart, body and soul are captured by Reyna... Reyna with no last name and a secret life that hides a terrible bargain, one written in family blood.
978-1-931513-62-3

MAKING UP FOR LOST TIME by Karin Kallmaker. Take one Next Home Network Star and add one Little White Lie to equal mayhem in little Mendocino and a recipe for sizzling romance. This lighthearted, steamy story is a feast for the senses in a kitchen that is way too hot.
978-1-931513-61-6

2ND FIDDLE by Kate Calloway. Cassidy James's first case left her with a broken heart. At least this new case is fighting the good fight, and she can throw all her passion and energy into it.
978-1-59493-200-7

HUNTING THE WITCH by Ellen Hart. The woman she loves — used to love — offers her help, and Jane Lawless finds it hard to say no. She needs TLC for recent injuries and who better than a doctor? But Julia's jittery demeanor awakens Jane's curiosity. And Jane has never been able to resist a mystery. #9 in series and Lammy-winner.
978-1-59493-206-9

FAÇADES by Alex Marcoux. Everything Anastasia ever wanted — she has it. Sidney is the woman who helped her get it. But keeping it will require a price — the unnamed passion that simmers between them.
978-1-59493-239-7

ELENA UNDONE by Nicole Conn. The risks. The passion. The devastating choices. The ultimate rewards. Nicole Conn rocked the lesbian cinema world with *Claire of the Moon* and has rocked it again with *Elena Undone*. This is the book that tells it all...
978-1-59493-254-0

WHISPERS IN THE WIND by Frankie J. Jones. It began as a camping trip, then a simple hike. Dixon Hayes and Elizabeth Colter uncover an intriguing cave on their hike, changing their world, perhaps irrevocably.
978-1-59493-037-9

WEDDING BELL BLUES by Julia Watts. She'll do anything to save what's left of her family. Anything. It didn't seem like a bad plan...at first. Hailed by readers as Lammy-winner Julia Watts' funniest novel.
978-1-59493-199-4

WILDFIRE by Lynn James. From the moment botanist Devon McKinney meets ranger Elaine Thomas the chemistry is undeniable. Sharing—and protecting—a mountain for the length of their short assignments leads to unexpected passion in this sizzling romance by newcomer Lynn James.
978-1-59493-191-8

LEAVING L.A. by Kate Christie. Eleanor Chapin is on the way to the rest of her life when Tessa Flanagan offers her a lucrative summer job caring for Tessa's daughter Laya. It's only temporary and everyone expects Eleanor to be leaving L.A...
978-1-59493-221-2

SOMETHING TO BELIEVE by Robbi McCoy. When Lauren and Cassie meet on a once-in-a-lifetime river journey through China their feelings are innocent...at first. Ten years later, nothing—and everything—has changed. From Golden Crown winner Robbi McCoy.
978-1-59493-214-4